George Lamming was born and educated in Barbados and he later taught in Trinidad and Tobago for four years. In 1950, at the age of twenty-three, he went to England and shortly after arriving wrote his autobiographical novel *In the Castle of My Skin,* which was awarded the Somerset Maugham Award for literature. Apart from *Natives of My Person,* he has written four other novels – *The Emigrants, Of Age and Innocence, Season of Adventure* and *Water with Berries* – and one non-fiction book – *The Pleasures of Exile.* He has travelled extensively throughout the Caribbean, Africa, Europe and North America and, in addition to writing, has worked as a broadcaster and held lectureships at several universities. He has been the recipient of a Guggenheim Fellowship, a Canada Council Fellowship and a Honorary Doctorate from the University of the West Indies.

Also by George Lamming
and published by Allison and Busby

Season of Adventure
Of Age and Innocence
The Emigrants
The Pleasures of Exile

NATIVES OF MY PERSON

GEORGE LAMMING

ALLISON & BUSBY

LONDON · NEW YORK

This Allison and Busby edition first published
in Great Britain in 1986 by
Allison and Busby Ltd
6a Noel Street, London W1V 3RB
and distributed in the USA by
Schocken Books Inc
62 Cooper Square, New York NY 10003

British Library Cataloguing in Publication Data

Lamming, George
  Natives of my person.
  I. Title
  813[F]   PR6023.A518

  ISBN 0-85031-695-2
  ISBN 0-85031-696-0 Pbk

Printed and bound in Great Britain by
Billings and Sons Ltd, Hylton Road, Worcester.

for Margaret Gardiner
and in memory of Richard Wright

I
Breaking Loose

ONE

The wind was rising again. It rode up the mainmast, and a sail struggled lazily into action. But the ship didn't stir where the cables held it fast to the rocks on the shore. The afternoon had brought an early darkness down from the trees. The clouds swung low, then divided, and a fleet of shadows passed over the men on the deck. They were eager to be gone; but no orders had been given for them to depart.

'What news?' a man asked.

'None.'

'Nothing at all?'

'Why does the Commandant hold us here?' his neighbour enquired.

There was a note of distress in the man's reference to the Commandant; but no one was able to answer its appeal. They were making silent calculations about the length of their delay.

'Is it some strategy?' a young man tried to suggest.

'What about the officers?' the next voice said.

'I think the officers are also in the dark,' the young man replied.

They were afraid and obsessed by their failure to discover what might have gone wrong. It was going hard on two months since the first contingent of mariners had assembled on this forbidden coast. The recent laws of Lime Stone made it a capital offence for trading vessels to trespass on these waters. But the crew had arrived at intervals of two or three days, collecting in different places before following the directions of the Commandant's secret agents who had brought them as far as the Aberlon forest.

The final reckoning was more than one hundred and fifty men: shipwrights and common hands; carpenters and smiths, cooks, masons, the painter and the powder maker. The Commandant had recruited every skill which he required for the immediate restoration of the ship. By daylight and in the dark, the men had laboured for the better part of six weeks to make the *Reconnaissance* worthy of seas some of them had never sailed before. There were older men who knew from previous experience that a voyage to the Indies would be long; but no one could predict the perils of this particular enterprise. For it had begun in fearful secrecy; and it had no precedent in the lawful history of those trading adventures which had brought such wealth and power to the Kingdom of Lime Stone.

They had slept with the rigging and tackle of their trade ever since they arrived. The air had grown familiar and sharp with the smell of pickled onions and beef, cider and cheese. A perfume of sweet oils would drift up at night when the wind ferreted among the casks of prunes and dried pears. There was honey in the breeze. The holds were laden with provisions that amazed every eye. But it was twelve days or more since the last consignment of cargo had been reported by Steward. Every detail of their preparations had been complete. But the Commandant would not give the order to hoist and sail; nor could any of the officers explain why they had been detained. The Commandant kept his silence; and no one dared enquire why he was waiting.

The tide quickened and came high up the bow, rubbing its weight against the waist of the ship. The men heard the timbers shake and cry. They were gazing towards the officers' quarters, hoping for an order that would release them from the coast. But each glance grew more submissive, and their heads turned elsewhere when they saw the Commandant emerge with the ship's boy from his cabin.

He was wearing his tunic of black velvet with nine silver buttons that measured him from the collar to a thick, deep hem showing where his thighs began. The sleeves sailed full and loose to the elbows, sloping narrow down the rest of his arms into a cuff of white frills that closed over his wrists. His trousers were a fine blue fabric, made wide as a frock in the seat, and moulded into breeches from the knees to the sharp, fine laces of his black leather boots. It was unusual to see him without his hat of sealskin decorated by a startling plume of ostrich feathers. But there was no change in his mood. He was neat and severe. Now his hair was naked and shifty in the wind. His eyes grew small and vigilant, searching the movement of the men below. His cheeks stooped wearily over the space of his jaws. A scar had ruined the calm and massive base of his chin.

He had begun his promenade on the stern deck. The boy came close behind.

'You understand the meaning of this Voyage?' the Commandant asked, resuming their previous talk in the cabin.

'I understand,' Sasha answered, coming to a halt. 'Completely understand.'

The boy would have been at a loss to say what it was he understood; yet he wasn't lying. His experience was average. He had been picked up during a recent revolt in the northern Region, and later pressed into service by one of the Commandant's agents. Innocent and deprived of all human rights, he could never think of his rescue as an act of theft. He was scarcely ten years old. But he said he understood and meant that he was learning to be happy where he was. Without a word the Commandant was applauding the boy's reply. He had collected another loyalty. This was the solitary thought which now accompanied his reflection on the weather: the boy understands. Sasha's gaze was aimed at his own feet.

'Sir,' he said, reading his naked toes as he spoke, 'when do we sail?'

'Soon.'

'Very soon?'

'Eleven is an unlucky date,' the Commandant said. 'Tomorrow may bring us a safer number.'

'Yes, sir,' the boy said. He could appreciate the value of luck on the eve of his first voyage.

But Sasha was growing conscious of the men whose eyes were set on him from below. He was dressed in a long nightshirt smartly gathered up at the hips, and saddled by a fine marlin that went many loops around his waist. He was lean and less than four foot under the black serge cap. His eyes were a vivid blue; but his teeth were raw as nails, and his gums showed the soft, dark shades of charcoal. There was a boil like a small black currant festering at the corner of his mouth.

'Sir,' he said, dipping his chin to show a deeper respect, 'I think the men are afraid we may never sail.'

The Commandant appeared to smile from the corner of his marble eyes.

'Are you afraid?' he asked.

'No,' said Sasha. He had jerked his head up high to answer also with his eyes. Bright-nervous and without doubt, they swore all his allegiance to the future.

'But you are anxious for the men,' the Commandant said, and continued his scrutiny of the deck.

Sasha was cautious. He wanted to answer with his head that he was not.

'Why are the men afraid?' he asked again.

Suddenly the Commandant had given all his attention to the sky, as though the history of his crew was clearly written there. He was still ignorant of their names, but he knew their condition like the back of his hand.

'They have to get away,' he said, and paused to take a closer look at the boy. 'Do you understand?'

'I understand,' said Sasha, 'understand completely.'

But he would have been at a loss to say what it was he understood.

Sasha didn't risk any further questions. He had sensed some change of mood come over the Commandant. He had almost forgotten the boy as he followed his memory back to the ships he had formerly put to sea. Then families had assembled in a magnificence of ceremony to celebrate the glory of rewards that were to come. There would be a blaze of trumpets, and a pride of banners dominating the bay.

Suddenly the Commandant gave his attention back to the deck, where a man was exercising with a pair of oars. And he thought he was about to witness the future of the ship in action. Their departure would pass without a splendour of farewells. For whether they knew it or not, they were about to violate the most sacred law of the Kingdom and its House of Trade and Justice.

This awesome institution was the vital centre of all commercial affairs. Its rules were rigid and elaborate, covering hundreds of clauses that master as well as mariner was expected to know before he went to sea. When ships returned with gold and the rewards of glory, it was the House of Trade and Justice that decided on the final distribution of their booty. On arrival or departure every item of cargo had to be listed with the House; the names and particulars of each crew must first be registered under oath in the voluminous literature of their records. All ships, whatever their business or. command, were the national property of the House of Trade and Justice. They decided the value of all currency that circulated in the Kingdom. People might praise the daring and industry of the nation's parliament; but it was the House which received their ultimate obedience.

It was the heart and flesh and conscience of the Kingdom of Lime Stone; the source and agent of every national triumph. To provision a ship and undertake any Voyage without the recorded authority of the House was a crime on the scale of treason. And no courts could intervene in its decision.

The Commandant watched the men pick their way about the deck and wished it were possible to commend their defiance. But it was too soon for them to earn his admiration. He knew why they were here. They had sprung from every corner of the Kingdom, a fairly typical reflection of the continent of Lime Stone. Unfortunately born, or with appetites out of all proportion to their status, they had found in the ship their last chance of rescue from the perils of the land. Some had no memory for the laws which ruled their Region, and so regarded the sea as their safest home. Others had to flee from the ancient afflictions deriving from religious contention in the Kingdom. But hunger had recruited most of the men. And all were driven by a vision of gold.

'Gold, gold!' His lips began to fret. 'Gold, gold, a vision of gold.'

Suddenly his eyes had grown fierce and irritable, as though some novel rage was moving gradually beyond his control. The boy looked up in alarm. But the spell was brief. The Commandant's temper had subsided. A bar of sunset struck across his brow. He made an arch with his hands above his eyes and followed the tedious journey of the trees into the sombre zone of the Aberlon forest. In the distance, beyond the final spire of the hills, he could detect a castle go into hiding. The mouth of a cannon closed behind a pearl-grey wall of mist. Memories of gunpowder and the sound of battle prevailed against the rising tide of the wind. He watched the sun slide back of the cliffs, huge and powerful in its decline, like the head of a bull just slain. The cliffs stood out, white forks of limestone soiled by shadow, their radiant peaks rising through the last stages of sun burning out in the background.

'Shall I go now?' the boy asked.

But the Commandant hadn't heard. He was exploring the sky for contours of a landscape which had endowed his birth with honour. He had inherited a name which, on a date now remote and memorable, his ancestors had conferred on a castle and a battle. He had held the most envied command of forces at sea and on land. Lime Stone was famous for its seafaring sons. Many had won royal praise and honours for their exploits. But none had ever aroused such excitement, such a national admiration, as the Commandant coming back from battles with the rival continent of Antarctica. He was once the pride of the Kingdom's applause.

'Lime Stone!' His voice was offering some personal sacrifice to the sky. 'The Kingdom of Lime Stone.'

The words had made fresh discovery on his lips. Each syllable, savoured in silence, became a jewel of sound dissolving in his ears. Lakes of sunlight dazzled his tongue. He set his glance on the boy; and in that interval the past had fled him through a harvest of names. He was patrolling the fields of his own childhood, hearing the voices of his ancestors come loud when the wind swept over the rich acres of the Kingdom. Their tears could tell the rain where it was falling.

As the Commandant walked towards his cabin, the men stared up from the lower deck, observing the natural reverence of the boy, who was pacing a stride or two behind. The crew saw the boy halt abruptly at the door. The Commandant looked over his shoulder and hailed him forward; but Sasha couldn't move. His gaze had fixed him to the shore where a man of extraordinary height had appeared. The man was bending carefully down to examine the cables which held fast to the rock.

'Sir, sir,' the boy cried.

'What is it?' the Commandant asked, and retreated a stride.

'There,' said Sasha, pointing. 'What is he doing there?'

The Commandant didn't answer. He screwed his eyes into focus, taking full measure of the man. Then he took the boy's arm and lowered it gently down his side. The crew had become feverish with rumour. They saw the man stand and stretch like a mountain of cloud beside the rock. He was making some signal towards the ship.

'Sir,' said Sasha, but he had run out of words. He was amazed by the way the Commandant appeared to dismiss the presence of the man on the shore.

'The officers,' he said.

'Shall I call the officers, sir?' the boy stammered.

'Yes, yes,' the Commandant ordered. His voice was firm and casual as rock. 'Priest, Boatswain, Surgeon, and Steward. In that order.'

Then he dismissed the boy and entered the cabin alone. He shut the afternoon light out from the room, and his taste for solitude prevailed.

'At last,' he said, leaning his body into the chair. 'Pinteados is here at last.'

TWO

EXTRACT FROM THE VOYAGES OF THE COMMANDANT,
A NOBLEMAN OF LIME STONE

On the fifty-sixth day of our laborious waiting, my chief agent and pilot Pinteados arrived. His report was there to confirm that all arrangements had been completed on land, and from every source of our own choosing the news was reliable and good. First and foremost in all our calculations was the safety of our sister ship, the vessel Penalty, *then lawfully moored in the capital harbour and waiting in disguise until all agents under the pilot's direction had discharged every item of provisioning.*

15

Avoiding all conflict with the Law, Penalty *had put out to sea, though some portion of her cargo was to enter without a truthful declaration of content and purpose. In all matters affecting my ultimate ambition, Pinteados had become the very shadow of my ears on land, as he was now to prove the eyes that would steer me from the thieves of the sea. A foreigner, it is true, not being of the soil of Lime Stone, and my enemy in battle not so long ago, but loyal and daring wherever his new interest decides.*

Afternoon it was, with the sun low, yet spreading no more warmth than the islands of ice off our northern cape, when my judgment warned me against further delay. Summoning the officers according to my custom each day, and learning individually their report on each division of the crew—split into four for reasons of easier management and command—I gave Priest the order to prepare a service that would be brief and true; for it had become the habit of certain tedious masters to prolong these blessings beyond the endurance of the crew.

Yet there was to be one more occasion for delay. I decided within the hour to surprise the officers by calling an urgent council for the second time. But this was strictly a matter of strategy; for such a meeting had no other purpose than to train them to the habits of emergency, since men who fear adversity must learn to live crisis as if it was a normal blessing. It was always my deliberate policy to excuse Pinteados from these meetings so that any untoward discovery of his presence on a vessel decorated in the banners of Lime Stone might not fetch the extreme punishment if he could prove his ignorance of our deliberations; nor could the officers take vengeance by reporting statements he was in no wise able to offer in their presence.

I could not but accept a total responsibility for Pinteados, on whose foreign head the threat of execution would be instant if the laws of the House should prevail. Nor was it any less my intention to choose my own death if by capture or interference of any kind my ambition to reach and settle the Isles of the Black Rock did not go forward; for these isles would soon become the only kingdom on earth which my heart yearned to inherit and enjoy.

Under my grave command, and by the loyal direction of my officers, Steward, Boatswain, Priest, and Surgeon, I had deter-

16

mined to cause this crew of former strangers to break free and
loose from the ancient restrictions of the Kingdom of Lime Stone;
and I declare it was my pride and no less to build from this
battalion of vandals and honest men alike such an order as
might be the pride and example of excellence to Lime Stone
herself; that I would plant some portion of the Kingdom in a
soil that is new and freely chosen, namely the Isles of the Black
Rock, more recently known as San Cristobal. For I have seen
men of the basest natures erect themselves into gentlemen of
honour the moment they were given orders to seize command
over the savage tribes of the Indies. Here is a perfect school in
the arts of conquest and command!

More than twenty summers ago, it was this same isle of gold
that gave me my first glimpse of the yellow metal. My very first
Voyage it was, when I was eager and knew what it was to be a
beast before the prey of good fortune; second to none in exercising the terrors which forced the Tribes to volunteer their services
to us and all men who had brought them no less a reward
than a knowledge of the true light. We had to drive them like
cattle from the fields and pastures, leaving ripe grain to rot, and
a mighty famine that would overtake even the unborn; but such
was the necessity of circumstances if the mines and rivers were to
yield the yellow fortune before the rival thieves of Antarctica
were upon us.

Now my ambition is in reverse; and I reckon it is a more
noble preference to plant some portion of Lime Stone in the
virgin territories of San Cristobal. This purpose I declare to be
absolute and true. Moreover, the fabulous mines are now empty
and only a source of false report, offering little else but the
fruits of nature and the broken skeleton of the ancient Tribes
who celebrate their slow but certain extinction.

On the fifty-eighth day in the late afternoon of that autumn,
the pilot Pinteados took his place beside me, obedient as before
to my orders. We were about to hoist. The ship Reconnaissance
had come back to life, restored to perfect worthiness in all her
parts, a great castle on the water, all sails ready to roll her away.

The wind was marching everywhere. It churned the sea up.
A lather of foam washed against the rocks. It would be days

before they could complete the final bend of this coast and straighten safely on their course. This was the rule of the currents on this stretch, hazardous and contrary.

The Commandant stood beside the pilot, talking with his hands; yet hardly aware of any human presence. It was the temporary collapse of the sun and the sombre vigilance of the cliffs that held his attention. Night was at once his greatest risk and his only safety. Passion was his guide, his solitary and lofty defence against any manner of danger that might intervene. Pinteados remained silent, reading the hard, squat hands of the Commandant. For a while Pinteados would alternate between feelings of insult and admiration. The way the Commandant had taken charge of everything, making the pilot's skill appear almost irrelevant!

His hands were talking again. The thick blue sleeves of the overcoat floated and clapped against his arms. The wind had gathered power, hitting harder into the sails. The ship pitched, diving and halting as the currents pressed, lifting the underbelly sideways.

'Better be drowned than jailed,' a voice shouted from below, but its sound didn't reach far into the wind.

'Your grave will be a shark's guts,' its rival prophesied. 'Tell the Commandant to let you leap. Better drown early than too late.'

'Leap your own gizzards. It was a whore vomit you up first.'

Ropes swung and snapped, lashing a black fury ahead of the night.

'Praise your stars,' another voice came, 'it is a lucky chance that saved your throat. Knives have been waiting to slice you on land. The Commandant will get you to hell sooner than you deserve.'

'Slice, I'll slice you otherwise,' a muscular voice came back.

The wind had hurried seaward. The mist moved back from the high-spiked fortress, and the castle showed half a face. The mouth of the cannon was still closed; but the cliffs of Lime Stone were dissolving into night. The huge head of the sun had fallen off, rolling out of sight among the stern black fortress of rock. The Commandant felt the weight of those rocks in his eyes; but he brooded on the cliffs. Out of sight, all things would be stored in his memory. He felt at home on this rebel tide, where the stage was set for a drama that would resolve all his previous conflicts with the Kingdom. He would reduce every danger to negligible size, simply by naming it another example. His defiance was enough protection against any adversity; it was the source of his claim to the future. All his ambition had taken up residence in that other kingdom that was about to come: the Isles of the Black Rock, more commonly known as San Cristobal. He shared his wishes with the continent and the ship, and the huge promise of the islands ahead, borne from wave to wave, faring him forward.

The wind was collecting the men's voices below deck, so many bundles of words quickly torn open and emptied by the gale overboard. They were slowly learning hope; but their attention was still quick and eager for any rumour. The wind struck with such fury that the younger men feared the weather might never pause.

'The pilot has a good eye,' one mariner ventured. He needed encouragement. 'They say he has a most worthy skill.'

The wind buried his voice, but he kept up his effort to enquire about their safety with the pilot.

'They say he has put many a ship out of danger,' he said again, 'that he has a fast eye for any change of weather.'

He heard his neighbour cough and spit.

'It doesn't make for safe companionship,' the other voice said.

'Not safe, you say?' The early note of panic was not concealed. 'They say he has a sharp eye.'

'And so he must,' the neighbouring voice came back, 'but he doesn't spare a word that would help you see inside him. Keeps everything shut tight.'

'Except his eyes,' the younger man replied, trying once more for assurance. 'They say he keeps a sharp eye.'

'I see his mouth move,' his neighbour said, 'but not for the making of any sound. Don't you call that most unnatural? He is no native to our habits.'

'But he has a good record.'

'Not native, I say,' the other man went on. 'Not native to Lime Stone, where the word is necessary as blood. We call on it in and

19

out of season, for good reason and bad, or no reason at all. But this pilot is the enemy of all sound.'

The younger man was still trying for luck.

'Maybe he makes exception of the Commandant,' he said. 'Some talk must pass between those two.'

His neighbour came near to agreeing.

'A syllable at a time,' he said. 'It's how he breaks the enmity with his tongue. One syllable at a time. Yea or nay. He wouldn't let an answer reach much further. Very dark on the inside.'

'Sometime, somewhere, he will release his tongue,' the young man offered.

'I would prefer it after we arrive,' the older man warned. 'Not a syllable before our arrival. It must be a proper night inside his head.'

'But a clear eye,' the younger man said. 'They say he has a sharp eye in any weather.'

The pilot could see where a blade of rock carved open the last neck of light which lingered on the receding coast. His eyes were clean and sharp as the wind, holding a critical vigilance over the long night of blue fog which chased ahead. He was counting weathers in his head as he watched the ocean wait like a forest to receive them. But silence weighed like an anchor on his tongue. His skill was superlative; but much more fearsome was the union of power and silence which the crew had recognized in Pinteados and the Commandant; a similarity of forces that was truly fearsome. Grave, dominant, and yet flexible. Whatever records of the past might show them to be different, now each knew he was a man who could bury a secret. They were partners in some confidence that the crew might never share.

EXTRACT FROM THE VOYAGES OF PINTEADOS,
A NATIVE OF ANTARCTICA

Rumour will make any true history of my record impossible to tell; and it is many a season past since I renounced all effort to make known the facts of my exile from the land I was once so happy to love and serve. To what purpose and for what author-

ity shall I speak? Since the famous Treaty between my native
Kingdom of Antarctica and their ancient enemy Lime Stone,
all ears are finally closed to any interest in my travails. Let it be
so; for I welcome no allegiance to either or any sovereignty, but
celebrate the privilege I was to find in being foreign in Lime
Stone.

I was thirty-five years and at the summit of my skill when
negotiations for the Treaty struck a blow to my conscience; for
it was against the true interests of my kingdom. But I had no
force to make my wish a real danger to those who were in the
power. I spoke my heart for all to hear, and such honourable dissent was to be my miserable undoing. That I, Pinteados of
renown, supreme among the pilots of his Kingdom, should be
offered up as sacrifice to the rumours of the day, which ignoble
rumour would have the common people of Antarctica believe I
was a spy and traitor during the whole history of my spotless
career; that I should be put in the stocks like a common criminal
and my head shaved for every witness to see the degradation!

After these humiliations done to me at Mona, the smallest of
the Black Rock then under our command in the last voyage of
battle before that famous Treaty, there was not a vessel under
the seal of my native Antarctica that would welcome me; not a
jail in my native land that did not have orders to make room
for me.

But like the man of Scripture, heaved up from the grave of
the whale's black bowels, I made my resurrection among the
living in the Kingdom of Lime Stone, a continent at ancient
enmity and then in actual warfare with my native Antarctica, and
where the sound of my name alone would be sufficient reason
for punishment by death. I had to learn the fearful discipline of
silence, to sojourn unknown and in the society of men who from
various causes, personal or civic, could ask no protection of rights
in their own native continent. Such were the political divisions
of Lime Stone at this time where the old families were in mortal
conflict with the rising power of the seafaring merchants.

I reckon there is a price for every act of justice; and I declare
it an act of justice that the Commandant should come to my
rescue at this point of such grave crisis in my life. It was so I
came to accept his recognition of my skill as pilot who has dared

many hazardous intricacies of coasts unknown and barely known. Grateful I was for this resurrection from idleness, for I had not so much as viewed the sea in three years when I gave the Commandant my word and sworn contract as a man capable of revenge that Reconnaissance could expect the utmost of my skill and no more.

My favours to him complete on land, wherein I did execute plans unknown to all official records, including safe dispatch of the vessel Penalty, I gave him my word I would enter no allegiance of any nature with his crew, who will never know the true source and origin of their own recruitment for this adventure. I swore I would ask no questions in affairs that do not concern my skill as pilot, and I endeavour not to provoke any interest in my own history.

THREE

Night had given them safe cover. The cliffs had turned black. No eye could detect where the highest peaks rose to join the wide ceiling of the sky. The men were moving noisily about the crowded furniture of the decks. They collided in the dark. There was a coarse and jovial exchange of oaths. Words came from them like an act of breathing, and they were reckless in everything they said.

Somewhere the sound of a flute trembled on the wind. A voice was trying to challenge the flute with music of its own. There was a brief rivalry of song and flute, until the wind exploded afresh and tore each note into a fragment of echoes that died on the swell of the sea. Then a babel of voices arose from the mess deck, contentious and drunk with the power of their sound. They were celebrating their escape from the land, speculating on the fortunes that would reward their labours. With every league of distance, they seemed to gain fresh triumph

over the silence they had endured while they waited on the coast.
The darkness was restoring their manhood; and each tongue had
discovered the music and speech of its Region. They were no
longer fugitives from danger, but men surprised at last by the
immense and novel promise of freedom which the ocean was
about to offer them. It was a delirium of the tongue that had
overtaken them, spontaneous and utterly beyond their control.

FIRST VOICE: I know a future when I feel it. The moment we
arrive, I will set myself up in style. Order my affairs like I was
Lord Treasurer to the House of Trade and Justice.

SECOND VOICE: Would you know the name of the man you
mention?

FIRST VOICE: Gabriel Tate de Lysle, to be sure. Same as the street
where I was born, and not the mere street, but the orphanage
and hospital as well. Every place of charity in town they
christen after him.

THIRD VOICE: But you have no name to give.

FIRST VOICE: I know a future when I feel it.

SECOND VOICE: You dream to be Lord Treasurer to the House?

FIRST VOICE: Now, there is a man who knows how to live, tames
his thirst with the best foreign wines. That's Gabriel Tate
de Lysle as I've heard it said of him. Doesn't touch water if
he can help it, though he bathes twice a day in pure goat's
milk, once in the early morning and a last time at night, with a
staff of virgins in attendance, and the most delicate perfumes
the Kingdom can purchase.

FOURTH VOICE: Where does he hide his wife when the virgins
arrive?

FIRST VOICE: Wife, you ask? What's a wife before such privilege?
Such power keeps a wife like you would have a cow or a dog
or some such animal of convenience. Why should a man hide
his domestic beast when he gets down to private business?

THIRD VOICE: A business of the private parts, you mean.

SECOND VOICE: You dream this enterprise will bring you similar
fortune?

FIRST VOICE: I dream to lie in his kind of bed. The moment we
arrive you will witness me order my affairs to that end. I know
a future when I feel it.

23

THIRD VOICE: You have no future, I say. There is only rot and wind inside you. Like the crops you eat up North. Won't last or flourish in any weather.

FIRST VOICE: It's what you feed on down South, child seller. I know you—you couldn't eat if we didn't plant.

THIRD VOICE: No perfume will ever clean what's inside you, I say.

FIRST VOICE: Shit cleaners, that's what you are down South. Up North we breathe air. The Kingdom would starve if we didn't plant and reap. A mountain people and proud. What we pass out wash down on you. It's a cleansing wind off the sea, yet I can smell you here.

THIRD VOICE: You're worse than a smell, mountain coon. Your women say it and they ought to know. Nature didn't make you complete.

FIRST VOICE: Whores! They are only whores who drift South. All kind of refuse like what we pass out after feeding.

THIRD VOICE: Some drift from high places.

FIRST VOICE: It's the way with mountains. Everything is high, whores and all.

THIRD VOICE: Every other birth in the North is a whore birth.

FIRST VOICE: One out of two for the North, you say. That's more than the South can claim in wedlock where every wife is a harlot before her wedding.

And now there came a very strange absence of sound, as though the wind had got caught and strangled in the huge thicket of the night. The voices had gone dumb, fearing some warning of danger in this sudden drop in the wind. One sailor was talking quietly to himself like a man who has no wish to be heard.

'What affairs can they order?' he was saying, his voice held safely to a mutter of the lips. 'They don't know when talking should stop, or what to say when they start.'

He was alarmed by the attention he risked bringing on himself. He was reluctant to be noticed. There was a thumb of light pointing down from the lantern. He was going to apologize, when he felt a breeze tickle his nostrils. He was making his escape up to the quarterdeck. His hands breathed a smell of turpentine, and resin and fresh paint. He couldn't avoid the

24

corporate freedom?

odours of his trade or the secret visions that resided in his brain. A man who could see things, he had an eye and an ear for knowing what was happening beyond.

But his flight to peace was a failure. The breeze had flared into a gale that punched him around the ribs. Argument was more boisterous above. He was speechless when he heard the new voices. They were disputing the virtues of their respective Regions. He admired the spirit of the men, the fierce pride of Region that ruled their temper, but he couldn't approve the way they let passions endanger their unity. They were hot with abuse for each other. He wanted to get out of their way; but the voices were pursuing him.

FIRST VOICE: The South is not the North. That is a fact.

SECOND VOICE: Give us another fact.

FIRST VOICE: The East is not the West.

THIRD VOICE: You are a man of facts.

FOURTH VOICE: He allows no contradiction when he speaks.

SECOND VOICE: Give us another fact since you are a man of facts.

FIRST VOICE: The Lord Treasurer to the House of Trade is no common sailor from the North.

THIRD VOICE: Gabriel Tate de Lysle is from the South. I know that as a fact, since I grew up from the orphanage which carries his name.

SECOND VOICE: Gabriel Tate de Lysle is from the South, it is true. But his whores come from the North. That is more than a fact.

FIRST VOICE: North or South, it does not matter.

SECOND VOICE: I recognize you to be from the East.

FIRST VOICE: It does not matter where I come.

THIRD VOICE: You are not from the West. That is a fact.

FIRST VOICE: The West is also full of whores.

THIRD VOICE: Whores in the West, I agree, but they come cleaner than the East.

FIRST VOICE: Whores are whores, whatever Region you find them. That is a fact.

SECOND VOICE: And so are whoresons.

FIRST VOICE: So are whoresons, I agree.

SECOND VOICE: You call me a whoreson?

do women have any other name?

25

FIRST VOICE: A whoreson is a whoreson, whatever Region the whore lies down. That is a fact.

SECOND VOICE: And you are a whoreson from the East.

FIRST VOICE: I agree. We are whoresons, whatever the Region.

THIRD VOICE: Your mother was a whore, you say?

FIRST VOICE: My mother was a woman.

THIRD VOICE: And so was mine. But I was not born to any whore.

FIRST VOICE: North or South, I say you were born to a whore if your mother was a woman.

The sea whipped up a cold, burning spray across the deck. The ocean rose like a huge fist of wind pounding their ears. The night was salt and heavy in their throats; the man with the soft, apologetic voice was hearing himself go astray again.

'It's a bad contamination,' he said. 'The sea never made worse argument against itself.' He was talking to himself as he put fresh distance between him and the men. But his eyes had led him into collision with the powder maker, who stood alone, searching the sea for some glimpse of traffic other than the ship.

'Who's that?' the powder maker asked in a voice which seemed to demand explanation.

'It's the painter,' said Ivan.

'So it is, and I can smell you. Baptiste has a nose in his face.'

'I don't mean to offend you,' Ivan apologized.

Baptiste put out his hand, and the painter drew near. They were the oldest members of the crew.

'This sea has a taste like sulphur,' said Ivan; 'it's no ordinary current here.'

'You imagine things,' said Baptiste.

'Like brass after a mighty fire,' said Ivan, crouching his shoulders against the wind. 'You do not taste it?'

'You think there was fire on this water?'

'There is a treasure of bones below,' Ivan said. 'That I know.'

'I know what I see,' Baptiste muttered, 'and there's nothing but night and the wind at war.'

They walked a few steps away, increasing their distance from the men who were still in a fury of argument over the rival vices of their Regions, alternating between the vileness of their women and the terrible divisions that threatened the Kingdom.

'Is there no man among them to spare the land a tribute?' Ivan asked, still talking to himself.

'What's there to spare?' Baptiste countered. 'They are feeling a freedom they never know on land. North and South, it makes no difference when the powers trample over them. They spare everything except people.'

Ivan wanted to avoid any talk that might put him at odds with Baptiste. He detected something like rebellion in the speech of the powder maker, but an unspoken comradeship had been building up between them during the long wait on the coast.

The voices were unnerving the painter again, waging their war of self-esteem with increasing fury. Ivan feared the liberties they were taking when they spoke of the division of loyalties in the Kingdom; they were too daring with rumours of ammunition and murder between the Regions. Now they were in an ecstasy of promise, surrendering all sense to a wild dream of gold and glory that presented the Lord Treasurer to the House of Trade and Justice as the summit of achievement. They were on their way to similar fortune.

'They take great liberties,' said Ivan.

'They have been silent a long time,' Baptiste answered him. He was scraping phlegm from the pit of his throat.

'I suppose each has to try his voice,' Ivan suggested, and waited for the powder maker to come to his aid.

'And they may never talk again,' said Baptiste in his stern and melancholy grumble. 'They think they are seeing the last of tyrants. But there are tyrants above us, and if I know my way about the ocean, we may yet be hanged.'

Ivan heard the wind like a warning of trouble. Although he refrained from sharing any judgment on the Commandant and his officers, Baptiste had aroused his fear. The wind went on making a bugle with his ears. His secret was leading him into some visions of a Region beyond the ship. Perhaps it was the cause of apprehension among the men; after all, it had given him anxious moments in the past. Now the secret had become a difficult burden to bear, and often too delicate to share with Baptiste: this feeling, almost a certainty, that he had never experienced anything for the first time. It might have been the second time or the third time, but never the first. Baptiste had

once argued with him that they could never have met before
this voyage, since the painter's travels had taken him East.
But Ivan's conviction rested on a different kind of evidence.
He was sure he had seen many of this crew before. And it was
the same with places. The more improbable the circumstance
that he described, the more convinced some of the men would
become that it was true. He had powers that were not natural;
he could see things. They said he had an ear for knowing what
was happening beyond. His modesty, however, was no less a
power than his secret; habit had trained him to serve.

'There's trouble in the House of Trade,' Ivan whispered.

'Are you seeing things again?' he heard Baptiste ask.

'I know what I feel,' he said, and was about to let the matter
rest. But Baptiste had relaxed his manner. Ivan heard him
chuckle.

'Such a feeling will deceive you one day,' Baptiste said. He
was smiling.

'I feel,' said Ivan, and let his fingers ramble over his mouth
before he continued, 'I feel we have set out against all custom.'

'Maybe,' said Baptiste, as though it were a matter of no importance. 'But hunger makes a man practical. My appetite can't
recognize what is ordinary law. That's certain, and you can ask
any of the common hands below.'

'You have a light tongue,' Ivan scolded him. 'To call the
authority of the House of Trade and Justice an ordinary law.'

'What is that about the House?'

Ivan felt his hands tremble.

'This ship is not on their record,' Ivan said. 'I feel it in my
bones.'

'Not on the record of the House, you say?'

Both men seemed to ponder the enormity of their meaning.

'I feel it,' said Ivan. 'It's outside the knowledge of the Lord
Treasurer to the House.'

Baptiste was spitting into his hands, cupped close over his
mouth.

'We do not make decisions,' he said. 'For or against. I come
from a Region where men live outside the attention of the House.'

Ivan was startled to hear such talk.

'You know there is no such Region,' he said.

28

'I know what I see,' said Baptiste.

'But in Lime Stone,' Ivan struggled to argue, 'the House of Trade and Justice is supreme.'

'I know what I have seen,' Baptiste replied. 'The poor live outside that House.'

Ivan was suddenly terrified of this line of talk. He was hoping the men's voices would return to protect him from the dangers of what Baptiste was saying. He called the powder maker's attention back to the boisterous revelations which the men were making about their Regions.

'How they spill and flow with rumour,' said Ivan. 'You'd think they were outside of affairs. Foreigners to events that shake the Kingdom.'

'It is a privilege of common folk,' said Baptiste. 'They can be free with what they know.'

A silence like worship had come over Ivan. He wanted some protection from the blasphemies which Baptiste was preparing for his ears. And he feared for the safety of the men. He felt the wind shake his knees, as though some force beyond the sky was calling him to prayer. But he couldn't find the words that would give his faith its lasting weight. For a moment he wished he had the eloquence and learning of Priest. Then he would intercede on behalf of the men who were like children in the wildness of their speech, yet innocent before the dangers of what they were saying.

Since Ivan had never learnt to read, he felt disconnected, like a man who was vaguely conscious of being in the wrong place. He had no knowledge at all of his parents, and he often talked of his past as though it were an adventure he had heard about someone else. It included an orphanage, escapes from official guardians, a boyhood briefly rescued by priests who had taught him the mysteries of the faith through the fabulous pictures of saints and angels. He had preserved a radiant memory for those colours. The Church was the only experience that acquired the weight of familiarity; and even when he talked about the Church, it was as though his memory had taken refuge in the future.

Brooding on the treacheries that might lie ahead of the ship, he hoped for some miracle that might convert the experience of the powder maker into a source of protection.

the religious discourse seems to come out of nowhere

'Baptiste,' he said, in a voice near to plea.

'You're seeing things again,' Baptiste joked.

'I know you have been out to the Black Rock before,' Ivan said. 'You have a long knowledge of the Tribes in those parts. I rely on you to keep a watchful eye on the men, in particular the younger men.'

'That's the Commandant's burden,' said Baptiste.

'Burden, you say?'

But the powder maker's attention had been taken elsewhere. A sword of lightning had struck a long, deep scar through the night. Above the mainmast they saw a wheel of fire spin briefly into flames, then spread like the branches of a tree, scorching the night. Ivan began to pray.

'Rain,' said Baptiste, 'I am going below.'

FOUR

EXTRACT FROM THE VOYAGES OF STEWARD,
A NATIVE OF LIME STONE

The tempest came over us without much previous warning. The winds were contrary, but not of great danger in the opinion of those who had crossed these straits before. We were three nights away from the coast, and in no great discomfort when we heard the thunders break through with a sound like volcanoes, and the cables down the mainmast went wild, splitting into pieces and lashing like whips against the sails. The winds now started to come at a great speed, and fierce beyond my ability to relate, swelling the sea to a dangerous height everywhere. We lost two men swept clean overboard before any witness could detect with certainty where the bodies disappeared below; nor would it have been a great help to learn their whereabouts, since it was impossible to lower a boat in such seas. The crew showed no commiseration for such loss, being all in mortal fear that some lack of proper attention to duty could bring them a similar doom.

The men gave such an example of fortitude as I do not remember in a lifetime; in particular Boatswain and the powder maker, now putting their long experience to great purpose. The tempest was with us for two days; and as if it was our destiny to be alert at all times, the Commandant did not let us relax with the calm which followed after. The moment the ship was at peace again, and proving reliable beyond belief, he summoned the whole crew, officers and all, to hear a declaration that he had put down in writing, as is his custom; and through which each man could acquaint himself with a knowledge that was truly surprising.

Of the Commandant's general character none may now be in doubt, and one detail has been especially observed and reported on by all. He appears to have little taste for personal fortune. The conditions of service that he there made known to officers and men alike are proof that no common greed supports his intention; his general purpose is to explore and settle the territory commonly known as the Isles of the Black Rock, or more lately named San Cristobal.

We were confounded by such a generous offering as he made. Surpassing the charitableness of all previous voyaging, he allows to the common sailors two-thirds the value of any booty that may fall with honesty into such worthy hands—such as meeting by chance some abandoned treasure at sea. The officers, who are in number four, not including Pinteados our pilot, and each having separate authority over his own division of men, will share equally with the Commandant in the total and absolute fortune of the enterprise; on completion of the said Voyage to San Cristobal, each officer may claim a just share of ownership in Reconnaissance, a ship of most lasting worthiness, provisioned and furnished with a completeness of articles surpassing all previous experience of any who man her. And in return for which the Commandant then demanded that each man in good health would give as recompense his voluntary service for five years in laying the foundations of a new and enlightened society on the Isles of the Black Rock.

We could not believe what we were witnessing when the

Commandant said that he would first put the matter to the
opinion of the men, who with one voice applauded before cele-
brating with music and dancing so generous a blessing as the
Commandant had seen fit to bestow on their labours. In the even-
ing we held a short and solemn service wherein the Commandant,
with the ship's boy in close attendance, read the lesson himself.

They had recovered from the ravages of the storm. Two boats
had been battered to fragments by the winds, but the crew had
cleared every trace of wreckage from the decks. The pumps were
still again. The clouds looked like curdled milk where the morning
rolled across the sky. The carpenter, who was stooping amidships,
had been mending the broken ribs of a small boat that was now
restored, whole and ready for any emergency.

Pierre dealt a final blow to the nail, and watched the head
sink below the mellow stave of ashwood. Alternately coarse and
gentle, his weakness was a certain violence of temper. In the
evenings he would exchange anecdotes about his sexual adventures, hoping to rival the exploits of older and more experienced
men. The carpenter was young, his fists were efficient, and his arms
strong. Although he said he hated fighting, he left no doubt
about his readiness to defend his honour, but it was his flute that
had made him a great favourite among the men.

Pierre let the hammer fall to the deck, and observed the splice
of joints he had made down the spine of the small boat. A sudden
boredom had come over him. He would have liked to find a
partner to wrestle with; but any sport that resembled a fight was
strictly forbidden on the ship. As he stood erect, flexing his
muscles against the wind, he saw the fisherman appear from the
stern.

Marcel shook the sleeves of his canvas coat, and pondered
why he had come out on the open deck. He looked like a tree,
standing impervious to the traffic of feet and the noise of the
wind. Pierre watched him, and felt some stroke of mischief urge
him to get the better of the fisherman. The boy, Sasha, sat on a
bench, splicing a rope, and admiring the way Marcel could hold
his balance before the wind. Slow and casual, with an infinite
sense of freedom in everything he did, Marcel was walking across
the deck. He came towards the boy, but paid him no attention;

36

indeed, he had scarcely spoken to any of the crew at any time. The boy watched him in awe. Marcel was medium height, and had lost one ear; his head was bare, clean as glass all over, except for a soft black fence of hair that wheeled over his ear and met in a widow's peak at the back of his neck.

The boy stole studious glances at the fisherman and wondered why no one ever paid him much attention, since it wasn't easy to ignore his presence. But that's how it was with Marcel. The men moved about him like an obstacle that gave no trouble for the moment. Pierre, however, suspected that the fisherman might be a devil: there was a hint of deformity in his stance, and his calm had the force of a sign that no one could decipher. Marcel never spoke unless it seemed to be his duty to do so. But he attended to his affairs with a certain promptness. Perhaps this was the single feature which might have brought him to the men's attention: this natural promptness. It was said that he hadn't seen his family for more than a month in the last twelve years. Although his experience of voyages was wide and eventful, perhaps the equal of Baptiste's—they had never shared in a previous expedition—Marcel wouldn't allow any questions that might force such evidence from him.

Along with Baptiste and Ivan, he had been given the task of reporting to the officers on the general state of the ship. Every morning he would start briskly on his tour of the kitchen, inspecting ovens and all cooking arrangements. Then he visited the areas of the deck where the men of his division had slept. But there was no evidence that Marcel ever reported any lapse of duty among the men. He might tidy any disorder which he found, and never gave anyone the opportunity for saying thanks. It was simply known that Marcel had done it himself, and the matter ended there. But his appetite was a match for any three men; he liked eating in great quantity, and had been known to save the midday meal so that he could do greater justice to a double portion at night. Yet this oddity of taste had seldom elicited comment from the men.

Sasha tried not to meet the fisherman's eyes. When he turned his head, he saw that Pierre was halfway towards the bench. The boy watched the two men, giving the better part of his attention to the fisherman's boots. He would have liked to distract

him with some question, but there was such a look and power
of command to Marcel that his presence made Sasha cautious.
In silence, he was trying to make some sense of the difference
between Pierre and the fisherman.

Pierre was lean, athletic, with remarkably brilliant eyes set
deep in his head. His hair was heaped high above his brow, and
was clasped at the middle; the rest grew like weed down the back
of his neck. It made the boy think of a bird's nest, deserted
and in ruin. In spite of a certain bluntness of speech, Pierre was
a great favourite with the men, who had started to collect near
the bench where he had made his challenge to Marcel. Sasha
thought there might be trouble, got up, and moved a short distance
away.

'So what's your Region, I ask?' Pierre insisted.

Marcel seemed to take an eternity before he spoke.

'What's your question?'

'Your Region,' said Pierre. 'I ask what's your Region.'

'It's a lawful part of the Kingdom,' the fisherman said.

There was a chuckle from the men.

'You shave your answer very clean,' said Pierre. 'It leaves nothing for a stranger to detect.'

Marcel scratched his ear and looked out at the sea. Pierre felt
the first warning of an insult.

'A man ought to know his neighbour,' he said, half in rebuke.

'There's time enough,' Marcel answered. 'I figure we'll travel
through more days than any journey your memory can compare.'

Pierre had never made a voyage before; the men pressed closer,
observing a point of scarlet spread over the carpenter's nose.
His temper was beginning to make him stammer.

'Come, come, come on, what's the secret?' he shouted. 'I am no
agent of the House of Trade and Justice.'

'I am no enemy of the House,' said Marcel.

'Did I accuse your Region of enmity with the House?'

'I didn't name my Region,' said Marcel. 'You have no target
to accuse.'

A loud sucking of teeth came from the crowd. They were impatient to see how Pierre would resolve this challenge from the
fisherman.

'I am from the East,' Pierre said in defiance.

34

'It's a lawful part of the Kingdom,' said Marcel.

'Who said it wasn't?'

'Couldn't tell. I never heard otherwise....'

Pierre bit on his lip. A vein began to swell and wriggle up his throat.

'You sound like a man of the South,' said Pierre.

'That's a lawful part of the Kingdom,' the fisherman answered.

'Some say the South was the first cause of division for the House,' Pierre went on. 'They rob the old families of the North out of their inheritance.'

Although the fisherman made no comment, Pierre decided that he had to press for some kind of concession. Voices were coming to Marcel's support in an improvised chorus: 'It's a lawful part of the Kingdom, a lawful part of the Kingdom, a lawful part of the Kingdom.'

'So tell me, then,' Pierre insisted, 'if all is lawful, how do you explain the subversion that divides the Kingdom and shakes the foundations of the House?'

'Look to the foundations of the ship,' the fisherman countered, 'the ocean isn't easy where we are.'

'The Commandant decides those matters,' said Pierre, 'or **do** you oppose the action of the Commandant?'

'What did you say?'

'I ask,' said Pierre.

'What is it you ask?'

'Do you oppose the action of the Commandant?' said Pierre on a note of triumph.

And for a brief moment it seemed that Marcel became uncertain. He was familiar with the minutest ways in which rumour could begin and soon grow fatal. Sasha noticed that the fisherman took his leg down from the bench and turned for the first time to look Pierre directly in the eye.

'Is that your thinking?'

'I ask,' said Pierre.

'With some inclination to believe,' the fisherman parried.

'I ask,' Pierre insisted, and his voice was climbing to a scream. 'I ask if you are against the Commandant's action?'

The fisherman had no idea why Pierre had started on these interrogations, but he was conscious of the men's hunger for

35

rumour. It was a special greed of the ear that he had always recognized in men of the sea. Sasha wondered what the fisherman was going to do. Then he witnessed a perplexing turn of events: the fisherman turned his back on Pierre, deciding to reply to the men.

'I'll give you an answer you may not care to hear,' said Marcel, observing their eyes. 'It's right I should arouse a foul suspicion. But what's worse is a man who will identify with every Region while hiding the particulars of where he came; such a man is a dangerous neighbour. Any answer he makes could be a risk to your personal safety. A watch must be kept on such a man. You must keep a watch on me.'

The men remained speechless. They looked at each other and at the fisherman as though his words had set a stupor on their senses. They didn't know what to make of these warnings which Marcel had made against himself. Pierre's mischief had misfired. The carpenter was timing his retreat away from the bench; first a solitary step back, then turning sideways and in slow motion like a crab, before completing the next stride forward.

'No fun,' Pierre said, as though in compensation for his subtle defeat, 'such a man has no fun in him. Just keeps himself to himself. '

He was looking for an ally to share this judgment of Marcel; the men, however, had begun to separate, moving in the opposite direction across the deck. The fisherman was leaning against the rib of the ship, meditating on the heave and swell of the sea. He saw a huge mackerel surface and briefly float before diving out of sight; and his eyes grew gentle. His gaze was soft, almost affectionate in its concentration on the water. The boy had returned to the bench, observing with relief the air of composure that had suddenly come over the fisherman. He would have liked to talk to Marcel, but the fisherman seemed so lost in wonder, and utterly beyond the reach of anyone who saw him.

Sasha felt uneasy sitting so near him, and felt immense relief when he saw Pierre beckon him forward. He hurried towards Pierre as though he had suddenly become an ally of the carpenter, whose fingers, lean and nimble, began to trot up and down the hollow body of his flute. Pierre's mouth grew small as a baby's and his eyelids trembled when he piped his breathing gently down the narrow tunnel of the instrument. The boy heard the wind float each note away, and a great affection welled up in him. It was the kind of moment that gave Sasha his knowledge of the men. He was always trying to sort out the different meanings in the men's conversation and their furious argument. Pierre gave him little difficulty; his directness struck sharp and clear, like the arrival of sunlight on the deck. There was nothing obscure in the carpenter's wildest outbursts, no trace of a shadow in the general sway of his words.

The music had come to an end. Pierre took the flute from his lips; and Sasha couldn't restrain his laughter when he saw the carpenter wildly applauding his own performance. He had brought a sudden joy to the troubled air of the deck.

'No fun,' said Pierre; 'there is no fun in the fisherman.'

But Sasha didn't offer any comment of his own. He knew how far his loyalties should go.

'I am off,' he said, and thanked Pierre for playing the flute.

'Off, you say. Off where?' Pierre teased him.

'To the Commandant's cabin,' said Sasha.

Pierre slapped him on the shoulder with the flute, and shoved him gently forward.

'You'll be an officer before this voyage is over,' said the carpenter.

The boy gave sound to his delight. He didn't ever want to stop laughing.

EXTRACT FROM VOYAGES OF MARCEL, A FISHERMAN
AND NATIVE OF LIME STONE

I reckon two weeks of regular winds would bring us to the Azoros islands and put the ship on a right latitude for the Isles of the Black Rock. But the pilot was avoiding the shortest and most natural route. I was sure of it even before I went to Steward's cabin to make my regular report that the ovens were not working well, which was a cause of great embarrassment among the cooks. Steward was in deep study over his maps as always. You would think he was keeper of all the ocean's charts, the way he blinds his eyesight with reading the latitudes and revising the false markings of charts too old to be of present use.

Steward had no heart this morning for talk of ovens and the blow they were dealing to the pride of the cooks, but did me the great favour—or so he would believe, being a man of exceeding conceit about his position—to instruct me in the latitudes where we were coursing. I did not want to answer that I was familiar with the knowledge he was so kind to vouchsafe; for I have lasting reason both to remember and forget the coast for which we were by present direction bound.

In my Fourth Voyage under Master Cecil, of late and unhappy memory, I was left behind, after our miserable defeat off the shoals of Guinea, which soon came into the possession of Antarctica before the native Tribes returned in a surprising vengeance to drive the pirates of Antarctica off their land. Master Cecil, of late and as I say most bitter memory, was a man of infinite avarice and crazy no less; for he did against all reason bring his only daughter out on a voyage when he was commander-in-chief of San Cristobal, the same daughter as was to become wife to Gabriel Tate de Lysle, now Lord Treasurer to the House, a girl of exceeding beauty and great spirit; after which the young woman went almost mad what with living so near the blasphemies of the savage Tribes under her father's command. She took to melancholy ways and afterwards did go for her safety, it was said, into a nunnery, where religion worked a cure in time to make her some years later bride to Gabriel Tate de Lysle, the said Lord Treasurer to the House of Trade and Justice.

I did not report any serious portion of my knowledge to Steward this morning, since I find no solace in sharing grief with men above or below my station; but it was the smell of these winds coming from the Guinea coast that lit up my memory and sharpened the agony I was to endure after our defeat under the late Master Cecil. I did not think it a necessity for him to put me ashore along with other good citizens of Lime Stone who gave nothing but honourable service before they died in the miserable prisons of Antarctica. I alone was to survive, if my enchainment in a box no bigger than two casks joined together can count for surviving. It was then that I lost all my hair due to the compulsory shaving, which was their manner of punishment. They scraped my eyebrows clean off, and every grain and curl of hair wherever it grew, even in the most private parts of my person.

thereby hoping to diminish my dignity in my very eyes.

There were six of us surrendered as ransom to the enemy in place of twelve slaves of Guinea which were the property of Master Cecil and which he was resolute he would not part with. I did not conceive then how a citizen of Lime Stone with such service to his name as I had could in honesty be held of less value than a heathen black of Barbary; but so it was to transpire that I with five others was to be handed over like a box of cargo, since Master Cecil had a preference for the safety of twelve black slaves which he in his own right did exercise.

And after my shaving was complete, they brought us some medicine of local herbs, a most foul mixture it looked, but even worse than any damage to our palate was the potency of its concoction. Two of the men died within the hour from overdose; and I with the rest lingered, but without sleep for four days, after which time the remaining three died, broken by such long exhaustion. I was to spend nine days altogether, wide awake and without any power of my own to bring sleep to my eyes. It is a torture too evil to believe, counting first the seconds, and then the minutes in every hour from sunrise and all through the night for nine days.

When the mixture wore off, I went into a great sleep, but I know only what they told me when I came awake, since I had no certain knowledge how long I slept. Nor was I sensible of any injury which they had performed on me when I was asleep and without all trace of feeling. It was only when the sun started to burn a fresh wound over my temples that I tried to touch my ear, which was no longer there. They had cut off one ear, so that my fingers could find nothing but a hole no bigger than the head of a nail open on the left side of my face. I was a prisoner in solitary enchainment for six years, not uttering so much as a syllable to any man. And there I might have remained forever if Lime Stone and Antarctica did not make the great Treaty, after which I was released into fresh captivity when revolt in the northern Region of Lime Stone began to shake the Kingdom.

Ever since which calamities I have come to learn and admire the silent fortitude of the fish which war without mercy in every zone of ocean and which I value above the careless depravity of

*man or woman. I will not speak therefore out of idleness like
younger men do; and rather than talk with a light tongue, I
would choose not to have any tongue at all.*

FIVE

Baptiste came up from the mess on to the main deck. He stood
alone, admiring the belly of the sails blown to their full girth
about the fourth mast. The huge spar rose at a slant from the
stern of the ship, a giant thigh of oak planed and coated black.
The ropes stretched and shivered from the press of the wind.
The sea was calm; and the sun came over without any trace of
heat. The light was weak, uncoiling from a long, dark chain of
clouds that chased after the ship. The men were emerging from
below, parcelling their duties out with care, selecting different
areas of the main deck where they were used to assemble after
eating.

There was a flavour of smoked herring on the powder maker's
breath. He was washing his teeth with his tongue, sucking the
wind through the wide gap that drew attention to the shocking redness of his gums. He was short and thick in the shoulders,
with muscles that twisted like a rope down the back of his neck.
His arms hung loose, and curved like a bow at the elbows. His
brow steered high and away from the wide bridge of his nose,
and with his eyes set like pebbles far back in a pink marsh of
hairy sockets, he had the look of a hunter wherever he went. He
turned his gaze from the spar of the mast, out across the water,
where a huge body of feathers had just come into view, and started
drumming with his hands over his stomach as the corpse of the
sea hawk floated up from the afterwash of the ship. There was a
smell of land in the breeze.

Pierre had come up quietly behind him. He heard the footsteps and knew by the whistle of the carpenter's flute that Pierre

40

What hawk?

was near. But he didn't relax his gaze from the carcass of the hawk, dipping out of sight and bobbing as quickly back on the misty lather of the sea. The feathers had been picked clean from the head; the skull had shrunk to a small flat cake of bone that looked like chalk. The solitary eye was the size of a bead, streaked with a pale gold splinter from the sun. The current carried it forward, pushing the sleek body of feathers around and over. The left socket was empty, and the light showed the bird's cheek tinted green with little flakes of blue like the scales of the flying fish. The corpse worked a curving magic on the powder maker's attention; perhaps he saw in it some terrible omen of adventure. He was fascinated by the previous carnivals of slaughter which the sea hawk had survived until the ocean took its body. Then the sound of voices came near as the men assembled in their chosen groups on the deck, and Pierre lost interest in the flute. He pushed it under his belt and joined Baptiste in a long, close scrutiny of the dead hawk.

'The fish will get that lot,' said Pierre.

Baptiste nodded as though he found it hard to believe that he was seeing the end of the hawk's career.

'A great explorer,' he said, losing sight of the carcass; 'I've seen him in every bay known to man.'

Pierre was cuddling the flute against his middle. He was going to whistle a tune; but the huge carcass of white feathers had put a similar spell on him. The powder maker was saying something about the strange way the body of the hawk had survived. The head had been nibbled into decay. It would soon fall off, leaving the fabulous body to float its white feathers over the sea.

'A terrible explorer,' said Baptiste; 'the fish are afraid of him alive, and I reckon it's the same now he is dead. Take a look at that, I say. Dead or alive, he can put an awful fear in little fish.'

A breeze was grinding over the sails. There was a new sound like the echoes of an organ in the rigging. The light was getting stronger as the sun pushed through the small peaks of cloud, slowly falling away. Most of the men were now on the main deck, reminiscing about the night before. Some were making enquiries about the latitude of the ship. No one could mistake the change in the air. The winds were more amiable, and the sky looked so much softer.

'The heat will soon be on us,' said Baptiste, 'blistering heat, I tell you. It will set a furnace in your brain if you have never been out before.'

Pierre was laughing. He was greedy for romance, taking joy and danger with the same tendency to welcome the unknown. Baptiste would often scold him for a lack of attention to matters of weight, but he had taken a liking to the young carpenter.

'I am sure you've been in these waters before,' Pierre said, out of respect for the powder maker's silence. Baptiste had returned to his brooding on the sea hawk.

'There's no end to mystery in this zone,' he said. 'Even the fish have a superstition of their own. Like how you see the hawk. They are afraid to take his corpse to pieces. Same when he was alive.'

Pierre was about to fit the mouth of the flute between his lips; but another glance at the dead hawk had restrained him. The powder maker was saying something, chewing his words until there was no sound but a sucking of his teeth in the wind. The corpse of the sea hawk had set a strange look of melancholy on his eyes, but the prospect of land had brought a moment of ecstasy to his ambition, and this influence was also working subtly and surely on the carpenter.

'There's no way of telling,' said Baptiste, 'no way at all of telling how nature works in these zones. Soon you'll be seeing creatures who resemble you in every way except one. Civilization didn't touch their skin at birth. Strange creatures, I tell you, of land and sea.'

'Would the fisherman know these parts?' Pierre asked.

'He is most familiar with this zone,' Baptiste said.

'There's no fun in him,' said Pierre, and flexed his muscles.

'You must not offend Marcel,' Baptiste warned him.

'He has no fun in him,' Pierre insisted.

'And maybe there is a reason,' Baptiste said, showing great patience with the young carpenter. 'Marcel knows these zones, which you have yet to learn.'

He paused, looking away from the dead hawk and into Pierre's eyes. The carpenter was doubtful whether he should prolong his smile.

'You are too young to have much history,' Baptiste said more sternly.

'I have a lot of history in my hands,' said Pierre, and jabbed his fists into the wind. 'Like my grandpa before me.'

Baptiste was familiar with the carpenter's pride of ancestry. He had come from a long line of craftsmen, and he felt a deep sense of their achievement, the conviction of his own skill in making things. It was his grandfather's phrase that had influenced his boast: he had a long history in his hands.

Pierre was cuffing the yards of hair that flew like sails about his head. His back turned to the corpse of the sea hawk, he was looking directly at Baptiste; and his eyes grew suddenly warm and affectionate with memory. They showed his eagerness to challenge any pride of which the fisherman might boast.

'We couldn't read until my father's time,' said Pierre, making a bid for the powder maker's attention. 'Couldn't tell cow from dog without a picture. But Grandpa could smell a good chair. Knew whenever a leg went wrong, however perfect it might stand up. He put many a royal backside to sleep in comfort.'

The claim to privilege had pricked Baptiste's attention. He was plucking a hair from his nostril.

'What is the proof?' he asked, continuing his scrutiny of the dead sea hawk.

'Word of mouth,' said Pierre; 'all my past comes by word of mouth.'

'You can't be sure,' Baptiste warned, forcing the root of a hair out of his nose.

Pierre was agitated by the powder maker's doubt. The wind bruised his eyes, and a patch of skin showed red like a coin on the curve of his cheek.

'My breed didn't tell lies,' he said with some show of indignation. 'Not as how I might go easy on the truth for a night or two. Eating up a whore I never knew. Just making it sound so in the telling. But the old ones in my line didn't need lies.'

Baptiste helped his tongue through the gap in his teeth before he spoke.

'They had no ambition outside what they did,' he said. He spoke as though the ocean had become his audience.

'Ambition, you say,' Pierre said, and swore an oath in the wind. The old pride of ancestry was coursing hotly though his veins. 'You mistake the rank of person Grandpa would serve. Nothing

43

less than royal they were who employed Grandpa. That's what he would always say, and he told no lies. It didn't pay to give service to men of your own station, he'd say. He wouldn't labour for those who sit on stools, I tell you.'

'Pierre!'

The voice struck with anger through the carpenter's ear. A little tube of veins spread over the powder maker's throat. Pierre remained silent; he had made Baptiste turn sour, but he wasn't sure why.

'You have opportunity,' said Baptiste, growing more sober, 'but you don't know what to do with what you have.'

Although Pierre was grateful for the change of mood, he hadn't got over this pride of ancestry which ruled his tongue.

'I have my hands,' he said meekly, appealing to the powder maker to respect his meaning.

'I have nothing but my head,' Baptiste said sharply.

'That's not so special,' said Pierre. 'You have hands too.'

'Opportunity, Pierre'—the powder maker smiled—'opportunity is what you must learn to make.'

The voice had become friendly, almost solicitous in its advice. Pierre was feeling his confidence return.

'And you,' the carpenter said, 'when do you plan to make opportunity for yourself?'

Baptiste heard the wind make a sound of water in his ears. He was schooling Pierre in an art for which there was no name.

'It's not like your Grandpa's chairs,' he said. 'Once you decide to make it, then opportunity is happening all the time. The making starts when you decide. But it is only a special moment that shows you what you do.'

'I think you had a lot of moments,' Pierre said, making his peace with the powder maker.

'There is only the special moment,' said Baptiste, 'and it is in front of me still.'

He admired the candour of the carpenter's eyes, yet he always restrained his speech when he was urged to praise a younger man. Instead, he turned his head away from Pierre in time to see a wave hoisting the corpse of the sea hawk high into the air. The current had rolled it over, so that it floated breast up to the sky. The wind ploughed over the wide tent of feathers, but the white breast barely stirred. Pierre shared the powder maker's fascination with the majestic corpse of the white sea hawk. He was fresh to the wonders of this foreign zone, and had never conceived of any kind of beauty that might be found beyond the territory of his native Lime Stone. The bird was dead, however; and he suddenly felt his pride of ancestry restored, as though the death of such a marvellous creature had suddenly freed his confidence again. He ran his fingers over the mouth of his flute and heard a tune ripple across the lateen sail.

Baptiste was quiet for a while. He shook the sea spray from his eyes, then heaved his hair up and away from the sweep of the wind. Pierre was waiting for him to speak. He had always found some moment of enchantment in the powder maker's talk. But Baptiste was deep in thought, his head up, blinking his eyes while he stared towards the top of the mainmast. The great square sail stretched and trembled in the wind. Although he felt the lasting power of the timbers, it was the spectacle of the boy, Sasha, now perched at the highest peak of the mast, that struck him with wonder.

Sasha was hugging the ropes, bobbing to and fro against the final joint of the mainmast. An ensign flew a blue tail about the boy's head. Baptiste thought it was the corpse of the sea hawk that held the boy's attention. But he was wrong: Sasha's gaze had covered a greater range. He was surveying the horizon, where he thought he saw a peak of snow rise and flutter over the very edge of the ocean. Was it a deception of the clouds? Or was it land? The boy didn't know; nor had he heard any warning that they might be approaching land. But the wind was teasing his eyes, casting doubt on his vision of a peak of ice that spread a white fire over the rim of the sea. He was getting ready to descend, agile and careful in every movement of his limbs. He drew his fists tight over the ropes, and his legs were splayed full length until his feet closed and came level over the first coil of the ladder. Already he was at home in every part of the ship. Baptiste hadn't spoken ever since he saw Sasha. The carpenter's voice now struck him like a blow.

'The boy likes it there,' said Pierre. 'He hauls himself up the yards and finds a lookout at the oddest hours.'

Baptiste watched in silence as the boy descended the mast;

then his eyes travelled wearily back to the flutter of the ensign above the head of the mast.

'Could you challenge the wind up there at his age?' Pierre asked, and looked where the boy was about to leap to the deck.

But the powder maker didn't answer. The spray was getting into his eyes again. There was a screen of mist shivering across the dark girth of the mast. Baptiste felt a fresh sting of spray, and saw the timbers multiply as though the ocean had begun to shroud the oak with leaves and branches he could identify. There was a gradual spread of forest where the masts emerged from the swaying cradle of the ship. Then he saw the boy and his eyes were clear again.

Sasha was walking up from the stern. He was looking for Ivan, who might explain the mystery of the snow peak coming over the edge of the ocean. But Ivan was absent from the deck; the boy's next choice fell on Pierre. He was hoping the carpenter would play the flute. Baptiste measured every stride of the boy's approach, and suddenly felt an ancient bitterness threaten his sight.

'I was the boy's age when the Law took my father,' he exploded. 'Your grandpa had an easy time making chairs to entertain those devils.'

'Devils,' the carpenter began to stutter. He had grown fearful of the powder maker. His eyes were like daggers where they saw the boy not far from Pierre. Sasha, nervous, was about to retreat from the small gathering of men. But Baptiste ordered him to come forward. Although he wanted the boy to hear his grievance, he continued to direct his anger at Pierre.

'I was the boy's age,' he said again, and it seemed his voice was about to fail him. 'The Bishop of the North always wanted to lay my mother. She was a temptation in his eyes right up to the day Papa caught him battering her like a ram—under his own roof. Like a man's house was no more than a kennel.'

Pierre drew closer, and struggled to show his regret. Baptiste was wiping the back of his hand across his brow.

'How could any woman be more than a whore?' he asked, fixing Pierre with his gaze. 'When such an animal wears the cloth of a priest, and the highest of his rank in the Region, he was. But Papa was his equal, all right. He laid a hot poker to his cleric arse, and

46

turned him cripple with blows. Couldn't walk, I tell you. The sol-diers had to lift him out. Soldiers, yes. The village was like a garri-son when the news got out. Papa had to run. He just turned wild, like the dogs in the North. The Law was chasing after him every-where. Papa had to travel by night with nothing but dirt and damp for company, knowing from the start that he was right, and refusing to give himself up, since he didn't stand a chance.'

He stared vacantly up at the head of the mast.

'But my mother would never forgive the old man,' Baptiste said, 'because he wouldn't let the matter rest there. He took to robbery like a holy vocation. All around the markets without security. And my mother couldn't forgive the old man for being a thief. Maybe it was safer to whore than steal.'

His eyes grew bright.

'But the best part of his ambition was still to come. What a seed the Kingdom planted when Papa was born, my first and only hero.'

He was wiping his face with the palms of his hands, sawing his short, thick fingers over the bridge of his nose. But there was a look of applause in his eyes now, as he turned them from Pierre to the boy. Sasha listened in awe to the powder maker's history of his father.

'What a seed the Kingdom planted,' said Baptiste, and a stroke of sunlight caught the filed edge of his teeth. 'Sometimes he would slip in at night, travelling like a beast on hands and knees. Mad, my mother said, he was mad to plot a raid on the Bishop's palace.

'That's what he had come to say. That's why he had come home, to tell me his ambition. I remember how we waited for news, and every failure of the Law to find him would fill me with praise. We didn't know what he was going to do with the Bishop's palace, but I remember how we waited until that night, the biggest calamity came on the village.'

The powder maker started to pound his fist on his stomach.

He said: 'Papa had set fire to the church, and the palace where the Bishop lived. The Bishop's palace went up in flames; and heaven came tumbling down in my hands. I never saw my father since that fire, but the flames never went out in my head. Never.'

Baptiste paused, as though he needed time to recover from the ecstasy of memory that had brought his father back to life. He looked like a man emerging slowly from a trance.

Then he said in his familiar manner: 'I was no bigger than the boy here.'

Pierre had grown apologetic. He was regretting every moment of privilege he might have known. He looked towards the boy for some relief, but Sasha, afraid to make his presence felt, was begging his body not to stir while they waited to hear the powder maker. A shadow like a mountain tottered down the deck; the boy thought he caught a glimpse of the snow peak melting in the wind, but he daren't enquire about what he had seen. They heard the powder maker clapping his hands, as though he was free at last from the memory of his father, free from the flames that took the Bishop's palace. Baptiste was looking up at the mainmast again. Now he drew near to Pierre, steering the carpenter's head up and around to where the ensigns flew.

'My very first voyage was under Master Cecil,' Baptiste explained, 'half brother to the same Bishop and a proper bastard he was, in fact and performance as well.'

The powder maker kept Pierre's head pointed towards the top of the mainmast.

'He had me bound right there, I tell you,' he said, 'right where we watch the boy make his lookout. Had me triced by the legs and hands, waist belted firm with rope to the mast like it was Calvary. The same Master Cecil, now dead like the brother he was bastard to. He made a proper crucifixion of my legs and hands just where we watch the boy settle his lookout. I made my bed on the mast, and there also I had to feed. The mariners brought me cider and biscuit twice a day. Right there, on the masthead, in the most violent rain and wind, the late Master Cecil had me lodge and live. Every other week, day and night till that Voyage was complete.'

He was staring at the ensign and counting the resinous joints of the mainmast. Pierre watched the powder maker's eyes and saw where the spray collected and settled like tiny beads into his sockets. The carpenter's hands began to shake with rage.

'What was it you do to merit such a punishment?' Pierre asked.

Baptiste felt his lips part, as though they were urging him to smile. His voice was softer now. The shadows were crawling out of his eyes.

48

'It was a natural crime,' he said, glancing from Pierre to the boy. 'I was my father's son. So it was. One week out from Lime Stone it was, when the news reach Master Cecil that I was a son to the man who put fire to his brother's palace. I was my father's son, Pierre, and so intend to be. There is more than fire to come, I tell you.'

Ivan had appeared on the quarterdeck. They watched him linger until he saw the powder maker, stern and melancholy, brooding on the water. The boy was relieved to see the painter making his way towards them; Ivan could be relied on to bring a moment of calm to the air of grief and fury that radiated from Baptiste. But Pierre was less relaxed. He was still feeling the indignities of the powder maker's story, and wondering what might have happened to Baptiste's father. Did the Law ever find him? Did they kill him without making any further announcement? Or did the powder maker's father die alone and undetected, after his long weariness through the forest and valleys of the North? It was the first time Baptiste had made the young carpenter go soft. Pierre's gift of mockery had deserted him.

They saw Ivan sieze the rib of the ship's side and pull his way forward. The painter was gazing ahead at the enormous frame of the sea hawk. He was caught in the majesty of the ocean, infinite with wonders no mortal brain could conceive. The boy kept his eyes on Ivan as though he knew by instinct that the painter would be his safest guide through the extravagant spirit of Pierre and the gravity of the powder maker's mood. The men called Ivan the quiet one, just as they had come to regard the ship as a reliable one. There was a hint of weariness in his walk, a warning of age in the stoop of his shoulders. But his eyes were large and young in their gaze. It seemed they could change colour with every mood of the weather. Sasha was sure he had seen wrath in them the morning before the storm. His skin was spidery with lines like a chart of veins and scars all over his face.

Ivan had arrived. He turned his wonder away from the white corpse of the hawk and spoke to the boy.

'What opportunity do you wish for, little one?' Ivan asked.

Sasha tried to be silent without giving offence. Nor could he bring himself to look up and smile at Ivan. He was still hearing the echoes of the powder maker's voice tell what happened to his father. The boy was afraid to speak while Baptiste was there. He looked up at Ivan quickly, and as quickly dipped his chin to show his respect. Ivan smiled, and addressed his wish to the empty sky.

'With a different birth I would have gone for the Church,' the painter said.

Pierre was making himself ready to pounce on the painter's words. His eyes were weighted with rage as he stared at Ivan. His old habit of mischief had been put to flight by the powder maker's memories. The Church of Ivan's wish had suddenly become a charnel house where chastity and prayer assumed the force of crime. The painter's voice grew meek. His eyes would soon apologize for Pierre's irreverence.

'It is the knowledge I would be after,' said Ivan, begging the young man to give his meaning proper attention. 'There is knowledge abundant in the Church.'

Pierre was struggling to restrain his abuse. He liked Ivan, and at any other time would have given way to the painter's need for religion, but Baptiste had now achieved a greater claim to his sympathy. There was an element of revenge in Pierre's need to abuse the painter's wish; he would have liked to put a lasting curse on the austerity and solitude that Ivan would soon count among the blessings of the Church.

'You want to be a corpse,' Pierre said; and considered the effect of his words on Ivan.

'To be let into the mysteries,' Ivan said very quickly, and made a sudden appeal to the powder maker. 'Even Baptiste will tell you there's more in these ocean seas than ordinary intellect can catch. You may wrestle like a fighting man to find the truth. But in the Church alone there be a special kind of grandness that can raise you up. Just to walk in a great and holy knowledge.'

Baptiste kept his silent vigil on the huge white bulge of the hawk's carcass. No one could say what he was thinking; but he heard Pierre suck his teeth and spit down at the painter's feet.

'They are no good, those priests,' said Pierre, and wished the powder maker would intercede. 'Baptiste here can tell you a story that would rival the devil for wickedness. He would eat it up, the joy it would give.'

'The priest is only a man,' Ivan said, on the verge of stammer, as he tried to defend his meaning of the Church. 'Only a man, I say. But the knowledge he can gain belongs to the Church.'

'There are certain things they ought to know,' Pierre shouted; and the note of disgust was no longer forced.

'You don't need to know everything,' said Ivan, bringing a note of apology to his plea. 'There's a kind of knowledge which doesn't need every truth. Just a few and deep.'

'You stay with the Church,' said Pierre. 'You'll be a corpse before long. That is for certain.'

Ivan tried to answer, but he couldn't get any sound out of his voice. He was suddenly grave and cautious, almost doubtful of the consolations he was about to attribute to the Church. He had become conscious of Baptiste. There was a look of rebellion in the powder maker's mood. His eyes were heavy and accusing as he stared across the water, devouring the white opulence of feathers on the hawk's decaying frame. One look at that fallen monster was enough to make the painter believe that Pierre too might have a secret of his own. Ivan wondered whether Pierre had the power to predict; the prospect of dying had frightened him.

Pierre was about to revert to form, rumbustious and blunt. Sensing Ivan's discomfort, his old instinct for mischief had quickened. He relished the look of a momentary defeat in Ivan's vague and disconnected gaze across the water. It quickened Pierre's arms; set a patch of fire on his thighs. He had begun to exercise his arms, lifting his elbows slowly up from the waist; then he quickened the movement of his arms, thrusting them out and hauling them in, erecting his arms like masts from the deep cradle of his powerful shoulders. The exercise was swift as the movement of eyelids, natural as breathing, and beyond ordinary notice. But Ivan was soon consumed with admiration. He was bearing witness to an amazing strength of limb. It was an older man's nostalgia for powers he could only boast of having known.

'The devil,' said Pierre, talking to his body and aiming his judgment on the Church, 'the devil would eat it up. Eat the lot up, I tell you.'

He continued his abuse of Ivan and the Church; but there was no pause in his exertions. He was so possessed by the fever of his body in motion that he didn't pause to enquire why Ivan had suddenly started to bellow orders: 'Down, away, up and out.' The first among the men to see the Commandant appear on the stern deck, Ivan was stricken by the need to be doing something. He was terrified of the warning in the Commandant's gaze as the sun struck his shadow on the men below. The Commandant's presence had suddenly given Ivan's idleness a weight of guilt that deadened all his movements. There was a feel of iron on Ivan's tongue, until Pierre's body suddenly came to its rescue. He was shouting like a lunatic at Pierre's hands: 'In and out, away, up, I say, and in, out, away.' But the sound surpassed any actual words the men could hear. The men were seduced by that power of command which went like a bellow from Ivan's voice to the docile energy of Pierre's body.

'Excellent, Ivan!' they heard the Commandant intervene. 'You read my orders well. Drill him again, Ivan. You read my orders well. Fitness, I say.'

Ivan couldn't read; but he had seized the chance to protect his own idleness from the Commandant's scrutiny. He was improvising a great variety of instructions that he kept bellowing at Pierre. The orders struck like darts at Pierre's hands and his legs. The Commandant looked on approvingly; and the men on all decks gravitated towards this arena of the main deck where the power of the painter's secret was beginning to disrupt their belief in their own senses.

But Pierre's body was there for everyone to see. It had become a machine, perfect in its timing, as it illustrated the exercises which Ivan's voice was dictating. Both men had become some force other and larger than their actions: as though the body and voice had assumed an independence of their own. Pierre's body did not now belong to him; nor was Ivan capable of feeling ownership over his voice. They were simply there, movement and sound manipulated by a process of obedience which was beyond the understanding of either man. Pierre and Ivan might have been spectators at a distance from their own behaviour, stupefied witnesses of a performance that had now achieved a spell over the crew. Everyone joined in the exercise, as though the order of fitness had found its true medium in Ivan's voice. The crew watched, at first overcome with admiration for the suppleness of Pierre, until this sudden discovery of perfection in Ivan's tone of command seduced them forward, mounting a slow rhythm with their arms until some fury touched them from within, and they heard the painter's voice plunge them into a frenzy of gymnastics. Ivan was transformed. There was a moon madness in his gentle eyes; and his voice carried the touch of brimstone to the bodies of the men. The officers had appeared on the quarterdeck. They were gazing at the scene, satisfied and stunned by the efforts of the crew to bring the supreme order of fitness to perfection.

It was a supreme priority on the aftercastle where the Commandant watched with his feverish eyes. The ostrich plumes flew high above his hat. His gaze was steady, at once remote and eager in his vigilance over the ship, now charging forward into a blaze of white fire falling from the clouds. The sun began to burn the painter's ears, warning Ivan to rest. He could feel the heat chisel an opening in the back of his skull. He was about to faint when he heard the Commandant's voice climb beyond his own with the order: 'Rest! Rest! Rest!' The word came through in a sound that stilled Ivan's voice and brought a halt to the movement of arms, restoring the men to an ordinary awareness of where they were and what they had been doing.

Months later they would still wonder how it had happened, confirmed in their view of Ivan's secret power. But Baptiste resisted the call to any kind of magic; although willing to applaud Ivan, the event made the powder maker puzzle for a long time over the power of the Commandant.

'I'd say this for him,' Baptiste was brooding. 'He despises common folk, and he does so with a fine courage.'

The exercises had come abruptly to an end; but the men didn't relax. They could still hear the Commandant's voice like an echo of brass summon them to halt. Some were naked to the waist, glistening with sweat. The wind crawled lightly over them. The sun was high; and the light made a thin drizzle of mist drifting everywhere. But they were unaware of the weather as they watched the Commandant and waited for an order. He kept them waiting while the officers took up their positions. They were getting used to the threat of emergency. The Commandant watched them come near; then he gave his closest attention to the men.

'You had fair warning,' he said, recalling the punishment which the ship had taken from the storm, 'yet there's always a first time, and it could have been worse.'

His tone was light and affable, as though he wanted to put them at ease. The wind began to polish the ostrich feathers that rose from the side of his sealskin hat. His manner was jovial.

'It could be worse, I say,' he added, 'much worse. Some of the strongest vessels went under in those straits. It's a graveyard, but the safest way for our purpose.'

He was moving his lips as though he wanted to smile; then he clapped his hands for warmth and looked up at the sky, huge and serene above the head of the mainmast.

'It's a graveyard in those straits,' he repeated, steering his fists into the pockets of his black velvet tunic. 'But you won't go under. The ship, I say. She will yet stay afloat.'

His hands suddenly emerged from his pockets, and he clapped them against the wind. His glance worked its way from the men to the officers and back. They were trying to judge the purpose of his visit. He had already shown his appreciation of their work during the storm; and nothing eventful had happened since.

'It was the safest way out for our purpose,' he said again; and there was a new look of triumph in his eyes. This was the deepest impression he had made on them while the storm was raging: this feeling of exhilaration and assurance that came over him when the danger was most evident. It was with him now, although the weather was serene and the ship drifted forward without any trace of an obstacle in her way. But something had changed inside the Commandant. The men noticed a slight strain in his eyes. His hands were working their way out and up from the tunic. He stood still, weighing a fist against the palm of his hand. And his voice was graver when he spoke. The tone was more urgent, and the officers realized that the old, austere habit of command was about to possess him. They were suddenly in terror of some danger he might have kept hidden from them. The jovial air had gone forever; and the crew heard him in silence.

'I know there is argument among you about the divisions in the Kingdom,' he said, and fixed his stare on the men below. 'You rival each other for a pride of Region, even where the claims are about supremacy in vice, or nothing but scandal. I suppose it be natural that habits you learnt on land may travel with you when you put to sea. But there must be a limit to the power of every inheritance; and if you inherit nothing but division and discord

54

from the Kingdom, I declare it to be an order that you abandon
these legacies to the sea. Be rid of them at once, here and now, and
bring to your habits the same stern discipline I saw the painter,
Ivan, impose upon your bodies. We have broken from the restrictions of the Kingdom. Your loyalties must now be wedded to this
ship and the future we are preparing for the Isles of the Black
Rock. I order, therefore, an end to division and discord on this
ship, and I hope I may have no cause to repeat this warning.

'I know you by circumstance if not through each individual
name, and it is such circumstance I ask you to consider. It is right
you should know the state of affairs in the Kingdom of Lime
Stone, but wrong, and will be fatal, let me warn, if you use such
knowledge of fact or rumour to undermine the purpose of this
enterprise. Let each examine the man next to him and you will see
many an ear burnt clean through with a hole. This is no accident,
nor is it some fanciful decoration a man might wish upon himself.
It is, as every victim knows, the mark of the tramp, ordained by
law to warn the general public against his company. But in the
North alone I reckon nine out of every ten common men now
wear this signature of danger and disgrace.

'Who then are the general public but a mass of tramps?

'Of every age and sex you can see them plundering nature in the
countryside. No sheep can trust the wool it wears when the Kingdom's army of vagabonds grows so large; men made barbarous
and bitter by their hunger, eating rats and feeding off the very
roots of plants not yet a day in the ground. Not a rose, dandelion,
or the wildest undergrowth of weed can escape this savage massacre of men who battle with the swine for their daily meal. From
childhood to the grave there are men who have never known the
ordinary smell of bread.

'That such distress should be average experience in the Kingdom of Lime Stone, held in awe and admiration for her wealth
and power over the ocean seas!

'This is the cause of the Kingdom's division, where the ancient
families of the North, liberal and generous by tradition, have had
to make grievous revolt against the greed of the rising merchants
of the sea, who now seek to put the entire fortunes of the Kingdom under the sole and tyrannical control of the House of Trade
and Justice. That was the question which tormented the old

families of the North when they refused to put their ancient seals to the famous Treaty between Lime Stone and the rival Kingdom of Antarctica.

'I was against that Treaty and suffered with honour for my dissent. I have no special love of war, but I will not respect a peace whose solitary purpose is commercial greed. The conflict was sharp and must remain a poison in the heart of every Region until that question receives just and final answer.

'Should the great fortune, natural wealth and fortune of the Kingdom be planted so heavily in the merchant adventurers over the ocean seas? Or should the Kingdom's needs at home come first? This is the question which broke the troubled conscience of the Kingdom, and drove the loyalty of the North into such grievous revolt against the expanding greed of the South and that new pestilence of sea merchants who would rule the affairs of the Kingdom through the sole, invincible authority of the House of Trade and Justice.

'Nor must you believe that the special circumstance of my birth is the cause of any loyalty to the old families. It is true I was born to the North, an heir to vast fortune before I was nine; and my achievements, which no citizen of Lime Stone dares deny, had their first sponsorship from the North. But gratitude plays no part in my defence of the old families.

'My case is against the new barbarism of the sea merchants in the South, where every ancient decency is abused and dismissed by deeming it out of date; while the Lord Treasurer and Council of the House can excuse every known corruption by giving it the dignity of a prudent action. Prudent, I say. That is the name for every robbery which gets the signature of the Lord Treasurer to the House of Trade and Justice. Gabriel Tate de Lysle, I say; the name I hear you revere; a man who believes it is never prudent to utter any truth which goes against the trade and justice of the merchants in the House.

'It is not prudent to relieve hunger among the massive armies of tramps who populate the countryside.

'It is not prudent to favour the Regions beyond the South with some just portion of the Kingdom's fortunes.

'It is not prudent to recompense the widows of men who died in battle over the ocean.

'Nor prudent to give decent burial to citizens whose honour made them argue that the Old Families are not without just cause for complaint.

'Nor will it be prudent, I warn you, to plant the treacheries of that merchant breed on this enterprise.'

Suddenly the Commandant's gaze had left the men, to dwell for a while on the officers. They were astonished by the candour of his address to the crew; but his eyes were now wholly occupied with searching the faces of the men whom he had chosen to manage the general conduct of the ship. And they were agreed that he had made no great distinction between them and the harsh origins of the common crew.

Boatswain was trying to draw attention to his loyalty. He stood, shaking his head to emphasize his approval of everything the Commandant had said. He would have liked the Commandant to acknowledge his admiration for the courage and kindness of feeling that had started them on this Voyage.

Steward was calm, beyond anyone's detection as he felt again the weight of private dangers he had left behind. He was searching for compliments with which he might later reassure the Commandant of his loyalty.

In the terrible division that had shaken the authority of the House, the officers were careful not to make their sympathies known. Without a previous acquaintance, there was no way of knowing whether you were confiding in an adversary.

Steward's emotion was great. It made him search for some object to occupy his hands. He had groped his fingers under the tunic to comfort the wedding ring which hung from a chain around his neck. He saw the Commandant more clearly now, and felt the magic of the man's daring touch him.

Surgeon appeared more confident. The Commandant had transported him into the future: the end of the Voyage that would establish men of skill whom fate had deprived of a chance to realize visions in the native soil of Lime Stone. He was hoping to get a glimpse of Priest, who stood a little behind him; but he didn't want to distract the Commandant's gaze.

Priest stood far back, alone, his hands prepared for an act of blessing. He felt a solitude like the ocean swell around him. There was a film of mist over his eyes, so that he saw the sea achieving the contours of the land, dark and uneven where the wind ploughed it at intervals as far as the eye could see. Nature couldn't distract his attention from the bold passion of the Commandant's words, however, and he was glad for an order that would end division among the crew.

The men were eager to applaud; but the Commandant had raised his hand for their attention. There was a slight change in his tone of command. The voice seemed more piercing, yet without any increase of sound.

'You must feel this journey to be for a purpose beyond the price of gold,' he said. 'The metal is a small matter beside the true heart of my enterprise. The whole enterprise is a waste if you do not feel this purpose. We have broken loose and will continue free from the ancient restrictions of the Kingdom. This is the essence of the matter. Whatever you were before, the question now is what you must become. Such freedom is a vocation you have to learn and plant, now and long after the enterprise is complete.'

He swept a hand impatiently across his brow, then closed his fists and weighed them quietly down the pockets of his tunic. He leaned his shoulders back and cast a glance up at the head of the mainmast. Now he was searching the ranks of the crew for a sign of the boy. They were still waiting, proud and fearful of the eloquence that had put a lasting silence on their lips. They saw him get ready to speak again, and the ostrich feathers struck a splendour like rainbows in the sun.

'Within a matter of days,' he concluded, 'we drop anchor off the coast of Guinea. We shall water and then sail fast for San Cristobal.'

He didn't linger a moment after he had made that final announcement. His stride was large and swift. They watched his back swing wide like an eagle's wing and disappear behind the spar of oak which rose outside his cabin.

Some of the crew began to applaud now he was absent. Their voices passed like a friendly exchange of gunfire.

'A fine courage,' they heard Baptiste cry out.

The remark seemed to find its way very slowly into the men's understanding. It was unlike Baptiste to yield; but they had seen a momentary admiration in his glance now set in wonder on the

Commandant's cabin. Ivan was getting his hands ready for prayer. Pierre looked unnaturally subdued. The boy was so happy to be on the ship that he was getting ready to cry.

'A very fitting knowledge he has of matters,' said Ivan, 'of many matters. Great and small.'

'To speak of the Kingdom in such words,' Baptiste whispered.

'A fitting knowledge he has,' said Ivan.

'A fine courage,' Baptiste gravely acknowledged, 'a very fine courage, indeed.'

SIX

The crew had laid bets about the distance from the bay; but no one had anticipated what would happen. The Commandant's predictions had gone wrong. The ship made no progress towards the Barbary Coast. One morning the men stood aghast on the decks as they watched the masts and sails disappear in a thick shroud of mist and fog. The winds grew more feeble every hour, until they finally died away. But the sea was not visible for eleven days. The calm had set a deep slumber on the sails. There was scarcely a whisper of sound from the water. The men grew fearful of this zone of ocean which seemed to disrupt the regular course of nature. They moved like worms about the decks, tunnelling their way through the long night that had descended without warning on the ship.

The Commandant didn't leave his cabin. Sasha kept watch at the cabin door, alert to any orders which the Commandant might have him pass on to the officers. But the Commandant had no orders to give. He had surrendered the ship to the judgment of the pilot, and he left the crew alone. He kept the horn lanterns alight at all times in the cabin and passed most of his waking hours on the second bed, which rose no more than a foot from the floor. It was made of purple heart, a wood he had brought home as souvenir of his long sojourn on the island of Dolores, and was quite narrow, barely the width of his body. Sometimes he let the boy, Sasha, sleep there. Otherwise it was reserved for occasions that forced him to reflect on the great dramas which had filled his life. Sometimes he found it difficult to tell where the frontiers of sleep had joined his dreams to a vivid consciousness of being at the centre of events that had come back with omens of the past.

Although the fog had buried the ship, the Commandant showed no signs of apprehension about the future. He spent many hours at the council table writing up his elaborate accounts of people and events that had made some lasting impression on his command. Then he would retire to the small bed and brood on the curious pleasure that the fog had bestowed on his cabin. His memory became a vast museum of evidence, which he alone was able to excavate. The calm which had set such deep slumbers on the sails had brought a feverish delight to these days of waiting. He saw the charts spread out around the cabin; but his heart was now anchored at a different latitude. The islands sank slowly into a huge, burning range of woodland, where winds rode with the music of bees across the moors and forests he had inherited. He watched his youth stagger with bliss across the years.

His Fourth Voyage was complete. He was twenty-nine; and already he wore the most illustrious laurels the Kingdom could confer. He had come home. There was no corner of earth more precious than this great woodland in the North. Childhood had made these acres sacred. The summer came early and hot as the torrid lands from which he had returned. The mornings would wake him to the noise of bees. He heard the winds racing over the moors. The trees swayed and sailed with a fleet of leaves over the lake. The gardens had recovered from the frost of a bitter spring.

He lay full length on the bed and watched the pyramid of fruit that rose from the silver platters on the chest. The orchards had made their harvest ready for his return. The apples were red and fresh as blood. A peach had split open at the stem; she must have arranged the peaches in the same crystal bowl his mother had used for apples. He saw the delicate udders of the pears breathe and swell with sap. A soft, sweet stain of pear skin clung to his teeth. He was chewing slowly on the tissue of the pear, feeding carefully as a child on the fruits he had seen his parents plant. He was learning to eat again.

'It's getting dark,' he said.

He watched her body of black velvet dance across the room. She was tossing her hair over her shoulders. She stretched her hands out to light the candles. The gown opened at her throat, and came apart down to her waist. Her skin was soft and clean as daylight. She walked past the bed to light the candles on the cabinet to his left; and he followed the black gown of velvet, bringing her body near. The sleeves were frilled with cloth of gold. Her hair was held with scarlet ribbons. The candle waxed with a brief flare. A petal of yellow flame started a fire in her large brown eyes. He waited for her to come back to bed. But he was suddenly afraid to speak. He was afraid that any word might ruin what he was feeling for her. He saw her turn. There was a glow of summer dusk in the room. The wooden panels started to flower with emblems. The tapestries came to life. A trinket of emerald began to sparkle on the mantelpiece. He saw her turn and smile. She was wearing an apple leaf above her ear. She leaned close and kissed him on his throat.

'Three hundred and six days,' she said, and kissed his throat again. 'That was the shortest voyage.'

He was nibbling at the ribbons that fell onto her neck.

'You mark the days on the calendar?' He laughed and tried to bite the ribbon from her hair.

She was cleaning his eyelids with her lips.

'I collect the days,' she said.

'Collect the days?' he said, and laughed aloud, and slipped the gown from her shoulder.

'I collect the days,' she said again, and took her head away. 'My calendar is a crystal jar. One jar for every voyage you made against my wish.'

His hands grew cold. There was a hint of trouble in her eyes. She was looking at him with strange intensity. He wanted to escape this passionate scrutiny that made his hands go cold.

'And my second voyage out,' he teased her. 'How many days by your crystal jars?'

'That was the first for me,' she said. Her voice was prompt.

'It was the second of my career,' he said.

'But the first for me,' she insisted, and brought her head down on his shoulder. 'I didn't want you to go again.'

'How many?' he said quickly.

'One thousand and one days,' she said, munching at his ears.

'You keep my journeys in a jar.' He laughed.

'The middle voyage was the worst,' she said. Her voice had suddenly failed. He thought he heard her sob.

His absence was like a season of plague. Daily she would watch from her window on the high bedroom floor how the moors rambled for miles, desolate and empty of any human sound. It was impossible to endure the acres of woodland, turning like the ocean, tedious and dark and without horizon. She would count the leaves of the oak and the elm to remind her of him. She went swinging her luck on the apple boughs, hoping to keep a proper number of the days since he had gone. Her memory was not reliable; his departure had made her suddenly forget the use of numbers. Later she began to gather the leaves, storing each voyage in her crystal jars.

Now he was here beside her, home forever if he could be made to keep his promise. It was his last voyage. She felt a pride of conquest. She was divorcing him from the sea.

'Let me look at you again,' he begged; and she heard a cry of hunger in his voice. She knew every cadence of sound through which his need made itself known. He turned on his side. The bed floated like the timbers of a ship under his body. The air swayed with tides when his eyes found the soft white column of her throat. The candles had started to build cones of yellow flame above the deer horns that held them. They played a game of shadows over her mouth. Her lips were like the corners of the moon, full and perfect in their curve. An emerald was smouldering in her large brown eyes; the light made them dance. He felt a slow dizziness steal over his gaze. This absence from home had starved his eyes. Now they went wild as fish, nibbling at the warm rose flesh of her cheeks. Some old, forgotten urge began to stoke his appetite. It made his mouth tremble. He let his hands go free, probing slowly through her hair. His mouth had found a soft, fresh crater under her arms. He wanted to speak; but this wildness of appetite had throttled his tongue. She took his head between her hands. She was stroking his neck; her mouth had made a harbour in the large, wet sockets of his ear. She was searching his muscles with her lips, grazing slowly over the rich black hairs that covered his chest. He heard the sigh and suckle of her breath roasting his loins; feeding on the very root and tide of his strength. She had made a feast of his body. There was a hammer of fire pulsing through his thighs. He felt his flesh go soft and tender as a sponge. There was the familiar sway of tides riding over her eyes. He could scarcely see her now. He had no power to stir an eyelid, no trace of command over the sweet idleness of his hands. He lay still and limp, and heard his strength crumble like some precipice of weed on the ocean floor. His body was sinking beneath the timbers of the bed.

The light danced over the tapestries that hung from the walls. He could see where the flame leapt from the candle, and fell like petals over her mouth. There was an early tremor on the curve of her lips. Something was going dark behind her eyes. Every beat of her heart became more sober, as though she felt some menace in the silence that had sealed his lips.

He drew the small table near. She sat up beside him and watched his hands collect a pair of emerald dice from the drawer. The table was laden with souvenirs of each voyage. The candlelight poured silver over the furniture of the room. A fortune of stones was gathered over the mantelpiece.

'You know where the river bends at Belle Vue?'

She nodded and watched a pebble of sapphire turn to stars between his fingers.

'And San Souci? You were with Master Cecil at San Souci.'

She didn't answer. He was weighing the grains of rubies, puffing his breath over the shadows that smouldered in his hands. He hadn't noticed her silence; but he could feel her gaze hold vigil over his hands.

'This little jewel is from the Demon Coast,' he said.

He was flecking the dust from the paw of a silver dog.

'Souvenirs of you,' he said, and smiled up at her.

She was catching for breath. He squeezed her arm and kissed her on the nose.

'Souvenirs of your conquest,' she said.

He was quick to forgive her meaning, and without pause he

63

hurried to correct the impression that his gifts had made on her.

'No,' he told her, showing some hint of rebuke. 'They are souvenirs of you.'

'These treasures are not of Lime Stone,' she said. 'How could they hold me in your memory?'

He was too sure of his feeling to start an argument. He begged her to close her eyes. He was raising his body from the bed, straining his reach to seize the purse of black sealskin under the table.

'What are you doing?' she asked, pretending to be blind.

'Now,' he said, 'now you may look.'

He was weighing the necklace of pure silver over his hands. A large cameo of rubies hung at the end. The face was set with pearls at the centre. She sat beside him on the bed, aching for speech. The stones set a blaze on her eyes. She leaned forward to touch them.

There was a sensation of heat in her fingers. He closed his hand around the back of her head and guided it forward and onto his chest. She heard the sound of rivers winding down her neck, and felt the cold clasp of the silver hug her throat.

'There,' he said, and tossed her head back, surprising her eyes with the small mirror which he took from the table. He held it before her face. Her eyes were drunk with the glow of the pendant. She saw a firmament of stars blaze from the glass. The light had made a well of silver between her breasts. There was fresh moisture in her eyes.

'You were the reason I took them,' he said, and drew her face towards him. He was kissing the moisture from her eyes.

'Took them,' she said, trying to catch their reflection in the mirror.

'At San Souci,' he said. 'The Tribes left these stones behind after they fled underground.'

She watched his eyes burn with triumph; but she didn't speak. He was still holding the mirror up. She was blinded from the sparkle that scurried like rats' feet over the glass. It seemed the mirror would crack from the glow of these treasures. She couldn't speak. She wanted to ask him about San Souci and the Demon Coast, and the flight of the Tribes, but she was speechless with wonder when she saw her throat imprisoned with such splendour. He wouldn't take the mirror away. He would allow her no respite from this tyranny of beauty that ordered her eyes to bless the treasures he had brought.

'You were the reason I took them,' she heard him say again; and his voice had driven every cry of the mines from her memory. She had forgotten her questions about the Tribes and the flight of the families from the mines at San Souci. She could hear nothing but her breathing and the delirious beat of her heart as he held the mirror before her face. He had come home. He was there beside her. She had divorced him from the sea, and forever.

She took the mirror away, and let her head fall into his hands. She made a kitten of her body, crawling sleek and small into his arms. She could feel the hairs of his chest climb into her ears and her mouth. She could no longer remember the name of any tree or the number of leaves that filled her crystal jars. She was a colony of joys given over entirely to his care. Some tyranny of love had condemned her to his need. She felt the warmth of his body alert her tenderness. His flesh was rising again, making its press against her arms. A wave of heat was coming up from his loins. She could feel him go hard with longing, as though his appetite had opened like an ocean, soothing and merciless in its greed. His desire was about to drown her where she lay. And her wish was certain and swift as the touch of silver burning her throat. She felt him come massive and firm as a mast inside her; weighing her slowly with his loins, and thrusting her gently forward; until she heard and felt the wash and lather of the ocean spread over her. His flesh had entered her through every pore. There was a sound of rivers streaming into her ears. The plumes of his ostrich feathers had taken her by the hair and launched her body like a sail before the wind. She made a noise like a wounded bird.

'What did you say?' he asked.

'Say, say?'

'What did you say?' he asked again; and craned his weight up to catch her gaze.

'Say?'

'Yes, what did you say?' he repeated. 'I heard you say something.'

She was slowly getting the better of this stupor that made her stammer.

'I think I was crying,' she laughed.

'Crying?' he said; and his voice had found its customary stern-
ness. 'Why?'

'Why,' she droned, as though her voice was coming from the
distant spaces of the moors.

'Did I hurt you?' he asked; and she knew he had gone soft and
nervous for her safety.

'No, no, never,' she said. She was eager to put him at ease.

He was waiting for her answer; but she had pulled him forward,
pillowing his head on her breasts and sifting his hair between her
hands.

'Why were you crying?' he was determined to know.

'Because I am happy.' She laughed. She was dragging her legs
out from under his body. She sat up, bit his chin, and kissed him
at the far corner of his neck before closing her mouth over the
wide cave of his ear.

He was afraid to speak; but he knew he had to. His silence was
always a warning of danger; and he was silent now. He was so
afraid to speak; but he knew he had to.

'I am glad I make you happy,' he said.

She looked him straight in the eyes, recalling his own method
of summoning attention for his orders.

'You'll never leave me again,' she said. 'Never. It's not a favour
I ask, but the contract we agreed.' She was staring at him. 'That
was your last voyage to the Isles of the Black Rock. You will never
leave Lime Stone again while I am alive. Never.'

She too was afraid of his silence; and she wanted to speak. The
candlelight was making pockmarks all over his face. He was chewing his lips, ploughing up the heavy shrub of eyebrows with his
thumb. It was awful when his silence attacked. It grew like
some fatal cancer of the tongue. Afraid for their future, she decided to coax him back to some region that would make words safe
and easy. She took his hand in hers, and ran her mouth over his
fingers. She was munching the soft rise of flesh at the back of his
palm.

'Tell me about the mines at San Souci,' she said. 'Are any
families of the Tribes left on the Demon Coast?'

She saw him smile and knew he was relieved by her interest in
his triumph over the seas. But he was slow to speak. He looked
suddenly weary.

'My darling,' she called to him, making a chain with their arms. 'Tell me, my darling.'

But he was suffering his old sickness of the tongue. He felt the chain of arms enclose them; but his attention was taken entirely by the treasure of glowing silver that burnt her throat.

'Let us sleep,' he said; and his voice was ever so old, as though his weariness had grown beyond belief. 'Let us sleep now.'

And she fell silent on her face, chewing the sheets, and digging her nails without a sound through the wet groves of her hair. His silence was like some germ of the soul whose range of infection knew no frontier.

Sleep now, let us sleep. Now. Let us. Let us. Now. The bed was sinking slowly, bearing his slumber deeper and further away. A ball of cannon rent the cloud. His dreams were striding with martial fury across the sky. Now. Let us now. His tongue had come alive elsewhere. His eyes worked like flares searching the white sheets of sand that spread out from the coast. The islands tossed about like a string of pearls over the sea. He was choosing the safest shoals where his men might lower the boat and ride to war. They didn't like this emptiness in the air; no sound, not a face anywhere. He was anxious for the younger men. Four voyages had made him old. They envied him his honours at such an early age; and envy made them eager to be his equal. But his gifts of command were a right at birth. After three nights awake, they could find no trace of the Tribes. One legend says, sometimes they vanish. He saw her father arrive. Master Cecil stood beside him, twice his age, but never his equal in the skill of conquest and command. 'I wonder what strategy their cannibal brains are up to now,' Master Cecil said, 'if hiding can be called a strategy. It's clear as day. But we shall find them.'

He saw the old man waver. Master Cecil was anxious to go home. Living had turned him to a shell. 'Or should we try for another peace?' Master Cecil was asking him. He would make the old man yield to his decisions. He knew her father would have to give way to his wish, here or at home. 'I've made four journeys to this coast,' the young Commandant warned, 'and each time peace was a way to drive us off. Antarctica never gave me so much trouble.' The old man restrained the pride he felt in this stripling from the North. He was yielding his authority to the youth. 'What are your orders, then?' The young man's plans were ready. They kept him company in the day; shared his dreams when he brought his weariness to bed. 'Send your men with dogs to search the usual places,' he said. 'San Souci, Morne, Belle Vue, Chacachacare. Multiply the dogs on the Demon Coast. The rest can follow when it gets dark.' The old man had found new boldness in this boy's inspiration. 'Is that all?' a soldier asked; and Master Cecil looked at the young Commandant, brooding on the emptiness of the air, the lack of sound in the trees. 'Allow no arguments,' the young Commandant said, 'and shoot if the distance is too great for capture.' The old man called the men to attention. He was giving the benefits of a longer experience. 'Take a sample of the Tribes for torture,' he said, and glanced at the young man in command. 'Torture,' the young Commandant mused; it was a strategy which hurt his pride. But the old man wished to remind the soldiers that he was senior in command. 'This is not ordinary war,' he advised, 'there are no rules.' He didn't wait to hear an argument. A division of men assembled around him. They followed him down the bend of the river. The young Commandant was happy to see him go. Here and at home the old man had always got in his way. He turned to address his men. He chose a middle-aged subordinate to channel his orders through. The men had come rigid with attention. 'Away from Lime Stone,' the young Commandant was saying, 'you and I are no different in what we are doing. Whatever our rank, our business is the same. You must make that clear to every man.' His glance fled like an arrow down the docile rank of soldiers. 'I know when to speak to them, sir,' the officer said, as though he had to defend his age. The young Commandant heard him out, then addressed himself directly to the men. 'We must prepare for any strategy the Tribes might play on you. When you arrive, they may pretend that they do not see. They will behave as though we are not here. While you occupy the island, you may see them go about their ordinary business in canoes, collecting fresh leaves for fire, offering prayers as usual in some barbarous ceremony. We are not going to be deceived. So my first order is this: on arrival in the hinterland where they now hide, every Chief of the Tribes to the number of twelve must be captured like a slave and held until the population is under my command. This has been a very long journey; but I want to make it my last.'

My last, I want to make it my last. I have reasons, I have. I have a reason why my voyaging should end.

The timbers were swaying with his body as though the bed had gone soft as cloud. The wind stripped the branches bare, plucking the leaves like feathers where he floated high up and tall as a ship. His hands were hot from the sun's rays. He saw the sky come close and simple as a hat to cover his head. A soldier arrived; there was trouble. The man was clutching at his throat. 'Water, a little water,' he begged. The man struggled to say what he had seen; but he was losing too much blood. 'Where were you when the arrows hit your throat?' the Commandant asked. But the man couldn't talk. A shout came up behind them; another soldier had arrived, panting like an animal. 'Dog, the dog'; he coughed, and his tongue tripped between his teeth; 'the dog—vanished, gone, sir, the dog gone.' The Commandant was furious and ordered the men to douse the soldier's face with water. 'Do you believe in "things", things not natural?' he shouted. The man began to tremble. 'I'm all right in my head, sir. But the dog just vanished.' The man was hysterical. He slapped the man's face, shouting close to his ears: 'Have you ever seen an animal fly? Wings on a dog, you imbecile.' The man's mouth started to bleed from chewing at his lips. The young Commandant glowered, but was patient as a nurse when he spoke again. 'Let us take it slowly,' he was saying. 'You had a dog with you?' And the man stammered, 'As you ordered, sir.' 'And suddenly there was no dog,' the Commandant repeated. And the man muttered, 'As I said, sir.' The Commandant's patience was at an end, and he began to shout. 'It flew away, vanished, turned to air in front of your eyes?' But the man had collapsed before he could finish. The dogs were disappearing, and the men under Master Cecil had not come back.

'The graves,' he whispered in his sleep; 'it was a strategy of the graves.'

At San Souci and Morne the dogs had disappeared in the largest numbers. Later he discovered what had happened to the soldier who couldn't explain why the animal had vanished. The man was lucky to survive. Panic, however, had prevented him from investigating where the Tribes had begun their strategy. The place had no name until the young Commandant called it Constance Creek, or the Creek of Deception. There appeared a stone built like a gate into the ground. The land was safe above the stone; but the men moved inland at their peril. The Tribes had gone underground, and turned the earth into a cemetery. At San Souci and Belle Vue the soldiers slid like worms into their graves. Everywhere. Even before his fourth arrival, the Tribes had dug the graves; and the men under Master Cecil were buried alive, dying in the dirt, with the dogs their only company.

'The graves,' he was whispering in his sleep; 'it was a strategy of the graves.'

His heart could never forgive this defeat. He had seen the sea cover many a man in battle. That death was bad enough, but you could at least challenge the water for rescue. Not here, not at Morne or San Souci, nor Chacachacare and Belle Vue. The sea was never so treacherous as when he saw men disappear into the earth that looked, until they fell, safe and flat as the palm of his hand. How could you move to help them? To the left the innocent patch of grass was cover for your own grave. To the right the same was waiting if he dared move. He stood alone on a footpath he dared not measure with another step, caught between his pride and their dying; and wondering what was the nature of that patience that had prepared the Tribes for this strategic burial of his men and those who went with Master Cecil. Although their arrows were no match for Lime Stone's ammunition, nature had intervened on behalf of the Tribes. They knew the coral face of their land.

'The graves,' he was whispering in his sleep. 'It was the strategy of the graves.' Now he would never leave them alone. Already his brain was mounting the assault that would follow on his return. The Tribes would never hear the last of this young Commandant.

The pillow was wet where the smooth, strong base of his chin had settled. The night was droning a slow wind up from the moors. There was a treasure of naked flesh in his arms, heaving and sobbing like the wind. But he couldn't feel her legs grow tight and quivering between his thighs; his desire had taken root elsewhere. An imperial joy had shipped his pride over the ocean seas. Her breast shook and heaved over his arm. She was kneading her hands down the root and testicle of his strength; his sperm, however, was nurturing a different soil, his star was ascending a foreign sky.

He heard voices come from the Creek of Deception, a ceremonial call of drums riding up from the river bend. They were refusing to die. But the future was against them. Only he could rescue them from the perils of staying alive. One legend says they vanish, later to return. They would witness many deaths until their animal perseverance came to an end. He was giving his warning to the stones and the trees and the fresh river water that flowed with gold. He was warning the sky to yield. These Tribes were treacherous in every crisis, yet he admired the patience that made them wait. But resistance was a liberty he could not allow. He would never understand their cannibal refusal to surrender; servitude could hardly be a punishment in their animal state. But Lime Stone knew when a duty had to be done. The Kingdom was generous in her rewards, never forgetful of courtesies she had received. He was young; but he knew whose cause the future would purify. He was begging the stones and the grass to tunnel his message underground. They had no reason to resist. With a little luck he would put the gifts of the Kingdom at their service; correct their tongues, which knew no language; introduce them to some style of living. Lunacy, he was warning the sulphur peaks of the cliff, it was lunacy to desecrate such gifts with an open insult, to resist. The Kingdom would ask no more than a painless subjugation to a contract that would leave them free. They were entitled to their usual share of things. Nothing would change except increase of crops, which the natural vegetation now conceals. But if this stubbornness grows, if they continue this insult underground...

'The snakes,' he was whispering in his sleep; 'my answer will be the snakes. The snakes. Will be my answer.'

A hand was uncoiling around his neck. But he didn't stir. Gently, with the slightest rustle of the sheet, she had begun to take her body from his embrace. She had released her legs from under the warm weight of his thigh. Her hand was sliding free, until her wrist came up against his ribs. He was breathing hard. She could hear him shrug in his sleep. She let her wrist pause under his ribs, and waited until his breathing grew quieter. She didn't want to wake him; besides, she knew it wouldn't be long before he discovered that she wasn't there.

Now she wanted to be alone. She had to go before her emotion got out of control. She levered his body forward and made a passage under his back. Her hand had come through. She sat up for a moment and let her legs hang down the side of the bed, measuring each phase of her retreat. She wanted to be alone. Her knowledge was unbearable while she lay so close beside him. Yes, she knew what his silence meant; he wouldn't have to tell her. Their contract had been broken. He would sail again. Her triumph had been premature. That's why he hadn't spoken. He was afraid and ashamed to let her know what he had decided. He would leave her again to ramble daily through the windy desolation of the moors. After his second departure she had almost gone mad with hunger for his body. As each day increased her need for his presence, she took to walking through the vast acres of woodland, pretending that he was there, stride for indolent stride, beside her; embracing the apple boughs as though they were his arms spreading a miracle out from the trees. She shuffled the leaves, making little fingers with their stems. But the middle voyage was the worst.

She was ready to move again. She lowered her body, coming down on her toes. There was a shuffle of silk cloth under her feet. She brought her heels down and waded her hands like oars through the dark. She heard his body turn and root for fresh space over the bed. She came to a halt and stood still, waiting until it was safe to stir again. She started to paddle her way forward. She found the door, and made her passage sideways and out to the narrow corridor that led to her room.

This was her refuge when he was away. His absence had made it sacred with living. She took all her meals in this little cabin of space, furnished with miniature ships, stones of emerald from the new lands; every item of seafare that would bring him near, and hurry his return to her arms.

She had found the candles. She lit them and waited for the light to show the mouth of the horn that held them. The room became a large box crowded with charms that had long ceased to console her waiting. There was a sudden burst of candlelight on the floor. It swept her small bed, twisting slowly up the beams that supported two rows of shelves. This cabinet, sacred as a chapel, was where the three huge crystal jars were stored. They kept measure of the days he had gone. The crystal could not predict when he would be back; but she could rely on the leaves to tell her how many days he had gone. She was taking them down, each jar bearing its own label of the voyage it contained. She sat on the floor. Her hands were shaking when she stretched them forward to remove the lids. She had to wait. She tried to read the number which showed up on the shoulder of the middle jar.

'You're mad,' the wind was warning. 'Love has driven you mad.' She could hear the sound come up from the moors to storm the window. There was a rattle of locks. She watched the crystal jars, each with its separate cargo of leaves that numbered the days of the voyage it contained. Her ordeal had been the same after each farewell. The pattern didn't change. She would pluck a leaf every day from the date of his departure, and each day was a mile away from the day before. Who could ever guess her motive when they saw her striding through the wood? She had covered every acre of ground in her pursuit of leaves to measure his days over the sea. Until it was no longer a souvenir of absence which she observed. Gradually her mood would change. After a month of leaves her emotion achieved a new release, and each day became a promise of his return. She would begin to smile again. The servants overcame their alarm for a while. They would hear her laughter in the distance as she made her way back to the small cabin of space where she lived alone.

She was taking a leaf out of the jar on her left. She removed the film of paper that wrapped each leaf. The green heart of the oak and elm had shrunk to a crisp brown skeleton of veins. They would crack and shrivel at the slightest touch of her hand. She took the paper away and let the thin ghost of the stem snap and topple onto her hand. She saw the little dry spine divide into two. Her hands began to tremble. There was a spasm of fever in her fingers. She couldn't bear it any longer. She was crushing the fragments between her palms. One mile and one day had been strangled with the once green leaf between her hands. She looked at the middle jar; but she could hardly endure her fury. She was reading the label with its number of days. The mist had grown heavier over her eyes. She could see nothing but a crust of leaves shivering inside the crystal jars. The middle journey bore the largest cargo of days. They were the bitterest leaves her memory could recall. He had been gone for one thousand and eleven days. It was a week after Christmas when he came home.

She didn't want to take the lid of the middle jar away. She turned her eyes up to the ceiling; then she stared towards the window. There was a drop in the wind, as though the moors had gone elsewhere. The silence fell like doom over her little cabin of refuge. She could hear nothing but an echo of her footsteps trampling over the years. She had walked two hundred and fifty days of miles before the first cargo of leaves was complete. It was her maiden voyage in keeping his absence at bay. She was brooding on the middle jar again. It was the most horrible passage of her waiting, one thousand and eleven miles of days.

The wind was probing the window again. The locks began to shake. There was a sound like cables lashing outside the house. The tears fell like beads onto her hands. He had broken their contract. She had lost her duel with the sea. He would sail again; that's why he hadn't spoken. She could smell his silence like a season of foul weather. The muscles were seizing up in her throat. She stared at the smallest jar in disbelief. It held the lightest cargo of days; exactly one hundred and eighty leaves. She had thought she knew why he had made his fourth voyage short; he had decided to bring their separation to an end. His silence, however, warned her she was wrong.

She pushed herself up from the floor; but her gaze continued its vigil over the crystal jars. She knew she would bring him awake. She didn't want him to come near her now; all her feeling had gone out of gear. She didn't know what would happen next; but a storm of hatred started to swell her hands. Her feet were kicking at the jars. The ships and the emeralds began to tremble at her touch. He had deceived her. She would wager her soul to find proof that he had deceived her. He knew that he had not come home to stay. He had bribed her into a crooked certainty that she had divorced him from the sea. And he knew. She was swearing on her life that he knew. He knew he would sail again. It was the jar with the lightest cargo of leaves that finally broke her spirit.

The wind was raging up from the moors. There was a noise of bees in her ears. She heard the trees collapse from the crash of flying crystal. Her hands had gone amok. The little cabin became a pyre of glass and leaves. She couldn't stop her hands from smashing whatever came within their reach. The little ships and the stones of emerald pitched like comets across the room. She could hear nothing but the large noise of bees increasing their mockery in her ears. Her tears had frozen her still.

Suddenly the room was quiet. She pressed her arms over her breasts and watched the rubble of leaves and crystal crowd around her feet. He had arrived in the doorway, but she couldn't tell the difference between his body and the night that led beyond it. Everything had become useless and ordinary as space. Even his voice. She couldn't identify its sound.

'What is it?' he went on asking. 'Tell me, darling, please tell me what I have done. What have I done now?'

He was moving towards her, picking his way slowly over the rubble of leaves and broken crystal. The floor was a battlefield of mementos. The room was getting smaller, as though the ceiling was about to crush his height down to the level of the chair and the small cedar bed. He looked to the bed for some hope of rescue. He struggled towards the chair, trying to achieve some action that was simple and domestic, like sitting down. He was lowering his body into the chair when he heard the violent twist of the lock and the slam of the door shutting her out.

She had gone. Suddenly she was not there. He waited for the sound of footsteps on the landing; but wind was pounding at the windows. The noise drowned his ears. He couldn't recognize the room since she had left. She was not there. The light was winding thin shadows over his hands, twisting like snakes up the golden lapels of his gown, and he tried to curb the tension that shook his knees. He paused, reflecting on the broken neck of the crystal jar which lay at his feet; he was hoping for some respite from the tension of the room. But the door had given way to her force.

She was there. But she came no farther. She was standing where she entered the room, her body held erect and still, in an attitude of strained and dangerous compromise. She had come back; but he couldn't predict the moments that would follow. She had given him no time to learn what he should say, to prepare himself against her rage. Her arrival was always too soon. She remained standing where she had entered the room. Time crawled under his skin, flooding his pores. Although he wanted to speak, as he saw her body grow like a column of black velvet up from the floor, it struck him dumb. This silence had become his role, his prison. Any effort of speech would be a blasphemy in her ears.

'What have I done?' he asked. His voice was working on its own; the words carried messages against his will. 'Tell me. What is it I have done?'

His innocence had propelled her into battle. She was staring at him; her glance grew hard and fierce. Some vengeance of the heart was waging war in her huge brown eyes, now sparked by daggers of candlelight. She didn't speak. She required no word to complete the meaning that her eyes declared. He felt her eyes reduce him to a captive target.

'*Now,*' he said again, 'what is it *now?*'

His voice was low, offering some hint of apologies to come. But there was no change in her method of attack. She remained standing, the sparkle gathering into a fire from her eyes.

'I must talk to you,' she said. Her lips barely moved. The words might have been relayed through her. Speech did not relax her.

'I say I must talk with you.'

'What have I done?' he said more firmly, and he was suddenly a man about to defend his honour. While he made no claim to innocence, he remained forever unaware of any guilt that might attach to his actions.

'About us,' she said, 'about you and me.'

The manner was conclusive. What else could there be to talk about?

'What about us now?' he asked, like a prisoner who had been kept in the dark.

His body was rooting about the chair for space. A fragment of crystal from the jars was scraping at his heels.

'What are your plans?'

'My plans,' he said, talking quietly to himself.

'Will you sail again?' she asked and fixed her stare between his eyes.

'Those are my orders,' he said.

'Your plans, I ask, what are your plans?'

'I have no plans outside my orders,' he replied.

Her glance travelled up the chair, crawled slowly over his throat and down to the pile of glass and leaves at his feet.

'Am I outside your orders?' she asked, her voice now calm and remote as the sky.

'You want to speak about the Voyage?'

'I want to speak about us, about the contract we agreed.'

She never moved while she spoke; not a muscle stirred to shift the weight of her body. It was this still, statuesque posture of arms and body that confused him; the immobile carriage of her head and throat, wearing the necklace like a chain of nails. Her voice was calm yet violent in the urgency of its appeal. It gave her the momentary power of some enemy he hadn't known before. But her hair fell wild as roots over her shoulders.

An hour ago she had tamed his hunger with her body. He had grown dizzy from the touch of her hands nursing his ears, coursing like candle flame down the warm arch of his spine. Now he could scarcely believe what he was seeing. There was a dangerous stranger lurking behind the terrible calm that came over her voice and her eyes.

"But she is beautiful," he reflected, and suddenly called a halt to his longing. He was afraid of what he knew. Her rage would reach its peak at any sign of his submission. He warned himself against forgetting what he knew: the swift, unerring assault that would meet any gesture that showed him yielding to her demands. "She must know," he was trying to say, "she must know that I want to stay."

'Whatever I do,' he said aloud, 'you know very well how I feel.'

'You have decided,' she said coldly; 'you have decided to sail again.'

He didn't answer; but she was ordering him to speak, as though his silence could no longer serve as a reply.

'I say you have decided,' she said again.

Nothing registered with him except the fact that she had not moved; the patience of hands and feet to stay where they were while murder raged in her voice, and her gaze drilled into his body.

'What are you?' she asked. 'Tell me what you are.' He might have been a foreigner she had discovered on the moors. Her hands began to tremble; he heard her voice sharpen its edge. 'You wear the highest honours the Kingdom can offer. Men of every rank admire you. Now, tell me how you do it. Tell me.'

He rubbed his heels together and mused on the plunder of crystal jars on the floor. He had anticipated her assault. He knew what was coming. 'How?' he heard her shout at him. 'Tell me how you do it.'

Her ignorance now hurt him.

'I know my work,' he said with great patience. 'It is more than many a man can say.'

'Work,' he heard her grumble.

He had always taken pride in this conviction. But his confidence didn't have the effect of subduing her. Now it seemed to increase her contempt and give a greater power of argument to her abuse of his achievements. 'Work,' she shouted, 'a butcher's skill. You call it work. You call your butchery work?'

His body came rigid on the chair.

'You are not worth the meanest of your men,' she was accusing him. 'Work, you call it. You will sail again, I know. So tell me, answer me now. What will you kill when all the mines are empty, when every offspring of the Tribes is dead and buried? Tell me. You will sail, I know. So answer me now. Whose women will you murder next? Tell me, answer me, before you sail. Whose children will you strangle next?'

He wanted to stir from the chair. He couldn't move. He tried to speak; but he was alarmed by this force of malice which had conquered her feeling. This drama had never lost its magic of terror. Familiar as bread, it brought new treasures of destruction whenever they fought it out. But he couldn't summon the urge to fight her now. Again he could feel his nerve fail; this failure had achieved something unique, a novelty he could not name. He had lost the urge to fight her back. 'A murderer,' he heard her repeat, 'a murderer's work.' He would have preferred her to spit at him and take her leave on that note of final contempt. There was nothing to rival the malice of her voice drilling these intimacies deep into his ears, menacing the source of all his confidence. He was making an old man's noise with his mouth.

'I loved her,' she heard him mutter. But she had taken charge of his emotion, as though she knew what gifts his nature would not allow.

'Love,' she said, instructing him in the harshness of his own feeling. 'You will never know what it is to love. Never. Not you.'

His voice was working on its own. He heard it say: 'So what would you have of me?' It seemed he had found some logic that might rescue him from her rage.

'Sail,' she said. 'You must sail again. Go feed on your humans. That's your work. Like the vultures over the Demon Coast, you feed on humans. You must sail to your work.'

'Is that all you can say for me?' a voice was coming to his defence. He had forgotten the nature and pain of insult. She had made him forget.

'Name any monster,' she cried, 'and he is no match for you. He will never be. A human-eater is what you are.'

A voice leapt from his throat against his will.

'And your father?' he was asking the broken shoulder of the jar. 'Do you feel the same about your father?'

For the first time she moved; it was hardly movement. He didn't see it happen. The slam of the door was the first evidence that she had departed. She wasn't there. 'Gone,' he heard himself say, but he didn't trust the relief his eyes had brought. He had to look again. She was not there.

He looked at the door; and stared for a while, as though he had to carry out an experiment with his eyes. He forced himself to recognize where she had been standing. The place always preserved a quality of discovered ground. He was musing on the relief that her absence had brought him. Always it came like a great soothing wave of sleep over his eyes, cooling the furnace of words she had made in his ears: this immense relief at finding that she was not there. He made to get up.

But the door was suddenly thrust wide open, and her voice had stormed the silence of the room. She had returned. She was there: the body slightly bent and quivering like an animal in its pride of wildness, timing the impulse to pounce.

'If you prefer a murderer's work to me,' she said, 'then you must murder me.'

His silence had grown like a fortress about him. He had no words; no way of telling how long she would stay, or what new danger her fury was preparing. Murder was always present on her return, and she left it behind whenever she went. Gone, his eyes were blinking, she had gone before he could prepare himself. She was not there. But every whisper of the door warned that she would be on her way again.

The wind was rising. It came hard and high over the house, then floated without any trace of sound beyond the horizon of the trees. His eyes were fixed to the spot where she had stood. The room was suddenly still. He couldn't move. A clock struck in the hall; he didn't know whether it was the third or fourth chime which he had heard. The night was roasting slowly in the little room, sizzling his skin up with its fierce heat. She always took her share of space when she went. She was somewhere outside. On the great wooden staircase? Or in the hall? Or had she gone on her ramble across the moors, defying every danger with her vagrancy? But he couldn't move. His feet had grown soft and hot. There was a feel of burning rubber at his heels. This temperature was worse than the torrid ocean seas that he had sailed and conquered for his Kingdom. He could feel the little room draw its walls together, closer than a box. He tried to push himself up and walk towards the window. He had to make sure it was still there. It seemed the box was making space for his height; but nothing changed. The window was there, a frame of blistering candlelight. He wished the light would burst its shutters and let the air come through. Every whisper warned she might be on her way. He wasn't ready to cope with her return; and yet he needed to have her back. He had never known any human absence that aroused in him such fear and expectation. Although her departure came as a relief, her absence was unique in its affliction.

The heat was attacking his eyes again. He could barely see the rubble of glass and leaves on the floor. 'Let nothing ever happen,' he heard himself say; but his voice worked on its own. A spell of dizziness closed his eyes. He was dreaming of the ocean, and the rival prize of islands, stealing their temperature into this room. An entire garrison might desert; or a sudden flight of population deprive his work of any meaning, leaving him nothing to organize or control. He would be able to endure such contingencies, brood on them until monotony made them trivial examples of inconvenience. But her absence was unique, a creation without any parallel of anguish. He was muttering more freely now, hearing his voice alert him to some danger.

'Let nothing happen to her,' he said; and the thought now made him ready for vengeance. He felt his nerves come steady. His muscles found their steel, he was discovering some portion of his strength. He sat at the edge of the basket chair. 'Let nothing happen,' he cried; but he had started to cheer himself up. He was trying to detect some failure in her. There was some defect in her virtues. She had become a victim of passions that confused her. Her virtues were flawed by some error of indulgence. She knew why he had to sail. He had found the urge to argue, now that she wasn't there; and he started to calculate the punishment that her absence inflicted on him. He lay back on the little bed.

'If this would last one night.' He was trying to speak in her defence. 'But she will begin again. She will begin exactly where she left off. It's always the same, only a little worse each time. The last departure was bad; this will be worse.'

His hands were sweating floods. He pulled himself forward and looked down at the shambles she had left behind. He wanted to make himself ready for her return; but the heat had trapped his brain. It made a furnace of the leaves and crystal fragments of the jars. The sweat started a ring of clouds around his eyes. He had never noticed the rigours of climate in the torrid zones. Work was his atmosphere. It reduced everything to normal, and made him impervious to discomfort. He would hear voices complain about the humid pressure of the days, the sweating nights. Words in his ears! A habit of noise that might protect men from the dangers of their trade. Work made him blind—until they met. He had never known the face of weather until she came into his life.

'From the very first day we met.'

It was easy to remember, but he couldn't get further with his reflections. He was trying to shield himself from the dangers of what he knew. He couldn't cope with her rage. He had no skill to curb the passions that made her wreak such damage on his need. The ocean had chosen him for the Kingdom. He had a destiny across the seas, a duty that the future would purify. And yet she let her rage denounce him as a common criminal.

He was wiping his hands over the lapels of the gown. The mist grew dense over his eyes. He heard himself stammer again, as though his voice was working on its own.

'She is a virtue I cannot satisfy,' he said. 'And she will never change.'

There was a note of finality in his voice. Her departure had brought a momentary relief; now her absence reminded him of danger. It would be worse when she got back. He listened for some whisper from the door, but the wind had come hard again. It was mounting the chimneys, lashing the trees with a burst of showers. He started to push himself up again; the damp had unsettled his hands. He struggled to get his balance. There was a crush of leaves and glass under his feet, and he heard the rain come harder.

'There's too much error in her virtue,' he was whispering. He might have taken a risk with his convictions, and surrendered his duty to her judgment. But he was afraid of her virtue. It threatened him with destruction. She was too hard in matters of self enquiry. An impossible vigilance reigned over everything she did. It was some part of her fascination and power over him; this fierce and punishing scrutiny that she turned on everything he said. She had made him a prisoner of speech.

He felt the islands thaw and float their torrid moisture down on his hands. There was a bubble of lava spreading at his back. He knew he had to sail again.

Was it an hour since she had gone? Was it the third or the fourth? He was struggling through the last rays of candlelight towards the door. He heard the rain shake the roof as he came out to the landing. He was discovering his strength again as he moved to the safety of the bedroom. He pushed the door forward; but the floor was slipping under his feet. He looked again as though he thought his eyes had deceived him: she had come back. He took refuge in the chair. His dagger had fallen from the small table onto the floor. He picked it up to give his hands something to do, making himself ready to speak with her. But something had changed. He couldn't believe what he was seeing. Her eyes looked old. There was no magic to her mouth. Rain was racing down her cheek, forming like icicles at the curve of her lips. He wanted to take her in his arms; but he couldn't move. He was afraid to stir lest he disturb some delicate balance of sanity that now made her calm. She was still, almost serene in this attitude of remote and mute endurance. She was bearing some agony of spirit that was beyond his experience. Although he wanted to speak, his tongue lay wet and dead. There was a feel of sponge in his mouth. He watched her from the corner of his eyes, afraid that she might detect his glance. He had no answer for this long and desolate struggle raging inside her skull. There was some catalogue of miseries reflected in her eyes.

She looked up from the bed and glanced about the room as though she couldn't tell with certainty where she was. She was trying to find her bearings. She felt the soft, sleek shuffle of silk under her feet. The tapestries hung like banners around the room, purple and blue in the candlelight. The colours were spinning before her eyes. She saw the face of a blue dragon loom out of the tapestry on her left. The mantelpiece was laden with souvenirs, trinkets and stones of emeralds laid out like pebbles on the shore.

The rain was washing the moors. She heard the echo of her footsteps labouring past the trees. She was counting the days she had crushed to fragments, the miles that her hands had buried beneath the splinters of the crystal jars. A flood was taking her last cargo of leaves across the moors: one hundred and eighty miles of days; but the middle voyage was the worst.

'And the women of the Tribes,' she said. 'Are there any families left on the Demon Coast?' Her voice was calm. She wiped the icicles of rain from her mouth. 'Their punishment was worse than mine.'

She had come to a point of speechlessness. She recognized what she wanted to say, without fathoming the doom that it implied. She had known a separation of her own; she had also borne witness to the madness that a separation could afflict on the women of the Tribes who had to wait. She was there. She had seen them. She had watched the women wait, labour and wait until their bodies grew frail as bramble that the wind would break. She had no name for what she knew; no word that was large enough with truth to tell reliably what she had seen. The middle voyage was her worst, the heaviest cargo of leaves her hands had gathered. But she had never known the curse of toil enforced on her waiting. She had seen the women of the Tribes go in droves, herded like cattle across the farms, digging the earth with sticks and naked hands.

She was counting the leaves that numbered his days away. She saw the dragon smile through the blue thread of tapestry. It was the lightest cargo of leaves that broke her spirit. She saw the smallest of the crystal jars open in fragments over her hands. The splinters pierced her ears, made a hive of screaming in her head.

'My father was in command of the Demon Coast,' she said.

The name had alerted him. He made his body rigid in the barrel chair. His nails were digging quietly at his thighs. He looked ahead and down at a stone of emerald on the floor. He was afraid of questions, hers and his own. But he wanted to let her know that he had heard. It helped him to let her know that he had heard.

'Your father,' he said, and kept his glance on the glittering stones. 'Have you had news of Master Cecil?'

Suddenly he wanted to make some apology for his effort to speak. He was terrified of the consequence any question might inflict. He had lost the power to predict where words would lead her.

'Have you had news?' he asked again. But she knew his motive. Words were now a way of protecting him from speech. He would let her answer come to his aid. She would contribute to the fortress of his silence.

'I was there,' she said, talking to the stones on the mantelpiece. 'Ten thousand women died in a single month. They had not seen their men after my father took them away. Ten thousand in one month.'

Her voice had lost its passion. He couldn't tell what feeling stirred behind those memories. There was such infinite patience in her speech. He kept his head down, reading the dull glitter of the stones. He heard her father's voice, grown feeble from the stress of onerous command. His nails were making a chart of rivers down his thighs.

'I thought the small jar was my last triumph,' she said, and looked up at the canopy that covered the bed. Her eyes travelled slowly down the cedar posts. She looked beyond the bed, letting her eyes roam towards some object that might halt her gaze and hold it. But she had scarcely seen his body in the barrel chair. Her eyes were spread with a tangle of mist and tears.

'Ten thousand mothers in a month,' she cried, and her breath came hot as lava from her nostrils. 'The corpses of the children went without count. We couldn't number them where they lay.'

She heard the rain beat on the moors outside. The middle voyage was the heaviest cargo of days her legs had covered when he went away. She saw the largest jar of crystal break and spin with leaves. One thousand miles of stems collapsed in her hands.

'The women of the Tribes were ignorant of the plough,' she said, and suddenly paused and brought her fingers up to touch her lips. 'For eight months of the year, heavy with child inside them, almost to the very day of their delivery, the women were the only hands left to work the farms. Ten thousand mothers dead in one month. My father had taken their men away. Ten thousand! And the children; we could not count the children where they lay.'

She clutched at her hair, prising the roots up from her skull. Her eyes were blind with mist. She saw the canopy above her like a sky at night. The wind had lifted; and the rain came softer on the moors. The cloth of silk was crawling leisurely under her feet. She was looking for some object that would anchor her gaze. She saw the candelabra climb like horns above the mantelpiece. The silver lay careless as pebbles where the river bends along the Demon Coast.

'No family here,' she said, 'no noble in the Kingdom would deny my father is a decent man. A loyal husband, indulgent to a fault in affection for his daughter.' She turned to see the body in the barrel chair. 'Ten thousand mothers in a month; and drowned their children every one before your bullets cut them down. We couldn't count the children where they lay.'

The wind had died. She heard the last sound of rain outside on the moors. But the echo of her footsteps now traced her voyage through the trees. She had gathered the last cargo of leaves.

'I didn't know,' she said, clutching the collar of silver at her throat, 'and never would have known that this could happen under another sky. It is not possible ever to believe unless you see. But I was there. Because of you I was there.'

She was suddenly frightened by some memory that had fled her from the Demon Coast. She wanted someone to come to her aid, wanted to hear him speak. She was counting on her fingers like a child, caught in a forest of numbers that made no sense. Feeling some calamity which lay outside his power to conceive, she shifted on the bed and pushed herself forward to see him more clearly in the chair.

'How many are we in Lime Stone?' she asked. 'Here in Lime Stone, how many are we?'

He was startled by the nearness of her voice. His hands went to work again, tracing a stream of red veins over his thighs. He couldn't be sure what she was asking; what demon had driven her to make a trial of the Kingdom's triumphs over the ocean seas?

'How many?' she asked, and her voice had come near to a shout. 'How many are we here in the North?'

He turned his head away from the stones and watched the prancing fervour in the dragon's paws. The tapestry was floating blue candle flame down from the beams which held them high.

'In the North, you say?'

'Here in the North,' she answered quickly, 'how many are we?'

'The population of the North,' he mused.

'People,' she said briskly; 'how many people in the North?'

And he detected a nervous impatience in her tone. But he

hadn't lost his nerve. His delay was reliable. He was earnest and grave in moments of delay.

'One million and a half,' he said. His voice was firm and clean, his tone exact.

She sat still, repeating syllables she couldn't calculate. Million and one month, one hundred months, ten thousand. How many? How many are we left? How many would we be?

He watched her now, and felt a little safer while she was brooding on her hands. But he was afraid to trespass on her silence. His fear warned him to be sure. He had to know where she was leading with this wild arithmetic.

'It wouldn't take longer than your life at sea,' she said, and brought her body down the bed to see him at a closer range. 'Not longer than ten years.' She had anticipated the extinction of the North.

He had become afraid for her; she had gone dangerously beyond her senses. He watched her for a moment, and felt some weight of guilt oppress his eyes.

'What do you mean?' he said, touched by the fierceness of her eyes counting joint after joint on each finger.

'Ten years,' she said. 'No longer than your life at sea.'

'What do you mean?' he said again. 'Tell me, my darling, what can you *possibly* mean?'

And it was the emphasis his voice had fixed on 'possibly' that made her scream. He had never heard this sound from a human voice before. She had leapt with a tiger's fury from the bed. She trembled in every limb where she stood, screaming her life out in his ears.

'Mean, mean, mean, you know well what I mean.' She wheeled her body around and boxed the air with her fist. 'Imagine ten thousand mothers died each month. With twice as many children buried. Imagine that here in the North. Ten thousand by the month. It would bring the Region to an end. And in less years than you have been at sea. Can you imagine this Kingdom without the North? Can you? But with ten thousand mothers dead. And in a month!' Extinction was now real as the air she breathed.

She had brought him to his feet. He stood erect, aghast at the sinister labyrinth of reasoning that had seized her brain; she was not herself. He was sure her mind had passed beyond the limit where she could judge what she was saying. What demon in her brain could make her conceive the liquidation of the North, whose ancient families were the very heart and history of the Kingdom? He moved to touch her, to caress her back to sanity. And in a blinding flash of blood he felt the dagger split his chin. Her hands were swift as lightning. Transfixed, he didn't stir a muscle in his body. He couldn't feel the drip of blood slipping past his throat. She had gone. The door shivered and shook with the fury of her voice screaming her misery over the moors.

'Ten thousand mothers died on the Demon Coast. Ten thousand in one month.'

The room closed over him like a tomb. The blood burnt his chin. His hands were light as feathers; but a weight of iron hung over his eyes. 'Let nothing happen. Let nothing. Happen to her.' A voice was delivering him from the fortress of his silence. The rain had ceased. The night was dumb. There was no stir of vegetation anywhere.

That summer of his fifth Voyage out she came back to her little cabin of space where she would store fresh leaves and watch the days accumulate in her crystal jar. There was fever in her eyes, and a wish that reconciled her to his going.

'Whatever you are,' she said, 'I love you. It is you I love.'

Voices grew louder everywhere. The ship's bell rang again, calling the men to the decks. Sasha wiped a cloud of mist from his eyes and cast a glance at the water. The timbers made a shudder under his feet, and the carpenter's flute sent out a hard, high sound like the clap of a hand. There was a fist of light pushing slowly through the gunport. The moon was riding low, a huge glow of flame that cut full speed through the silver nets of cloud. The men were getting drunk with song as they watched the last strips of fog dissolve. The wind had come awake. The sails began to shiver. The boy was waiting to break the news. The calm had lifted; and a breeze rode easily over the bow. Sasha came closer to get a view of the Commandant stretched full length on the small bed. The boy thought he was asleep; but the Commandant's eyes were open. He was watching the charts emerge from a distant fog of moors and woodland, while vaguely aware of a chorus of bees droning up from the decks below. He saw the islands sink beneath her eyes, burning like stars whenever she laughed. She was there, a cargo of green leaves in her hands, and her voice like a summer of bees now borne from wave to wave was calling him to his final safety. The boy walked quietly back to the door.

It was the woman's voice that had brought the Commandant up from the small bed. Awake, he had swung his legs off the small bed. He stood for a moment considering the charts, though he saw the boy linger at the door. He glanced at the large globe on the council table where the last rays of the horn lanterns had begun to fade. The boy watched him bend slowly into the chair. He had sent no orders to his officers; but the boy decided he would wait until he heard the order to dismiss. The Commandant had taken up his quill, and the boy watched his left arm curve like a bay around the sheets of paper.

The boy came nearer and stood, waiting. This was routine, he would stay there until the Commandant was ready to give an instruction; it was as though he had already begun to perform the instructions he might receive.

But there was a difference in this waiting. Sasha felt that he was bearing witness to something that he couldn't, for the moment, understand. Some magic radiated from the Commandant's face. His eyes were soft, the brow untroubled, as though the entire cabin was under a spell. The air was calm, almost serene. The Commandant became conscious of the boy, and looked up to acknowledge Sasha's presence. This act of recognition gave the boy a feeling that was near to thrill. Sasha smiled as the Commandant waved him towards the small bed; he alone knew of the gun the Commandant kept underneath it. The boy felt he was part of some deep kinship, some conspiracy of knowing. He couldn't say what such knowledge was about. But it was there, like a memory that had temporarily lost its content. He felt proud to be on this ship, in this enterprise, with this Commandant; prouder than any man or officer he had met.

The Commandant was writing. Grave and patient, he had crouched his shoulders low over the council table, and it seemed that he would go on writing forever.

SEVEN

Daylight had taken the boy by surprise. Sasha was recovering slowly from the trance of strange weathers that had left a veil of shadows over his eyes. The ship had come safely through the long dark tunnel of fog and mist, and the mornings began to pour with rays from a hard blue rock of sky. The forest rose like a tide of green fire down the coast. The boy couldn't recall when the sun had first appeared. But it was there, large and fierce, striking a million fists of violent heat upon the deck. There was no interval of dawn under these skies. The night seemed to loiter for a while. The moon would dip out of sight; and soon a terrible firmament of rays had set a lasting fire on everything it struck. He was afraid to touch the timbers or the shrouds that seemed to scorch his hands. His heels were soft as tallow from the heat. The air sizzled like water coming to the boil. The boy didn't think it was a region where men could live; he was sure the Commandant wouldn't let them linger here very long.

The ship was anchored at the mouth of the river. Sasha had watched all the anchors lowered; two at the bow and three of smaller bulk at the stern. He was curious and vigilant as he watched the line of the shore recede far inland. He had never seen any other coast or river but those of Lime Stone. Now there was no sign of a house anywhere. Trees appeared in the distance, incredibly tall and heavy, with fruit at the top, their leaves thin and sharp like the blades of spears. And everything was still. There was scarcely a breath of wind, but the air had started to hum with a soft pulse of song. A flock of birds chased in circles over the ship. They were smaller than any he had ever seen; bright with colour and swift as flies as they swept past the ensign that fell slack and still from the head of the mainmast.

The boy watched the river grope around the ship. The water

was dark and still as mud until the surface began to stir. A large family of reptiles was migrating from the shore. The boy couldn't tell whether these monstrous creatures would swim or fly until he saw the river shake and tremble from the lash of their tails. They were longer than the yards that held the sails; and the bodies spread thicker than the timbers of the ship's mainmast. Sasha looked up at the masthead, which the birds had suddenly deserted. They rose and pitched through the air; then straightened their wings, cruising like tramps across the sky. But the river made him shudder. He watched the crocodiles churn the water up. They were feeding on some huge, black bulge of flesh that looked like the carcass of a horse. He was afraid to be alone; but the Commandant was busy. He had not yet sent the boy with orders to the officers, for he had been holding long council with the pilot. It was an hour or more since Pinteados had entered the Commandant's cabin. The boy kept watch outside the door.

The officers were in separate conference, for the sight of land beyond this river had aroused a new promise of fortune. Priest had gone to confer with Surgeon, while Boatswain accepted Steward's invitation to join him in his cabin. Boatswain knew the secrets of the coast. Such knowledge was worth a fortune in gold; he was careful whom he chose for company.

Steward showed no sign of discomfort from the heat. His cabin was ablaze with sunlight. The sweat dripped from his hands, and the mirror went dark under a new cloud of steam. But his eyes were gay. He was combing his beard, lifting the red tail of hair high up between his fingers. He plucked at the ragged end of beard and wiped the cloud of steam from the glass; the smooth turf of whiskers made a fence around his face, and his cheeks showed two peaks of flame. His mouth was thin and dry. Boatswain sat in the far corner, admiring Steward's taste for order. His clothes were always neat, and he made his orders brief and precise. Steward finished his toilet, wiping a fresh ring of cloud from the mirror.

'Put it under cover,' said Boatswain, mopping his brow with a sleeve. 'In an hour you couldn't tell whether it's glass or iron. This climate turns everything to rust.'

'You've been on this coast before,' said Steward, polishing the mirror over the breast of his tunic.

'Rust, I tell you,' Boatswain answered. 'In less than an hour. I've seen it happen to the most steadfast metal.'

Boatswain pulled a bottle from above his hip, and raised it up to his mouth. But some force of elegance in Steward's glance had suddenly stopped his arm. Boatswain coughed and slapped the sweat off his neck. Steward made a casual signal with one hand to the cups on the table. Boatswain looked distracted as he rose slowly from the bench, measuring his stride towards the table. He had grown formal and nervous under Steward's glance. He noticed that his tunic was open to the waist, and his stomach seemed fat and coarse with hair. Steward's neatness held his attention, like a charge against his own exposure. It was an effort to remember that he was an officer. He was pouring the drink into the cups. He watched Steward from behind, admiring the carriage of his shoulders. Curious, his eyes grew small and enquiring, as though his mind worked on the subtleties of breeding he had observed in Steward. It was the privilege of learning. Boatswain made a formal offer of the drink, but Steward was putting the mirror into the chest. Steward paused, musing on the screen of charts which showed around the cabin. Boatswain thought he had detected some rebuke in Steward's delay. He kept his head down and waited, concentrating his furious attention on the cups.

'You've never travelled this far before,' Boatswain said, making a point in his favour. There was a hint of superiority in his experience. He took the cup from the table and stretched his arm slowly out to Steward.

Steward took the drink, made a nod to register his thanks, and quickly turned his eyes back to the charts.

'I couldn't make that boast,' he said, conceding the advantage of travel that Boatswain enjoyed. 'My knowledge comes largely from the charts.'

'It's a privilege,' said Boatswain, sipping his drink, 'to have such a knowledge of maps.'

He considered the atmosphere that reigned over Steward's cabin. It looked like a school for pilots. The timbers showed screens on every side—large squares of canvas cut to fit the size of each chart, and fastened with tacks as a shield against the rough surface of the wood. The charts were spread full length, smooth and clear, over each sheet of canvas. There were smaller maps on the table. The cabin seemed to crawl through a network of lines and spheres. The lettering was fine, climbing with names and signs like an infinite line of ants, marching in curves, halting to make green angles for a space that showed the size of an ocean. The ink wriggled like worms where a range of mountains was thinly scribbled. The room throbbed with Steward's passion for cosmography. He had no rival to this dream that would complete his knowledge of all the globes and charts he had compiled; every item of evidence that travel and arithmetic had discovered in the four known continents of the world.

Steward turned to check his memory by the charts. He was nursing his lips with the tip of his tongue, soothing the pink flakes of skin that peeled off his mouth. His cheeks were flushed with heat. The lobes of his ears looked soft and tender from the pressure of air in the cabin. But the charts occupied his mind. The sweat had clogged Boatswain's nostrils. A roll of mud came away in his hands when he scraped his neck. Although he wanted to go out to the decks for a breath of air, he couldn't resist this curious passion that held Steward to his maps, comparing the charts that showed the latitude of this river.

'Do you know the more recent maps?' Steward asked as he now remembered that he was not alone.

'I couldn't make that claim,' said Boatswain, helping himself to another drink.

He walked slowly towards the porthole, clutching at a rope which stretched full length across the cabin. He cleared the mist from his eyes and turned a lazy glance down at the water. The surface was torn open with river life. The reptiles went crazy in their pursuit of food. He glanced over his shoulder to see Steward tracing his fingers over the lines on the chart.

'There is a town where the river widens,' said Boatswain as though he wanted to give substance to Steward's devotion.

'Twenty miles down,' said Steward, and smiled at the direction on the charts. Boatswain felt humbled by the tone of precision. Steward's voice was still telling the distance by the charts.

'And you've never travelled this far before,' Boatswain said, paying his tribute.

'All my knowledge comes from the charts,' Steward answered, and looked down at the chest.

'And most reliable too,' said Boatswain, guiding his glance into the cup.

He felt so meek before the magic of Steward's passion for learning. Boatswain grew cautious with his secrets. This coast was a memorable frontier in his life. He might have made his fortune here many years ago; but he held no rank of any substance in those days. He was a common sailor who failed to qualify for anyone's attention. It was impatience which had contrived his failure. Not greed. He could never think of his ambition as an example of greed. He watched the clumsy labour of the river, heavy and tedious under the heat. Like the pile of years he had lost to the sea. He could have built a kingdom from the early plunder of this coast. But he was a common sailor then. His skill couldn't thrive without that magic of breeding which he observed in Steward. His skill had deceived him. It had made him too eager to impress those who were in command. A lack of patience had finally trapped him into misfortune.

He forced a smile at the charts, as though he wanted to pay just tribute to Steward's devotion. He started to scrub his neck again. His eyes were quick and careful when he looked at Steward. "A friendly man," he thought as he mused on Steward, "but there is too great discretion in his bearing." There was something which warned that friendship was a matter for care. You had to achieve it slowly and according to the interests which he disclosed. Boatswain settled for the charts as the safest guide into Steward's confidence.

'With such a knowledge of maps,' he said, and his breath formed bubbles over the wine, 'you would be worth a fortune to the House of Trade and Justice.'

Steward's eyes suddenly closed over a peak of ice indicated on the charts. He was cautious in reply. Boatswain noticed his reserve. It was the certain effect of any reference to the House. It made Steward consider the attitude he thought safe for the circumstance in which he was called to speak. Boatswain's mouth made a noise of sucking over the rim of the cup. The steam was floating huge pimples of sweat down his chin. The pimples thawed and salted the wine.

'They say that's how the Lord Treasurer started his career,' he said. 'It was a knowledge of the maps which did it.'

Steward's body grew erect. Boatswain saw him turn from the chart. His eyes were drawn narrow and grave with brooding. He took a stride forward and rested the cup on the table. But he was slow to speak.

'Such a wealth of maps,' Boatswain said again, 'they say these paved his way to the House. That's as I heard it said by those who knew Gabriel Tate de Lysle.'

Steward's hand felt for the chain around his neck. There was a fresh print of colour on his cheeks, but his voice was cold when he spoke.

'Gabriel started here,' said Steward, and quickly snatched at the cup on the table.

'Gabriel,' Boatswain was whispering to himself. He was astonished by this intimacy that Steward assumed in his reference to the Lord Treasurer to the House. Yet it was done with the tact and calm of natural breeding.

'The Lord Treasurer,' Boatswain said again, hoping to confirm what he had heard.

Steward's beard seemed to crackle with flame. He had put the cup firmly back on the table. The wine left a stain over his lip. But his reserve was like a hard red mask of sky, remote and free of trouble.

'The Lord Treasurer started here,' Steward said, 'on this same coast. It was Master Cecil made him a gift of Guinea slaves. I believe it was this same coast.'

Suddenly Steward called a halt to what he knew, and turned quickly back to the charts. He might have been talking to himself. If his voice was low and casual, his meaning had been planted with care. Whatever the risk, he would not allow any rumour that praised the Lord Treasurer's knowledge of maps.

There was no need to emphasize his certainty. He noticed Boatswain's reluctance to make further comment on what he had heard. Boatswain filled his cup again and started a slow retreat back from the table. He heard a stale wind roll inside the cavern of his stomach, and let himself gently down on the bench. He didn't want to probe further into Steward's association with the Lord Treasurer; such curiosity might prove a risk he couldn't afford. He heard an echo of the Commandant's warning about the merchants of the sea, and he wondered where Steward stood in the affairs of the House.

'I feel the pilot will sail upriver before the day is out,' said Boatswain. He was scheming to bring Steward's attention back to the charts. And Steward was agreeable. It was so much safer there.

'There is conflict about the size of the creeks,' said Steward. His voice had grown more lively as he walked over to the gunport. The first whiff of breeze came up from the water. He swept his hands up his throat and hugged the red tail of his beard. It was soft and moist with sweat.

'The pilot knows his way,' said Boatswain; 'that's to be sure.'

'He's been out here before?'

'That's a certainty,' said Boatswain. 'Antarctica once ruled this coast. The late Master Cecil suffered his last defeat coming up those very creeks. It's a certainty the pilot would know.'

He had aroused Steward's enthusiasm for greater knowledge of the creeks. Steward dried the sweat from his beard and came back to the charts. He was selecting two copies from the pile of maps on the chest. He came towards Boatswain and spread a map with infinite care out on the table.

'There's conflict somewhere,' he said, inviting Boatswain to join him in scrutiny of the map. 'The late Master Cecil made it ten miles at the mouth. What would you say?'

'It's bigger than the figure he puts,' said Boatswain.

'Twenty-five, to be exact,' Steward replied, hoisting the second map for Boatswain to examine.

'I wouldn't be exact,' Boatswain said, 'but your figure comes nearer the fact.'

'And the pilot would know?'

'I dare say he would,' said Boatswain gloomily. 'Pinteados served with the enemy when Master Cecil was put to flight up those creeks.'

He was scrubbing the back of his neck with his hands. He dried them on the front of his canvas jacket and reached forward for the bottle. Steward declined his offer of another cup, but Boatswain leaned the bottle away from the maps and poured himself what remained. He stooped his heavy shoulders forward and put the empty bottle on the floor. His eyes were moist and thick with mist. He felt a gradual sluggishness drag at the roots of his tongue, but his memory was ripening fast. He heard the distant rapids of the creek hurry him to speak.

'Some say he did a treacherous thing,' said Boatswain. 'Master Cecil, I mean. He was forced to ransom a man or two, and with just cause, I say. Though some would have it otherwise. Adversity will not always make for an honourable decision.'

Steward was reading the fine inscriptions on the chart, exploring for the creeks that had put a final blemish on Master Cecil's career. He read the small arrows of ink crawling everywhere:

River is safe at the mouth, navigable for five days down if winds be favourable and do not veer. Ten' days further the tides may subvert, cause being great ridge of rocks that continue east for miles. Shipwrecks be numerous here. Not worth the meagre traffic in slaves.

Steward's eyes darted from the intricate markings on the maps, to study the melancholy warning on Boatswain's face.

'But what could Master Cecil do?' Boatswain insisted. 'Tell me what you would do if you had to choose in such a conflict of loss? Would you risk the safety of a whole ship for a small portion of the crew?'

He paused to let the wine make a passage down his throat. He was about to gargle, but he saw Steward's studious eyes alight with attention, and swallowed the wine.

'There was no food for a crew that size,' he said, 'and the water wouldn't last to the Isle of Dolores more than a thousand miles away. There was no keeping the crew with so many mouths to feed. And that's what had to be, I swear. He cast lots to decide which men he would put to ransom. It was a fair way to decide a fate, seeing the odds were not in his favour. And certain slaves he took in exchange for a man or two.'

Steward relaxed his gaze and crouched his shoulder over the second map. The line of ants was crawling with tiny signals again; an empire of dots roved under his eyes:

Two days favourable winds and waters will divide. Many freshets

NATIVES OF MY PERSON

*join river at this bend. Town is docile, safe, and plentiful in
foods. Nuts and spice a common delicacy ten miles inland. Perfect
for watering and fresh provision. Inhabitants will war if there
be cause, but have no heart for victory. A good traffic in black
cargoes.*

'What would I do?' said Steward, and surveyed the cabin.
'They say he gave half the crew as spies in exchange for the
Guinea slaves.'

'A wicked rumour,' Boatswain quickly denied. 'It was twenty
men and no more he gave in exchange. That's a certainty, I tell
you. The rest offered to turn themselves loose, seeing they were
too many mouths to feed. They offered free and of their own
accord. I tell you what I see. I was there.'

He watched his eyes dance a shadow over the wine. The sedi-
ment spread like a fungus at the bottom of the cup. A large
bead of sweat slipped from his brow and shook like a pebble
over the last drain of wine.

'There's no knowing what common hands will report,' he began
to fret, 'and when the charge touches one of high repute, there's
no limit to the crimes they will imagine. Deliberately imagine, I
tell you.'

He thought he might have said too much; still, he had spoken
on behalf of authority. He was going to stretch his legs, but his
knees had grown soft and merry from the wine. He decided to
steady his balance with further speech, and Steward listened like
a boy in love with school.

'A similar travesty fell on the Commandant's head,' said Boatswain, musing on the last trickle of wine slipping down the cup.
'At San Souci it was. After we had freed the Tribes from the
rival thieves of Antarctica. Stubborn, I tell you. Those native
beasts were a stubborn breed. They'd rather eat the metal than
guide us to the mines. We had to open them up with knives, it's
true, but a gentle influence will not work on that kind of creature.'

Steward leaned his shoulders near. He was eager for some reliable history of the Commandant's career. He inspected his cup
for wine, then decided that his thirst could wait.

'You were at San Souci when we won it?' he asked.

'Under his command,' said Boatswain. 'The Commandant, I

mean. I came between him and his grave at San Souci.' There was
a note of nostalgia in his voice. Steward saw the look of admiration startle his eyes.

'They say he surpassed Master Cecil,' said Steward.

'In every way,' Boatswain replied. 'And at an age that made
him the envy of all ranks.'

Steward was curious to find the latitudes that showed the Isles
of the Black Rock, but Boatswain's story delayed his urge.

'They put it out as true report,' Boatswain said, 'how the Commandant murdered a whole town. But it was suicide that took
the largest numbers. They were a stubborn breed, making a joke
of suicide, killing themselves to make a mockery of our conquest.'
Boatswain slapped his hands in fury against the table. 'There's
no limit, I tell you, no limit to the charges they will imagine, no
limit, I tell you, when the charge touches one of high repute.'

Steward wanted to probe Boatswain's career from Guinea to
the Isles of the Black Rock. The man had served under the most
famous names in Lime Stone's history of conquest. Steward was
elated by these adventures. This moment of revelation—even
intimacy, it seemed—made him take pride in the great events
that had conferred such fortune on the Kingdom. His attention
was good as witness to what he had heard, for there was a way
of listening that made him feel identified with Boatswain's
experience.

'You have a wide experience,' said Steward, as though it was
a dismal shadow of what he really meant.

Boatswain wanted to thank him for his attention. Proud of
the enthusiasm he had aroused, he felt a greater confidence in
the destiny that had brought himself and Steward together as
officers in this enterprise. He had a dread of making error, however, particularly an error that might have its origin in the kind
of confidence he now felt in Steward. To give too generous
approval, one that circumstance might later force you to withdraw. Many voyages ago, before he had fallen out of the memory
of those who knew him, Boatswain had suffered this conflict of
feeling.

Abruptly, as though there was a great variety of examples in
his mind, Boatswain said: 'There are differences in character
that you can never reconcile.' He had startled Steward by this

philosophic turn of thought. 'In the battle at San Souci I made mention of, and again in the battles for the neighbouring Isle of Dolores. It would come as a problem to perplex the wisest judgment. This difference in character you can't ever reconcile.

'The Commandant had a rival in Dolores,' he said, 'Badaloza by name, and a man of similar fame in Antarctica. But most different in tone of character, I tell you. Badaloza would say to his officers: "I meet a man. Circumstances make him my company, but he is a stranger. Then I follow one rule of friendship: that man is a crook until time proves him otherwise."'

Boatswain screwed his lips and smiled in disgust.

'The Commandant was the opposite,' he said. 'You were a man of honour until conduct proved it otherwise. Take the example of this ship. That he should allow us equal ownership in what the enterprise will achieve.' He paused and stared hard at Steward.

'True,' said Steward.

'But there can be grievous error either way,' Boatswain reminded him.

Steward parted his hands and swizzled the tail of his beard between his thumbs. He pondered the low ceiling of the cabin, searching for compliments that might assure Boatswain of his loyalty. Yet he felt a natural aversion to any style of praise that might appear to be flattery. There had to be some obvious source of truth in any assertion he made. He was as meticulous in his judgment of men as he would be in the scrutiny he brought to the conflicting evidence of various charts. This was where his confidence lay: in the globes and spheres of his mind. In the dreams of his boyhood. Through the industry of his maturer years. His passion for learning the intricate perils of other men's travels. He couldn't resist the thread of ink scrawling dim messages over his eyes:

Creeks navigable for seven days. Delicacy be fish and safe for provisioning. Canoes abound, being only known means of journey safe to inhabitants. Slaves given as token of respect or in exchange for mere trifles. Infidels show great love of knives and bells. Marvellous bay for traffic in the flesh.

He looked up from the map, considering what tribute Boatswain deserved.

'Your experience is wide,' he said, ironing the moist turf of beard down his chin. 'I judge you are worth a fortune to the Commandant.'

Although Boatswain was appreciative, suspicion made him cautious of praise.

'You flatter me,' he said.

But Steward had hastened to make himself clear. He felt a mild resentment that Boatswain might entertain some doubt about his motives.

'My meaning is particular,' he said, feeling the sweat itch his chin. 'I notice how you lecture your men when they speculate on the divisions in the Kingdom. It's a clear case of knowing what words are right for the occasion.'

'I allow no dispute that does not relate to duty,' Boatswain intervened. There was an unexpected sharpness in his tone.

'Exactly,' said Steward, pondering this change in Boatswain; 'exactly what I mean.'

The wine had started a small fire in Boatswain's throat. He held a cough back, and whipped his tongue over the roof of his mouth. He was grateful for the attention Steward had given to these accounts of the voyages he had made. A just tribute to his great experience; it made for solace and a revival of confidence, whereas others might have sought to restore that familiar process of rumour, casting doubts on his worth. He had made seven voyages in as many years; but adversity had pursued him everywhere. Younger men began to treat his misfortune as an example of failure.

'I repeat, you have got a way with men,' said Steward, as though he wanted proof that Boatswain trusted his judgment.

'Each man to his own way,' said Boatswain. 'You have a manner yourself. Especially with the Commandant. I watch you.'

'He has an eye for worth,' said Steward. 'He knows a worthy man when he finds one.'

'That he knows,' said Boatswain with emphasis.

He wouldn't be drawn into further judgment on the Commandant. He was pumping the flesh around his knees, timing the moment it might be safe to stand. But his thirst was sharp. He was making some private appeal to the dregs in the cup. His glance caught the empty bottle on the floor. His eyes were bright and lucid as the rays of light striking through the gunport. But he heard a noise like bees crawling somewhere behind his ears. Was it the gradual influence of the wine, or the dizzying sting of the heat in his ears? The sound was getting louder while the silence lasted. But Steward had gone back to devouring the creeks and waterways. The maps were growing with messages further on. The black line of ants continued:

Creeks reach far inland. Much store of gold employed by inhabitants to adorn coffins of their king. Great trust in idols and terrible fierce when in battle. Slaves plentiful but difficult to maintain.

Boatswain heard his ears hum and spin. He decided it was the heat that had started this clamour in his head. The noise was coming now like a march of feet. He felt a pressure of hands closing hard over his throat; there was a hammer of church bells on his skull. He saw the timbers twist and sink above his head. The cabin was about to burst with the violence of the heat. Steward looked up from the charts, detecting some sign of terror in Boatswain's eyes.

'Are you ill?' he asked, and pushed himself up briskly from the chair.

His voice had joined the sound of bells in Boatswain's head. The sweat grew large pimples over his face. Boatswain was nodding his head, denying any charge that he was ill; it struck him as an accusation that Steward had made against his health. He was working the muscles of his mouth, loosening up his tongue for danger. He had to make his suspicion known before the rule of friendship could prevail. He looked at Steward.

'Would you be a friend of the Lord Treasurer?' he asked. 'Tate de Lysle, I mean. Would you know him as a friend?'

Steward was slow to reply. His hands found the edge of the table, and he lowered his body onto the chair. He was alarmed by this personal obsession with his past. His hand found the chain that hung around his neck, and he probed his finger through the circle of the ring at the end of the chain. The charts warned him to be careful with his answers. Boatswain was probing deeper into his past. Steward's reluctance had given him grounds for what he feared. Was he an agent of the House? What was his role in the enterprise? Suspicion had made him bold in his interrogation of Steward.

'Have you ever had any association with the House?' Boatswain asked.

But Steward didn't yield. He grew fearful of Boatswain's motive: was he an agent of the Commandant? They had similar cause for alarm. Steward's voice was irritable; but habit had trained him to curb his anger. They heard a sound of voices from the deck.

'With your permission,' Steward said, and stood, bowing his head in deference to his guest, 'I have matters to attend.' He paused and waited for Boatswain to stir from the chair; then added on a note of great urgency: 'And so have you.'

Boatswain had suddenly lost his urge to put Steward's loyalty to the test. He had also heard the warning sound from the deck. The crew had gone wild with shouting. There was such a fury of voices trailing their echoes up to the cabin that Boatswain thought the men had answered a call to revolt. Boatswain was timing the moment he should appear, for he didn't trust this boisterous tendency he had observed in the crew. He looked at Steward as though he had suddenly found a cause for proving their loyalty to the ship.

They were waiting for a pause; but the voices had increased their fury. Now the noise changed. It was no longer contentious and wild. Although the sound retained its force, the feelings of the crew had grown more sober. There was an interval of waiting, as though the men had suffered a temporary loss of speech.

A huge flock of sea fowl appeared overhead. A solitary voice rose from the quarterdeck: it was Ivan announcing the vision that had struck a new radiance across the sky. The voice rose quick and clear, a spasm of joy ascending from the painter's tongue. The moon had warned him of what was to come. He saw his prophecy roam like meteors over the sky.

The crew's emotion changed with every new wave of fowl that swept high through the air. They saw an infinite fleet of wings spread everywhere. A head of green feathers was diving down, plunging deeper through the air until the legs opened from under the orange wings and straightened upward. The

103

beak was the length of a man's middle finger, and narrow as
the eye of a needle. The bird paused in its descent; then made
an apron with the slow, wide spread of its wings. The feathers
opened and closed to the rhythm of the wind. The body began
to turn slowly in the air; then a frenzy struck its wings, and the
feathers spun fiercely and still as a top. The needle beak was
plummeting dangerously down towards the deck. The wings
folded up, gathering the fragile yards of legs into the smooth
white turf of the huge breast. The bird flew blind as a bat and
finally tangled its neck between the shroud of ropes which fell
from the sails. Sasha saw the body hang long and heavy as a
man's from the gallows.

The men watched from the decks, alternating between feelings of wonder and fear. The ship might have been in danger.
A procession of giant fowl was drawing near, following in the
wake of the fallen bird. They spread out like a fleet, immense
and slow in their laborious drift down to the water. They made
an arc over the mouth of the river, covering miles and miles in
every direction, until it seemed that the ship would be marooned
in a vast lake of feathers. Too numerous for ammunition, it
would be impossible to kill them off. The men trembled and
prayed for a miracle that would rescue them from this terrible
avalanche of sea fowl descending on the ship. These birds were
harmless except in their numbers; they would feed an army for
many years. But the men ran for cover as the first wave of wings
crashed over the deck. The bodies began to pile high, like the
total death of an army. They spilled from the deck, rolling in
huge numbers over the ribs of the ship, then sank with a great
rush of water into the deep bowels of the river.

The officers had appeared on the quarterdeck, all except Pinteados, who remained in the Commandant's cabin. The boy
Sasha had come up with orders for Boatswain. He was to recruit
the men for immediate repairs to the yards and spars of the ship.
Boatswain read the note and considered the chaos below. There
was a great tangle of rope everywhere. A small lateen sail had
been torn from its cordage. The ensigns had fallen from the
masthead, and the ragged tatters of a banner were floating over
the plucked white feathers of the sea fowl. The river showed
under a wild illumination of colours like a garden of carnations

crushed and scattered by the winds. It was hours before they could clear the decks of this multitude of wings, broken and breathing to the last. The men laboured all afternoon, fearful that new armies of sea fowl would arrive.

But the crocodiles had appeared, and the face of the river soon changed colour. There was a current of blood wherever the crocodiles surfaced to swallow the scarlet plumage of the drowned sea fowl. The sunlight poured like rain over the glistening acres of carnage that covered the mouth of the river.

'With your permission,' said Boatswain, as though he had found an opportunity for rebuking Steward, 'but I have urgent business to attend. Most urgent business.'

He had recovered his confidence. It seemed his memory had suddenly made the savagery of the coasts a familiar sight. He smiled up at the sky and the burning horizon of the trees. Steward felt a lack of experience stab at his pride. Away from the charts he seemed to lose all trust in his eyes.

'Business, you say?' His question was an offer of apology.

'I lead an expedition tomorrow,' said Boatswain, and narrowed his eyes to warn against the difficult stretch of shore.

'Tomorrow,' Steward echoed him, fighting to discipline his stammer. 'Lead the expedition, you say?'

Boatswain lowered his glance to inspect the river; then shook his chin as though he was talking to the drifting carcass of a black sea fowl.

'The same creeks?' Steward asked. 'The same as Master Cecil fled?'

But Boatswain didn't answer. He was enjoying a mild triumph over the man whose formal knowledge of charts couldn't tell the true secrets of this coast.

'With your permission,' said Boatswain, and smiled again. 'I have business to attend.'

Steward watched him turn away. He felt alone, almost deserted by his passion for the charts. He had to steady his hands. He found the wedding ring that hung from the chain around his neck. He felt its circle of gold shiver and sting like heat over his finger. He saw the sky come close. The sun was making a furnace of the capes and spheres he had never found. The charts crackled and smoked like a rubble of parchment in his hands. He closed his eyes over his wife's ring and spat at the river.

EIGHT

EXTRACT FROM VOYAGES OF PIERRE,
A CARPENTER OF LIME STONE

It would take the greater part of a long life to give a complete account of my first days on this coast. The fog that put us out of sight for eleven days was truly fearful, and then the great wave of fowl striking like a hurricane over the decks came near as any tempest to burying the ship alive; for their numbers with such a vast proportion of wing and body did put a wonderful terror in every heart, so that no man could resist the necessity to find a comfort in his religion. We were now holding chapel with regular fervour, begging Priest to intercede on our behalf should our God in a harsh moment of his judgment deem it wise to abandon us to this great pestilence of devils which live in the river and forest beyond. There be such creatures here as no man can in his ordinary language describe, monsters that do try to resemble men as though the power of Satan was marvellous enough to rival the Almighty. I saw creatures that would swim one moment and take to the air in the next, huge giants with the face and shoulders of horses, but turning to human shape at the waist and standing upright on occasion like any man would do to show the full measure of his height.

This river was of the substance water, and that is the only certainty my eyes would verify, but for the general properties of life and motion I could not describe its true nature. For the hours would often deceive us, exceeding the customary limits of day and night, so that it was only the men of previous experience who would decide which light was born of the moon and which was sent by the true rays of the sun. But for many a day or night we would witness the same rays of pearl and silver spread a wide bright drizzle over the sky. We lost five able men, and so quick was their decline that Surgeon could not explain except to say the cause of death was due to some excess of surprise.

There was a monster in bulk and appearance like unto the rhinoceros, but of more fearful proportion, as we were to prove when he swam up to inspect us and we saw the full measure of his bulk from head to hind come near to the length of the ship. We were in constant danger whenever he swam near, fearing the slightest collision would break the ribs of the ship in half. Boatswain was eager to release some shot and scare it away, but the Commandant advised against any action that might provoke the monster to release his full fury on the ship. This beast was black from the horns to the hindermost part which made a downward slope broad and thick as a wall covering his feet. The eyes did not appear where his face would be, but opened at the sides where you would expect the ears of a beast. His favourite pleasure was to yawn, and we could see the long white tusk which seemed to be the only manner of tooth he carried in the huge cavity of his mouth.

There are Guinea legends which say these beasts were human in a previous life and had to suffer the loss of their nature as a penalty for grievous crimes done in their name and to rivals they could not endure to be near. Which knowledge did have the effect of making for a greater penance in some of our men. My feeling soon began to show greater respect and a wonderful admiration for those heroes of Lime Stone who had left the comfort of a prosperous home to dare the wonders that occur in these frightful zones. It would be more easy by far to settle for the peace of a farm, knowing the calamities nature will contrive to test the courage of men who adventure on behalf of the Kingdom. So did I think with my heart as we made ready to explore this coast.

We were now four days on this river according to the measurement which Steward was careful to make, he being a man of studious zeal in the notation of latitudes and distance on the charts. They say this passion for maps was with him even as a boy, and only some grievous robbery done to him in the past was the cause he be not more widely known for his knowledge of the waterways of the world. He was much in the company of Boatswain, who would support with details of his own experience every measurement as well as the manner of the wind as shown on the charts.

The days were regular again, with a natural dark coming as it should after daylight, and everything seeming more favourable for our progress. There was a fresh current in the water, and a regular breeze that made fair sounds with the sails at night. The moon was the beauty it would be over Lime Stone, but of a proportion much more vast than I remember it. The sky was never without a great multitude of stars like the firmament of Scriptures, and we had good reason for praising God, who did bring a great peace to bear on the heavens and the waters below. But not all was joy and a sweetness of climes. For there be some strange substance in this breeze, which though it fall soft and sweet on the ear, seems to leave a most subtle infection in the blood and cause much violent subversion to the nerves. In the space of few hours several of our men did collapse for want of breath though the wind was plentiful; others had to suffer the most violent fits of vomiting; and seeing we did not partake of any natural foods off this coast, the opinion was that there be certain infection in the breeze. It is a common danger to men who travel on this coast, and some tell how the late and famous Master Cecil did himself yield to the infection which for a while did infuriate the old man's brain. We were now much instructed by previous experience of those who had come slaving on this coast. However, my friend and much beloved senior in years, Baptiste the powder maker, would console any who gave way too soon to fear by citing example of known recovery.

There be a place of cure in the capital of Lime Stone for such as may be stricken by this malady of the breeze; and it be said that at Severn—for that is the true name of the place where they go who become infirm of mind—at Severn, I did hear it said by more who know, how the largest portion of inmates be those who did give their talents to the ocean in seeking fresh glory for the Kingdom before this said affliction did overtake their senses.

As we made progress into the deeps of the river, this sickness

*did increase our cause for worry, and Priest, already overburdened
by constant prayer on our behalf, was now in frequent session
with Surgeon debating their remedies of body and soul. Yet six
men did nevertheless expire, and more were good as dead, being
put out of service by this infection which is the cause of deep
weariness and makes the limbs a great burden to lift. It is thought
to spare those who have recovered once before, and I declare it a
truth that no sign of discomfort was seen in my friend Baptiste
nor the fisherman Marcel who went about his business like he
was ignorant of any cause for alarm. So too was Boatswain who
now became more swift of foot than before, and growing increasing haughty and harsh in his command. He was now in charge
of the first expedition which lowered boats at dawn and charged
with speed for the blacks.*

*They were standing on a hill some twenty in number, upright
and powerful in body but with surprising harmony in every limb,
and no more so than when they took to their heels, recognizing
what new dangers they did face. At first they didn't understand
what damage our shot could inflict, seeing that ammunition was
still foreign to their ways, since bows and arrows be the only
known weapons they take to war. I was amazed to see them
dance at the first shot of fire, believing our arms intend some
kind of greeting, until a shot found mark and tore a hole in the
chest of the man who was coming forward. The rest were still
laughing and shouting like they would put some spell of jubilation on our men, until they realized their leader could not stand
up for the great quantity of blood which his insides did expel.
It was a wonderful blow which struck him through, so that his
bowels were pouring onto the ground. It took such calamity to
make them understand it was the work of our shot which did
blast him to bits, and then they made up the hill swift as hare,
with our shot hard in pursuit. We were sorely winded in our
flight after them, but our men had a mighty heart for the chase,
mindful of their share in any cargo that was honourably taken.
We were after them, preserving our shot in case their numbers
did multiply, which without warning they did.*

*And now a most terrible battle was raging, with arrows com-
ing fearful and fast where we lay. But the sound of shot put
them to fright, and soon the arrows subside and we watch them*

assemble like they would hold council what to do. We released one shot more that did straight open the throat of a woman, which tragedy seemed too great for them to contain and thereby made them decide to seek in peace what we were after. We held our shot, seeing that they made no move forward nor back, but went down low like an animal about to urinate, and it seemed that in this position they would remain until we arrive. We spread out over a wide radius so that any charge might be met from several points of vantage. However, they were not desirous of attack, losing all heart after the shooting of the woman, who, it seems, was of some importance to their custom. They remained in their squatting position and howling like dogs, yet with some harmony and purpose to what they were saying. They were now one hundred and more, men and women, and all naked as the ground where they began to roll screaming and tearing at their hair. We sent a scout forward to investigate if they would be ready to follow, keeping our harquebuses ready for action should this lack of fight be a trick to lure us into danger.

But we had no further cause for alarm, seeing they had no heart for the slightest sign of retaliation. There was one who did speak some words of our language, having done some previous business with ships of Lime Stone; and knowing our purpose before we did even declare our terms, he came forward wearing his hands like a cross before his face. He did ask permission to bury the woman who looked to be dead for a long time, but fearing such request might be a way of springing some fresh surprise on our men, we did not allow any delay, and ordered all without exception of age or sex to march before us towards the river, where we had ample reserve of men waiting to come to our rescue should some untoward event come upon us.

It was a wonderful silence which went before us like they did forget even in a second what they left behind; which did make us surmise that they be a people with little or no memory for what takes place in their life, such was their obedience as we loaded them onto the longboats which would carry us but a short distance to the ship. They were one hundred and seventeen at the first reckoning, but twelve died not long after, and from what cause we were not able to detect, seeing as no incident, however small, did occur after their capture. We made a lasso around them eight or nine together, and hauled them up in bundles onto the deck, where they did remain chained for safety at the ankles until the Commandant was ready to give the final order for their care and maintenance.

But we did suffer an even more grievous loss of fortune which the daybreak now showed on the water. We thought the chains were security enough, and that no slave could move without carrying the burden of the one bound fast at his ankle, since the obstacle of one body was equal to a chain of twenty, making it impossible for anyone to escape without causing the total loss of all. Which indeed is what did happen; for they be a people not adequate in the powers of reason which is the cause of their doom.

Forgetting all encumbrance, they did make a leap overboard in the night, which was an act no less than suicide; for it was impossible to swim with such an encumbrance of chains and their imprisonment one to the next. It was a spectacle to arouse our pity, seeing their remains, which were torn up and eaten to fragments by the crocodiles that prowl here waiting to feed from the ship. For a mile or more around the river we saw such a spectacle of blood, with limbs floating everywhere like logs, and the red fragments of skullbone and ribs we could scarcely recognize. A most horrible sight was this great inconvenience which came without warning on our first labours up the coast. It made for a sudden convulsion in the boy Sasha, who did take to the Commandant's cabin where he remained laid up in a convalescence which lasted for the whole period of our traffic on the coast. This decision to leap was beyond our reason, so that we did surmise—and ancient wisdom also confirms—how this blackness of hide which resembles skin must be nature's way of warning against the absence of any soul within, which is the clear cause of their ignorance, just as a true Christian countenance resembles the colour of the sun, thereby giving a power and beauty of light which adorns the skin and supporteth all pious reason; being yet further proof that there be nothing that appears by accident or indolent chance in the purpose and harmony of our Lord's creation.

NINE

The river had come awake with sound, a tireless fluting of invisible lives that crawled miraculously up from the mud and slime of the shore. The light gathered like clouds, spreading a drift of bleak shadows over the coast. The wind blew a croaking noise through the trees. There was a constant dirge and whistle of leaves. The dark was about to close the portholes. Soon it would plunge with all the force of night into Surgeon's cabin. There was nothing visible but the startling whites of his eyes and teeth. He sniffed at the air and breathed the heavy smell of rain. Lingering at the door, Priest watched the fugitive pearls of drizzle fall on a vague traffic of hands below. A trickle of rain was blown into his eyes, and coursed slowly down to the tip of his nose, soft and warm as sweat. He couldn't distinguish any face he knew. The deck grew black with shadow. His eyes warned that he was weary, but he was muttering prayers for the men below. He thought of them as the eternal poor of the earth— his flock, who had come together for reasons known only to themselves, and many for no reason he could tell. The coast, however, had given their presence some holy purpose. 'It is with these men we may have to make common cause,' he said; but his voice was low. The night had brought a feeling of dreadful solitude.

He turned from the door and walked slowly back to the table. He was reluctant to speculate on the future of the crew; this climate had put a strain on their powers, and softened the most stubborn pride among them. He was enjoying the authority of his holy office. His gifts were now in great demand, for he alone could exorcise the demons that troubled their sleep. He heard Surgeon move about the cabin, sat down, and waited for a light.

'It is an atmosphere for a man who knows how to meditate,' Priest said. 'But we must not fall into too deep brooding.'

He heard Surgeon laugh from the corner. Introspection was not a habit that Surgeon encouraged. His laugh would have deceived anyone about his age. He was much younger than Priest, though not so young as his health declared. He prolonged his laughter, as though he had to assert some boyish pride in his sufficiency; it seemed the dangers of the river had increased his sense of achievement. His was the gayest face among the officers. Priest envied this note of jubilation in his voice.

'The enterprise is not orthodox,' said Surgeon, 'and that's what I admire. No limit to our freedom here. Ordinarily we would need a licence to traffic for the flesh on this coast.'

Priest considered his meaning, then nodded gravely to himself. He was considering the exact shade of agreement he might offer.

'The conditions are unique,' he said. 'That I will not argue.'

He heard his breathing weigh on the silence that followed. The pause was like a warning from the corner, where Surgeon remained in the obscurity of the shadows that collected above the chest.

'I have never held a post of such command before,' said Surgeon, as though he wanted to share some confidence.

'Nor come this near to fortune,' Priest answered gravely. 'Not that I count most on that.'

The laughter came up from the corner again.

'But it is not against your calling,' Surgeon suggested. There was an obvious hint of mockery in his voice.

'Not against,' said Priest, rubbing his hand over the table. 'Although such fortune can increase the chance of error.'

'Error,' Surgeon was echoing him.

'Yes, error,' said Priest. 'That I have seen.'

Surgeon had arrived at the chest. He paused to consider his reply.

'I could have such errors multiplied a million times,' he said.

There was a noise of chains falling in the corner. Priest felt it his duty to curb the younger man's ambition.

'The black flesh is a terrible temptation,' Priest warned, folding his frail arms about his shoulders. 'You might find such cargo too great a strain for a man of principle.'

'The Church has never ruled against such a harvest,' said Surgeon, heaving the chains back onto the chest. 'And I smell a plentiful harvest ahead of us yet.'

'But the principle,' Priest insisted; 'the traffic must be conducted according to some principle.'

Surgeon was laughing again. Priest heard it like the voice of a wayward child. Although the young man's errors might be easy to forgive, his energy would require some measure of restraint.

'The principle,' Priest was repeating. 'There must be a code for the conduct of such traffic.'

'Every new plan makes for a new code,' said Surgeon. His voice was hurried. 'It is a law of movement, you might say.'

He was laughing again. The cargoes of the coast had aroused his enthusiasm for adventure. He felt free at last, as though this radical change of climate had released some resource he hadn't suspected in himself.

'Find a new plan and you find a new code,' Surgeon said.

He wanted to draw Priest out on the ethics of adventure across the ocean seas. Different latitudes might require different laws of living.

'Find a new plan, and I find a new principle,' he said, as though the challenge was especially intended for Priest.

Priest smoothed the heavy lapels that fell down his chest.

'You wouldn't instruct your men along these lines,' he said. He felt it his duty to remind Surgeon of their status on the ship. They were officers in command of men whose loyalty was never an absolute certainty. Authority didn't work like the tides. But Surgeon couldn't restrain his impetuous temper.

'You'll find the men need no instruction there,' he said, working his hands in the dark. 'Invite them into a plan, and they will invent their own principles as they go along.'

Priest wouldn't take the challenge. And Surgeon was suddenly quiet. His hands rambled in the dark. Priest heard the chains swing in the corner. A light flickered up, then blazed above Surgeon's hands as he secured a chimney to the lantern. There was a quick rattle of wire and a sparkle of flame. The cabin emerged in a sudden glow of yellow light, showing the black face of the porthole and the thick wall of night filling the door. It had achieved an atmosphere of comradeship.

'It's a comfort to be here,' said Priest.

'It will be greater comfort after the cargoes are taken,' Surgeon said. He was walking back from the cabinet. "He has a masterful way," Priest thought, observing the care with which Surgeon had gathered a bottle and two glasses in one hand.

'It wouldn't be a crime,' said Surgeon, and smiled, indicating a glass for Priest.

'To the enterprise,' said Priest, and raised his hands as though he was about to pray.

Surgeon was too attractive to be tedious, but his exuberance was making Priest weary. Perhaps it wasn't the younger man's fault. Priest had become very sensitive to the smallest changes in his body; seeing the veins swell like roots over his hands, he thought his bones had begun to rust. His ears were alert to the creak of his joints. He couldn't resist this habit of observing the gradual process of change that aged his body. His nails had begun to curl and shrivel like bits of bone sinking into his skin. In all weathers, the light over his eyes was frequently grey. Brief spasms of cramp would seize his muscles without fair warning. The movement of his bowels was less regular than he would wish. He wasn't an old man, to be sure, but a sense of age weighed heavily on him, holding a curious mastery over his judgment. Like the power of sin.

But he found a surprising joy in his office when he ministered to the crew. It was a profound consolation to know that the souls of the ship had been entrusted exclusively to his care. He was holding service twice a day, discovering new texts of Scripture for his purpose. He had become more eloquent than ever on the perils of those who had answered the call to the ocean and dared every manner of tempest in the name of God. His experience was now offered entirely to the service of his Lord. It had brought him the greatest consolation to observe the men who were yielding to their daily exercises in meditation and prayer.

Fear had made them meek. They grew more docile as they drifted deeper into the savage bosom of the river. He knew the nature of such conversions. He had seen it happen before; but it was his duty to make the fruits of his wisdom survive these days of crisis. This interval on the river was a happy omen. It was easier to reveal the necessity of faith, to school them in the habits of obedience. And he used his experience with great effect. Now they knew without exception that there was some lasting purpose to their labours. The coast had restored them to the need for faith. He had instructed them in the rewards of sacrifice; for that was how the dead would be remembered. Their death was the price of an enterprise that would stand as a memorial to the Kingdom. Those who survived would know why they were spared. The future would bring certain glory to every rank.

Priest had forgotten the discomforts of his body for a while. He drank in silence, savouring the sting of the liquor and praising the agreeable calm that had settled on the cabin.

'The earth brings forth one wonder after the next,' Priest said, playing his eyes over the wine. He held the glass under his nose, inhaling the sharp fragrance of the liquor.

'Think of the fortunes this has made,' Surgeon reminded him. He had raised his glass to ponder the rays that sparkled from the surface of the wine.

'You should think of the pleasure God allows us,' said Priest.

Surgeon leaned the bottle deep into the mouth of the glass and poured himself another inch of wine.

'They say it opens the appetite,' he said, and waited for Priest to confirm this rumour.

But Priest had withdrawn into some deep cavern of memory. He heard the triumphs of the past assemble to pay service to his endurance. His experience was full of unfamiliar dangers. He had survived revolt at home and a great variety of pestilence over the ocean seas, carrying the Gospel like a sword among various and forgotten heathens. Now he travelled under a new name. The music of the rain, strong and steady where it poured outside the door, made his memory fertile. There was a wash of rivers in his ears, the march of floods that had once drowned the most ardent flock of missionaries who had ever sailed these creeks. He used to be the shepherd of this coast. His youth had been a battleground of faiths. He had given his blessing to the traffic in black flesh; but he would always maintain that it contained a soul. He sipped the wine and pondered the turbulence of his past. Those were glorious days when faith was a weapon in his hands and men waged a war with words to justify some divinity of right over these black cargoes. He had won the issue both ways. The black flesh was a challenge which nature had flung back in the face of God, the last experiment in grace. Priest could hear his rivals yield. If piety could be planted where there was none, then conversion through ownership should be allowed. The shepherd of the coast had won. But at the height of triumph, his first life died. He saw the shadow of Lazarus collapse into the mouth of his glass, and knew he must distract himself from these thoughts of the grave.

The rain had gathered power. It struck with terrible violence down on the ship. Priest felt the jolt and sway of the river lift them up and sideways. The light made a chase of flames over the ceiling. It was a great comfort to be here, nesting in the cosy silence of Surgeon's cabin, yet he couldn't avoid the clink and rattle of dead bones blown from the coast. He had witnessed a pestilence of floods in his time; seen the best harvest of his brothers drowned before his eyes. Alone, in the savage wilderness that covered the earth beyond this river, he had continued his mission. His existence had astonished the heathens who survived. He shone like a miracle in their eyes, a great white spirit that had sent some lasting torment on their dreams. They would collect around him like flies, begging for the life eternal that he taught. He had converted them to the doctrine that a time would come when the laws of the earth would give way, and their hands would learn to work like wings, soaring them through the remotest spaces of the universe, a dream beyond any magic they could conceive. It was then he discovered the true depth of his talents, the unique power of his calling. And then his first life began to die. Perhaps his triumph was premature. Like the coast itself, there had been no limit to the service he could render. His faith fell like an axe on the innocent flesh of the infidels. He had dispatched many thousands by the month. From the coast to the Isles of the Black Rock his triumphs had become a legend. Grown careless with every wave of fresh achievement, he had forgotten his loyalties to any temporal powers. He was supplying Antarctica with slaves, increasing the fortunes of the enemy. An astonishing wave of cargoes crossed the ocean for the early settlements of Antarctica. He had betrayed his loyalties to the Kingdom of his birth, and soon he had to flee. He became a fugitive for Christ.

"So slow," he tried to argue as he heard the punishing blast of rain outside. "Lime Stone was so slow to take the challenge. What difference could it make which temporal power came to the rescue of those black cargoes? But a soul was buried somewhere in that flesh, struggling like a foetus to survive the menacing blackness of their nature. And Lime Stone would not listen, had grown too indolent to see the challenge. It made no difference what temporal power completed the work of our Lord. A soul in sin was better than the doom that threatened eternal darkness. I had to make the enemy my ally in God's service."

No one really knew how he had escaped the temporal law of Lime Stone. But he took example from the Scriptures and lived again the miracle of Lazarus. He simply went dead, and let rumour sanctify his sojourn among the savage heathens of the coast. Legend had made him both pirate and saint. It was the general belief in Lime Stone that he had been eaten alive. Relics of burnt flesh had been sent back as evidence of his ritual killing. The resurrection of his bones was occasion for a national shrine in his native village, where they wept for the feast the infidels had made of his bones. His body, however, had survived. He had been born again, disguised by age, and travelling under a different name.

Priest looked up from the glass. He saw Surgeon's handsome face, the smooth bronzed cheeks soft and fat under a glistening down of hair. There was an orchard of curls rolling black waves over his head. The light made a silver spray at the back of his neck. His eyes were young and full of mischief; but there was such energy and daring in his brow, now shaded by the thick, black lock of hair. Priest was afraid of the restless temper that showed in Surgeon's eyes, so eager to claim his right to the future. Priest felt a shudder run through his hand; he seized the bottle and poured a large drink into the glass. He didn't let Surgeon's smile distract him. He drank with impatience, then brought the glass slowly down from his lips. There was infinite care in the gesture that turned it without sound back to the table.

'We could take a fortune from this coast,' Priest said, hoping to free himself from Surgeon's gaze.

Surgeon's voice grew cheerful, almost wild. Priest had detected this weakness in him. Surgeon allowed his dreams to hurry his speech. There was no pause in his enthusiasm for the future. A pioneer in the cause of colonies, he was eager for any enterprise that would start life afresh.

'Virgin lands,' said Surgeon, as though he could predict the end of their enterprise. 'It's the most blessed territory, I tell you. A man can start from scratch, turn any misfortune into a fact of triumph. They are idle of mind who do not fathom the privilege of starting from scratch. Take the hospital, for example.'

Surgeon was taking a sip of the drink. A bead of wine hung from his lip. He licked the moisture back into his mouth. There was a look of exhilaration in his eyes. He had a lucid vision of himself established on the Isles of the Black Rock, known everywhere as a founder of hospitals, a pioneer in the most novel arts of healing. Infirmity had suddenly assumed a startling pride of place in his affection.

'A man comes with sickness,' he said, tasting the sprig of hair over his hands. 'He must leave us whole again and with some knowledge of his healing. The surgeon and the sick become equal parts of the same learning. Each man recovers, and with some new knowledge of his body. Such experiment is rare. You can only manage it in virgin lands where you have the chance to start from scratch.'

The light made a flutter like bats' wings over the ceiling of the cabin. Priest felt his eyes brighten. The timbers of the cabin looked near, strong and reliable as the masts of the ship. He wondered when these ambitions had started in Surgeon. Was it the influence of the Commandant, who had called on them to break free of the Kingdom? Or was Surgeon a man with plans of his own?

'I would expect to hear no less,' he said, cuddling his fingers around the glass. He couldn't restrain the hint of praise in his voice. He started to drum his fingers on the table, then stopped, as though his thought had found its abrupt and natural climax.

'It is in that sense the harvest rules out the strain of our cargoes,' said Priest. 'I would expect no less from one of such imagination.' He was worried lest he appeared too fulsome in his praise.

Surgeon heard him through, and considered the absolute stillness of the glass in his hand. He was in a mild trance of triumph.

'The Commandant must have known how he was choosing,'

Priest added, seeking to reduce Surgeon's stature in his eyes. 'I would think such a calculation was in his mind.'

Surgeon turned his glance abruptly from the glass. He had been alerted by Priest's reference to the Commandant. The name left a spasm in his ears.

'I should not think he would act without some calculation,' Surgeon said, and warned himself to curb any freedom of judgment he was about to express. His silence was now abrupt, making Priest reluctant to pass any further comment on the Commandant. It was the natural habit of caution that had been cultivated by these officers. They could not be sure what points of contact their lives might have forged in the past. The manner was tentative, burdened with loyalty and the vaguest hint of compromise, but protective and alert to the possibility of some unfavourable detection.

'True,' said Priest defensively, 'there would be no chance to start such a school of healing from scratch. Not back in the Kingdom.'

Surgeon didn't care to speculate on his chances in the Kingdom. He showed his preference for what was ahead.

'Too fierce competition does not make for safety,' he said, 'and safety is a prize beyond any fortune. Hence the blessing of virgin lands, where the new man meets the new endeavour. To know there is not a plan to push you out.'

Priest was reminded of his own exhortations to younger men who had tried to plant the Church over the ocean seas. He grew careless in his desire to exchange a confidence.

'I think that was the sickness of the House of Trade and Justice,' he said, forgetful of his warning to avoid the past. 'Men could not be sure of the ground they stood on.'

Surgeon was quick to evade any answer that included mention of the House.

'A clean rivalry is welcome,' he conceded, 'but the atmosphere must be loyal.' He paused and tried to weigh the silence that had briefly closed Priest's eyes. 'Herein lies the advantage of starting a commonwealth from scratch. A few men, once planted in abundant spaces, have little cause for rivalry.'

Priest grew silent, yet found some gesture that would show his approval. His fingers continued to drum their satisfaction on the table.

Surgeon recognized the meaning of this pause. He was arguing with himself whether he should make some reference to the House of Trade and Justice. Yet he was fearful of any talk that turned on the affairs of the House. His skill had gained him acquaintance with men of importance there; and he believed Priest's calling might have served a similar purpose. But they had never shared in the same patronage; nor had any previous allegiance brought them together. He couldn't .be sure where Priest had placed his sympathies in the battle that waged between the families of the North and the southern merchants of the sea, and this calculation reminded him that Priest was still a stranger. He had no special faith in the reliability of Priest's vocation. From the Guinea coast to the Isles of the Black Rock there were many priests who had traded as agents of the House. Yet Surgeon felt an urge to take the risk. He wanted to probe Priest's connections with the House. He was going to name the Lord Treasurer to the House, emphasizing that the nature of his business was never more than that of a surgeon. He would leave himself free to shift ground according to questions Priest might ask. He saw the light throw a circle of shadow under Priest's eyes; and suddenly his attention was distracted by a sound near the door. The rain alternated with the pound of fists.

'Who is it there?' Surgeon shouted.

The figure appeared out of the night. The wind was pushing the carpenter from behind. He shook the rain from his hair, and made his apology through a nervous chatter of teeth.

'Speak up,' said Surgeon, rising from the chair. 'What do you say?'

'Ships,' Pierre said. 'The watch send word they have seen four ships.'

'Did you say four?' Priest intervened.

'Yes sir, four,' the carpenter answered. He was reversing on his heels towards the door.

"Antarctica?" Surgeon mused; then asked aloud: 'Would Lime Stone send four ships to pursue us?' There was great agitation in his voice.

'These could be Antarctica,' said Priest; 'the Treaty grants equal rights for traffic on the coast.'

'In the black cargoes as well?'

'What other virtue would the Treaty have?' Priest said, protecting Surgeon from his fear. 'The black flesh is now the only rival to gold.'

He pressed the glass to his mouth and watched the carpenter disappear into the rain.

TEN

EXTRACT FROM VOYAGES OF PIERRE,
A CARPENTER OF LIME STONE

So many rivers seem to meet in this great waterway that no charts agree on the names that do belong to each separate divide; we went with the current some forty leagues where a bunch of small islands did appear, thick and green with foliage everywhere. We saw no face on these islands, but there did appear a small boat which they use for fishing, and each even to the smallest child had a wooden spear which they throw with the bare arm at their prey, and a marvellous aim they possess, seeing that they were in motion with the current rocking their boat sideways and each standing upright whether he be paddling forward with the oars or heaving their spear at the shifting target under the water; they did seem so harmonious in their relations that I surmise they were of one family, but on enquiry we did ascertain how five were taken by force from a rival tribe of savages and put to service the needs of their heathen master. Boatswain was in command of the new expedition, which was beyond our expectation, so easy and fruitful it did prove to be. We ordered the master to release his captives, which we did load onto the deck within the second of giving the order, and thereby found ourselves provided with most reliable guides for the remaining part of our enterprise down the main heart of the river.

These were less wholesome than any we had seen higher up the coast, and of a more frightful blackness of skin so that the white of their eyes would sometimes make a fearful glitter, like a midnight snow frozen bright and stiff on the ground. They suffered barbarous mutilations of the mouth with bits of animal bone pierced through the lips, this being some mark or signature which denotes the true worship of their ancestors; and it did appear that the children, there being four of these, were taken into slavery even at birth. I was not at ease while they were with us, fearing the evil power of spirits which legend declares often reside in the eyes of their infants; but there was no treachery in their guidance, seeing how we did reach after two nights and some mornings downriver a huge encampment of prisoners—I reckon there were beyond one thousand—now chained in captivity after some local wars, which are continuous and without mercy among these savages. The true cause whereof I have heard many expound, but there is no saying which account is the more to be trusted.

Here on the coast at Xavier at latitude thirteen and a half degrees there did live a thrifty band of savages with all the appearance of civilized arrangements like courts where their King held parliament and supervised the laws and punishments of his people; but abundance of gold made his subjects lazy, so that they were soon victims of their waste and the lust which can subvert the senses, living without proper observance even of their own barbarous idols, and allowing intercourse, it was said, between themselves and certain spirits or gods which assume any shape or part of the flesh as they wish. There be infinite numbers of half-caste as well, which, as I must mention here, was due to the licentious conduct of Antarctica. But these savages had lost whatever dignity other men are quick to defend; so that their defeat was like the shift of sand which the tide makes loose. They were up for sale, everyone, and on their own lands, which they say were given by the gods who make fire.

Four vessels of Antarctica did appear, and after making their greeting with a double shot of ordinance, made busy with the traffic of the blacks. Here was a sight so wonderful in the extremity of grief and endurance which these infidels did show. Some could not put any mastery over their primitive feeling, and losing all control over their fear did howl and grovel before they would allow their bodies to be sold. But they had no authority over their own flesh, and after severe penalties of whipping and scalding of hot fats on the back would peacefully yield and watch their purchase take place. The Captain of Antarctica had found a great barter, since I reckon there be well over one thousand of slaves which his vessels were well furnished to receive. We did feel a great envy seeing this prize escape us, but the Commandant gave no orders for traffic until the vessels of Antarctica completed their purchase. Yet there was no need for haste, seeing as how these people are infinite in numbers though the climates be so hostile to any natural living, which was yet just proof of the mysteries of our Lord's creation that He should allow the likes of men to endure, and in such abundant health, the great pestilence of heat and sickness as to be found nowhere else save on this coast.

There be one moment of auction which I did not hope to witness and which after wiser reflection I reckon to be further proof of the mercy which God may yet bestow on these unfortunate creatures of the Guinea kingdoms. Some difficulty did arise when a family of one woman and two sons, after much dragging and beating, did come forward and stand for auction, the father being already taken aboard one of the vessels. The woman was wild and showing such a fury of strength as did surpass that of any man, biting and spitting and screaming her refusal in the Captain's face; and like it was a final impertinence to those who would separate her from her man and sons, she thereupon began to empty her bowels, excreting filth and passing out a mighty stream of her urine for all to see and in a manner which held no hint of discretion for those who witness such bestial forms of showing grief; but such must be the sorrow of knowing she would never see her offspring again, nor would father set eyes on son, nor one brother on the next ever after; for it be the custom of experience on the coast to distribute this human livestock in a manner which will not allow common speech and understanding between one slave and the next. Such *was the extremity of her fury that no one could bring her to order when she saw her sons taken away, and each dispatched on a separate vessel. It is indeed a cause of some pain to behold such a division of blood wherein the root and branch of one family tree be torn up and discharged into exile which only death will end. It was a sight most wonderful in extremity; yet nothing to compare with the rejoicing of the Captain and men from Antarctica now safely returned to their ships and furnished with a fortune in the black flesh as would fetch more millions of currency than my simple brain could comprehend. Herein lies the great power and wealth of Antarctica, which did reign supreme in the continents to be discovered, until by the grace of God the seafaring sons of Lime Stone through courage and a natural Christian piety did stamp their signature on the waves; which be yet further proof that God will work on the hidden resource of His elect when the time be ready for Him to order a true fulfilment of His purpose.*

And so should it be, seeing that Antarctica, our chief rival in these adventures, did leave wherever they go a most terrible record of debauchery and unjust licence over the victims of their rule, encouraging their heathens in the doctrine of idols, and making men more savage than they were before Christ was crucified. Their blasphemies in war and peace did surpass all outrage; for it was told us on authority how they would defile their blood by unholy concubinage with the women of this black coast, and wherever their ensigns fly you may witness, as indeed on the river we saw, how they spawn a numerous population of half-castes which do confuse the issues of government and rule not only on this coast but throughout the domains they possess on the Isles of the Black Rock.

For it be said by wiser men than myself that unless a man be powerful in the discipline of spirit, his nature will change with every radical change of sky, becoming loose and base if it be the will of the stars to captivate his lust. And such is the dismal record of Antarctica on this coast and wherever their banners stand throughout the Isles of the Black Rock. Against the will of God and the sacred needs of their own blood they do enter into the most uncritical acts of fornication with these heathen women, blaspheming against their body and in a manner not fit even for the pleasure of beasts; for such is known of their custom that they would forsake all normal practice in the arts of love to enhance their pleasure by entering into the most bestial experiments of lust, like fitting their organs through the mouth and up the fundament of the woman's hindmost parts. It is a matter not fit for record, nor would I mention it except as a warning to more noble natures, for it be known these heathens do have a power which may bind some Christian natures against their wish. So great is the trance they set on the men of Antarctica that many are known to forsake their natural wives and take to permanent residence on this coast; and indeed many examples can be found of men who could not overcome the first taste of black women on this coast, but did seem to enter a trance of passion which did make it impossible for them to redeem their Christian nature; wherein it is a fact that they never allow their wives to travel as company or otherwise along these coasts, fearing that a similar spell of lust might excite them to entertain the heathen blacks who go naked everywhere like beasts, though some in imitating our own discretion do try to decorate their organs with various articles of nature like leaves or grass, and thereby hide the grossness of its size, for they be creatures with truly massive instruments which they can erect at will, and without encouragement from the other sex, causing in all Christian men a most terrible fear for the safety of their lawful wives. But such is the justice of our Lord that He does punish this unholy lust by planting a lasting madness in the brain of such men who spawn the earth with a mixture of breeds which are a torment against all code and decree of Christian piety; for it is a most lasting shame for a man not to be able to acknowledge the sons or daughters sprung from his own loins; which shame no Christian of Antarctica will confess when the charge of fathering these half-castes be put with the evidence made known to everyone.

But there be no great inconvenience to body or soul which may not also be the cause of greater glory and reward from God; begin a great increase of knowledge on my part, and such as would mould my present desire, which be to study and acquire a true management of these heathen peoples and to help to plant the banners of Lime Stone wherever there be a single cape or for here in the dark and savage zones of this latitude, there did *gulf without the blessing of a true Christian light. It is in the great heart of the ocean ways with their full dangers of uncharted rivers that we bear witness to the true power and mastery of our Lord; and so with patience and zeal for his office Priest did instill deep in my understanding the true value of error in the eyes of our Creator; not that I would resign all judgment to the full authority of the Church and its messengers, there being many such who will not qualify for the paths which lead to salvation; but it was the infinite trials of the coast which did bring a new light to my understanding wherein I did recognize as never before the full measure of God's mercy bestowed upon me, Pierre, a carpenter who was not one then known to be meek or humble in the presence of authority.*

A single life is too little time to put on record the great conversion to knowledge which displaced my former ignorance. For now I did learn to discourse, following the instructions of Steward's learning, how the great globe of the known world was divided up, into what latitudes and distances, with what pestilence of climates, what treacheries of unknown waterways, creeks, and streams, what hidden chain of mountains divide the earth, and by what right and justice the powers and princes hold dominion over what they discover in the continents where science did not yet reach; and men believe the torrid climates rain too great fire, making it impossible for ordinary men to inhabit these zones. And believing, as the Scriptures say, that charity should have first birth in a man's native home, I did reckon it a just cause for Lime Stone to claim unto itself whatever fruitful lands might multiply the wealth and glory of our Kingdom, for in the arts of peace and Christian rule we have no equal.

That there be great perils of sickness and battles I will not argue, but not so great as to distract us from the great benefits which will reward a true endeavour. Herein is an opportunity made ready for the talents of men who if they only knew would not delay to make this adventure the true crown of their life's fulfilment; for here is a people which without too great encouragement of words or by the mere threat of sword and the sound of gunshot will prostitute themselves before us, granting free access to command their continent as we wish. Those who have not seen the waste of such chance will never believe how easy it would be for Lime Stone to add vast continents to its present ownership; yet there be many, I am told, who hold high office in the Kingdom and use their authority to discourage this great discovery of fortune. Not knowing that conquest requires no great strategy where these heathens, much divided among themselves through greed and a lack of common inheritance in speech, are not capable of unity enough to withstand invasion. There is abundant report how the thieves of Antarctica, selecting with care the black chieftains of different realms, will provoke these infidels to enter battle against themselves, wherein the contestants have nothing to gain except small tokens of payment for the prisoners they so joyfully put up for sale; so much that there be wise heads which fear that such good fortune may not last forever and the time will yet come when combining their full strength of numbers, which far surpasseth ours, the heathens could with little risk of life resist our trespass on their coast and hinterland, which would be a most sinful betrayal of the mercy granted us by God; for it be a fact reported widely by men of Lime Stone no less than those of our rival Antarctica that the heathens transported across the ocean seas to the Isles of the Black Rock do rejoice in their new habitation, enjoying for the first time a great liberation from the terrible iniquities of their own rulers in whom there be neither truth nor fair dealings in the management of their subjects; which be yet another example of proof that no enterprise, however strange and extreme in present agony, does not accord with some larger purpose of our Lord, seeing how, as every true report does give, those heathens transported under the rule and law of Lime Stone do show a great improvement in their nature, which being slow to change, may yet if it be the will of God approximate in time to some resemblance of a true Christian piety. All which knowledge and surmising have come to me through close attention to the teaching and experience of the officers who serve under our great Commandant; which men, and in particular Priest, being more skilled in such wisdom, did not fail to train and instruct us day and night in the small and larger points of ethics and obedience which we would have to practise and apply on arrival in the Isles of the Black Rock. I know now, through the grace of our Lord, that this great mercy did not fall upon me by chance, that I, a carpenter of little *worth or promise in the Kingdom, should bear witness to such momentous enterprise, which privilege is not given to many men of Lime Stone to enjoy.*

ELEVEN

The river was everywhere. Green precipices of leaves splintered and fell amidst the turbulent screams that rose from the decks of Antarctica's four ships. The black cargoes of flesh were slowly borne away; but the coast shook and trembled as a giant stride of sound made a fury of wailing through the forest. It seemed the trees were about to make sacrifice, as each leaf and branch tottered before the sudden crush of a gale. The wind went mad. There was a throttled murmur of drums echoing from afar. Soon the coast was empty, and a shower of leaves came tumbling down across the river.

The *Reconnaissance* lingered within an arc of white fire that lifted sunwards, burning the air. Ivan had followed the sails of Antarctica's vessels, heaving and dipping before the river spray. He tried to watch this race of water and fire until a swift sensation shut his eyes: a fine, furious drilling ache chiselled away at the back of his skull; and he felt his body lean like a corpse onto the deck. His hands were operating on their own: hot, fragile sticks of bone searching vaguely through his blindness. Now he felt a nerve breathe somewhere under one eyelid; and the river shook the vessel. His hands had collapsed like bramble down his sides. Time afterwards—maybe hours or a second, he could not tell—the men were reviving him with rum.

'It's the only medicine for this devil climate,' Duclos, the first cook, said. He was a man of frivolous manner with a kindness of heart which his colleagues welcomed and suspected at the same time.

'The Devil's climate,' the cook repeated for want of something more cheerful to say.

'What is?' the painter's stricken voice was trying to ask. 'What is? What is?'

'That sun there,' said the cook, Duclos, searching his memory for legends of the river; 'they say the sky itself will turn to ash if it comes too near this coast.' He was hoping in his curious way to distract Ivan from the dangers of the heat.

'One last swig and you'll be asleep,' he said, 'like an angel. A babe not yet born.'

He was forcing the liquid past the painter's lips; but Ivan showed no sign of recovery, and the cook was seized by a sudden panic. 'Ivan, Ivan, Ivan.'

The word turned itself like tape around his tongue, but it had lost the power to name. Duclos began to fear for his own sanity. Was it really Ivan whom he was nursing back to consciousness? A slight shudder was struggling with the painter's fingers. The rum had finally stung his palate. Though he made an effort to talk, his tongue was stiff. There was a taste of sulphur at the back of his throat. Ivan was trying to recall the moment he felt the clap of heat on his head. There was no warning at all, no draining of strength emptying his arms, no gradual dying of touch escaping from his fingertips. There was nothing but the clobber of the sun's fist and his sudden transport into a furnace of pain. The river had been swallowed by the screams of the cargoes of black flesh borne in triumph through the darkness, and he had felt his skull open wide.

Now he tried to work his hands up from the deck and over his head, tracing a line of hair. Gently he swivelled the lobes of his ears. He pressed his fingers against his skin, feeling for the bone that would identify his cheeks. It was the cautious probing of a man who wanted to check that nothing was missing.

It was difficult to swing his body around, and he was hoping to avoid too great attention. He hadn't yet recognized the cook nor any of the men who stared in awe at his frailness. But it wasn't his weakness of limb that he wanted to hide so much as his fear of having to explain what might have happened. He was terrified by this assault of the climate on his senses, and his imagination began to order events as best he could remember them. Was it the vision of the black cargoes that had blasted his sight? Or the news of tragedy, which he had learnt from one of Antarctica's vessels? Soon it would be his burden to bear report that the Kingdom of Lime Stone might be in civil strife. He thought he should force himself to sleep and wait for some more reliable sign of recognition. The sky looked black beyond his feeble glimmer.

'Ivan, Ivan,' the cook repeated, 'Ivan.'

But another voice had broken into the scene on the deck, shattering the cook's obsession with madness and dying.

'Every man to his business,' Boatswain was shouting.

The cook was searching for the right tone of entreaty, but Boatswain's voice had found its flint. 'To his business, every man.'

The men started to disperse, slowly, reproachfully, leaving Ivan splayed across the hatch. Boatswain dictated a final glance at the cook, who seemed to linger.

'Every man, I say,' the voice ordered again.

There was iron and the smell of blood in its sound. Boatswain was not simply giving an order. He was also offering himself as an example of how orders should be given. He had taken the Commandant's model beyond perfection. For a moment no one could imagine a time when Boatswain might have done anything else. It was as though this moment of authority was his entire history of work, his total existence.

'Let him rest,' Boatswain continued, measuring what tone of concern his voice should offer Ivan's body. 'Until he be fit, that is.'

It wasn't clear whether Ivan had heard. He lay where the men had deposited him, light, immobile, beyond sensation. Boatswain was about to go, but he was carefully timing the proper stages of retreat. For he had caught the stern, melancholy eyes of Baptiste returning his stare. No word passed between the powder maker and Boatswain, who was now marching briskly, decisively back to his cabin. Baptiste walked slowly over to the hatch and sat beside Ivan. He said nothing. He just sat there, like a man keeping watch, silent, purposeful.

There was a fretful wind coming off the river. Baptiste reflected; was reflecting, as though the black coast had driven him forever inward. This weight of self-enquiry had become his habit, his way of being. If the Commandant symbolized and enacted the essence of command, the coast with its cargoes of black flesh had precipitated a tendency to reflection in the powder maker. For him—

ever since the arrival of Antarctica's vessels—even eating, working, and breathing were an expression of reflecting. He pondered the mournful silence of the coast, and couldn't distinguish whether it was ambition or fear that spoke within him:

... to die, I, Baptiste, the powder maker, I'm going to die, and Duclos with his life of mending the timbers of ships he has known, Duclos, the cooper, and senior cook, Duclos is going to die, and Pierre trading his loyalties for a favour from above, green and youthful, Pierre the carpenter will die, Pierre and the fisherman, Marcel; carpenter and fisherman will die; and the men without any certainty of skill, the men, long idle, cast away, recruited in secret and by intrigue over many a morning when nothing could happen except God, the idle and the castaway driven by order of their circumstance to sail for a purpose not to their knowing, not necessary to know, invited by circumstance to set sail, journey called duty, destination glory, the men are going to die; like the Commandant; the Commandant is nothing, just a hole, a hole that takes in what it takes in and lets it out again, lets out orders, just a hole, in and out. The Commandant shits in my ears, every time authority is ready to relieve itself, the hole opens, I hear authority shitting in my ears; the Commandant is going to die. I am going to die, that is why Duclos is here, and Pierre and Marcel, and maybe Ivan is dying, maybe not, but Ivan is going to die, that is why Ivan is here....

'You talk to yourself?'

The voice had startled Baptiste. He looked everywhere except down at Ivan, who had spoken.

'I gave you up as dead,' said Baptiste, recovering from the shock of Ivan's voice. 'Who is it talking? You or your ghost?'

The interval of banter was wasted on Ivan, who persisted with his question.

'I ask if you talk to yourself?'

'How do you feel now?' Baptiste asked, and there was a curious blend of kindness in his anger. 'It was a stroke that put you down.'

'Where is Pierre?' Ivan asked, as though there was some special warning in his enquiry.

'You are still drunk,' Baptiste answered, determined to ignore any reference to the carpenter. 'The sunstroke turned your head, put you down. Flat out. A daze it is. That's what you have. A small daze from the Devil's Coast.'

'It is the news from Lime Stone,' said Ivan, trying to raise himself up from the hatch. Although he had faltered, he refused help from Baptiste. He insisted on proving his strength. But his efforts were undermined by memories of Lime Stone.

'Go easy,' said Baptiste; 'you don't owe nothing nowhere.'

'Have you heard what calamity hit the Lord Treasurer of the House?'

'Calamity, you say?'

'The Lord Treasurer has lost his wife,' Ivan whispered. 'Given up for dead.'

Baptiste probed the roof of his mouth with a dry tongue.

'The Lord Treasurer is not the first man to be a widower,' said Baptiste.

'But murder,' Ivan exclaimed, and trembled from the knowledge he was imparting. 'To murder the Lady of the House!'

Baptiste yawned, then quickly made the sound of a rat trap with his teeth.

'Go easy, Ivan,' he said, his voice held to a whisper, like a man obeying the rules of conspiracy. 'I say you owe nothing nowhere.'

But Ivan had recognized that Baptiste was not quite so remote from the meaning of such news. The powder maker had felt the weight of what he heard.

'The Lady of the House,' Baptiste intoned.

'Declared murdered,' Ivan informed him, 'and her body not yet found.'

'A dangerous funeral she will make,' Baptiste said coldly.

'You know you speak too lightly,' Ivan reproached him.

The painter tried to raise himself up, and suddenly slipped.

'I say go easy,' Baptiste rebuked him, and the note of impatience was not lost on Ivan. Baptiste watched him sprawl flat over the hatch. A muscle throbbed and hardened under the powder maker's skin. 'Conspiracy is conspiracy, and in affairs of state...'

'But the Lady of the House,' Ivan interrupted him. 'We speak of the Lord Treasurer's wife, Baptiste.'

'I say there is no limit to what rivals within the House will do,' Baptiste argued. He was making an obvious effort to control his temper.

'But such fatality will make for a very raw future,' Ivan reminded him. 'Already the authorities have hanged all suspects. Or so the Antarctica crew assured me.'

'I believe it,' Baptiste said, and let his glance wander past the pyre of leaves that multiplied their flames along the burning coast. 'Be grateful you are not in your Region at this time.'

'But the search!' Ivan coughed as he tried to rise again. 'The search for evidence will not end at the shores of Lime Stone. That you know.'

'Be grateful you are alive,' Baptiste said. 'And let the House of Justice look after its own dead.'

The painter's vision was guiding him to some region beyond the ship and the river. Baptiste brooded on the silence that had, for a moment, separated them. "It's true," Baptiste reflected. "To murder the Lady of the House—such a calamity could make for a very raw future." For a while he remained under the spell of Ivan's knowledge, pondered the news that the ships of Antarctica had brought, and tried to calculate the difference in time between their departure from Lime Stone and the discovery about the Lady of the House. He could not, however, afford the luxury of sympathy for any loss the Lord Treasurer had suffered. He preferred to admire the spirit of those who had taken such risk; but he couldn't be sure of their motives. He imagined his father's dead hand emerging from the grave to complete its act of rebellion.

'The Commandant is just a hole,' Baptiste said aloud. He had alerted Ivan's fears. The spell of the painter's knowledge was broken.

'What do you mean the Commandant is a hole?' Ivan said, rehearsing his effort to rise again.

'And the Lord Treasurer,' Baptiste added. 'Just a hole, like what you bury things in. A hole with two ends.'

'You are mad,' Ivan said quietly, 'just absolute mad.'

Baptiste had decided against any argument with the painter. He would leave Ivan to wrestle with the extravagance of temper that made him say such things. Suddenly Baptiste got up to go; but the weight of Ivan's news had come alive again. He paused against his will and watched Ivan closely. Could it be true that he was gifted with superior powers of vision? Suddenly some vague strategy had begun to take shape in the powder maker's mind. The officers would have heard the news that the ships of Antarctica had brought. He was reflecting on the way each would react; and his instinct for strategy had now sharpened into a decision. He would persuade Ivan to consult with the officers on behalf of the men. It was important that they knew the officers' reaction to this news about the Lady of the House. He started to walk away, following the bend of the coast where the shadows were gathering for the early night. Soon there would be a total darkness over the river.

Ivan was hardly aware of the powder maker's absence. He was repeating his earlier attempt to sit up, muttering about the madness of what Baptiste had said. 'The Commandant is a hole, the Lord Treasurer is a hole—what kind of craziness to say, not about the men in question, but just to say such authority is a hole.'

At last Ivan had achieved his wish. He sat erect, astonished by the swift revival of his strength. He could see the sky darken and descend like a lid over the forest. He heard the distant warning of a bell, and saw Sasha appear on the deck. The boy approached Baptiste, saluted nervously, and quickly passed a sheet of paper to the powder maker. Baptiste considered the orders, which were written in large bold strokes. He recognized the Commandant's lettering, then glanced at the irregular signatures that identified the officers. The pilot's name was absent. Already the men were collecting in small groups where Ivan sat. Baptiste took his time, carefully measuring each stride towards the men. They had anticipated danger, some threat of punishment in the orders which Baptiste was about to read. His voice was barely audible.

Contrary to your expectations, and notwithstanding the bold expeditions made by Boatswain among the natives of this coast, our vessel, Reconnaissance, *will receive no cargoes of black flesh but proceed with its original crew for the Isles of the Black Rock.*

Any plot by officers or common hands to bring into personal possession such cargoes of black flesh will be considered a capital

*offence against our orders. The punishment will be death, and
without the customary delay of open trial.*

Winds being favourable, Reconnaissance *will sail by the first
sun tomorrow, which by our reckoning we notice is Christmas
Day.*

The orders were received with a mixture of alarm and regret.
What other purpose could this hazardous passage to the Guinea
coast have had if there were to be no capture of black cargoes?
They had seen the ships of Antarctica sail with a fortune of
black flesh, and felt the Commandant's orders reduce their
hopes to a total waste. But no one dared register his disappointment. Even Baptiste withheld his opinion on the orders he had
read. Ivan was afraid the powder maker might make some aspect
of his rebellion known; but Baptiste was careful whom he
spoke to when he was reflecting on the Commandant. Now he
was reflecting on what he felt. He was not afraid of the Commandant. Nor did he hate him. And—so far as his judgment
could discover—there was no evidence of envy in his reflection
on the Commandant. The Commandant was simply a fact that
he had to confront, like this perplexing decision to deny the
Reconnaissance of its just reward in the cargoes of black flesh
that had brought them to this coast. He was deaf to the fretful
murmuring of the men as he tried to imagine the Commandant
in more normal circumstances of daily living: among his friends,
entertaining children, coaxing a woman out of worry.

But tenderness towards authority was a risk he would never
take, and suddenly he curbed such speculation and transferred his
attention to Ivan.

'I think it will storm,' he said. 'What do you say?' He might
have been pleading with the painter for some clue to their future.

'Use your powers,' Baptiste scolded him. 'Will it storm?' He
was making secret reference to the news about the Lady of the
House.

'I say it is too soon to predict,' Ivan insisted.

Baptiste was going to press for an answer, but the men had
come to his relief. Their eagerness for prophecy was beyond
belief. They had seen in the painter's sunstroke some possible
sign of revelation, a baptism of fire that had cleansed his mind

and ordained his vision with greater powers of prediction. Ivan could see things. He was the man to be consulted. Even Baptiste, they felt, who was so sceptical and by nature dangerously irreverent, was waiting on Ivan for a sign, a clue that would open them to their future.

'I'll say this,' Ivan conceded; 'there will be a moon tonight.'

'And when will the moon come out?' a voice was begging.

'That I cannot declare,' said Ivan, suddenly embarrassed by the authority they had conferred on him.

Baptiste was shaving his jaw with the sheet of paper.

'What use are your powers?' he asked, feeling the urge to argue.

'You are impatient,' Ivan said. His tone was gentle, solicitous, an affectionate reminder of his comradeship.

But Baptiste felt more secure in his role of rebellion. He was rubbing the Commandant's orders over the base of his buttocks.

'A hole'—Baptiste was laughing—'just a hole that lets out orders.'

The men couldn't follow the powder maker's meaning, but Ivan was apprehensive. It seemed a most inappropriate occasion for Baptiste to be light-hearted.

'A joke is a joke,' Ivan insisted, 'but what we know is no joke.' And Baptiste ran off, his laugh like a harmless roll of thunder awakening the sails. For a moment he seemed to enjoy the effect of his irreverence on the men. He returned as quickly, smiling at the studied gravity of the painter's bearing as he looked about him, anticipating the arrival of the Commandant. Baptiste lowered his body and brought his head a whisper away from Ivan's face.

'You must discover the officers' feeling,' said Baptiste, 'about the Lady of the House, I mean.'

'Later,' said Ivan.

'Before we sail.'

'We must speak later,' Ivan implored him, reluctant to share this confidence with the men. He had no gift for intrigue, but an instinct for protection urged him that the men were safer in their innocence of what he knew. He wasn't sure whether Baptiste had heard him; the powder maker had gone off on his own. A wind shook the river and caused a wreck of bottles on the deck. They made an echo like bells at odds with their chiming. Just sounds in disarray. Baptiste stood alone, his body loose and light against the curve of timber where he leaned, now helpless to restrain his reflection on the coast, and the fateful news about the Lady of the House.

"I am going to die." He smiled, as though he had discovered some joy in such knowledge. "Like the Lady of the House, Baptiste is going to die, but I feel free, ever so free."

His eyes flashed fires of ecstasy through the sombre folds of cloud that opened and closed over the silent forest. The afternoon was over; darkness was finally stealing over the river.

'Ever so free,' said Baptiste, 'so free.'

He heard deep soundings of the river in his ears, the measured rhythm of vast silences that rose from beyond the origin of the river. There was a moment of enigma, the signature of mystery written across the invisible sky.

He heard the muted voices of the men, perplexed by the Commandant's orders to sail without the promise of fortune in the cargoes of black flesh. They could detect no fragment of reason in such a decision. The Commandant had shown surprising generosity in his arrangements for distributing the fortunes that came within the ship's possession. And he had made history with his offer of future ownership in the vessel *Reconnaissance*. And suddenly—without warning—he had deprived them of the first certain gift of fortune that the enterprise had brought them. It was like a breach of contract, supervised by a man who had lost his memory. They couldn't comprehend such lack of reason.

But Ivan was trying with the utmost discretion to console them with some explanation.

'It is a rough experience that makes him act contrary,' said Ivan. 'He has been through as many wars as he has years.'

'Maybe this coast put a spell on his reason,' someone said.

'A fine courage he has,' said Ivan, as though he hadn't heard the man's misgivings. 'He should have gone for the Church, such a knowledge of matters he has.' The painter paused, then added with gravest acknowledgment, 'Of many matters, deep and small.'

Baptiste had joined the men, but no one noticed his arrival.

The painter was the focus of their attention.

'They say he made his second journey under a cloud,' said Ivan, 'a quarrel of some magnitude in the family. Cursed his own blood and took to military exile over the ocean seas.'

The men recalled with awe the Commandant's fearless denunciation of the House, and the bold concessions of loyalty he had made on behalf of the ancient families of the North.

'And the Church too,' said Ivan, now worried by a conflict in his estimate of the Commandant. 'He would curse the clergy whenever he set sail.'

Some vague feeling of admiration had stirred in Baptiste. He couldn't contain the urge to speak, to argue some flaw in the Commandant's gifts of leadership.

'But his long absence from command,' Baptiste intervened, and the men were startled by the note of rebuke, startled and yet grateful for some challenge to the Commandant's judgment. 'Who has set eyes on him since we ventured on this coast?'

There was a murmur of approval. It was true that no one, except the pilot, Pinteados, had spoken with the Commandant since they entered the river. He had left the decision for the capture of black cargoes to Boatswain and the young carpenter Pierre, who had suddenly blossomed into a man of imperial action.

'You know how he occupies his time in his cabin?' Baptiste continued, and felt a sudden thrust of envy.

'That is general knowledge,' said Ivan; 'always writing. He covers more paper than the forest has leaves.'

The painter grew feverish with wonder at the Commandant's ability to endure the patience and solitude of writing, almost without end.

'Every manner of account,' said Ivan, 'every journey from the first to this moment. What the natives of these coasts eat in the morning, and how they worship according to the movements of the sun until they become cargoes of black flesh. He will just write it down, always this writing things down. Like the men of the Church.'

For a moment the painter was stunned by this vision of ink, large and inescapable as the coast, making black rivers everywhere, increasing the mysterious power of the word on paper.

'And what use is all that report?' Baptiste intervened again. 'What use, I ask you.'

Ivan was slow to speak. This question had plunged him into a region of knowledge he did not care to share. He was afraid to meet the challenge of the powder maker's question.

'There be others who know the use,' said Ivan, hoping to avoid a conflict with Baptiste.

'But the Commandant,' Baptiste insisted. 'Why this excess of writing in the Commandant?'

'He may yet turn to the Church,' Ivan parried, 'in the end.'

Baptiste grew restless, as though a hunger for facts and answers had attacked him. He had recognized the voice of the cook, Duclos, whom he knew to be a man of many voyages. He started to bully the cook into an alliance.

'What do you say?' Baptiste was ordering him.

'Say?' the cook repeated, rearranging his hands. He was startled by the threat of authority that Baptiste assumed. 'Say? You ask what I say?'

'Yes, what do you say?' Baptiste insisted.

'About what?' The cook was whispering.

'About these habits of the Commandant?' Baptiste said, ordering him to have an opinion. 'About such long absence from the deck. This excess of writing. Or the strange order that *Reconnaissance* receive no cargoes of black flesh?'

The cook began to sweat. 'These matters are too deep,' he whispered.

'Come on,' Baptiste pursued him. 'You travel with the Commandant before. So speak. What do you say?'

'Many moons back,' Duclos began, as though he was making an apology. 'I didn't hope to welcome another voyage with the likes of him again. He is one who causes great drama wherever he sails. Never taken a ship out but some terrible disaster of sickness or battle makes news back home. There be masters who win praise and honours for their exploits, but none could ever arouse such a wondering and speculating how he survived such obstacles in triumph. He carries a demon of victory inside him.'

Duclos stopped abruptly, as though he was astonished by his own eloquence and the men's attention. Or the thought of demons occupying the coast may have forced his thinking into more sober regions. Surprised and apprehensive, he was like a man caught by his own conscience in the act of betraying inner secrets.

'But I couldn't choose,' said Duclos, indicating an end to his speech. 'He knows my personal history.'

Baptiste was waiting for him to continue. Was it a blank or eventful passage of silence? No one could tell. Duclos could have held their attention, made his name as one they heard out to the awful end. But nothing came from him except the foreboding sound of the word 'demon' when he said finally: 'And now this news of murder. The Lady of the House reported dead.'

The syllables carried echoes of brass over the river, prophesying blood for those who followed the Commandant.

Marcel, the fisherman, joined them, and the tension broke for a while. Slow, casual, with an infinite sense of freedom in everything he did, he had leaned his body on the bench. Then he said, as though he were talking exclusively to the sea: 'There will be many lives lost for that one Lady's life.'

But he didn't finish. The bell was calling the men to their evening meal. The dispersal was swift; Baptiste had lingered behind with Ivan and Marcel. This corner of the deck was almost deserted, where Ivan waited to welcome the moon.

'There be two men I would give a fortune to fathom,' said Baptiste.

'Only two?' Marcel asked.

Baptiste tried to smile. Halted by Marcel's calm, he recognized again the strange attraction Marcel had for him.

'Yes, there be two only,' he said. 'You and the Commandant. In that order.'

Marcel chuckled, a sound of marbles or dry bones rolling briefly to a stop.

'In that order?'

'Yes, that order,' said Baptiste.

'You won't fathom the Commandant,' said Marcel.

'And why do you say that?'

'I just say it,' said Marcel. 'That's as it comes to me.'

'Too deep? Is that your meaning? He is too deep?'

'I wasn't giving a special or particular meaning,' said Marcel. 'I was speaking as it comes to me, and I say you won't fathom him.'

'What do you say about all that writing?' Baptiste asked. 'How do you fathom his reason?'

'Fathom,' Marcel parried, 'there you go again with your "fathom".'

'There must be a reason,' Baptiste insisted, 'what use is this writing to the Commandant?'

'Use?' Marcel said, his voice raised in vague alarm.

'Yes, what use?'

'I don't fathom a use,' said Marcel. 'It is how he must spend his time.'

'You don't find it strange?' Baptiste asked. 'Why spend his silence that way?'

'He cannot talk with anyone,' said Marcel, 'so he must talk with himself. Every man has to talk. With friends if there be any. To himself if he be without. The Commandant writes. So!'

'And if he couldn't write?' Baptiste enquired.

'Then he would not be the Commandant,' said Marcel. 'Maybe; I don't boast a certainty.'

He looked to Ivan for some sign of agreement.

'But why?' Baptiste insisted. 'Why? Why?'

'It is a woman,' Ivan said quietly. 'Some woman is his reason.'

Ivan glanced up at the sky and detected a spear of light drilling small holes through the cloud. Then he joined in the dispersal. Baptiste remained. He was reflecting on Ivan's reference to the woman, and the sound of the bell came crashing into his ears again. He called out to Marcel. The fisherman was leaning against the waist of the ship. Tense and remote, he was keeping a private vigil as he gazed down at the half-face of the moon riding on the water. Baptiste came up and stood behind him.

'The moon is out,' he said. 'As Ivan promised.'

'Take a look,' said Marcel, hugging the powder maker's shoulder to him. 'Down there!'

'Where? I can't see anything in the water.'

Marcel never deflected his glance as he raised his arm and straightened it, instructing Baptiste where to look.

'Bring your head around,' he said, offering his index finger as a guide. 'Lift your eyes and watch my finger. Now, glance where the finger moves. There, exact where I am pointing now.'

Baptiste had grown docile as a child.

'A fish,' he said, seizing Marcel's hand.

'So you see it,' said Marcel, and took his hand away.

'Yes, I see it, all right.'

Marcel was living the mysteries of his fishing trade.

'Believe me or not,' he said, as though the fish would be his surest evidence, 'we have been watching each other for many a day.'

Baptiste made a shy, ambiguous laugh.

'It's true,' said Marcel. 'She keeps a watch on me, and I keep a watch on her. A cat-and-mouse manoeuvre, you might say.'

'You think the fish knows it is Marcel up here?' Baptiste asked. There was something of mockery and admiration in his voice.

'To be sure, she knows,' said Marcel; 'that's what I mean. She may not know it is the actual, particular me you call Marcel. But she knows the fisherman in me. She can smell the fisherman in me.'

Baptiste wanted to offer some contradiction, as he often did when Ivan troubled their attention with matters beyond ordinary ways of knowing. But there was a quality of certainty in Marcel which made him resist this urge to argue.

He simply said: 'You love the life on water.'

'For fishing, yes,' Marcel said. 'It's a holy feeling for the night to catch you out in that dark, just you and a population larger than all Lime Stone swimming deep under and around your boat. Everywhere you can feel the ocean waiting like a farm.'

Marcel talked as though he had the power to summon some multitude from the sea to bear witness to what he knew.

'You should try your hand at fishing,' he said.

His voice had stirred a strange jealousy in Baptiste.

'All my fish are on land, Marcel,' the powder maker said.

'I don't trust land,' said the fisherman, 'nor the two-legged animals that crawl over it.'

'Don't talk like that,' said Baptiste; 'two legs always make a man.'

'No difference between two legs and four,' Marcel argued, 'not after you've had experience of all the animals.'

They were staring through and beyond the last ridge of shadow on the coast.

'A man's a man, Marcel, two legs always make a man, and nothing but a man.'

Marcel had sensed the hint of reproach in the powder maker's voice. Marcel was confident; but his mood had grown sombre. There was a militant eagerness in his challenge to Baptiste.

'But the natives of this coast that leave as cargoes of black flesh,' Marcel said, 'have they two legs?'

'Of course, each carries two legs,' Baptiste said.

'And hands, eyes, ears that look like yours?'

'To be sure,' said Baptiste.

'But would you think of them as men?' Marcel asked.

Baptiste had curbed his defiance. A monstrous darkness filled his eyes. Now he was candid and cautious in reply.

'Perhaps not in the way I think of you and me,' he said, 'but there must be something of the man in them. Like the fisherman in you.'

His reference to the sea had softened Marcel's temper.

'You dream again,' the fisherman said.

Baptiste felt his passion for argument return. 'Did you hear how they cry?' he asked. 'Did you hear how the cargoes of black flesh cry?'

'So do the four-legged animals,' Marcel intervened. 'I see them multiply, and sometimes they too look sad and cry.'

'Strange you should talk like that,' said Baptiste.

'It's true.'

A silence came over them, secret and tense as unknown danger. Sprung from similar adversity, it seemed they had nurtured a different relation to their experience. A tail of light wriggled on the water.

'Two-legged animals,' Baptiste mused, and his voice was remote, almost mechanical. 'Once I heard my father say that's how the House of Justice thought of him. "Baptiste," he used to say before he got drunk, "Baptiste, my son, your father is nothing but an animal any king can tame with food and water." '

'I am no king,' Marcel answered, and turned his glance in search of the fish.

'Then you must talk like a man,' Baptiste said.

There was a blaze of starlight. The new moon was coming up over a purple hump of cloud, kissing the water with its shadow. They heard a sail clap, and watched how the river was combing the drowned reflection of the moon, dancing and waving like a woman's hair over the body of the fish.

TWELVE

'Would someone be there?' Surgeon shouted, and his voice had found the severity that marked all his orders. He saw the figure appear out of the night, edging a way nervously into the dining cabin. Priest recognized the painter.

'Is something wrong below?' Surgeon asked.

Ivan was apologetic and obviously frightened, so frightened that he thought it necessary to give his name. Soon he was hurrying with an answer.

'Nothing in the nature of disorder,' Ivan said, 'but an argument among the men.'

He shook the rain from his hands and drew nearer.

'I should have known you might be busy,' he said, and glanced at Priest.

The officers had met to celebrate the eve of Christmas. Boatswain was absent, and it was thought that he was still trying to overcome the Commandant's orders that there should be no cargoes of black flesh. It was surprising injustice for the hazardous expedition he had conducted beyond the coast. The painter observed the troubled, almost sullen expression on Steward's face. He was the only officer who had not raised his eyes to see who had entered the dining cabin. He sat at the far end of the dining table, where the candle showed half his face in shadow, and made little rings of flame that trembled over his hands. His glass was empty.

'I should have known you might be busy,' the painter said again, as though he couldn't afford the luxury of a pause.

'What argument?' Surgeon asked. 'You say there is some argument among the men.'

'It turns on a point of learning,' said Ivan, 'and your opinion is as final an answer as we'll settle for.'

Now he was cautious in his choice of words. He was about to launch into the tragic news from Lime Stone, but the word 'fatality' felt like wire wrapping around his tongue. "I refer to the fatality," he was about to say; and suddenly remembered the strategy that Baptiste had urged, and which the men approved. They wanted the officers' reactions to the news about the Lady of the House; the painter was to pretend that the argument had arisen over the Lord Treasurer of the House. But Ivan had no gift of intrigue. He was still trying to find the safest explanation for his arrival in the officers' dining cabin. He recognized Surgeon's interest in his presence, the razor sharpness of that officer's eyes rebuking his delay. The painter stared briefly at Priest, hoping to avoid the acute attention Surgeon had directed on him.

'What is the cause of your argument?' Priest asked. He, too, was curious about the general opinion among the men, and apprehensive of the painter's curious gifts of perception. He thought the painter would discover the secret of the officers' solidarity in his presence; for it was agreed that each would pretend an utter ignorance of any news from Lime Stone.

'We do not enter into any dispute dividing the House of Trade and Justice,' said Ivan, making sure that his visit was not connected with the policy of the House.

He watched Priest, and felt a momentary protection in his memories of the Church.

'The argument is a matter of learning,' Ivan repeated. 'If the Lady of the House be truly declared dead, can the Lord Treasurer make a legal marriage before the body is found? Some say he should not, since her death may remain in dispute. Others say he can, since confessions have been made and certain men executed for her murder.'

Surgeon looked to Priest, as though he were inviting him to take the issue over. It would have been simple to dismiss the man on some pretext, and let the matter rest; but Surgeon wanted to put Ivan to some test. He had some doubt that this might have been the whole purpose of the painter's visit. He was indicating that Priest might give an opinion; but Ivan had taken a few paces nearer the table and started to speak.

'And if the Lady ever turns up,' he said, 'what would her position be after the Lord Treasurer had taken a second wife?'

Surgeon found his curiosity sharpening for a reply.

'There is always a chance she might have been spared,' said Ivan. 'I mean...' He was fighting to overcome a slight stammer. 'I mean, it is just possible. Until a body was found, it is just possible.'

'Spared?' Surgeon's voice cut in. 'By whom? What are the men's views on this matter? Spared, you say. By whom, I ask?'

The painter was slow to speak; but Surgeon indicated that he was waiting for an answer. Priest had confirmed his own interest in what Ivan might have to say.

Ivan felt that they were trying to trap him. He could no longer distinguish between Surgeon and Priest in the matter of his own safety, although he would have taken a risk with Priest. Now it seemed that they were not only waiting to hear him, but he was under orders to speak. The situation confused him. He had come for an answer that would have been accepted. His role of delegate would have been concluded. Now he had been dangerously elevated to a different status. They were seeking his opinion, inviting him to interpret the various opinions of the men below; and every effort to speak warned him that he might be informing on his friends. Would he be allowed to report an opinion without naming the person who held it? It seemed impossible to draw the line between messenger and agent. And the curiosity of Surgeon emphasized this fear in him. It reminded him, too, of the trust which Baptiste and the men below had placed in him. If he were chosen to get an answer from Surgeon, it was simply because the others believed that he was the safest person for such a mission.

Now he heard Surgeon's voice, almost impatient, it seemed, when he said: 'Well, what are the men saying?' And Ivan was reminded that his silence might be taken for concealment. He was trying to bury secrets which his superiors ought to know about. This made for the greatest risk of all. The messenger, who might have turned informer, had suddenly blossomed into an agent of mutiny.

'There's nothing said that goes against your interest, sir,' he said, trying to address Surgeon and Priest at the same time.

There was no stir of life from Steward's corner of the table.

'All the more reason you should speak,' said Surgeon. 'What are the men saying down below?'

Ivan started to regret the mission that had brought him to the officers' dining cabin. He noticed everything now; how Surgeon leaned back in his chair, easy and relaxed, as though he had no worry about time and waiting. He noticed Priest's hands open and close, then the sharp, almost automatic clenching of one fist that brought the left arm up from the table. He looked in vain for some tremor of life in Steward. He would have liked to ask permission to go; but he stayed put, anticipating the catastrophe he might bring on himself if it appeared to be a gesture of impudence.

It seemed that the officers had forgotten his original question about the marital status of the Lord Treasurer. Indeed, they showed no interest in reviving it. And Ivan kept muttering to himself, locking his lips between his teeth: "They want to find me out on some matter. They want to put me on trial, but there is no offence to my name, no offence at all." He noticed Surgeon again: now Surgeon was reaching forward, slowly wrapping his hands around the glass, tilting it lazily to his head. Priest was digging a finger into his ear. Steward's silence grew more ominous.

Ivan wanted to return to the question he had put on behalf of his friends; but he couldn't take such liberty until Surgeon had been satisfied that he had got his information about the men. 'By whom? Spared by whom, I ask?' Then there would be Priest. What Surgeon omitted to ask, Priest was sure to remember. Ivan experienced a double fear; partly the natural caution that mention of the House inspired in everyone, and the suspicion of disloyalty to his superiors.

'Some of us think,' Ivan began, 'but it is never clear who says what. That I must put a firm point on.'

'Some think what?' Surgeon pressed him. And the urgency of his voice revived Ivan's anxiety. The more direct the question, the greater was the danger for any answer he might give.

'Some think it is bad the Kingdom should be so divided,' Ivan said. 'The unity of the House will always go hand in hand with the safety of the Kingdom. We were unhappy about such divisions in the Kingdom.'

The painter stopped, and parted his hands wide, suggesting there was nothing else he could think of.

'I would add,' he went on, 'it was a reason some of us had for making this enterprise. Dangerous as the ocean and foreign parts might be, we felt a greater safety away from the Kingdom. But we wish it well. Maybe this very enterprise may make for a little healing.'

He paused to reflect on the wisdom of what he had said; then he thought that it would add the right authority to this view if he offered some word of applause to the Commandant. But he checked himself, fearing that this might have reduced the importance of Surgeon and Priest in circumstances that now seemed to be their entire responsibility. He decided to leave their supremacy unchallenged.

Then Ivan became contrite. He thought he might have found a way of turning attention elsewhere. It would also be in keeping with that importance of connections which he attributed to Surgeon and Priest.

'I was thinking what a grave error I have made,' he said, achieving an expression of penitence and failure. 'Perhaps it was a personal loss for you. I mean the fatality of the Lady of the House. Would you have known her, sir, even by way of your calling?'

He was looking at Priest, but he had intended the question for Surgeon. He noticed Priest's slowness to speak. It was like a call on Surgeon to state his relations to the House. He noticed too that Surgeon now avoided Priest's glance, as though he had been waiting to acquire a knowledge that it would have been imprudent to ask directly of Priest. Distracted, Surgeon's glance found the floor.

'Where there is a personal knowledge,' said Ivan, embarrassed by the silence he had caused, 'feeling is sharper than it might be for the general calamity. We on the outside think of the division of the Kingdom, but it might be different for you who carry the grief of a personal contact. You would forgive me if it is so and I make no mention of it before.'

Priest looked grave, wholly self-absorbed, yet alert to the casual, distracted air of Surgeon, who refused to come to his rescue with any knowledge about their relations to the House. These attitudes perplexed Ivan; but he attributed the cause to some grief that the officers had experienced by his sudden reference to the personal nature of the fatality. It seemed that this might be an appropriate moment to take his leave. Even if he were sufficiently important to press for an answer, it would have been heartless to do so, for he thought they had some cause to mourn the news of the Lady of the House.

'I am sorry to come at so wrong a time,' Ivan said, speaking directly to Surgeon.

Priest was unsure what he should do to facilitate Ivan's departure; but he was sure he wanted him to go. Yet relations between the officers were such that no one risked violating certain formalities. Priest had authority to give orders to Ivan; but he was reluctant to exercise this authority while the other officers were present.

And Surgeon was playing for time; but it seemed that all possibilities were now exhausted. He could make no further use of Ivan, who was likely to complicate the situation by prolonging his stay. Tentative, amiable, Surgeon crept his hand up over the table, guiding Priest's eyes to the bottle.

'You must be ready for another,' he said.

'Not a moment too soon,' said Priest, his voice as startled as if he had been awakened from sleep. His hands became more nimble, he had worked up a sudden and contagious passion for Surgeon's offer of wine.

'A little more, if I might ask it,' Priest said, and kept the glass under the neck of the bottle.

'You must sharpen your appetite for tomorrow,' Surgeon said.

'If we are gone from this coast,' Priest said, 'it would be a blessing to have Christmas dinner on the ocean seas.'

'To the future of your appetite,' said Surgeon.

Surgeon raised his glass. It seemed they had forgotten the painter, who stood, vague and silent as a shadow, waiting to be dismissed. Then Surgeon lifted his head towards Ivan and worked his eyebrows up and across. The signal of dismissal was emphatic as a voice; and Ivan retreated through the door. Priest drank again; and Surgeon shook the wine and watched it leap up the side of the glass. He made no comment on the painter's visit, nor did Priest appear to notice that the man had gone.

'To Christmas on the ocean seas,' said Steward, and raised his empty glass.

It was the first time he had spoken since they had arrived in the dining cabin.

2
The Middle Passage

THIRTEEN

The officers ate with all the formalities appropriate to their new status, each addressing the other by the title of his office. The Commandant was not present. Boatswain was overcome by the brilliance of silver goblets that contained the wine. There were three on the table at this meal. An abundance of fruit piled high into glass bowls. The forks were pure silver. They ate like men who had to prove their capacity. But Boatswain was a natural eater.

'The quantity has never been an obstacle,' he once said. 'It is the absence that has worried me. I have known absence.' And he gazed wilfully around the table as though he wanted to add: 'And so have you.'

Surgeon wore that blissful, remote look of a horse chewing in sleep. He had a habit of soaking the dry prunes in his wine; then he would suck for a moment before grazing on the acrid, black flesh. His temples inflated while he ate, as though tubes were pumping air up to his head.

'Would Surgeon have known an absence?' Boatswain asked.

'I could give you answers that would be more useful,' Surgeon said. 'I put the past behind me that very moment I gave the Commandant my word.' He tore at an edge of meat that clung fiercely to the knuckle of bone.

'I have heard you discourse on the past,' said Steward.

'My escapades,' he said, giving up the bone. The little thread of skin refused to be severed. 'I think Boatswain is looking for amusement.'

Steward, expert at timing his interventions, cut in with a request for more wine before Boatswain had time to decide what he was looking for. The table looked like a battlefield of bones. The brass lamp hung low, throwing a shadow of animal corpses over the busy, wet faces. The pilot was taciturn; his opinion held well within the limits of a controversial statement. He was so tall that even while he was sitting his head did not seem far from the ceiling. Yet his presence seemed to attract little attention; sometimes he would pass a whole meal without speaking.

Surgeon helped himself to another cut of beef and considered what remained on the dish. There was no shortage of supplies, but it was his habit to anticipate the end of each meal. He had such a relationship to food that he savoured the flavour of the meat while his appetite warned of its eagerness for the fruit that would follow. Sometimes he would satisfy this conflict by choosing according to the urge that was on him. He chewed meat and threw a prune in his mouth while he was chewing.

Surgeon's eating was a kind of performance in which he saw himself in many roles. Exclusive and indispensable. It was as though he existed in order to give food some useful purpose. He embodied all forms of appetite. When the ship rocked and the plates started to slide away, his chewing would come abruptly to an end. Then he would sit motionless, his jaws drawn tight, and wait until calm had been restored. His enjoyment required a settled state. Objects remained in their place, and responded to his urge. He paid little attention to the men until it was time for anecdotes. This had become the normal climax to their meeting in the dining cabin. But Christmas was a promise of greater expectations. There was an atmosphere of fellowship in the cabin.

'Did you visit your division this evening?' Steward asked. He could never divorce his pleasure from an instinct which called him to duty.

'The men are well left alone,' Boatswain said, 'from time to time, that is.'

'It was awful quiet today,' said Priest. 'They might have been at prayer.'

The men had not responded to the festivities of the season. They had been strangely silent all day. Priest wanted to offer congratulations on the discipline that had produced such conduct among the crew, but his attention was drawn to Surgeon, who was fumbling with a knuckle of bone. It made a sharp edge, pushing out from the side of his mouth like the end of a tooth. Surgeon helped the bone out of his mouth with his left hand, and knocked the knife against it as though he were passing some silent judgment on what he saw. It was bare, sucked dry of any moisture.

'Did anyone see the Commandant this evening?' Boatswain asked. He wasn't expecting an answer. The question was the way he often introduced comment on something he had noticed. 'He was patrolling among the division before the bell went. It pays to see things are kept in order.'

Surgeon concentrated on his plate. He scooped a small pool of bone marrow up with his knife and ladled it gently over his tongue. Then he took a mouthful of wine and rinsed his palate.

'It's the Commandant's habit to take a look,' said Steward.

'Also it keeps him in touch,' Priest said. 'He is never out of date with the general opinion.'

'Self-witness is the best witness,' said Boatswain. 'What I hear and what I see will never be the same report.'

He was sitting next to the pilot, whom he looked at for an opinion; but Pinteados didn't acknowledge the suggestion. He seldom spoke beyond the simple request to pass something. Even then, it had to be well beyond his reach. It seemed that he was averse to asking favours. But his silence showed no sign of a disagreeable temper. It was unusual and allowed, like his height.

Priest approved Boatswain's remark. He made his approval obvious whenever he wanted to add something that might appear to be an improvement. 'Self-witness is the best witness,' he repeated, looking across the table at Boatswain. Then he added: 'Better still is self-judgment.'

Boatswain had already turned his attention back to his meal. He had a habit of holding his head low over the plate while he cast his eyes up to observe those around him. He noticed the fanatical movement of Surgeon's jaws. Steward was licking the end of one finger. He was delicate and sparing in his actions. Boatswain had to suppress a remark on the contrast between the habits of these two: Surgeon grown frank and ravenous in expression, and Steward, who seemed to eat according to some rule of conduct.

Boatswain thought he admired Steward, although he found more delight in Surgeon's rawness. Priest retained an air of urbanity that made it difficult to tell what effect the meal had on his senses.

Boatswain raised his head slowly and let his eyes relax level. He couldn't look at Pinteados without turning his head; so he gave up the exercise. This was part of a childhood lesson: that you saw something intimately connected with a person when you watched him eat. That's what he had often heard by way of correction. Eating had often put a strain on him. He feared he might give himself away. Even when there was no flaw he was aware of in himself, he kept a kind of watch on the way he was eating.

Christmas and the holy memory of manger and cradle had brought his origins vividly to mind.

'You can tell a man by the state of his plate,' his grandmother would say. 'Some men would be happier set before a trough. The pig and the plate will not concur.'

It was not a rule Boatswain could freely apply on this occasion. Surgeon was not a man you could condemn to the indignity of a trough. If he resembled a pig in his eating, it was not for lack of breeding. He had chosen to show his pleasure that way. "To be in charge of your shortcoming," Boatswain was thinking, "that is to know how to do as you please." This appeared to be a point in Surgeon's favour. There was a great difference in the quality of the man who committed his error and the man who freely chose what his error would be, and how it must appear. In this case Surgeon might have been assuming too great a freedom.

But it was Christmas; and Boatswain heard again a cry of bells as he watched the officers through his memory of a holy manger.

Surgeon was belching into his hands. He looked at the depleted carcass of deer and shook his head. A glint, like the light of a coin, was sprouting water in his eyes. There was a moist feeling at the back of his neck, and a pulse prizing his flesh up somewhere across his shoulders. It was as though the jacket had been rambling like a wet hand over the column of his back. He was feeling an immense power generated from his body. He looked at the fleshless bones and said: 'Nobody will eat you again.'

'You are well satisfied,' Steward said, and smiled his pleasure at Surgeon's performance. It was impossible to ignore his capacity.

'What more could he be wanting?' Boatswain said.

Priest suggested a word of gratitude.

But Surgeon had taken a pipe from his tunic and started to

fill the bowl. He searched the bowl with his thumb before stuffing the tobacco inside. He pushed it in and out of his mouth for a while, licking the stem. Then he lit it and watched the first rings of smoke drift up to the ceiling. He was still feeling an inclination to investigate the bowl of fruit, but the urge was not so strong. He sucked on the pipe, tasting the early bitterness of the tobacco. Almost involuntarily, his hand went out and lifted another prune from the bowl.

Steward joined him. It was as though he wanted to keep Surgeon company. Boatswain poured himself some wine. Priest had leaned his head back as though he was giving some sign of his withdrawal from their company. The Christmas meal was about to threaten them with fatigue. Surgeon was deciding whether to yawn or belch.

But Boatswain had become exceedingly curious. He was looking for a chance to make some important observation, or embarrass the table by some urgency of question. He saw Surgeon expel something from his mouth; then he was probing the bottom of the bowl where the prunes had fallen. Surgeon's movements were too rapid, too purposeful to allow any intervention. Steward was too delicate, too elegant to be a target for disturbance; he could not be easily drawn where he was unsure of the direction you were taking. And Priest was beyond experiment. There was no special air of solemnity about him, but Boatswain shared in a heritage of respect for the office of the man who heard his confessions. He couldn't treat Priest too lightly without endangering the seriousness of any meeting he might have with him on some more important occasion.

He had to keep his respect for Priest, just as he had found it necessary to restrain his admiration for Surgeon. There was a limit to respect, just as there was a limit to giving of yourself. Boatswain wasn't clear what impression he wanted to make when he turned to Pinteados and asked him: 'And what really made you accept this enterprise?'

The entire table was alarmed by the daring of the question. It was not only a personal challenge to the pilot; it seemed to violate an unspoken code that the past of each officer was a kind of sacred ground where trespass was forbidden. Steward's gift of timely intervention had deserted him. But there wasn't the slightest trace of agitation in the pilot. He said quite calmly: 'Power; I have never had power over anyone. That's why I take the Commandant's offer.' He paused to consider his own meaning. 'If anything should happen to the Commandant, I am the one who will decide what you do next.'

Not a word was spoken to confirm or deny the pilot's explanation. But they all shared a similar objection to this claim. He had now become the absolute foreigner among them: a native of Antarctica who had earned the confidence of the Commandant by a mixture of servility and skill. His admission was at once frank and offensive. What might have been noted and forgotten as a mark of ambition was now felt by the officers to be a display of impudence.

Steward wanted to call this to the attention of the others; but his caution overruled the displeasure he was feeling. He watched Pinteados and smiled. Steward had perfected the habit of smiling when he judged a moment of crisis was upon him. His concentration had become too obvious. He reached forward and carefully selected an apple from the bowl. Surgeon was the first to break the silence.

'You have had power,' he said. 'Everyone here had power sometime. To have a woman is to know some power sometime.'

'No woman,' said Pinteados; 'I have no woman. I shall have no woman.' His voice was formal and precise.

'No woman?' Surgeon said, expressing astonishment on behalf of the officers. Their faces showed the right degree of alarm. Boatswain became hysterical with laughter.

Pinteados ignored their reaction. He might not have noticed it for the promptness of his reply.

'I had a grandmother,' he said, 'and she would advise from early. Never open any door you can't close. No woman for me. Then. Now. Or ever.'

Boatswain's laughter had broken the tension. There was something like delight in the feeling which Pinteados had aroused in him.

Surgeon brought his chewing to an end. It was sudden, like turning attention at once to some new undertaking. He spoke with the authority of his profession.

'Gentlemen, can you tell the pilot what he has missed?'

'Degradation,' said Pinteados; 'that's what I missed.' His words came fast as gunshot; and wilfully aimed at Surgeon.

The pilot's tone had forced a different silence on them. Steward shovelled the apple pips from the plate and slowly threw them one by one onto the table. It was the safest way to avoid offering an opinion. Pinteados drained his glass and motioned to the goblet at the far end of the table. He filled it slowly, fixing his eyes on the red stain that rose level with the rim. Surgeon waited until he had taken a sip.

'Never in your life?' he asked, and smiled. 'You have never had a woman ever?'

Boatswain forced back his laugh, then suddenly grew solemn and attentive. Something had changed inside him. His eyes were dark with self-rebuke. Pinteados hadn't spoken. They couldn't tell whether his silence was an expression of anger or some unexpected shame for the failure which Surgeon was attributing to him. Everyone looked to Priest, who had excluded himself; sabotaged any curiosity by a wilful refusal to listen. Their caution reflected some respect for Priest.

Steward had little taste for this kind of enquiry. It was too open. Words had a way of making uncomfortable raids on a man's privacy. He would allow for a confidence between individuals who had met for the purpose of exchanging difficulties; but this free exchange was against his own instincts. Yet everything seemed different with Pinteados. The pilot had come from a different way of living; and it was natural that his own code of privacy should not necessarily apply to the pilot. This must have been the force of Steward's reasoning; for he called directly on Pinteados to answer Surgeon's question.

'As a matter between men,' Steward said. 'What's your answer?'

Pinteados raised his glass and drank again. His movement was slow, deliberate, almost self-protective. He looked through the cloudy half of the glass, before returning it to the table.

'You want an answer,' the pilot said at last. 'Then tell me what use will you make of it? I put a price on everything. I put a price on my answer. Tell me what use you will make of it.'

Steward hesitated, then decided to turn the challenge away from himself.

'Surgeon might be able to help,' said Steward. 'His advice would be in order.'

He looked at the men for agreement. Boatswain remained unresponsive, and Priest appeared to be elsewhere. Surgeon considered how he might encourage the enquiry without forcing a quarrel. It was difficult to tell how Pinteados regarded this encounter. There was no food in Surgeon's mouth, but he had started to chew again—a slow, meditative grazing of his teeth.

Pinteados showed the confidence of the stranger who is not inhibited by error, since the rules that judge him make no claim on his feeling. Behaviour was simply a matter of memory. Any violation of custom can be explained as a lapse of memory. He wasn't unduly troubled by what Steward thought as a challenge to his manhood; it was an opportunity to confirm his own observations.

The pilot looked prepared for any difficulty that might arise. He noticed Steward had withdrawn into himself. It was his way of avoiding any possible embarrassment. But Surgeon was acquiring all the airs of his privilege, his eyes grown more inquisitive with waiting.

'Well, Surgeon,' said Pinteados, 'do we agree on a price? I will answer according to what you will pay.'

They considered it must have been the festive dangers of the wine which had influenced the pilot's mood.

'But we are men together, as someone said,' Surgeon began. 'Secrets are the price of friendship. That's what I offer you in exchange. My friendship.'

Pinteados was urging himself to say that he was not in need of Surgeon's friendship; but that would have put an end to their conversation. Here he recognized a limit to the kind of error he might commit. This would justify the penalty of silence and exclusion. He thought he had found a way around Surgeon's strategy.

He said: 'But I thought I had your friendship already.'

Surgeon recognized a blunder in what he had said. He hurried to correct himself, aware of the trap which the pilot's reply had laid.

'Of course you have our friendship,' he said, and looked at Steward for confirmation. Steward nodded.

'Then I receive nothing I do not have,' said Pinteados. 'Friendship is of one piece. It will not allow any dividing of parts. Is it not so?'

'Of course,' said Surgeon, 'and it does not demand a price of the friend.'

'I cannot agree,' said Pinteados. 'It is always demanding a price. That's why I avoid it. Too expensive an arrangement.'

Surgeon was becoming impatient. Like Steward, he was affected by the foreignness of Pinteados. What might have been an exchange of wit had grown into a devious calculation for some triumph against the foreigner. He would have liked an opportunity to subdue the pilot; to force him into some humiliation which would expose the national and ancestral differences between them. A fierce and rigid morality was working on Surgeon.

'I think we shall have to do without your answer,' he said coldly.

Boatswain was surprised by the tone of voice. He too was feeling the foreignness of Pinteados; but it urged him to come to the pilot's rescue.

'Let him put his offer,' said Boatswain.

'To be sure,' Surgeon urged; and there was mockery in his welcome.

'Thank you,' said Pinteados. The pilot's eye lit up. He had drained the glass. He signalled Steward to pass the goblet along the table.

Boatswain's enthusiasm had forced this conflict on them. If Surgeon had thought of withdrawing, he showed no signs of avoiding the issue. There was a call for the goblets to be filled; and the fellowship of Christmas seemed to prevail. Boatswain congratulated himself on the change he had brought about; but he warned himself against taking any futher part in their enquiries.

'And now to your question,' said Pinteados. 'It is more difficult than you know. But my answer will be of great importance for you. For everyone. But you especially.'

He paused and considered Surgeon.

'And my price?' he said, as though the question was directed to himself. 'I will trade one answer for another. We have a safety in friendship. Tell me this: what happened to your wife? You give me your answer, and I give you mine.'

Surgeon struggled to push himself up. He was staring at Pinteados. Then he sat down. He couldn't decide what his safest posture should be while he spoke to Pinteados.

'My wife?' Surgeon whispered, trying to choose his answer.

'Yes, your wife,' Pinteados said calmly.

The officers recognized that Surgeon was having some difficulty; and they resented the pilot's intrusion.

'There is a limit to what you should ask,' Steward said.

Steward was superb at showing his indignation. He was calling on Pinteados to withdraw the question; but Surgeon resisted this effort on his behalf. Steward's agitation had made him calm.

'My wife has been ill,' said Surgeon; 'that's what is happening to her. Illness. Does my answer please you?'

Pinteados didn't speak. He could sense the change of feeling among the men. He had committed an error which they would not accept, although they knew nothing about Surgeon's wife. Surgeon's tone of misfortune was enough to tell them where their sympathies lay. The opposition to Pinteados was shared by all.

'You have had my answer,' said Surgeon. 'I do not ask any part of yours in return.'

The rebuke was final. Surgeon got up again. He was making ready to leave the room. The men stood in support of Surgeon. All expect Priest, who had leaned his head sideways against the chair. He might have been asleep. The fellowship of Christmas was in danger.

Boatswain had already reached the door. No one got much farther. The men saw him stop abruptly; then his eyes started a signal message which they didn't understand until he moved back and made way for the Commandant to pass.

They had got used to the Commandant's habit of eating alone. Now his arrival had the effect of restoring the atmosphere to total calm. Surgeon's resentment gave way to an attitude of welcome. Pinteados remained in his seat until the Commandant had come fully into view. Then he raised himself halfway from the chair and nodded his respect to the Commandant. Priest was awake.

'Good fortune brings us your visit?' Priest said, coaxing his body up from the chair.

'Less than fortune,' the Commandant said, and they noticed that his mood was grave.

He remained standing long after he had signalled them to their seats. Boatswain was arguing with himself whether he should pour a drink for the Commandant. His eye caught Steward, and he decided to leave the initiative to someone else.

'You have eaten well,' the Comandant observed.

No one was ready to speak.

'Tomorrow, keep the closest watch on the men,' the Commandant said. 'I was touring the divisions a moment ago. There is a danger of illness down below.'

'No one reported,' Surgeon said.

The Commandant ignored Surgeon's complaint.

'Whose division?' Boatswain asked.

'What's the difference?' the Commandant said. 'The danger is the same. But it's not confined to one.'

'I don't understand why there was no report,' Surgeon said.

'Fear. They are afraid of physic,' the Commandant said.

'I shall investigate the matter this moment,' Surgeon said.

'Tomorrow,' said the Commandant. 'Tonight they will sleep better for not seeing you.'

He walked to the table and took his seat beside Pinteados. The pilot made room. Pinteados looked from the table to the Commandant as though he wanted to avoid any exchange of glances with the others. If the Commandant's presence had made them forget, it had the opposite effect on the pilot. The Commandant made himself at ease. They were waiting on the Commandant, who showed no interest in the wine which Steward had offered.

'You should let them know what we've seen,' the Commandant said, and looked at the pilot. He then glanced around the table as he talked. 'Pinteados was in Severn asylum when the last outbreak of plague carried a whole army of mariners inside.'

Surgeon was startled. He stared at Pinteados and then furtively at the others.

'The plague of madness,' Surgeon whispered, and fixed his gaze on the pilot.

'I was not of the victims,' Pinteados said. 'I was in hiding, if you want to know. The asylum is the safest place to go into political hiding. It is one place the authorities won't look for any criminal offender.' He paused. 'Did you want me to say that, Commandant?'

'Say what you like,' the Commandant said, 'but ... it's better they know what to expect.'

'Do you think such epidemic might be on us?' Steward asked.

The Commandant passed the question to Surgeon, who looked morose with worry. He was staring at the empty glass before him, and postponing the urge to look up at Pinteados. He couldn't resist it any longer.

'When were you in Severn?' he asked Pinteados.

'Same time,' said Pinteados, and returned Surgeon's stare.

The ambiguity was perfectly timed. Was it the same time as the general epidemic? Or was it the same time as Surgeon's wife?

The room was still. The debris of bones looked like skeletons on their plates.

Severn had become a forbidden name. Few people were sure where it was, but it was known that victims of the plague were quickly herded there. Even suspects were dispatched with the same promptness. But in the case of Pinteados, the contagion had been a lucky event. He had offered himself up and was officially received without any enquiries. He had calculated that the Law would not pursue him there; and he was right. His foreignness had become neutralized by the abnormality of those around him in Severn asylum.

'Tell them,' the Commandant ordered, as though the officers had to be prepared for the ultimate price of this enterprise.

'The Kingdom was truly represented in that hell,' said Pinteados, feeling his memory roam across a sea of turbulent faces. 'Citizens of every kind of breeding in the land. Whatever their status, their natures had gone contrary. But there was never any attack by one man on the next. You were safe from your worst enemy. Each man was safe from anyone but himself. No one ever interfered with me. Not even to raise an arm to threaten. Never. But they were a pitiful sight. Each would inflict damage on himself. Terrible wounds. Anything to hand was a weapon: spoons, knives, plates, stones, combs. And always the attack was inflicted on the man by himself. Without weapons, the fingernails were all they had to do battle with. Never a morning that I didn't see skin hanging like wet cloth from a face. The authorities had to keep nails cut low, almost down inside the flesh. But there wasn't much they could do about teeth. You could cut fingernails or put things out of hand's reach; but the authorities couldn't bring themselves to take out all those teeth. And it was a question of how they would eat. So the teeth remain the most terrible weapons. They would bite away at hands, legs, navel, and groin; heads straining and heaving to get at the belly. My fourth morning in the first week it must have been, I witness a man bite up his tongue to shreds. His mouth was like a fountain pouring blood with the bits of tongue falling in lumps onto his chest. It was difficult to do anything like punish, because the attack was never on a next person. Then it might be easy. If you see a man inflict damage on a next, you feel a good reason to beat him up in turn. To protect someone else was easy. It was within reason. But you didn't know what to do when the man was biting up his own tongue or tearing the skin from under his eyes. You just watch him until he pass out of sight. In my time I hear many sounds, animal and otherwise in battle or sickness and dying; but nothing to compare with the human voice when it start to scream out from the cells at Severn.'

Pinteados never took his eyes off his glass while he was speaking. It was as though he could see the faces swimming through the wine, surfacing in shadow to bear witness to his experience. He didn't see how the men around him had reacted; and it never occurred to him to find out. He was under the spell of a recollected terror. Priest's hand must have been weary from making the sign of the cross. Every fresh item of mutilation plunged him into a panic of crossing himself. The Commandant kept his glance on Pinteados, calm and attentive, as though familiarity had made him resistant to any shock. The others looked at the Commandant. It was his voice they heard while Pinteados was speaking.

'And this plague of madness,' Pinteados continued. 'It was deepest in those old mariners who had adventured on the coast for black flesh. It was like you had a campaign with a prize for the best performer, a campaign to disfigure the body until it was no longer a known part of the man it belonged to. And the prize going to the one who came up with the most unexpected mutilation. So that if one man did tear the flesh that is his nose, a next man would perform the same mutilation, but more spectacular. There was no limit to making one deformity surpass a next. Worse than witness the doing was to see the result. In sleep, I mean. When the victims were knocked right out with sleep. To see them there. Ever so still, breathing human again, but more cruel in the result of their butchery. You wonder what curse nature put on these poor wretches, now looking so defenceless, like they had been neglected for all time, just born without any connection to anything at all. Seeing them flat out there in sleep, still bleeding but feeling no pain, it seemed. That was worse, somehow. And knowing how each would start the butchery on himself when he was awake. The curse of the Black Coast we call it. That's how I hear the men of learning christen such plague.'

Pinteados shook his head, indicating that he couldn't go on. He was going to finish the drink in his glass, then decided against it. He stood up and asked the Commandant's permission to leave. The Commandant made no further comment, but quickly offered to accompany Pinteados back to his post. They walked out together.

Steward had lifted the neck chain out of his jacket. He was nervous, secretive, occupying his hands with the wedding ring which hung from the chain. He thought he could recognize his own sense of discomfort in Boatswain, who sat rigid in his chair, pumping his fingers lightly against his throat.

'What is your verdict?' Boatswain said, appealing to Surgeon. 'I mean, was it as terrible as he says?'

Surgeon gazed at the debris of bones on his plate, his attention deeply divided between what he had heard and what he knew.

'Yes,' he said, 'it is known to be a condition outside the care of ordinary medicine.'

'I would keep an eye on Pinteados,' said Priest; 'you never can tell how he might react in crisis.'

Surgeon welcomed this warning from Priest. He had found a way of turning attention to Pinteados.

'We must keep our eyes on the Commandant,' he said. 'His protection is also ours. Do not let this warning of illness distract you from more certain danger. I mean Pinteados.'

Surgeon could feel their curiosity about his meaning. Fear had made them eager for advice; and Surgeon was the most composed. When the Commandant and Pinteados left, his relief was immediate. It seemed they had taken his own sense of personal danger with them.

'How would Pinteados be a danger?' Boatswain asked.

Priest closed his eyes in reply. His memory was a cradle of bells announcing the Holy Birth, and the curse of the Black Coast and the future of the enterprise.

Steward had interrupted with a noise of his chair as he scraped it forward, wedging his body against the table. He was quick to share Surgeon's misgivings. But he would be slow to offer his support.

'Don't you think Pinteados a danger?' Surgeon asked.

And Priest had suddenly come alive as though the future had liberated him from all error.

'We must put him at ease,' Priest counselled. 'My view is, he may not be at ease. He's never talked this much before.'

'I would not prejudice the matter,' Surgeon said, 'but suppose anything should happen to the Commandant?'

Steward felt more assured now. The time had come for him to speak. He said in a dry voice: 'Pinteados said what he would do.'

'Exactly,' said Surgeon. 'Pinteados made his ambition clear.'

Boatswain shared their fears.

'You mean he really means what he was saying?' he asked. 'I didn't take his meaning literal.'

'We must not brood on every word that's said,' Priest advised. 'Any foreigner feels a little apart. He may be talking to make up for what he misses. Also, no man goes into Severn asylum and comes out whole again.'

'But the question is real,' said Steward. 'What should we decide if something went wrong with the Commandant?'

The question had to be met. Pinteados had spoken seriously. Surgeon had got them to thinking on this matter of command. Apart from its importance, it helped to put any speculation on an epidemic out of their minds.

'Do not invite disaster,' Priest warned. 'Together we will find a way out of any danger. Together, I repeat.'

Surgeon was hoping for a suggestion from Steward. If Priest provided a consoling influence, it was still far from adequate. It was in the nature of Surgeon's work to anticipate any event that might be wholly new. Steward continued to guard his feeling. He had a horror of talking out of turn. Although this caution was sometimes to be respected, Surgeon now thought it out of keeping with the urgency he had given to the pilot's ambition.

In assessing these loyalties, Steward came high in his favour. Priest could be persuaded if opinion went against him. But he was doubtful about Boatswain. And he thought he had detected some affinity between Boatswain and Pinteados. Now the question of command had been raised, he thought it would make for safety if Steward would state his view. A conflict among equals was always more difficult to resolve. Yet Surgeon postponed his wish to hear from Steward, and spoke directly to Boatswain, in whom he had the least confidence.

'I think you will agree I should have a word with Pinteados,' he said. 'According to Priest's advice, that is. We must put him at ease. Above all, this talk of taking over from the Commandant should not get to the hearing of the men.'

Boatswain was decisive on the matter.

'Whatever happens, keep the crew out of this,' he said.

This crisis had created a new kind of apprehension in Boatswain. It was as though he had seen for the first time the meaning of his status as an officer and a man on the inside. Formerly he had concentrated his mind on the freedom that had rescued him from the perils of the land. He was grateful to be gone from Lime Stone. The danger of the enterprise had been contained, diminished by the safety of distance. But Surgeon's warning against the pilot had suddenly put his role of authority in a new perspective. An instinct for compromise was beginning to form in Boatswain. He had to protect himself against any fall from authority; and he realized that he could not do this alone.

If the ship was a symbol of his freedom, it also reminded Boatswain of the disadvantage of being so close to others. He couldn't go into hiding; nor could he attempt any scheme on his behalf that would escape the attention of the other men. This closeness made for almost total exposure. Everyone was seeing, and all the time. In such circumstances, it seemed that his survival would always depend on forming some kind of allegiance. Surgeon had now presented the danger of Pinteados as proof of this necessity. Boatswain didn't feel any great affection for Surgeon; but he had yielded to his judgment. He agreed someone should speak to Pinteados; and Surgeon struck him as the most suitable person to reason with Pinteados on the necessity of compromise among equals. They had a common interest in survival.

Steward had returned the chain under his jacket. He felt more at ease since the Commandant and Pinteados had gone. And Boatswain's readiness to support Surgeon added to this assurance.

'We must not leave the impression that the pilot frightened us with stating such ambitions,' Steward said. 'And yet we must not appear to provoke a challenge for him.'

Steward talked like an apostle of the middle way. Authority had to make its thrust without taking the risk of meeting retaliation. He would agree that Surgeon was the man.

'Would you have any special knowledge of Pinteados?' Boatswain asked.

No one responded to Boatswain's line of enquiry. There was some danger in this approach. It was as though any cross-examination carried special risks each wanted to guard against. The circumstances were not right for using any discoveries you had made.

'I don't think I really care to know,' said Boatswain, hoping to distract attention from the risk he was taking.

And Steward hurried to agree. Boatswain was surprised by this sudden harmony of response from Steward.

'It would serve no good purpose to probe there,' Steward repeated.

Surgeon listened and kept his method of approach to himself. It was enough to know that the others were supporting his suggestion. He could talk with Pinteados more freely.

'I shall let it rest until morning,' Surgeon said.

'Would it not be better while the matter is fresh?' Boatswain asked.

Priest was inclined to agree with Surgeon. He was against pressing issues that might not after all be of great importance. He would have preferred to forget the whole episode.

'If Surgeon is going to do the talking,' Steward said, 'then he must decide what time is best.'

'Perhaps,' said Boatswain. Then he nodded in Steward's direction to emphasize his agreement. Again Boatswain could feel this new urge that persuaded him to come to terms. It was part of the necessity to survive. Surgeon rose slowly from the chair. His expression was grave.

'Now I'll take a look around,' he said. 'The night watch might have some news about the men.'

'You think it's really serious?' Priest asked.

'Depends how long the bleeding lasts,' Surgeon said.

'I was thinking about Pinteados,' Priest corrected.

Swift as clockwork, Surgeon's mind had shifted its attention back
to Pinteados. Steward had not been distracted at all. It was Pinteados who remained the decisive interest in his thinking.

'If I do not raise the matter again,' Surgeon said, 'then you know
there was nothing to it. I think we may have said the last about
it. Until tomorrow.'

Surgeon looked more cheerful as he turned away. They watched
him closely until he was past the door. Priest leaned his head back
and let his eyes wander over the ceiling. Steward poured himself
a drink, then offered to fill Boatswain's glass.

Surgeon had walked towards the stern of the ship. The darkness
sharpened his memory for any obstacles which might be in his
way. He knew the empty spaces of the deck. As he looked ahead,
hearing the wind and the low groan of the sea, his eye caught the
solitary glow of a lamp: a pale opening of light trapped in the
enormous space of the night. It was the only evidence of some
presence on the water; but it was also a reminder that Pinteados
would be stirring there. This was the pilot's retreat. Surgeon pondered the immense darkness which surrounded him, and the
fragile, solitary vigilance of the lamp showing its small nipple
of light.

There was no sound at all on the deck. The watch might have
been asleep. Even in the dark, Surgeon thought, there is no hiding.
If he followed his instinct and went in search of Pinteados, he was
sure that this simple meeting would be witnessed. He had authority
to send the watch away if he chose, yet it was this same power that
had created the attention of those who obeyed.

Surgeon was beginning to feel some nostalgia for the privileges
of being on land, where an arrangement could be made that
escaped attention. Distance increased the opportunity for independent action. But the ship reduced every movement to an
important occasion. The slightest change of plan invited some
speculation. Although he had said he would see Pinteados the next
morning, he was determined to see him tonight. And he was going
to treat this as a decision he had taken privately, a decision that
was within his rights, and beyond the power of anyone to question.
For Surgeon had no intention of raising the matter of the pilot's
ambition with anyone. His question was more intimate and more
urgent than the issue of command.

When Surgeon left the dining cabin, he had decided firmly on closing the matter of Pinteados' ambitions. He would present the previous threat of rivalry as a miscalculation on their part. He would argue that they had allowed the foreignness of the pilot to deceive their judgment about the seriousness of his talk. It was a normal error in any exchange with a foreigner. The language of feeling made havoc of the actual words that were used. It was the same with Pinteados. The fault was in their reluctance to see the pilot as a just part of that status which the Commandant had bestowed equally on all the officers.

Pinteados had revived an area of the past that Surgeon had thought remote and frozen by his absence from Lime Stone. Suddenly it had been brought back to life, with all the threat and confusion that marked Surgeon's curiosity. Surgeon wanted news of his wife because it was the only way he might ascertain what knowledge Pinteados might have of him. He had to be sure that she was no longer in his way.

When he thought of his wife, Surgeon could only remember the intolerable strain that her fidelity had imposed upon him. He was at once proud of his conquest and exasperated by his subsequent failure to find some honourable reason for abandoning her. He had devised the grossest schemes for provoking her to some action that would give him cause for a separation.

At first he had told her quite simply that he wanted to be free. He had married her because he needed her support, but the marriage had gradually withered away. Circumstances had reversed their roles. She who was so zealous for his success had become an obstacle to his progress. He had made no attempt to disguise this feeling. Every stratagem that would advance his reputation was later threatened by the irrelevance of their association. She was in the way, and he had told her so.

Then he would find himself in increasing conflict with his own desire. She would agree to live apart, but she had always made it clear that it was not her wish. If she chose against herself, it was because she wanted to choose on his behalf. This was a form of virtue that had assumed in his mind the terrifying threat of blackmail. He couldn't trap her into error, and it had proved futile to play on her jealousy. She had no instinct for complaint, no elemental sense of female grievance.

He had decided, as a matter of principle, to convince himself there must be some limit to any woman's humiliation. Rumour extolled his prowess with women; but she would react as she might have to a spell of treacherous weather—it was inevitable and beyond her control. Therefore, she ignored what she judged to be true.

After an absence that lasted for a month, he came in one afternoon and asked her to remove his boots. He had sprawled his legs out, and thrown his arms back in an attitude of total exhaustion. Stooping before him, she unlaced the boots, making her innocent enquiries about his health. He took the boots from her and leaned forward; paused in his movement, and then said: 'I have fucked myself to death this time.' He had waited for her reaction; but there was no evidence of feeling on her part. She might not have heard. His voice was casual in its disdain as he recounted the details of intercourse with women she had known. 'This is how it went,' he would begin; and she had remained transfixed, her stoop more pronounced as she heard him through. And when he had come to an end, she rose and stared through the haze of her eyes.

'You are not well,' she said.

In the weeks that followed, she was to hear him relate the incidents to his colleagues. This was the beginning of a new stratagem. To her surprise, he would invite the most distinguished friends to the house. She took no part in their affairs; but she had never lost her enthusiasm for his presence. If she could not see him alone, then it was better to endure his friends than brood upon his absence from the house. If she didn't like these men, she was grateful that they came.

It was her first lesson in concealing some aspect of her experience from her husband; and it had plunged her into a state of remorse. These gatherings never broke up without some incident between herself and one of her husband's friends. An effort to seduce her would always take place. But she had come to accept this insult as part of the bargain for keeping her husband at home. Firm, she measured her rebuke, fearing that an open accusation would lead to a scene and the end of these evenings.

Finally, one evening when everyone had gone, she decided to take what risks would follow. Surgeon was about to retire when she

asked to speak with him. He continued on his way, but she
followed him. She related every incident as best she could remember; and his laugh began, first a warning chuckle, and then
the gross crescendo of approval burst from his throat. The boots
had fallen from his hand, as he clutched at the post of the bed;
and his laughing grew louder. It was like the sound of demons in
her skull. His pride seemed to have given way to an orgy of self-
delight. She returned to the long room where they had gathered;
and his voice pursued her. This laugh that couldn't be brought to
an end; that had some root and history too deep and devious for
imagination to discover. And it drove her to a fury which blotted
out all reason. She saw the chairs and heard his voice; and when
she glanced for composure to the table and the glasses, they
seemed to rise and float on the sound of this laughing. Suddenly
a force of demons had blown her skull, and turned all her strength
into an arsenal of hands and feet. Destruction was everywhere.
When he came down the stairs and into the room, the silence was
intolerable. She was lying amidst the wreck of furniture and the
blazing fragments of glass. He took a look at her face and realized
there was no need to speak to her. There was a crimson print of
blood where the fingernail had spliced her lip; and her hands were
torn.

"We must get you out of the way," he said to himself. It was the
first time he had thought of Severn asylum as the obvious refuge
for her future.

"Out of the way. She is out of the way...."

These echoes from the past pursued Surgeon as he made his
way across the deck, and he had to remind himself that he would
have to bring a similar resource of will to this meeting with Pinteados. He must be impervious to anything that threatened him
with remorse. His business was clear: to judge how great a threat
Pinteados might turn out to be. He took a few paces beyond the
ladder, listening for voices on the deck. There was nothing but the
wash of the sea and the slow grinding of the ropes, as he pulled
himself up towards the binnacle. He paused.

Pinteados heard the footsteps come lightly up behind him. The
pilot didn't turn to ask who was approaching; and no voice identified itself. It was like waiting for the night that he could recognize

by the smell and temper of the wind. He knew it must be Surgeon.
'You think of power,' said Pinteados, 'and yet you were so afraid.'

'Afraid?'

Surgeon had given this question the right degree of curiosity
and alarm. A veiled surprise. The pilot could be right, yet the
statement was impossible of proof.

But the pilot was not impressed. He heard Surgeon's words, but
he never let their meaning interrupt his own view of the matter.

'Yes,' he said, treating the repetition as a point of emphasis, 'it
is a certainty you were afraid.'

'She told you that?' Surgeon enquired.

Again the tone was distant, denouncing any suggestion of
personal involvement.

'It was not necessary,' said the pilot. 'She knew I understood.'

Surgeon timed his responses with great care. It might have
helped if he could study the look in the pilot's eyes, or give some
meaning to the movement of his hands. But the night had
deprived him of these aids. They were both shapes that the light
failed to distinguish. Their only contact with meaning was through
this dark, evasive rivalry of talk.

'She was deficient in some necessary feeling,' Surgeon said.
'That was the source of her sickness.'

'She was never sick,' Pinteados replied. 'That is for certain.'

'You think my judgement was in error?' Surgeon said. Now his
tone seemed generous and sure.

'Judgment?' Pinteados said briskly. 'Hers was no case for your
profession. It was more like unlawful imprisonment.'

'You accuse me?' Surgeon asked.

'It was her verdict,' said Pinteados.

'But you admit you know nothing of women,' Surgeon said.

'You knew everything about women,' Pinteados said. 'But you
could not afford to learn about one woman. You were safe only
when they were plenty.'

'You prefer her opinion,' Surgeon said.

'She was the opposite,' said Pinteados. 'She knew everything
about one man. Her knowledge of the plural did not exist.'

Surgeon wavered. He was reluctant to pursue this rivalry with
the pilot. Instinctively he could feel these recollections of his life
determine his approach. She was out of the way. Remote, harmless,

176

frozen by time and absence from his native shores. Yet she appeared, in this grim silence, as the origin of all his difficulty. Now he felt himself yielding to the verdict that his artificial greed for women had always sprung from his envy and fear of what he had recognized in his wife.

Instinctively he had decided against a solitary failure. If he couldn't come to terms with his own chaos, he would have to create some flaw in her, some lasting deprivation that passion could not remedy. For she would never respond to the game of mutual abuse; and he chose a rational basis for his failure. It was a certain frigidity that had protected her against his will; a deficiency in some necessary feeling that had made her incomplete. Her passion had suffered some vital deformity he could not name.

Surgeon felt a momentary recklessness come over him.

'Perhaps Boatswain's question was in order,' said Surgeon. 'What is your interest in this enterprise?'

Pinteados would not be drawn.

'I report what I know,' he said, 'but your history is no part of my affairs. If you think otherwise, you are decieved.'

And Surgeon was relieved. The pilot's knowledge had become a threat to his self-esteem. Now he was persuaded to admire Pinteados for his show of detachment. It helped him to resist the tyrannical virtue of his wife. He could safely freeze her out of memory.

'I am grateful to you,' said Surgeon. 'Now we can place the tragedy at Severn in perspective.'

Pinteados didn't answer. It seemed that he had given his attention wholly to the night. Suddenly his voice surprised Surgeon. Grim and casual, it was contradicting Surgeon's expectations. Surgeon had been offering a private welcome to this silence when Pinteados intervened.

'She made me stay longer than mere hiding required,' Pinteados said. 'But it was worth it.'

'You are very patient with the sick,' said Surgeon.

'She was very patient with me,' Pinteados said.

'Patient?'

'Yes,' said Pinteados. 'She was the first woman I get to know in that way.'

'In that way?' Surgeon repeated.

'In that way,' Pinteados said. 'She was the first to open my door, as my grandmother would say.'

He paused, savouring the salty flight of the wind over his mouth. Then he added, like a man talking to himself: 'She was your fortune, Surgeon. You have deprived yourself.'

Surgeon didn't stir. His legs were firm as timber where he stood. His lips argued about the moment he would eliminate the pilot from the night. His hand was urgent on his hip, waiting. Another word would be enough for murder. The pistol was probing carefully through the dark.

Pinteados had sensed the danger in this silence; but his skill had made him safe.

'Impossible, Surgeon,' he said. 'You know it's impossible to shoot. There is no other pilot among this crew.'

A grim necessity had been made plain. Pinteados had to be kept alive. Surgeon's gifts of intrigue were powerless to subvert this fact. Alone, in the stern, Surgeon struggled to put an end to his resentment. "In that way," he reflected; "so the foreigner had known her in that way." Then he began to laugh. He was laughing. He could hear his laughter join the wind in a drunken assault against the sails. His reason had provided him with a necessary change of attitude. It was Christmas again. He felt light as air. The night was a huge arm lifting him up in a ritual of exaltation with the wind and the murmuring applause of the ocean.

Sooner or later she will deceive me. That was the judgment he had prophesied from the moment his choice fell on her. She would do that to me. Sooner or later. But he had never cocked his lust without the moral protection of a man who knew what to expect. Sooner or later.... Now, as always, it was late, too late for news of her sex to bring him harm. Least of all from the human ruins of the Severn asylum.

FOURTEEN

The boy sat in terror outside the Commandant's cabin. He thought he saw the sky tremble where it joined the sparkling cliffs of spray; and he heard the Commandant's voice, like the swell of the ocean, shake the timbers. He was afraid for Steward.

'I've sailed half the ocean in adversity,' the Commandant was shouting, 'and now you would warn me about a risk of life. So tell me, Steward, what would you be elsewhere? Under a different command? Under the command of the House of Trade and Justice? Do I hear you propose that?'

'I propose no such thing,' Steward pleaded, 'nor do I wish for a different command.'

Steward had begun to regret his request for this interview. He had always impressed his fellow officers as a man of great caution. Always he wore the aspect of one who had dedicated his entire life to the task of avoiding trouble. In any crisis he held his own judgment to a point safely short of danger. But the news from Lime Stone had worked a certain havoc on his habit of reticence. He had come, in secret, to advise the Commandant of some impending danger. But the interview had hardly got under way before it provoked a violent wrath in the Commandant, who had ignored all reference to the news Antarctica's ships had brought. He would tolerate no obstacle which came between him and the enterprise. Steward felt the same sense of vacancy, the same insult of irrelevance that the painter must have felt when he came to the officers on a similar matter. And the Commandant reacted as they had done. He behaved as though he was utterly ignorant of this recent report about the Lady of the House.

'Well, then!' And the Commandant was on his feet, threatening the proportions of the cabin with his enormous stride. 'If you accept my command, it follows that you accept my decisions.'

Steward struggled to find the right tone of apology; but his gifts of caution had deserted him.

'I was only offering an opinion, sir,' he said, avoiding any hint of argument.

'You came with rumours of danger to this enterprise,' the Commandant reminded him, 'and the ocean is no place for argument. A strategy, yes, I'll hear you out on a strategy that lends progress to my action. But I do not listen to an opinion that opposes my view. If you have a doubt, then you should have asked permission to depart. You should have had the courage to stay behind on the coast of the black cargoes.'

With all his skill of reticence Steward now struggled to deny such a wish.

'I am happy to be part of this enterprise,' he insisted. 'You have no evidence to the contrary, sir.'

He looked as though he might collapse from fatigue. Some shadow of pain was about to settle over his eyes. The Commandant had returned to his seat at the council table. Steward remained standing.

'Happy to be part of the enterprise?' the Commandant repeated, as though he wanted to deny Steward's statement all possible meaning. 'Then what is your fear? You speak as one who might be an agent of the House. Are you an agent of the House?'

In all the circumstances of his knowledge, the Commandant would have realized the hurt he had inflicted by that suspicion. Steward was too shocked to offer any defence. And the Commandant seemed, for a moment, to regret the rage that had come over him.

'I thought only of your safety, sir,' Steward said.

'Under whose law?' the Commandant challenged. 'Under the law of the House of Trade and Justice?'

The rebuke was like a final judgment on the quality of Steward's courage. There was the vaguest whiff of a breeze cooling the dense atmosphere that weighed upon the cabin. The Commandant barely moved his hands, indicating a seat at the council table. It was almost too close for comfort, and Steward felt a gradual ebbing of his strength as he sat beside the Commandant. But his eyes had rested on the huge chart that lay wrinkled and intricate with islands before him. He saw a chain of pearls which marked the latitude of the Isles of the Black Rock. And there was a sudden promise of glory in his gaze. For a moment he felt ashamed of his mission: that he should come with warnings of disaster where the archipelago of islands confirmed his wish for the future of the enterprise. He wanted to pass his hand over the chart, to touch the flame of sand and pebble which heralded their arrival. The Commandant could feel a new mood of daring radiate from Steward.

'Do you know this chart?' he asked, and his voice was cordial, almost affectionate.

'I couldn't make that boast,' said Steward, recalling the loss which he had suffered.

His progress had been interrupted by the intrigue of men whom he had trusted. There were thieves among his rivals for possession of the rarest charts. But he had borne his loss without complaint. Now he recognized a look of sympathy in the Commandant's glance. He wanted to share his misfortune with the Commandant. This would have been the perfect moment to redeem his error. He was too proud, however, to register a personal grievance. This was the secret which had made him such a willing recruit for this enterprise.

'Some call your conduct honourable,' the Commandant said, 'knowing the robberies others did to your kindness.'

Steward felt his caution return. He was unprepared for the Commandant's reference to his past.

'You made a grave mistake,' the Commandant said, 'sharing the labour of your knowledge with such rivals as you had within the House. A man must cage his mouth, explain everything except what he puts a proper value on. Such is the nature of the House of Trade, is it not?'

Steward had gone dumb. He was alarmed by the Commandant's revelations about his past. He was afraid to acknowledge what he had heard. But the Commandant was waiting to hear him speak.

'It's difficult to hold back what you know,' said Steward, warning himself against any abuse of the House. 'It's the price I will always pay for a certain enthusiasm. When any man takes an interest in what I do. A certain enthusiasm takes me along.'

'And right into your enemy's trap,' the Commandant reminded him. 'Just as you experienced, did you not?' he went on, not waiting for an answer. 'A thief will recognize no kind of ownership, least of all when the property is in the nature of a plan. Your story is example, is it not?'

Steward kept his eyes on the chart and begged his tongue to be still. His mood of buoyancy had been diminished by the Commandant's knowledge of his personal history. He wondered how much the Commandant knew about his connections to the House. He was afraid to acknowledge the truth of what he heard, but more afraid to appear, by his silence, to be on the side of the Commandant's enemies. He felt a need to make his loyalties clear, but he could never be wholly free of the fear that any reference to the House aroused.

'I would never complain,' said Steward, finding some refuge in his pride, 'not if there is proper acknowledgment. My achievement is the next man's, provided there is proper acknowledgment.'

But the Commandant was losing his taste for indulgence. He looked up from the chart, and for the first time gazed directly into Steward's eyes.

'In different circumstances, I would call such conduct honourable,' the Commandant said. 'But you couldn't complain. You could not afford to complain, could you, Steward?'

'Could not afford?' Steward heard himself ask, and watched the gentle shudder of his hands. A cramp had seized his muscles. 'It makes the burden greater when you complain,' he went on.

'Even when there is an act of robbery against yourself?' The Commandant asked, and refused to relieve Steward from the pressure of his gaze. 'Why didn't you appeal to the House for protection?'

He was surprised that the Commandant should make his meaning so clear.

'Appeal to the House?' Steward heard himself ask again. There was a note of stupefaction in his voice.

'Why not?' The Commandant was emphatic, unsparing in rebuke. 'The House protects all merchandise, including charts, makes a clear reckoning of what and how much come from whatever source, be it person or place, the labour of hands or brain. And the House is careful to protect men it employs, particularly in the skill of charts.'

Steward was in agreement; but he couldn't bring himself to

offer similar rebuke in any matter pertaining to the House.

'There could be difficulty in proving true ownership,' he said.

'You do not think the expert knowledge of the House could tell who did what in such a claim as yours?' The Commandant observed him waver. To say no would be to deny the majesty of the House. To say yes would be to accuse some dignitary of a criminal offence. And it was a dignitary of the House who had stolen Steward's rarest charts. But he didn't want to share such knowledge with the Commandant. He deflected his glance, and pondered the chart on the council table. It spread, wrinkled and intricate as the ocean, under the Commandant's enormous hands. "How could you prove personal ownership?" Steward heard a voice accuse; but he couldn't distinguish who had spoken; for he had heard the question put to him before, in different circumstances, even before his departure from Lime Stone. His hands had won a temporary victory over the cramp. He was polishing the wedding ring he wore on the middle finger of his left hand. It threw a spear of light across the chart. The Commandant watched Steward's feeble struggle with the ring, and realized that the officer's attention had strayed. He was under the spell of some voice that had pursued him across the ocean. "How could you prove personal ownership," Steward heard the absent and familiar voice repeat; and immediately his attention was rudely brought back to the chart and the council table, and the fruitful knowledge which the Commandant had at his command.

'You couldn't make a successful appeal,' the Commandant was reminding him. 'How could you appeal to the judge who was also the man you had come to accuse?'

Steward suddenly looked so ill that the Commandant thought he might collapse over the council table.

'I have known a struggle of my own,' the Commandant said, coming to Steward's rescue in an unusual way, 'and a sort of robbery, too.' He paused to observe Steward's gradual recovery. 'That's why the enterprise must succeed.'

Steward couldn't believe that he had heard aright; for it was out of character for the Commandant to speak from such an area of private feeling, and to confess to some robbery had the sound of defeat. And the likelihood that the Commandant had suffered some personal defeat revived Steward's faith in his own powers. He heard the sound of voices drift up from the men below, and felt a sudden pride of authority stir within him.

'I was in error,' he said, 'to come with warning of danger.' Although he hadn't finished, the Commandant intervened, schooling Steward in the secrets of command.

'You are at liberty to be mistaken,' the Commandant said, 'but error spreads, and there is no error without argument. I would rather lose half any crew in natural adversity than have a single example of doubt cast on my action. It must be the way of things. Under such a command as mine.'

Steward offered no resistance to this view; nor did he entertain any disagreement with the Commandant in such an arrangement for the general conduct of the ship.

'To be plain, sir,' he said, 'my mission was a private matter.'

The Commandant had come to a halt before the largest of the charts. He wheeled his body around, looked at Steward, then calmly walked towards the council table.

'A private matter, you say?'

'My wife.' Steward nodded.

'Your wife?'

'I can't be sure how much she knows.'

'Your wife, you say?'

The Commandant had taken his seat. Steward noticed how the moisture slipped and ran down the ridge of his brow, making small tides of sweat that washed over his nose and fell onto his hands.

'Your wife, you say?' the Commandant repeated.

'She has some knowledge of this enterprise,' Steward said.

'And you do not trust her?' the Commandant enquired.

His tone was solicitous, confidential. It had restored some confidence to Steward's sense of their alliance.

'She is a cousin of the Lord Treasurer,' said Steward. 'I trust her no more than I would trust a crew of strange subordinates.'

The Commandant was suddenly alerted by his reference to the men.

'Tell me, Steward,' he said, 'which do you really fear? Is it the woman? Or the men who are down below?'

'I can control the men,' Steward said briskly.

'And the woman?' the Commandant asked.

Steward had registered the challenge in the Commandant's question, and reacted as though it were a signal for some general emergency.

'Now I think only of the safety of the ship,' he said.

It might have been the Commandant who had spoken. Steward's judgment was stern, his manner of speech decisive and fearless.

'We sail on to San Cristobal,' the Commandant said.

'That too is my desire,' Steward said.

'But you do not look too well,' the Commandant said, and swept a weary glance towards the small bed on his left. 'Have Surgeon see you soon.'

Steward knew it was time to leave. His instinct for ceremony had returned. A stride from the door he halted and asked formally the Commandant's permission to go.

FIFTEEN

The ocean was everywhere.

Steward felt his skin ripple and flutter where his thumb was probing against his chest. He couldn't find a name for this sensation; but it was there, subtle and teasing: this feel of water spinning under his skin. He raised his hand; and it seemed the water had hardened into a knot of air. He was going to call Surgeon's attention to it; but he didn't know how to explain what he felt. Then everything was normal again. It was as though this moment was a play of imagination, warning him against the risk of immodesty. But he couldn't resist the need to come to Surgeon's rescue, to share some part of the humiliations which Surgeon had revealed after his meeting with Pinteados. It was like a call to duty, this appeal of Surgeon for some consolation against the malice of the foreigner. Steward was never more certain that any confidence he exchanged with

Surgeon would be in good taste. His own experience was sufficient proof.

'My wife was worse,' he said, 'much worse, since she was without any excuse of being mad. She had the same evil ambition as the pilot. To get a hold of power over me.'

'We must watch him,' said Surgeon, 'or he may put everyone in his debt. There's more to what he knows than we've yet heard.'

Steward was turning the ring around the top of his thumb as he considered Surgeon's warning.

'It was the same method she would use with me,' Steward said. 'My head was to hold no other memory but my debt to her. Whatever I remember was what I owe.'

His hand worked feverishly with the wedding ring while he spoke. He was trying to get it past the knuckle of his thumb. He watched the flesh where it bulged and squeezed, choking any further passage. Then he rubbed it against his thighs, palm upward. When he looked at it again, he saw the curve of gold burn dully; then the flame, swift as the clap of an eyelid. It was like a warrant, pursuing him, a signal of retribution that he had sworn to wear wherever he went. A scar that wouldn't heal. He would have had to endure it for a lifetime. But this enterprise had come to his rescue. It afforded him an opportunity, the only opportunity that would meet the situation. It was not only the chance to be away; it was the magnitude of the promise. Now he might even achieve the supreme luxury of hating her.

Surgeon said, 'You think she will wait?'

'She will wait,' Steward said. He talked like a man surfacing from a dream. The ring teased his eyes with its frail glitter; and the room seemed to fill with echoes of her voice: he could never tell whether her shouting was deliberate, or the result of a natural rage. But the neighbours, on all sides, were audience to her chastisement. Their listening had become as compulsive as her need to reveal his disgrace.

'You wouldn't have believed she had claims to respectability,' Steward said. 'The common whores were dumb virgins by comparison.'

Surgeon had contrived an air of professional concern. 'You think it was only the money she gave you?' he asked. And in the pause he added: 'Or was there some other dissatisfaction?'

Steward thought about it; but everything had suddenly become obscure, a little confused. He couldn't be sure of an impartial judgment; but when he spoke, he felt it was the truth as far as he could tell.

'She thought I had deceived her with promises,' he said.

'Was there another woman?' Surgeon asked.

'Not then,' Steward said, 'and now I have good reason to know she would not let that trouble her.'

'She wasn't the jealous sort?' Surgeon urged him on.

'Not in that way,' he said; 'that's why I see the money as a reason. It made all the difference. Never accept such help from a woman. Or from men of lesser breed. It will always backfire to your disadvantage.'

He was silent, observing the friction he had made with the ring against his knee.

'She believed I had more to offer in return,' he went on. 'But then I wanted her to see it that way. And I was honest. I reckoned it would be only a matter of time before my skill repaid her. It didn't work that way, however. And then my own plans started to let me down. She couldn't help noticing how rapidly my rivals had gone ahead.'

Steward relieved his thumb of the ring, turning it slowly until the hollow showed itself free. He exercised the knuckle, then returned the ring to his pocket.

Surgeon detected a slight change in his voice; the tone was sharp and hurried, as though an early hysteria was beginning to work itself out from Steward's nose.

'It is partly the time we live in,' said Steward. 'Every day you hear of a new adventure. East and west in every corner of the earth men are declaring fortunes that make your head swim. And the arrivals. Ships like *Intrepid* and *Salamon* coming home for the third time with proof of conquests. Men who had no names at all, scavengers, for all you know, now on full parade. Living in national applause and personal fortunes that would last many a lifetime. It made her hate the sight of me. I was her deepest failure.'

Surgeon intervened with some observation on the wind. He hoped this might bring a momentary relief to Steward, whose expression had grown rigid, a mask of resistance against the corrosive power of his wife's voice, spreading its ultimatum across the ocean.

'But she had connections,' said Surgeon; 'she might have opened a way for your plans.'

'I didn't want to tangle there,' Steward said. 'I couldn't count on any permanence with that lot. She pressed for it, all right; but power changed hands too fast in that circle. Before you signed up on your privilege, you'd find your patron had lost his place. The new man made no allowance. If your patron fell, then your allegiance made you enemy too. I can take a risk, but I need an element of certainty to go along with it. And she hated me for that too. Even more.'

Surgeon speculated on his own conduct in a similar situation. Of course, he would have taken risks in spite of the turbulence which threatened his patron's power. Steward was different; that was clear. Yet Surgeon wanted to satisfy himself about the meaning of this difference. It might have had to do with fear; but it seemed that Steward's reluctance might also have been evidence of an honourable character. A man with an instinct for permanence may also carry within him the virtue of loyalty. Surgeon turned his head away from the bunk where Steward lay, and wondered whether Steward might have had a type of ambition that protects itself rigidly against any false move—a man whose prodigious cunning warns him to wait.

Surgeon had become more optimistic. This was the first time he had felt his confidence return since the pilot's revelations about his own wife in the Severn asylum. He felt a momentary gratitude towards Steward. He was grateful and certain that he would be able to win Steward's support in any crisis that lay ahead.

Steward was more guarded now. There was no reason to defend himself against Surgeon; but these admissions of adversity gave him a momentary feeling of emptiness. As though he had been turned inside out. These recollections of his wife warned him against a total exposure. There had to be some residue of privacy that could serve as an inner anchor. A moment would come when he might be forced to retire there: to some refuge of his consciousness which had been fortified by silence.

He considered what he had not said. He had omitted to tell Surgeon that it was not only the fear of insecurity that made him refuse the wife's connections. That might have been true;

but it wasn't conclusive. What aroused her fury was his stubbornness. He wanted to do the things himself; and the patronage of her family connections, however fruitful, would have put the seal of failure on anything he had achieved. The threat of insecurity was small beside his profound and aggressive self-regard. It had made him more vulnerable to his wife's ferocious challenge, for she had been able to humiliate him beyond any defence when she advised that it would be better to be helped than to go under by the sheer weight of his incapacity. A superior birth had given her the right to pronounce on the practical limits of his ambition. She would assist what skills nature had provided him with; but she would not settle for a total loss. And this was what, in her view, he had become. He had to choose between this voyage and the truth of her prediction. Circumstances had left him without any more plans.

Surgeon felt a powerful allegiance bind him to Steward's predicament. Sympathy was too timid an emotion to pay for all he had heard. You had to advise, argue for some brutality of action.

'You don't have to return,' Surgeon said. 'Make her find you if she can. And there's no telling, but a way can be found to put an end to her search.'

'I don't want to escape from her,' Steward said. 'Let this enterprise work according to promise, and I will have my own weapons. Then I could smash her connections. You have no idea what that would mean. If I can come to a fortune by fair means. Just large enough for my purpose. I could smash her connections. Then see to it that she lives with that. In a hell of luxury. She will have everything. Jewels, silks; name it and she will have it. That's my last plan. To make the rest of her life the most luxurious mourning in history.'

Surgeon was startled by this burst of optimism. Steward's eyes lit up, darting and flashing with schemes of sinister vengeance, the vengeance of a destructive generosity. He would feed death where the appetite of her vanity was at its most voracious.

'And the beauty of it,' Steward said, wiping his mouth, 'she couldn't refuse. Connections smashed, yes. That will make for a torture right through her; but whatever the mourning, she couldn't resist such luxury. She is tied to luxury like a man to his tongue. That's why she was after me in such a terrible fashion.

My failure was taking her tongue away. Whenever a plan of mine collapsed, it was another piece of her tongue I had stolen. She couldn't talk except to accuse me of this robbery. It's the beauty of it. She couldn't refuse any luxury I bring back.'

Steward looked almost gay; and Surgeon wore an air of unrestrained heartiness.

'You have excellent reason for being here,' Surgeon said, giving some promise of fulfilment to Steward's intentions.

'It was my only chance,' said Steward; 'time wasn't on my side any longer.'

'It's only the beginning,' said Surgeon, buoyant and prophetic. 'Sometimes I can hear the applause from the future. Unanimous welcome. It makes you marvel at the power of chance. Just the one chance, the one in a million, that puts every misfortune in reverse. Men will look at you as though you were born again. Even men who knew you soon fail to recognize what they remember, because of the opulence which you blind them with.'

'To be fair,' said Steward, 'I think I have a weakness there. She spotted that from the first. I couldn't live much longer without some kind of applause. It always hurt to be out of it. You get to feeling robbed, like how she is with luxury, just robbed of your own portion of applause.'

'It is good to wait,' said Surgeon, 'and the longer you wait, the more marvellous the arrival. You learn to value your station far, far beyond any imagining others may have.'

Steward had taken the ring from his pocket. He slipped it over his little finger and tossed it around.

'What's worth doing is worth suffering,' said Surgeon. 'As true a law as any in nature.'

Steward was reflecting on his experience with some of the laws of nature. He heard a sound of bells outside and a noise of feet pounding near the door.

'You can't afford too decent feeling in this business,' said Surgeon.

Slowly Steward turned the ring around his little finger. It had become a prison around his flesh.

'What's worth doing is worth suffering,' said Surgeon again. 'As true a law as any in nature.'

'Nature,' Steward laughed. 'Speaking of nature.'

Surgeon heard Steward laugh again. It was casual and gay, as though his memory had returned some occasion of comfort and triumph. There was a sound of bells outside, and the pounding of feet near the door. Steward was waiting. He was in no hurry. He was preparing to relate the details of a drama that was evidence of his mastery over circumstance. He, too, had had his hour of dangerous triumph.

'Nature.' He smiled again. 'I too can speak of nature.'

The girl climbed over the wall, falling heavily onto the spikes of a fence. But her skin registered no pain. She was frightened beyond feeling. She was on her feet again, trampling the grass towards the house. There was evidence of her hair on branches that hung low, colliding with her head. She entered the house from the back, squeezing her body through the loose rails of a window. The kitchen was empty. She pushed open a door and followed the long corridor of carpet wherever it led her. The house had an air of neglected grandeur. Her eyes were unaccustomed to this opulence of space: the wide sweep of the stairway climbing in circles above her head. It was like a ship abandoned by the crew, waiting for cargo. She saw a door open.

'Is the master in?' the girl asked.

The woman took some time recovering from the shock of seeing the strange girl in her house.

'Who are you?' she asked, and it wasn't clear whether she was about to approach the girl or retreat behind the door.

'I would like to speak with your master,' the girl said.

'I have no master,' the woman said. She seemed completely recovered.

'Your husband, madam,' the girl said.

'What's your business with him?' the woman said. Authority had returned to her voice. Now she pushed the door wide open and advanced a pace or two towards the girl, who was slow to answer. Her mouth was dry. She could feel her tongue like a cake of sand against her teeth.

'I need his help,' the girl said.

'What's your trouble?' the woman insisted. The girl didn't answer. She was exhausted.

'I could get you whipped,' the woman said, 'and put away. You enter like a thief and have the boldness to ignore my orders.'

'I am no thief, madam,' the girl said.

'Then what's your business?'

The woman heard the footsteps behind her. The noise had brought her husband out.

'I could have been murdered all this time,' the wife said.

She was undecided how she should speak to him in the girl's presence; but habit had forced her to renew this habitual charge of neglect. She resented the girl's intrusion, yet she found in it an opportunity to challenge her husband for his attention. But the charge had escaped him. He was looking at the girl where the dress had been torn open, showing her naked calf.

'I am from the orphanage,' the girl said, 'I just ran away.'

'Order her back,' the wife shouted. She was enraged by this new failure to attract her husband's attention.

'I can't go back,' the girl sobbed hysterically. She saw the husband move closer towards her. He was slow and deliberate in everything he did; and the girl felt, for a moment, that his calm might have held a greater terror than his wife's outburst.

'Why did you come here?' he asked.

The girl started to retreat at the sound of his voice; but he held his hand out. She was relieved by the touch of his hand. It suggested that she was not in danger. Slowly he walked her past the wife into the room that opened off the corridor. The wife followed close behind. Her voice was fretful and nervous.

'I'll have the authorities know of this immediately,' she said.

The man didn't appear to hear. The girl was eager to gain his wife's sympathy. She wanted to speak, but she was busy working some moisture in her mouth.

'Why did you run away,' the man asked.

'It's the Tate de Lysle Orphanage,' the girl said; 'it's a criminal place.'

'Why do you say that?' the man asked.

'He is a criminal,' the girl cried, 'but everyone is afraid to tell.'

'Who is a criminal?' the wife intervened.

The girl hesitated. The man urged her to go on, but she kept her eyes on the wife, as though she wanted her to confirm that it was really safe to speak.

'I know he is your cousin,' she said, still looking at the woman, 'but it's not your fault he is such a criminal.'

Then the girl regretted what she had said. Whatever the truth of her accusations, the girl didn't feel it was in her place to make this kind of judgment. She rubbed her fists into her eyes, then lifted the torn half of the dress up to her face and blew her nose. The wife pulled up a chair and invited her to sit. The woman's manner had changed. She had become indifferent to her husband's aloofness: the girl became the centre of her interest.

'You are quite safe here,' she said. 'What is it? Why have you come?'

The girl was overcome with embarrassment. She wasn't sure whether she should continue; but she noticed the husband's impatience to hear what had happened.

'I'm ashamed to let you know,' said the girl, addressing herself to the wife, 'but it's the truth. Tate de Lysle didn't give the orphanage for a good reason. It was my turn again tonight. I could not bear it any more. He comes every night, madam. He does it to all of us. I swear it is the truth.'

The woman looked up at her husband and then at the girl. There was a mixture of alarm and exhilaration in her eyes. The girl was confused by this exchange of glance that passed from the woman to her husband. Her previous sense of danger had returned. She was about to deny what she had said; but the woman suddenly walked over and put a hand on her shoulder.

'Get her something to eat,' she told her husband. 'I'll see to the other matter.'

The wife was in control again. The girl could tell that something had happened, and it concerned other matters than what she had spoken about. The husband stood his ground for a while. A hand trembled over his mouth.

'Well, what are you waiting for?' the woman said. 'Don't you think she deserves something to eat?'

He was making an obvious show of resistance; but the woman didn't notice.

'I'm so ashamed,' he said quietly.

'Be ashamed for your own cowardice,' the wife said bitterly.

He was going to reply, but he changed his mind when he realized that the girl would be witness to any argument that followed. He smiled at the girl, and walked quietly out of the room and down the corridor towards the kitchen.

The wife waited until she was sure he was out of hearing. She was trying to test her confidence in the girl's story. Her mind worked fast on all the reasons why the girl might have chosen to seek protection. Would she have known of the enmity which existed between Tate de Lysle and her husband?

'Who really sent you here?' she asked.

And the girl suddenly burst into tears. There was a look of utter dejection in her stare.

'No one,' she cried; 'I came on my own.'

She took her fists from her eyes, and her head was carrying her forward, gradual and blind until she slumped against the woman's breasts.

'Come,' said the wife; 'come this way.'

She looped an arm around the girl's waist and coaxed her up the stairs. They struggled across the small bedroom, and the woman rolled her gently onto the four-poster bed.

'You need to calm yourself,' the woman said; 'calm yourself awhile.'

But the girl hadn't heard. She had lost all certainty of where she was or the reason that had put her to flight. She was alone.

The husband was not prepared for his wife's return. She found him in the kitchen muttering threats of retaliation. It seemed he had forgotten why he was there. He had put some fruit and cheese onto a plate; but his attention had taken him elsewhere. His wife's arrival was too abrupt for any strategy of self-defence.

'About the girl,' she said.

'What about the girl?' He had decided on a tactic of delay.

'You will go to the orphanage,' she said; 'you will go tonight. If Tate de Lysle visits as she says, fine. You will invite him here. You do not beg Gabriel to come. The invitation is by order. We demand him here.'

She tore a large brown loaf of bread in two halves and spread them on the plate. Some instinct warned him that he should walk away; but her mood was raw. He knew she would pursue him with the scene. And they were not alone. It might have been different if no one was witness to what they said. But the girl was in the house.

'Why should I bring your cousin here?' he asked.

'We will see,' she said. Her manner was conclusive.

There must have been something squalid in her calculations. He wanted to tell her that. It was his chance to make the charge; but he should do so without allowing her any argument in defence. Virtue was the sharpest weapon he could use.

'What about the girl?' he asked. 'Think of the danger to the girl.'

The point was lost. He was incapable of reproaching her. But he hadn't expected such malice of reply.

'The girl is worth more than any plan of *yours*,' she said.

He had felt the urge to strike her, but his hand froze where he rested it on the table. His rage had made him calm, almost reasonable.

'Why should I do this for you?' he asked her.

'For me? What have you ever done for me?' she said; and after a pause that let her scorn work deep into her meaning, she added: 'What you do now is for yourself.'

'I tell you I can manage on my own,' he insisted.

'And what has it brought you?' she said. There was a pride of mockery in her demand. 'What have you got worth talking about? Money? Answer me. Authority? Answer me. You do not even have a chart. Not a single plan that's worth my head of hair.'

'I have some pride,' he said and made to go; but she had surpassed him in her urgency of feeling. He talked like a man who agreed about his loss, and regretted that it was the privilege of such a woman also to know. There was no way to assert his pride against such an adversary. To win was to lose with dignity. He would concede an interest in her plan; he would pay her tribute for taking an initiative that he would be always certain to despise.

'So what will you bargain for?' he asked.

'Bring Gabriel Tate de Lysle here and we shall see,' she said. 'I'll take the girl some food.'

Alone, he heard her steps pause at the top of the stairs, then the throttle of the lock and a gentle slam of the door. She had exhausted his feeling, deprived him of any greater power for hatred. He had to think of some method of punishment that would reduce her to defeat in her own eyes. And it seemed that

195

the girl might serve his purpose. Her arrival might yet prove to be the gift which luck had bestowed on him. He decided he would go to the orphanage. Docile as a shadow, he would follow his wife's instructions; he would give her the satisfaction of putting him in her debt. Against all his instincts for justice, he wished that the girl's story was true. But he would make his own arrangements with Tate de Lysle. As a matter among men. And he would settle it against any advantage his wife had calculated.

It was after midnight when he returned; but his wife was waiting. And he was alone.

'Was the girl lying?' she asked.

'No,' he said. 'Her story is true.' His tone was free of tension.

'And where is Gabriel?' she insisted. 'Did you see him?'

'Yes,' he said. 'I settled it myself.'

The wife had never seen him so calm.

'What do you mean, you settled it yourself?'

He had taken a seat, appearing to treat every question as a minor nuisance. She walked slowly around the chair as she talked. His calm had wounded her. Her mood grew sore again; and he watched her turn, frantic, wheeling around the chair like a dog that was tethered to a pole, yapping and sniffing for attention.

'The girl will stay here,' he said. 'The Lord Treasurer and I have come to an arrangement.'

'An arrangement? You and Tate de Lysle come to an arrangement?' The voice was detached, almost mechanical, like her movement around the chair.

'Yes,' he said. 'The matter has nothing further to do with you.'

His wife had come to a halt. His boldness was getting the better of her. She glanced towards the stairs and recalled the dejected figure of a girl asleep on the four-poster in her room. She had been made speechless by this turn of events. She didn't know how she could begin to establish her right in this negotiation. It struck her as an intrusion: an arrangement with Tate de Lysle. She wished he would explain; but his silence was conclusive. He had deprived her of any further right to enquire. He had come to his own arrangement. As a matter among men.

But the girl was going to stay. She decided she would wait. While the girl remained, there was no need to despair of the result. She knew her husband's loathing of Tate de Lysle. Their enmity was too sharp. She couldn't imagine that her husband would be part of any arrangement from which Tate de Lysle could derive complete satisfaction. What conditions had her husband forced on the Lord Treasurer? In the circumstances, she thought she could afford to wait. It didn't matter if her initiative worked through others. He said the girl would stay. For the time being that was enough. Her duty was clear. She would see that the girl did not escape. The wife decided she would wait.

'Nature,' Steward smiled, 'speaking of nature.'

Steward was enjoying his private little laugh again. Boyish and triumphant, he had leapt off the bunk. He started a series of exercises with his arms and legs. He was aware of Surgeon's eagerness to hear him continue. But he would let Surgeon wait a little longer. He brought an end to the exercise, and returned to the bunk. Surgeon heard him laugh again, quiet, jubilant. Steward had found a novel comfort in re-creating this scene which had reduced his wife in her own eyes. He was offering this mastery of circumstances for Surgeon's admiration.

'She never saw me so calm,' said Steward, 'when I announced my arrangement with Tate de Lysle that the girl would stay. It was a matter to be decided by men.'

Surgeon approved. He had got a view of Steward that contradicted their previous acquaintance on the ship. There was a limit to Steward's caution. If his dignity had been assailed, he was a man who would be prepared to take risk. Surgeon had heard enough for his purpose; yet his curiosity was more precisely fixed.

'So what was the deal?' Surgeon asked. 'How did you square it with the Lord Treasurer?'

'In the event of any enquiry,' said Steward, 'our word would be enough evidence that the girl had come as my maid. She brought me joy, and it cost Tate de Lysle nothing.'

'A matter among men,' Surgeon said. 'You kept the wife in the dark.'

'In the dark,' Steward reflected as he heard the voices of the men on the lower deck. 'There is an order of person who must be kept in the dark.'

'I didn't think she would give in so easily,' said Surgeon.

Surgeon had a hunger for completeness. His curiosity was

subtly encouraging Steward to continue.

'She didn't,' said Steward. There was a sudden urgency in his voice. 'She didn't give in that easily. She bargained on the family connection and tried to make her own deal with Tate de Lysle. But he wouldn't hear of it. He was never available. Just avoided her like the plague.'

'She never thought of calling in the Law?' Surgeon asked.

Steward smiled. There was comfort and the savour of a recollected power. This, too, was power.

'How could she?' Steward said, as though he had been called on to give his own name: the matter was so simple. 'The Law would cancel any charge while the girl remained as my maid recommended by the orphanage. And I had taken nothing from Tate de Lysle. Not a coin. I was free. Could act as I chose. Everything depended on me. I could act as I chose, and that's what I was doing. How could the Law cancel the Lord Treasurer's recommendation of my maid?'

He lingered in silence on his recollection of the girl. He couldn't resist the image of her body trembling with innocence, an energy that was superbly lasting. He had recovered the pride and vanity of his youth. The girl became a pleasure beyond any greed his wife had known.

'And the beauty of it,' said Steward, suddenly conscious of Surgeon's silence, 'I never took a coin off that criminal Tate de Lysle. Wouldn't touch it. Couldn't let his power interfere with the freedom of my action. That's the beauty of it.'

'That could have made a difference,' said Surgeon. 'I see a difference there.'

'It is a miracle how a thing comes normal,' said Steward. 'The girl was more than I bargained for. While my wife waited for a turn of events, the girl took her place in the family, you might say. This maid was the richest prize of all my nights. A queen in her own right. Crowned by my pleasure, you might say. And under my wife's very nose.'

Surgeon was flexing the muscles of his jaws.

'It's what she was looking for,' Surgeon said. His tone was sour, contemptuous. 'Tate de Lysle must have scared her, and the orphanage was no proper atmosphere.'

Steward was quick to the defence of his memory.

'I was tender with her,' he said. 'That she would confirm.'

But Surgeon's view was fixed. He would remain loyal to his own experience.

'Maid or wife, it's the atmosphere,' Surgeon insisted. 'I reckon they will have it anyhow if the circumstance is right. You can be rough as a bull if the atmosphere is what they are looking for. It's the atmosphere that works the trick. The orphanage wasn't the atmosphere.'

Surgeon slapped his hands and turned his head away from Steward.

'The girl had taste,' said Steward, defending his choice, 'more than my wife could claim.'

'They learn fast,' Surgeon insisted. 'Find me any order of woman who will not whore if the atmosphere is right. Discover one, and my fortune you can have.'

Surgeon slapped his hands again; and Steward gave him a look that said they were agreed. They might have come together by chance; but they were now united by a common experience of private tyrannies. Surgeon sucked on his teeth. Steward had taken leave of his customary modesty. Any echoes of the wife's voice could be endured. He was under a spell of victory. He was free of any contamination that a favour from the Lord Treasurer would have entailed. And his pride was restored—whole, impervious to temptations that went against his nature—to do the thing on his own.

'It must have taken some courage,' said Surgeon. 'In a way, you were threatening Tate de Lysle. While you had the girl under your command, you were a threat to his reputation.'

Steward hadn't really seen it that way. His strategy had been directed at his wife. She had to depend on what he decided. The Lord Treasurer was a negligible target beside that single triumph.

'He didn't have to fear,' Steward said. 'I think he knew the sort of man I was. Wouldn't stoop in a matter of that kind. In any matter.'

Surgeon gave notice of his congratulation. He was clapping Steward on the shoulder as he rose and walked around the table.

'I say it took some courage,' Surgeon repeated.

Steward was grave. He considered the cabin. There was a deeper shadow now; yet everything seemed to strike him with greater clarity. Surgeon had helped to bring some things to light. The question of courage. He hadn't seen the matter in that way; and he thought: courage is failing to recognize danger. He had seen no danger at all in the compromise that joined him to the Lord Treasurer and against his wife. In spite of the power of the man. It was a natural pride which had shielded him from these apprehensions that Surgeon had raised; and the climax of Steward's thinking was sudden, pure revelation. He had been seen by others in a certain way. To earn an admiration that his wife could not afford to acknowledge.

'I think it was that girl who really saved me,' Steward said.

'So I was thinking,' Surgeon agreed. 'You couldn't create a victory like that on your own.'

Steward hesitated. There was an edge to Surgeon's voice. Dry, ironic. Some prediction of a flaw.

'I would expect this to be a matter between us,' Steward said.

'Strictly so,' said Surgeon.

There was no irony now. Surgeon's voice was cold, hard, decisive. A confidence had been sealed. Steward felt a certain lightness in his hands. The elements of comradeship were being forged. He thought he saw Surgeon smile; but there was no trace of ambiguity in his eyes. Everything was clear, acceptable. The ocean was on his side.

Steward felt the ring in his pocket. It was like a knot of feathers. It seemed larger. His thumb probed through the top. The scraping lightly touched his chest: up and across, tracing the circle of the ring. He thought of the Aberlon estate, with its wide river that sang all night. The lights were like jewels burning the air when Tate de Lysle was celebrating there. This was his wife's dream. She would stare over the valley and brood on those lights, feeling a sense of utter dispossession. She would never let it be known; but she often cried when she looked up at the hills and gazed on the luxury that might and should have been hers. This power of desire was greater than any rights that law or nature had ordained. Those lights blazed where an act of robbery was taking place.

"She will have it," Steward said to himself. "I shall put such luxury at her disposal. Install her there and remind her every blazing night who did the thing. 'Where are your connections now?'" And he could hear the sweet certainty of voice that answered: "Smashed. I did the thing, made you rich. I did it myself."

'There are certain debts you can't repay,' Surgeon said.

'Debts?' He couldn't say what had prompted this observation; but it seemed to be the natural climax to his plans for Aberlon. He would put his wife in a debt which was beyond recovery.

'There are few debts which power can't put an end to,' Steward said. 'I can feel it.'

'You will have to build an orphanage,' Surgeon said. 'I am the man to advise you there.'

'I'll put it in my wife's name,' Steward said. 'Every luxury I robbed her of will be restored. It's the idea of all times. The orphanage in her name.'

There was the sound of a bell ordering the divisions to assemble. Steward stirred on the bunk, and he felt again the flutter of air under his skin. But he wasn't inclined to ask Surgeon for an opinion. He was distracted by the voices of men below. They seemed to offer some fresh warning against the threat of Pinteados. He thought of the pilot. Surgeon sat on the chair, secretive and grave, brooding on the silence that filled the cabin.

'Are you fit enough to go down,' Surgeon asked, 'or might I look to that?'

'I'll be there myself,' said Steward. 'It's a question of duty.'

Surgeon was still occupied with Steward's account of his wife. 'You've got your men under control,' he said. 'I couldn't see anything going wrong there.'

But Steward had returned to his normal habit of caution. It was as though the men existed on the same level of threat as his wife.

'Never trust in your absence,' Steward said.

His skin was making bubbles of air again. He felt an ache wriggle up to his collarbone. Surgeon watched him rub his hand along his chest.

'It makes a difference to be there,' said Surgeon, 'but it's a duty to be fit. You're an officer. Remember that.'

'There is the reason I'm ready,' said Steward. 'No medicine like duty.'

Surgeon was conscious of Steward's resistance to his suggestions.

He decided to give up the attempt. It was useless to warn Steward against any action which he regarded as his duty. Surgeon had observed this tendency in Steward. He was fastidious, almost mechanical in his response to any occasion he recognized as duty. Everyone had noticed it. The men in his division often paid tribute to him for this zealous attention to the affairs of the ship. And it had finally sent Surgeon on his devious trail of detecting Steward's motive. "To see his wife in luxury of mourning," Surgeon thought. He had found no motive to surpass the power of Steward's wife.

Steward raised himself slowly up from the bunk and pressed his hands against his ribs where the knot of air started its pulse-beat again. He stretched and thrust his hands out, trying to subdue his fear by this show of vigour. It was a way of convincing Surgeon that he was fit. But it was also a way of proving to himself that he could assume his duties. He paid no attention to Surgeon: the swift flight of arms, the exercise of wrist was his method of summoning Surgeon's attention. Steward had a vision of the men in his division, efficient yet wholly dependent on his wishes. They would be waiting; and then he thought of the orphanage and the role they had played in justifying his belief in his command. A memorial to the men in his division! He would have graduated from the experimental status of an officer and a man on the inside to that of founder. He would enter history through the permanence of stone; and he marvelled at the way time could fix a name. He was a candidate for immortality. An orphanage in his wife's name and dedicated to the memory of those men who served in his division during the historic enterprise to San Cristobal. Already the future had selected him as a candidate for immortality.

He glanced quickly at Surgeon and was relieved to find him distracted by some other memory. Steward preferred not to be seen at the moment he had taken refuge in the future. A glance, unfortunately timed, might have exposed the secret journey which his ambition was making. He looked in Surgeon's direction again; and quietly he brought his exercise to an end.

'There is only one anxiety I have,' Steward said.

Surgeon looked at him, curious and attentive.

'It's the girl,' Steward said. 'It wouldn't do to have her around.

I mean, the best name could be soiled by the information she would have.'

His manner was oblique, cautious, as though he wanted to invite Surgeon's advice without making a direct appeal for it. And his expression showed that temporary worry of someone who saw a perfect arrangement threatened by some minor obstacle. It was as though he was arguing with himself that the future could not be left to chance. Surgeon appeared to wait. His face wore an air of regret.

'As fate would have it,' Steward went on, 'she left the house one night and never returned. I had a feeling my wife had put her up to it, but that wasn't so. She was almost more upset than I was. Strange, that. My wife wept when she discovered the girl had gone.'

Surgeon had given him his full attention. Now he looked knowing, as though he had found a new interest in Steward's drama. Any moment Steward expected him to advise. There was that look which suggested total involvement in what he had heard.

'They had started to behave as though they were twin concubines,' Steward said. 'You would not have believed it. A perfect accommodation was made. To be frank, it alarmed me sometimes. I started to smell a plot. But there wasn't any evidence. The little wench kept up her part of the bargain. Until she disappeared. Sudden so, like how she arrived the first time. And my wife wept.'

Steward looked astonished by his own fluency. Now he talked as though he had known Surgeon all his life. They might have been partners in the same escapades, so easy was this current of feeling that let him relay this secret life to Surgeon: a confidence that made him ignore Surgeon's brooding. Attention was enough.

'The girl would ask her price,' Steward said. 'That is for certain. With a fortune and the applause it brings, I am sure she would ask her price.'

'She couldn't,' Surgeon said. The words seemed to roll off his lips.

Steward smiled, startled by the certainty of Surgeon's manner.

'But you know how they are,' said Steward. 'What's there to prevent that girl spilling what she knows?'

And he waited, reflecting on the possibility and the assurance Surgeon had given him.

'She died,' Surgeon said.

'Died?'

'She was with child,' said Surgeon.

Steward had lowered his body onto the bunk. It was as though all his movements now operated without any decision on his part. Sceptical and dazed, he sat, staring at Surgeon, who showed no emotion at all. Steward waited, hoping for some further assurance that he had not mistaken what Surgeon had said. And suddenly he felt a certain elation. "Died," he kept saying to himself, and saw in this news a liberation from all his fear. He was elated by the very sound of the word, 'died', that seemed to form like the knot of air somewhere in his throat. It was a moment of ecstasy, speechless and surpassing all belief. And the spell was broken only by the slow apprehension beginning to cloud his judgment of Surgeon. Death had brought him a moment of elation, which now dissolved into some terrifying knowledge which Surgeon had. Steward, who had difficulty recognizing exactly the emotion that seized him at any moment, was afraid he might have been deceived. The girl's death had granted him a freedom that now opened another world of destructive possibilities, possibilities that might be contained in what Surgeon knew.

'She returned to the orphanage,' said Surgeon. 'That's where I saw her.'

He tried to avoid looking at Steward as he spoke. His voice had grown calm, and supremely confident, like the voice of Pinteados on the deck. Surgeon had discovered a source of consolation in Steward's perplexity. And he kept thinking of Pinteados: this must have been the pilot's feeling when he revealed knowledge of his encounter with my wife in the Severn asylum.

'I don't understand,' Steward stammered. He might have been talking to someone outside the cabin. The ring was swinging lightly against his chest, as he stared down, feeling increasingly the sway and rock of the ship.

'Did you know my wife as well?' Steward asked.

'Never met her,' said Surgeon.

Steward felt an immense relief. But it didn't last. He could make no claim to a lasting emotion.

'It was Tate de Lysle who summoned me,' Surgeon said. 'It was too late. I think she would have died anyway. But it was natural, the way she went.'

'Died?' Steward asked again.

'That's for certain,' said Surgeon. 'In childbirth.' He wanted to encourage Steward's confidence. 'That's out of the way, you might say.'

'Out of the way,' Steward repeated.

'But a man can never be certain,' Surgeon said.

He got up and took a few paces around the cabin. The movement seemed to bring Steward a little relief.

'But why would Tate de Lysle want to save her?' Steward asked. 'She knew enough to set his name on fire.'

'He wanted to preserve a scandal,' said Surgeon.

'To preserve his own scandal?' Steward asked, and looked to Surgeon.

'A man of your correctness might never stoop to guess what men like that can do,' Surgeon warned.

'But I had the bargain my way,' said Steward. 'What else could he do?'

Surgeon was reluctant to answer. But it was too late to abandon what he knew; and Steward was waiting. He had to learn what flaw in his arrangement had given the Lord Treasurer some mastery over him.

'You are an honourable character,' said Surgeon, 'but you were not without youthful escapades.'

'Escapades?' Steward stammered. 'What do you mean by youthful escapades?'

'The girl,' said Surgeon, making a mask of his hands over his face. 'The girl was of your own flesh. Tate de Lysle knew her mother's history through the orphanage records. The girl was your daughter, Steward. Forgive me, but I didn't want to go that far.'

Surgeon paused and averted his glance from Steward. He wanted to shield Steward from the extremity of the news. It was his duty to come finally to Steward's rescue.

'It is double fortune the girl is dead,' said Surgeon; 'that's out of the way.'

Steward's hand had found the chain. Nervously, scarcely aware of his action, he was making loops around his fingers. The movement increased its speed. The loops came tighter. The ring was like a print of fire at the centre of his palm. 'She', 'the girl', nameless, accountable. Her death had cleansed him of his fear, obliterated any debt the future might set against his pleasure. But the weight of incest now made him alien to himself; too large to be called error, it had emptied Steward of all feeling.

'It could have happened to anyone,' said Surgeon.

The note of optimism was exact. It had gained a victory over Steward's silence.

'I had no idea,' said Steward, groping out of his stupor. He was in search of something to explain.

'How were you to know?' Surgeon said, realizing the power that now served to bring him to Steward's aid. Every observation was an act of rescue, a gift which Steward clutched at in an effort to justify himself.

'How was I to know?' Steward asked himself; and his sense of injury grew steadily. 'I am not that sort of man.'

He was finding his way back to the self he had always tried to promote. He felt a gradual recovery of innocence.

'I've seen how the power of intrigue works,' said Surgeon. 'But it is not in your nature to calculate so darkly.'

He was genuine in this assessment of Steward. It required no effort to accord Steward the luxury of innocence. That is what had always struck Surgeon about the man. Whatever errors of judgment he might commit, Steward would always strive to achieve an essential purity of intention. It was his protection against abuse, a natural ingredient of his ambition to surpass himself.

'I repeat, it is a double fortune the girl died,' Surgeon said.

'To a man like me,' Steward said, 'that such a thing should be done to a man like me.'

His fingers were working the ring free. The movement was much slower, as though he had become minutely conscious of every twist of the chain, the slightest contact that the ring made against his hand. His manner grew noticeably more certain, almost purposeful, during this slow, reliable disentanglement of the chain. And Steward could hear the voice of his wife, now remote and frail in defeat. It gave a new energy to his determination. Fresh evidence of his right to justify himself.

'From the beginning she wanted to destroy me,' Steward said. 'I always knew that.'

'And they will use any weapons,' Surgeon encouraged him. 'The one certainty my own experience has proved. Any weapons.'

'To bring a man and his own flesh together,' said Steward. 'And knowing all along what trap you were setting for him.'

'You are well out of the way,' Surgeon said. 'The future offers whatever she would deprive you of.'

'And that's why she gave me back the wedding ring,' said Steward. 'She had a reason I could never guess.'

'Just put her out of mind,' said Surgeon, 'and out of memory, too.'

'The arrangement is worse than the deed,' said Steward. 'What I did in innocence is like nothing compared with what she planned.'

Steward had recovered his total self-justification. He could see now the completeness of a strategy to rob him of a view he had of himself. His wife had never respected this self that he had promoted. It was a threat to her own claim of superiority over him. And she had tried by an alternating strategy of abuse and flattery to disarm him. Even her act of generosity could now be seen as an aspect of this desire to subvert what he valued. It was entirely the conviction of his own worth that had helped him to survive this history of intrigue and deception.

"When the gift can inflict the greatest punishment," he thought. "That's the best time to make your power felt. Let this enterprise succeed, and she will have every luxury she thinks I rob her of. And so it will be. The supreme form of vengeance, as I plan it. There is an evil side to generosity."

'I'll make it worthy of her,' Steward said, pointing to Surgeon. 'Just let the enterprise succeed. Whatever luxury she desires. She will have it. I will provide it.'

'Let us try it again,' the wife said, taking the girl's fist in her hand. The quill rose like a root up from their knuckles. Slowly the wife eased her hand away and watched the girl's fist tremble and scrape the letters across the page. The girl continued on her own, steering the quill forward and hearing the low scratch on the paper. At first she could recognize nothing but a broken trail of blue lines, crawling like weed over the paper. Then she remembered where the intervals should be joined. She filled the spaces and waited. Then she smiled, astonished by what she had already known. At last she could write her name. She stared at the word and thought she heard the paper imitate a voice. The lines had grown into a face with little white paper mouths shouting her name.

'Madam,' she whispered, astonished by her own triumph, 'you were right. I have done it. I can write.'

She was still stammering her surprise when she turned and realized that no one was there. She was clutching at the quill as she swung over the bench and ran into the house.

The wife stood at the half-open window, watching the slow movement of the clouds. The light cracked and tinted the valleys with colour. Orange shadows assembled along the dark range of the mountain. The girl came up beside her; but the wife didn't turn.

'You are crying, madam,' the girl said. The quill fell from the girl's hand. The woman started to wipe her eyes.

'I told you it wasn't difficult,' the wife said. 'Now you can write your name.'

'But why is madam crying?' the girl asked.

Then she saw the wife turn, and as quickly the girl felt her body pressed against the woman's. The wife couldn't control herself any longer. She wept on the girl's shoulders.

'Please forgive me,' she said, pressing the girl closer to her, 'but I will explain. You must let me explain.'

'Madam,' the girl said. She was afraid. 'Madam!'

Then she was silent. The woman disengaged her hands from the girl. She was walking away from the window.

'I have never done anything that wasn't in his interest,' the wife said, 'never thought anything that was not to promote his ambition.'

The wife had opened the window, and the light spread over the huge and desolate four-poster that stood in the middle of the room. A chest of drawers competed for space, and an atmosphere of congestion pressed on everything. She had been living like a fugitive in readiness to move on.

'Somehow he knows I would never leave,' the wife continued,

'whatever changed, there was the certainty I would remain.'

'You love him,' the girl said, as though she spoke a language she had never heard.

The wife couldn't find any adequate answer for the girl's remarks. But it made her reflect on the stranger she had become in her own eyes. Ever since she could remember, her husband had trained her to feel and think of the future as the only important aspect of time. Every inconvenience pointed there. The most crushing disaster was simply some part of the debt which they paid for their arrival.

'I gave up everything,' the wife said, 'cut myself off from family connections, from any claims to privilege, so that he would feel complete master in our life. I wanted nothing but his happiness. And that is how I lived.'

'He thinks you are too ambitious,' said the girl.

'He thinks that now,' said the wife. 'It's because I know him better. It was Tate de Lysle who stole the maps and passed them on as his own property to the House. I could never forgive my husband for refusing to demand what was his. And when I tried on his behalf, he accused me of ambition.'

'Tate de Lysle is an evil man,' said the girl.

'Some nights I would stare across those hills,' the wife continued, 'and my eyes would fill with tears when I thought of my husband's refusal to defend his own work against the Lord Treasurer's robbery. He would rather witness his ruin than come face to face with the man who was bringing it about. And it was then I knew how much I loved him: this feeling that I would rather be raped by the Lord Treasurer than have him steal my husband's work. I would do anything to recover them. My husband said it was envy. That is what I was. Ambition and envy.'

The girl had grown melancholy, almost contrite as she glanced out of the window, trying to avoid the woman's eyes. She got the feeling that her presence was an additional burden on the wife. She felt an increasing weight of embarrassment and guilt.

'No harm will come to you now,' the wife said. 'Now that I know you.'

The girl would no longer be a pawn in their game with Tate de Lysle. She had decided to abandon all interest in Tate de Lysle and the future of her husband's maps. She looked at the girl and felt an immense gratitude for the accident of her arrival. Her presence was a gift, a relief from the wordless solitude that had imprisoned her in this room. This was her fortress and her prison. Until the girl arrived.

'You must make this your home,' the wife said. 'I want you to stay.'

But the girl had already decided that this was no longer possible. The wife's affection had come as the absolute proof that it would be wicked of her to stay. The girl was afraid to risk explaining her feeling. She knew what had started to happen secretly inside her; but there was no one to whom she could complain. The girl looked out of the window and let the sweep of the mountain range distract her attention from what she wanted to say.

'It has been so different these last few months,' the wife said. 'You have made this house into a home again.'

'Madam,' the girl whispered in an effort to disclaim any credit that the wife might attach to her stay.

The wife came closer to the window. She put her hand on the girl's head. They stared towards the mountain, ignoring the low sweep of houses below.

'I used to rant and rave like an animal,' the wife said, 'they could hear me all the way. Sometimes into the early hours of the morning.'

'You, madam?' the girl said.

'You never know what you will become,' the wife said. 'But I had to be that way. Not because I wanted my troubles known. But I would get a feeling like madness inside me, and there was no one to listen. Like how you are now, here with me. It is like being rescued from madness. Just to have you here, and knowing that you are hearing me.'

'Madam,' the girl said again, and suddenly stopped. It was beyond the girl to understand how she could have come to the wife's rescue. And then the girl looked towards the table and was about to ask the question which the wife answered when she spoke.

'Shall we try again?' the wife said, taking the quill from the floor.

The girl was ready. She would give herself to the wife's schooling once more. For the last time. It was the only way she knew how to say good-bye. By nightfall she would have turned fugitive again.

SIXTEEN

The ocean was everywhere.

Sasha was slowly becoming aware of something. Although he couldn't give this feeling a name, it was there, inside him, around him. Memory played little part in his experience. He witnessed events, and lived them while they lasted; but there was no lasting echo of the days he had left behind. He used to feel some pride in being so near the Commandant; now even this privilege had become a normal part of his routine. Something had begun to change inside him. Quietly and without notice, he was trying to sift opinions he had collected about the men; this was his private game.

'Ivan doesn't like fun. That's what's wrong with him. Always against fun.' This was a view he had heard about the painter.

This wasn't always true, however, since Ivan could be very amusing when he chose to be. Besides, the painter gave the impression that he enjoyed whatever he was doing. Yet there might be some truth in what many of the men had said.

'There's a sort of man who keeps himself to himself,' Baptiste would say, 'and Ivan is one.'

Yet Ivan was not secretive; nor was he without friends. Most people seemed to enjoy Ivan's company; but Baptiste might have had a point. There was a secret of some kind about Ivan. A sort of mystery, you might say. Unlike most of the crew, Ivan rarely showed any sign of being angry. Even if the rations were mean and the cooking was bad, Ivan would eat as though he hadn't noticed what others were complaining about. And always the painter's eyes seemed to reflect the colours of his brushes. It was difficult to tell when Ivan was working and when he was at play, making some private joke with the stir and sweep of oil and paint as he danced his hand up and down the timbers of the ship. He would spend a whole day on a single splice of wood, changing and repeating what he had done until no one could tell what was the colour when he began.

That was the secret, Sasha told himself; the painter was always playing while he worked. Although he worked alone.

The boy had set out on a secret pursuit of Ivan. He wanted the painter to become his private ally, and would seize every opportunity for conversation. Sasha did him small favours, the kind no one would ever notice, not even Ivan himself. The boy wasn't sure why he wanted to achieve this special friendship with Ivan, but this ambition, known only to himself, had made for a burning interest in the painter. Sasha had perfected this habit of collecting views, and had hoarded a great store of knowledge about everyone; now he had started to feel the power that secret knowing conferred on older people. He couldn't be sure when he got this feeling; but it was there. The ship had made him a man.

He thought for a moment of Pierre, the man who once stood for fun; it was a frequent topic of conversation among the men, the way the carpenter had changed. As for Ivan, he had the gift of knowing what others wouldn't dare think upon. But sometimes it was difficult to get the full measure of Baptiste; there was fairly wide agreement only that he was clever, and independent. He had ideas, and he didn't pay very much attention to what anyone thought about him.

From what the boy had seen and heard during the voyage, he was beginning to form a special attitude about people. It was an exhilarating discovery: this feeling that he, Sasha, would have a particular way of seeing those he had to live with. Already this discovery had stamped one firm impression on his behaviour. Living was a kind of private truce, like the treaty he had heard the Commandant speak about and which he couldn't understand until he related it to the men. You might hate someone; then you killed him if it was safe to do so. Otherwise you agreed to hate and go on living with the person. There were probably men who hated the Commandant, but they didn't think about it any more. The Commandant and their hate had become a normal part of their decision to carry on.

It was Ivan alone who eluded clear definition; gradually Sasha was arriving at another view: that the painter was a superior person. That is, he was different with a difference. The Commandant was different; but everyone understood the reason. He had power over the ship. You paid attention when he was present; obeyed whenever he gave an order. And the same was almost true of the officers. But they weren't different in the way Sasha now thought of Ivan. The painter was superior because there was some distance between him and what everyone thought they knew about him. Sasha thought he had found another secret. But it was not about Ivan. His game had led him to start a new pursuit of knowing. He wanted to learn about the distance he had noticed between the officers and the men.

Instinctively he felt his safest guide would be Ivan. He had found the painter crouched in the waist of the ship. The boy's presence was always an offer of help; and Ivan welcomed him. This pursuit was different, but nothing had changed; and Sasha waited until he judged the moment right to start his private game.

'I notice Steward's clothes always in order,' said Sasha.

'This ship's a dirty business,' said Ivan.

'But Steward is always clean,' the boy recalled.

'Work will never dirty Steward,' Ivan said.

His mood was prophetic; but there was also a note of restraint in the way he had spoken. Trying to play it carefully, Sasha felt his timing might have gone wrong.

'What sort of man is Steward?' he asked.

'Do you mean if I like him?' Ivan's answer was no more than a shadow of the boy's question.

'Do you like him?' Sasha asked. Curiosity had made him daring with his questions.

'You are a special one,' Ivan said, 'making everything your business.'

'Do you like Steward,' Sasha repeated.

'If I like Steward?'

'Yes or no?' Sasha insisted.

He had risked his luck too far. The ultimatum came like an

insult, a sudden burst of impudence from a boy who had forgotten his age. Ivan looked up, startled; then said, giving his attention to other matters, 'I mind my own business.'

'Not when you are reading the stars,' Sasha said.

The boy had forgotten himself. He was surprised by his own tone of challenge as he looked at Ivan. A little like the Commandant, he thought, and regretted this urgency in his manner. He was going to say he was sorry when Ivan took command and dismissed him abruptly.

'Go find work to do, and pay attention to your affairs.'

Sasha grew desperate. For a moment he wanted to press his apologies upon Ivan: he had made a mess of the asking game. Worse, he had taken a foolish liberty with his senior. Already he was trying to think of a way to redeem himself in Ivan's judgment. Whatever the value of the knowledge he learnt, he needed a favourable atmosphere. It was the same with all the men: his game was never without a bargain for friendship. He grew sullen in the knowledge of his failure; and regretful that it was Ivan who had been the occasion of his defeat.

Sasha was desperate for company, but there was no one he could approach for advice. It was important that the incident should remain a secret between Ivan and himself. Otherwise, it might mean the end of his private game. Alone, he struggled to think of a way that would return him into Ivan's confidence. Then he thought of the Commandant; but he could not allow the Commandant into the secret of his error. Sasha had counted the days, and it was the tenth morning since the Commandant had given an order to terminate all visits. Sasha was an exception. Now he wasn't sure that this privilege would still be his. Somehow his private game had made him feel equal; and as an equal he had failed. But much greater than failure was his shame at offending Ivan. To find a way back to Ivan was the only way he could save his world from ruin. So he decided on a greater risk. He would see whether his privilege still allowed him entry into the Commandant's cabin.

Later Sasha was sure he had scored a private victory. He had taken a blank sheet from the Commandant's papers. A letter seemed the proper way to reconcile himself to Ivan. He made a simple wish and an appeal. He wrote:

Dear Mr. Ivan,
I was wrong. Please I am sorry. Do not let the men know what happened.

Sasha

Without explanation, he had put the note in Ivan's hand and disappeared from the deck. It was Pierre who witnessed this exchange, and decided to make the content known; for Ivan could not read. At first the boy's error had struck the men as a wicked joke. But Ivan came to Sasha's defence. There was a reason for the boy's apology.

No one would believe Ivan's account of what had happened. There was so little to explain; yet Ivan had grown weary with explaining. It seemed their interrogation would never end. Sasha's closeness to the Commandant had given the message some sinister power of foreboding; and Ivan's failure to explain became an act of treachery against the men who were down below.

The cook, Duclos, threatened to bring the matter to the Commandant's attention. Pierre made more sinister promises. Most alarming of all, Baptiste had refused to talk.

'The boy is a rascal,' said Duclos, 'a filthy little newsmaker.'

Some of the men were quick to agree.

'I told you so,' Duclos continued. 'He is the ears and eyes of the Commandant. Always was, that boy.'

'Why make such fuss?' Ivan pleaded. 'It is as I say. He was just talking to me, asking questions like he always does. A pure innocence. No more.'

'But what is it he wants?' Duclos asked.

'News,' said the junior cook.

'What else?' Duclos insisted. 'He collects news. Always.'

'What I don't understand,' said Pierre, 'is the formal way he had to speak to you. Whoever called you Mr. Ivan?'

'But it is my right, no?' Ivan said. 'So how it happens I should not have the title of "mister"? And from a boy.'

'Is it only titles you want?' Duclos queried.

'Every jackass has his honour,' said Ivan.

'And every honour its own jackass,' Baptiste said.

It was the first time the powder maker had spoken; and the junior cook was about to laugh. But Baptiste generated a fury that put the seal of gravity on all their responses. Laughter would have been a miracle of achievement, like denouncing the Commandant in his presence.

Suspicious, persistent, each in turn collaborated in this effort to probe Ivan's silence.

'Are you a man to be trusted?' Pierre asked.

'Certainly not,' Duclos said.

Ivan was angered by this challenge to his honour, but he refused to answer.

'If you have some special knowledge,' said Baptiste, 'then spare us the suspicion and say what you know.'

Ivan watched the crusts of paint harden like scab wounds over his hands. He could feel his skin tighten. There was a sensation like fire burning low inside his mouth. It was not the first time speech had failed him in a matter that seemed so simple. He recalled the evening he had returned from the officers' dining cabin without an answer to the men's speculations about the Lady of the House. Neither Priest nor Surgeon would make his reaction known. The men had queried Ivan's delay in the dining cabin, but he couldn't begin to explain the complications into which Priest and Surgeon had trapped him.

Baptiste appeared to be the most sympathetic, and his questions were in the nature of a plea; but suddenly his manner changed. Some call of dignity had put an end to his patience. He thrust his hands out. His fingers struck like spears into Ivan's shoulder. Baptiste grabbed his arm and shook him.

'So what it is come over you?' he demanded. 'Your tongue is a leper? You don't let it travel with any news, not even how you feel? What prize you expect for playing dumb?'

The cook was prompt with an answer that insulted.

'He is no ordinary man on deck,' Duclos said. 'He is put among us for some purpose.'

'Tell us your business with Boatswain,' Pierre said.

'Yes, what about your visits to Boatswain's cabin?' Duclos insisted.

Ivan let the paintbrushes fall from his hands. It seemed that he might offer some defence of himself. For the past week, every morning at about the same hour, Ivan would abandon whatever he was doing and hurry to Boatswain's cabin. But he was under the strictest instructions to remain silent about any matter that had been discussed during his visit. The men had made no enquiries about his services to Boatswain. Until this moment when Pierre raised it as evidence for their suspicions.

'Maybe they will raise him to higher office?' Duclos teased.

The cook was confident about his verdict.

'Ivan and the boy, Sasha,' said the cook, Duclos, 'they are the eyes and ears of the officers.'

Baptiste heard some threat to his sense of rivalry.

'Remember, it is always the turn of the men when you reach land,' he warned. He spoke as though he would soon run out of words. But Ivan's caution was like the desert, calm and fruitless and unending.

'Where is the boy Sasha?' Baptiste asked.

He was trying to be intimate again, coaxing Ivan to share in the comradeship they had always offered him. But mention of the boy had aroused Ivan from his solitude. The men thought they were on the verge of some disclosure. But Ivan surprised them. He was protective of the boy and militant in his own defence.

'I am no man's keeper,' Ivan said, and immediately regretted his outburst.

'The men will see to that,' said Baptiste, 'the men are the real keepers. They know where to keep one who turns against them.'

'Why do you threaten me again?' Ivan asked.

'Not threaten,' said Baptiste. 'I predict. Like when you watch the stars, while I prophesy by the light of day. You see only at night; but my day lasts longer. I see more.'

'I trouble no one,' Ivan said, the note of apology taking over.

'You offend the men by your secrecy,' said Baptiste; 'you never give us warning you would go dumb. A man can't just change without giving some warning. You can keep your words to yourself, but not your action. And we do not like your action.'

'But I trouble no one,' Ivan said coldly.

There was no note of apology now. His voice was firm, clear, certain of his meaning. He rubbed his hand gently over the mark that showed where Baptiste had gripped his arm. You felt the painter was forgiving him what he had done. It hurt a little where he patted his skin, very gently.

Marcel was approaching. He seemed to be in some doubt where

he wanted to go; paused in the act of clearing his eyes and was soon directly opposite Ivan.

'I would like some of my fish tonight,' he said, addressing Ivan.

Baptiste laughed; and Ivan had the feeling of conspiracy being arranged against him.

'You should tell the cooks,' said Ivan.

'Is it safe for me to give orders to the cooks?' Marcel asked.

'Why do you ask me?' Ivan said. 'I am no cook.'

'Then I will tell the cooks.' said Marcel. 'Seeing that I have your permission.'

'I have no authority,' said Ivan. He was hurt by Marcel's teasing.

'Then I will tell the cook,' said Marcel, and continued walking.

There was a pause, almost tense, between Ivan and the men. Baptiste showed his regret.

'You see what I mean,' said Baptiste; 'you make us expect things from you. A man can't make his friends expect and then don't give.'

Ivan turned to go. This combination of Marcel and Baptiste in a similar mood of accusation had unnerved him. He needed to be alone, to feel innocent of their charge. They behaved as though he had denied them something; failed somehow in his promise. But he hadn't betrayed anyone, least of all Baptiste or Marcel. He felt hurt by what they were doing; and more deeply hurt by what they were thinking. He could not escape this knowledge, nor the feeling that he would have to say something if they were not to abandon him.

He could do it easily without the favours of the officers, of the Commandant himself; but the comradeship of men like Marcel and Baptiste was a debt he owed to life itself. Suddenly he remembered the sound of the words Sasha had written, and which had brought about such a mysterious change in everything that had followed: 'Dear Mr. Ivan, Please I am sorry.'

He meditated on the respect Sasha had shown him: a natural pledge of courtesy from a boy. He could not recall any other circumstance when the boy had called him 'mister'. But the interpretation the men put on it was quite different; and the difference had become independent of anything that had actually happened. This other meaning had taken on a life of its own. It allowed of no explanation on his part; and it was supported by facts of its own making. His visits to Boatswain's quarters, his consent to swear secrecy, and avoid exchanges with the crew.

And suddenly, in a fit of accusation he couldn't himself accept, he wanted to blame Sasha. If the boy was sorry, why didn't he just say so? Why did he have to write, to leave evidence, as they say, of words on paper? Now he forgot the resonance of 'mister', and thought on the substance of the boy's apology: 'I am sorry.' Ivan would have liked to meet Marcel and Baptiste on the same ground of confidence; but there was no occasion to justify this behaviour in him. There was nothing for him to be sorry about. It was so different in the case of Sasha. The occasion was right. He had taken liberties, and he had been rebuked for doing so. His apology was natural. The matter was clear. Ivan was debating with himself the necessity to maintain his dignity, and the increasing need to be free from this solitude which had made him alien to the men.

The men had begun to disperse, muttering abuse as they walked away. And suddenly the painter felt an overwhelming impulse to communicate with someone; to share this burden of innocence and guilt. But where should he begin? What secret could he share that would return them to his confidence? He was about to reveal this state of loneliness to Baptiste when the boy arrived with an order from Boatswain.

'He wants to speak with me?' Ivan asked.

'In his cabin,' said Sasha and disappeared.

Marcel stood beside Baptiste, silent, inscrutable. They watched Ivan enter Boatswain's cabin. His departure had heightened their suspicion, giving a sharper edge to the accusations they had brought against Ivan; but each refrained from offering any clue to what he thought. Their attitudes were like an old arrangement, warning that there were moments when comradeship could not survive if the closest ally dared to talk.

Ivan could feel the wind nibbling at the end of one ear. It might have been a welcome distraction in other circumstances; but Boatswain had threatened any pleasure the painter might have found in this weather. Boatswain was overwrought, haunted by fears he thought the painter might have divined. Such agitation was never evident when Boatswain gave orders to his division. He had learnt the strategy of command, how to establish, at a moment's warning, the measure of distance necessary to protect his authority.

Alone, Boatswain was a different man, coaxing the past to ignore his failures. Each memory was like a rebel he had to pacify. Sometimes the conflict put too great a strain on his judgment; he would be frightened by the fear of giving way, the failure to be an officer and therefore a man on the inside. Then he would submit his authority to the painter's gift of prophecy. Boatswain wanted desperately to know what future might have been hidden from the knowledge of those who were making this enterprise. This was his secret with Ivan. He wouldn't acknowledge his dependence on the painter, but the rumour of Ivan's powers was enough. Yet he didn't trust Ivan's relation to the men. Rumour always made Boatswain alert; his status as an officer, a man on the inside, warned him there were dangers everywhere.

Contrary to his custom on these occasions, Boatswain hadn't invited Ivan to sit. Now he could detect signs of weariness in the painter, who had been exhausted by his conflict with the men. Their accusations were still fresh in his ears. He struggled to share his attention between them and the sinister scrutiny of Boatswain's eyes. The cabin was like a danger in daylight.

'Do you put much value on your life?' Boatswain threatened him.

'But how have I gone wrong?' Ivan repeated.

'Yes or no!' Boatswain would not be satisfied by any answer that wasn't direct.

'Like the next man, I surely value my life,' Ivan said. He thought it was a harmless reply; but Boatswain appeared outraged. He had smelt some danger in what he heard.

'I do not ask your opinion of the next man,' he said; 'it is this gang feeling that will be your undoing. I ask you about yourself. Do you value your life?'

Ivan was pleading for time to compose himself.

'Yes, I do, sir,' he yielded.

'Excellent,' Boatswain replied. His answer was like an award he was offering the painter for his ability to recognize what he had heard.

He drew Ivan's attention to the side of the table, inviting him to sit. Again Ivan seemed to ask for time. He had scarcely found his balance on the chair when he heard Boatswain's voice seeking his assurance. Boatswain had suddenly turned cheerful, almost confidential.

'I had begun to feel I had left the worst behind,' Boatswain said.

Ivan offered his assent; but it struck Boatswain rather as a promise than a fact.

'Are you sure?'

'If you feel that way,' said Ivan, 'it will be so.'

'On what authority?' Boatswain asked. His query was nervous.

'You know your way, sir,' said Ivan; 'that's why we obey.'

'Forget the "we", Ivan,' Boatswain rebuked him. 'I warn you, it is the gang feeling that will be your downfall.'

Ivan was making an enormous effort to correct himself. This error in speech, he thought, was worse than the error which the men had attributed to his silence.

'I didn't mean it that way, sir.'

'But a word is a word,' said Boatswain, as though he were disposed to accept the painter's error. 'Such a word carries its own meaning.'

'I understand,' Ivan conceded.

There would be no further argument. Ivan could sense a change of temperature in the cabin. But he couldn't overcome his restraint in Boatswain's presence. The painter wanted to deny any feeling of cordiality that might grow out of this meeting. The slightest hint of a favour from Boatswain made him think of the men below. He couldn't allow their suspicion to be confirmed by any favours with which Boatswain might reward him. Every gesture of intimacy warned Ivan of betrayal. But he was under orders to obey. He heard Boatswain's jaws grinding like hinges under his skin. Boatswain had found temporary solace in the painter's company; but he was about to take a risk that could be terrible in its consequence. To trespass on the past, and with the painter as his guide: a man who was from down below. But Boatswain couldn't resist his desire to know.

'Be careful how you hear me,' Boatswain said, 'and put a proper value on your life. Is it true that you see a woman in the Commandant's life?'

There was a look of terror in Ivan's eyes. What trap was being laid for him now? To join with an officer in secret whispering about the Commandant! There could be no limit to the penalty he would bring upon himself. Boatswain understood the painter's awe; but he was too far gone to restrain himself.

'Well, tell it,' Boatswain whispered, 'tell it if it be so.'

Ivan was shaking his head like a dog in search of its ears.

'It's an order,' Boatswain reminded him; 'is it true you see a woman in the Commandant's life?'

'Such is the evidence of my vision,' said Ivan, 'but I myself cannot verify.'

'Could you identify?' Boatswain whispered, his hands cupped and calling to the painter for some proof of his powers.

'I receive no evidence that would identify,' Ivan said.

He watched Boatswain relax his jaws and hug his face gently with his massive hands. His hunger for secrets had been abated. He felt some jubilant future might yet be detected in the painter's moon. But he would abide with this promise. For the time being he would go no further.

'Enough,' Boatswain said, regaining his officer's certainty of command. 'You may go.'

'At your service.' Ivan bowed.

Ivan hurried from the cabin. He was hardly aware of his step, and walked into the boy as he crossed the lower deck. He was going to apologize, but he didn't know what to say. And Sasha was too afraid to speak.

SEVENTEEN

The little hills of cypress trees appeared, leaning away from the wind. A soft green haze stretched and shivered where the land caved into the valley. On the far side the crops changed colour: clusters of foliage, bright yellow, halted the wind. The citrus fruits hung heavy from their branches. As the ship narrowed the distance, the little port displayed its abundance of fruits. Docile and smiling, the native pedlars waited with their small cargoes of domestic objects: knives, wooden spears, a brilliance of stones gathered at random from the shore. The commonest sea shell had been polished to match the radiance of the sun. There was a small garrison of soldiers; but none were to be seen around the port. They had no warning of this visit. The natives, trained to centuries of patience and waiting, expected anything.

The men had collected on the near side, observing the lazy contours of the island. The Commandant's order was that no one should leave the ship. It increased their eagerness for the pleasures of the land. They had an urgent hunger for other company.

'I could make a break for it,' the junior cook said. He spoke in a whisper to Duclos, who pretended not to hear.

'The small part of an hour would be enough,' he went on; 'the smallest fraction of the clock hand would ease my feeling.'

'I see no human comfort over there,' someone said. 'Not a breast in sight.'

'You'll find them, all the same,' the older man said; 'the menfolk will show you where.'

Duclos overheard, and warned about the dangers this would entail. The males were known for their jealousy: ferocious and unyielding in their vigilance over their women, who were seldom allowed to show themselves in public.

'For every rule, there is one exception at least,' the junior cook said.

'And that will be your massacre,' Duclos said. 'I've seen a man lose all his organs for thinking that way.'

The cook was in meditation, letting his eyes rove from the traffic of pedlars on the pier to the slow, somnolent slope of the stunted grape trees in the distance.

'I wonder what it is the Commandant is expecting here,' the junior cook said.

'Hold your tongue,' Duclos warned. 'You make food, not plans. The Commandant has his business.'

'Maybe we take in water,' someone said.

'That I would know,' Duclos put in quickly. He preserved his rights when he was sure of them.

This had led to some cautious speculation among the men. The Commandant had given short warning that they would make a stop before the Isles of the Black Rock. They were less than an hour away from the little island port when they first heard the news. They had become exceptionally cheerful. Each anticipated a moment's respite from the discipline of the ship. But the feeling was brief, terminated abruptly by the Commandant's orders. No one was to leave the ship. They allowed their fancy to work on other possibilities: the length of their stay in the bay, the purpose of the delay. Ivan had been chosen to attend the Commandant during his visit ashore. The men gazed at the island: a near and precious gift which they had been forbidden to touch. They leaned against the side of the ship, measuring the nearness of the land and regretting their deprivation.

Someone had called out for Baptiste. They wanted to hear his opinions about the island. Perhaps he might have a hunch what the Commandant was up to. But Baptiste was not among the men. No one had remembered seeing him during the last hour or so.

'Maybe he went to relieve himself,' the first cook said. 'Always takes to relieving himself when he gets upset.'

'What's he got to empty that takes such time?'

'It's how he gets upset,' the junior cook said; 'takes a long time to settle again.'

'Then ask Duclos,' a voice said. 'He has experience of these parts.'

A few heads turned to Duclos.

'Yes, ask Duclos,' another voice agreed.

'I see Pierre had new instructions,' said Duclos. 'He is in the confidence of the officers.'

'Forget the carpenter,' said the junior cook; 'you have former knowledge of the island.'

Duclos was slow in reply. He watched the small boat wading forward, as it carried the Commandant to his meeting with the Admiral of the island. Duclos could barely recognize the shapes of the Commandant and Ivan, who rowed without any sign of effort.

'How strange a circumstance,' said Duclos, and stopped.

The junior cook puzzled over what he heard.

'Would the Commandant be safe?' he asked.

'Give thanks to the Treaty,' said Duclos, 'there was a time no man of Lime Stone would trespass on this southern coast.'

'Except by conquest?' the second cook enquired.

Baptiste had arrived. They felt his presence like a change of weather.

'How strange a circumstance,' Baptiste repeated, staring in unbelief at the twisting shoreline of the southern coast.

Then he broke his meditation to answer the junior cook; but he was brief, as though he was waiting for the right moment to explain.

'There was no conquest here,' Baptiste said, and turned his gaze back to the Commandant's boat.

In the historic scramble for Dolores, the island had never yielded all its territory to a single rule of law. When the navies of Lime Stone and Antarctica met in sea battles that had become legends, conflict always ended in a mutual agreement to withdraw. The garrisons of Lime Stone, however depleted in numbers, retained their hold on the northern portion of the island. Nor was Antarctica ever dispersed effectively from the South. A destiny of twin conquests marked the island's history. Lime Stone ruled in the North, and Antarctica retained its hold over the South.

The natives had acquired, from witness and custom, some of the characteristics of their respective rulers. The South was famous for its irreverence and its sensuality. The North had inherited deep traits of taciturnity and forbearance. Established conventions were safer in the North. At any rate, they enjoyed a more lasting obedience. The South, with its gift of self-mockery, always posed a threat to such conventions. Each region had a record of bitter struggle against the foreign rule of Lime Stone and Antarctica. But they had never allowed this common humiliation to unite them. In fact, natives of the North had been known to take some pleasure in the others' defeats. It was a common saying in the North: 'It is just that they should be restrained,' referring to some defeat of their kinsmen in the South.

Antarctica knew a similar support among their subjects; but it was not so open and reliable as the attachment of the northern natives to the authority of Lime Stone. The saying among the southern natives was: 'It is as well they should be taught.' There was a subtle difference in the feeling; it lacked the moral urgency that characterized the North. The situation had achieved its supreme irony in the attitudes of the foreign garrisons. The men of Lime Stone preferred the natives of the South. They thought them more open and more human; whereas their adversaries—the admirals and civilian authorities of Antarctica—spoke warmly of the prudence and good sense of the northern natives. As a result, one aspect of foreign rule—perhaps the one that was to evolve into a settled tradition—was the techniques of the bribe.

Bribery had acquired the status of a salary. It was the recognition men were paid for honest labour. And it was how they were persuaded from disloyalty. The supreme bribe was to bestow an honour, indigenous to the foreign power, on a native who had displayed some excellence of loyalty and achievement on behalf of the foreign power. He became an object of great attention among his own people. His company was a privilege; his praises were sung. The main reason—as the foreign rulers were to learn—was simply because the honoured hero used his position to arrange less glamorous bribes for his minions.

But the Commandant was exceptional in this respect. He seemed free of any illusions about the natives, North or South. In the course of his duty he had done whatever the situation demanded in the interest of Lime Stone. But a reputation for meanness had sprung up, largely from his refusal to confer honours. He executed, instead.

'Even his own men,' Baptiste said, recalling the young Commandant's ruthlessness. 'But you can't do that, sir,' a subordinate had pleaded with him during his first visit to Dolores.

He had called the garrison together, along with a select group of the natives, and told the soldier much older than himself to explain his case. The occasion was like a trial.

'The bribe is the only way to get them on our side,' the soldier had said. Whereupon the Commandant drew his gun and shot him in the neck. The man didn't die, but he was put on the next ship and sent, a cripple, back to Lime Stone.

These foreign garrisons had indulged in appalling cruelties against the native population, and were often barbarous in their habits of coercion, but the men of Lime Stone were shaken to the roots by the Commandant's action that morning. It was the absolute nature of the act that astounded. It had no history of anger, no evidence of a grievance that might have given it some logic in their thinking. It was only the solitary granite purpose of a man whose action was utterly identified with his purpose. The bribe was the greatest enemy of efficiency; and the young Commandant considered no action too extreme that would eliminate it from the land.

During his stay on Dolores—it lasted five months—the Commandant had turned the North into a workshop. Men seemed to communicate only through what they were doing. His reputation had spread some alarm in the South. The southern natives wished he might attack their foreign masters; and the latter, in moments of crisis, would frighten the population with the possibility of the Commandant's invasion. There was immense relief on all sides when he departed.

Baptiste had made a shade over his eyes as he followed the curve of the bay. He could see a vague movement of faces where the boat was being tethered to the shore. A boy's face appeared, gay as silver in the afternoon light.

'I heard that Lime Stone once took the southern portion too,' one of the men said.

'Official records may show it so,' said Duclos, 'but it never happened. That was the pride of Badaloza, heaven curse his heart.'

'What strange names they carry in Antarctica,' the man said. 'I have heard Boatswain talk of him.'

'He was the terror of Lime Stone,' Baptiste told them. 'The Commandant himself would not deny that.'

'I believe the Commandant was his match,' the man said.

'Equal, perhaps,' Baptiste conceded, 'but different.'

'Lime Stone was never known for their kind of cruelty?' the man enquired.

Baptiste was still guarding his eyes against the light, as he speculated on the lazy traffic of people beyond the shore.

'Not a cruelty by direct murder,' he said, glancing at the man who had spoken, 'but I think Lime Stone found a more terrible way to murder the natives of the North.'

'More terrible than the Commandant?' the man said.

'Lime Stone restored the Honours after the Commandant left,' said Baptiste. 'The Honours!'

He took his hands from his eyes. 'You'd have to witness by experience what I mean. To know a northern native who held the Honour of Lime Stone! That was a corpse you could never bury, a man in permanent conspiracy against his own soul. That became our method with the northern natives. And it worked, worked in a way superior to anything Heaven could invent. The ultimate and most terrible form of the bribe.'

The men watched Baptiste in awe. It seemed the Commandant's absence had brought him a novel liberty of speech.

'And that's a reason the Commandant had aroused the anger of the House,' Baptiste said. 'He was against paying the natives with the Honours of Lime Stone. Wouldn't contaminate the name of the Kingdom with offers of bribery. To gain the favours of natives, he could manage in other ways. It made him most unpopular on all sides.'

Sasha had arrived with a message for the cooks. Duclos took a final look towards the land, and then hurried away. The boy didn't linger. He bowed towards Baptiste, and crossed the deck to the other side of the ship.

'Where is Pierre?' someone asked.

'With the officers,' Baptiste said, but he would offer no further comment.

They watched the boy, who stood alone, gazing down at the water. Sasha was thinking about the effect of the Commandant's absence on some of the men. Steward and Surgeon had occupied the Commandant's cabin the moment the small boat started its journey to the land. It was the first time he had ever seen two officers together in the Commandant's cabin. He had observed the strong friendship which had grown between Surgeon and Steward. He couldn't account for Priest; and Pinteados was nowhere in sight. But he knew that Pierre was hidden in the bow. Stern and aloof, Pierre had put a temporary distance between himself and the men who were down below. It made Sasha puzzle again over the secret view he had of the enterprise: the way each man changed with some change in his visible circumstance.

It was dark and sweating down below. The heat grew like a fever in the belly of the ship. The cooks were busy severing two dry, stiff carcasses, hooked and swinging from a wet rod of iron overhead. The sweat ran like oil down their necks. They fought with axe and saw, cleaving and drilling through the splinters of bone. The smoked meat was bleeding some nameless substance over their hands. Here, in this echoing hollow of the ship now moist with heat and the smell of wombs, they hacked and parried with their tools, carving up huge rations of meat.

'I reckon we be a mouth or more extra this coming meal.'

'Thicken the slabs,' Duclos said. 'That's the order.'

'Pity such a feast should come at this time,' the junior cook said.

'You are still stoppered up inside?' Duclos asked him.

'And worse. A worse putrefaction you could never imagine.'

'Then loosen your innards,' the elder man advised.

'That will be worse than the sickness, I fear,' the young cook said. 'I may be the first to die from such a breeze.'

Duclos was laughing, but his voice was hoarse. He had to struggle to make himself heard.

'What a way to name such a wind,' he said at last. 'Breeze! Now I call that real delicate.'

'There's no record of high breeding in my line,' the young cook said, 'but I am delicate, as you say. Always have been.'

'Maybe they will raise you to higher office,' Duclos said, 'like Pierre. The carpenter has charge of the men below, according to the officers' instructions.'

'It's only for the afternoon,' the young cook said. 'And I feel safer here.'

They heard footsteps approaching; and they were silent. It was Pierre. He stared at the cooks, paced up and down for a while, and then left. They heard the sound again; but they couldn't be sure whether it was an echo. The younger man was going to take a look when Pierre reappeared. He made a brief inspection, but he didn't look in the direction of the cooks. Then he was gone. The cooks crept forward, puzzled and silent, trying to locate the sound of his footsteps. Then they saw his back emerge like a wall into the sunlight. A fierce brilliance had struck over the men who were overhead. Their orders were to scrub the deck before it grew dark.

'When does the Commandant return?'

'Let it be soon,' Duclos said, recalling the look in the carpenter's eyes.

*   *   *

The Admiral Badaloza rose very slowly; it seemed that he was taking an age to complete his height from the ground. His eyes, which were frozen bullets wedged into the wide scarlet sockets, never left the Commandant, and liquor showed in his cheeks. His greeting was elaborate, and graced with all the courtesies appropriate to the Commandant's reputation.

'Peace brings us together, at last,' the Admiral said. 'May it continue the whole of my life and yours.'

He paused, then thrust his arms out, inviting the Commandant to share his embrace. Brisk and equally courteous, the Commandant wore the look of a man on the move. He had business to settle that should be done swiftly and to the benefit of both men. The Admiral stood a step back, musing on the formidable presence of the man whom he had always had orders to kill. The Commandant remained motionless, as though he understood what his adversary needed: a moment to reflect on the change in their respective duties. It was as though he owed it to the Admiral to grant this indulgence. The Commandant's natural haughtiness of manner could never be wholly absent on such an occasion.

'What is the news?' the Commandant asked, and took the liberty to wave Ivan to a seat.

'When did you leave Lime Stone?' the Admiral asked.

'Six months but for some days,' the Commandant said.

The Admiral showed some reluctance to speak again. He didn't want to ruin this meeting with the Commandant. He hurried to the side where the Commandant was standing, and pulled a chair up to the desk. He made quick, noisy half-steps, as though some new excitement had overcome him. The meaning of this visit had begun to work on the Admiral's sense of gaiety. He had gone back to his side of the desk, but he noticed the Commandant had remained standing.

'What shall it be?' he asked, pulling open a small cabinet door. But he had failed to distract the Commandant's attention from serious matters.

'Admiral,' the Commandant said quickly.

The cabinet door swung back, and the Admiral's hand stayed where it was: an empty arc of bone tottering quietly down to his side.

'There is no time,' said the Commandant, 'no time at all.'

He glanced over his shoulder to where Ivan was sitting. The painter might have been without hearing for all the interest his face showed. He stared at the ground; later, his eyes were set on the ceiling. At last the Commandant sat. The Admiral's eyes were a little mournful; he was going to be deprived of this small celebration.

'But this is history,' he said, taking the Commandant's arm, 'when has such a thing happened before? That we sit here together. In peace.' He was embarrassed by the Commandant's lack of gratitude for this moment in history.

'It will take time before the meaning of the Treaty comes home to the masses of our people,' the Admiral said, 'but they will rejoice. As yet, they are not aware, so there is no jubilation. But that is a matter of time.'

The Admiral looked across at Ivan. His eyes were sceptical.

'He is safe,' the Commandant said. 'You can talk. But it must be brief.'

The Admiral wasn't impressed. He didn't support this liberality in the Commandant. Subordinates, however trusted, should not be present on such an occasion; and suddenly it occurred to him that the Commandant had forgotten to ask his permission to let them be seated.

'He is in my confidence,' the Commandant said; 'my fullest confidence.'

'I do not question it,' said the Admiral, 'but we do things a different way.'

'You have my word,' the Commandant said.

Ivan showed no sign of hearing what was going on.

'You will not drink a small celebration?' the Admiral offered.

'If you say there is no further news,' said the Commandant, and threatened to rise from his seat.

'There is,' the Admiral said; and his voice betrayed something of regret. 'There's a rumour of civil strife in Lime Stone.'

He was sorry he had spoken; but the Commandant's response had taken him completely by surprise. He seemed indifferent to the very name of Lime Stone.

'My mind is on San Cristobal,' the Commandant said.

The Admiral looked relieved. If the future of San Cristobal was all that troubled the Commandant, then there was nothing to argue about.

'Is San Cristobal in the news?' the Commandant asked.

'Skirmishes,' said the Admiral contemptuously, 'just skirmishes. But the garrisons have their orders.'

'The garrisons have not been withdrawn?' the Commandant asked.

'Almost,' said the Admiral; 'the order was that a civil commission of both our kingdoms would settle all affairs. There should be no troops when you arrive. Unless the skirmishes got out of hand. Then we shall join to finish them off.'

'And that is all the news?' The Commandant said. His voice was so low the Admiral wasn't sure he had heard.

'It is about the only news,' the Admiral said. 'We are safely at peace in these waters.'

He looked up at the Commandant, as though he had to remind him that it would be improper not to celebrate the occasion. But the Commandant didn't yield. He stood and raised his hand to say he was leaving. The Admiral looked quite overcome with disappointment. The scene would never be repeated. The Admiral raised his great body with the help of the table, and now his manner was less ceremonial. His movement was prompt. There was firmness in his grip as he shook the Commandant's hand. Decisive and brief. Ivan had already taken up his position at the door, waiting for the Commandant to pass. They saluted the Admiral, who didn't seem to notice when he got up. The Admiral was working his fingers around the key of the little cabinet door. He found a bottle and two glasses, set them down firmly on the table, and stared for a while through the open doorway. The Commandant had gone.

The Admiral lowered his body very slowly onto the chair. Then he was absolutely still until his eyes began to turn and squint, as though he was not familiar with the early twilight that loitered outside. The Commandant's departure had deprived him of his taste for drink. He couldn't detect any logic in such a visit. It was so brief, almost impertinent. And he wondered whether this might have been the Commandant's intention. Was there some hint of mockery in his questions about the latest news? The Commandant had showed no interest in the report of civil strife in Lime

Stone. What news of importance could he have that the Commandant didn't know?

The Admiral was beginning to nurse a sense of injured pride; and suddenly he regretted the Treaty that existed between their two kingdoms. It would have been the perfect moment to settle an ancient rivalry; to savour the pleasure of some personal retaliation. He wiped a hand across his eyes and brooded on the empty glass. He started to pour himself a drink, but the Commandant still occupied his thinking. This was no way for gentlemen of equal rank to conduct a welcome. He returned the bottle to the table and continued his reflection on the empty glass.

The twilight was building sombre shadows that stretched across his room. The Admiral watched the light fade like cloud over the walls where the portraits of famous heroes hung. They were the pride of Antarctica: names that had inspired the Admiral to his own achievements. He was making an effort to forget the Commandant as he looked at the history of conquests that reigned over the room. Suddenly he slapped his forehead and swore at his attendant, who had arrived in the doorway. The man was trying to attract the Admiral's attention; but he had observed the Admiral's mood and was afraid to break the news. The Commandant had returned.

Without any further delay, the Commandant had decided to come to the attendant's rescue. He didn't wait to be announced. The Admiral abandoned his interest in the dead heroes of Antarctica. He looked up at the Commandant, timing the moment for a rebuke; but the Admiral's indignation had deserted him. The attendant saluted and withdrew, leaving them alone. Ivan waited outside.

'If you would do the honour,' the Commandant said, 'to feast with us on the *Reconnaissance*.'

The Admiral hadn't quite freed himself from his early stupor. Now he saw the Commandant's arms stretched wide, offering the traditional embrace of welcome. The Admiral struggled to hide his alarm at this unlikely show of friendship. He was diffident and a little haughty.

'I will not leave without your acceptance, Admiral.'

The Commandant was overpowering in his new role. The Admiral couldn't decide on a correct response. He suspected some mischief in the Commandant; yet he felt himself under the spell of his rival's conviviality.

'Your departure was not so friendly,' the Admiral said; but he was careful to obscure any sign of irritation. 'I thought I had offended in some way.'

'And so you had,' the Commandant said, and curved an arm around the Admiral's waist.

'Offended?' the Admiral puzzled.

'In a manner of speaking,' the Commandant said, and paused. 'Do I have your permission to sit?'

'Your privilege and my honour,' the Admiral greeted him.

They sat, looking across the table at each other: the Commandant jubilant and boyish in his eagerness to please; the Admiral cautious and smiling.

'You look a year younger than when you walked out of this room,' the Admiral said. 'What is it about Dolores that pleases you so?'

'A jewel of discovery,' said the Commandant. 'It's a jewel, this island. Shared by Lime Stone and Antarctica alike.'

'May our great Treaty confirm what you find here,' the Admiral said. He gave his voice a little warmth. 'Shall we celebrate? It was my wish when you arrived.'

The Admiral seemed to lose his judgment of a proper measure. He was filling the glasses to the brim; but the Commandant did not restrain him. It would be his first taste of liquor since the *Reconnaissance* set out from Lime Stone. The Admiral raised his glass and invited the Commandant to lead the toast in honour of the Treaty that had brought peace to their kingdoms. He got up as the Commandant had done; but he noticed a change of mood come over the Commandant. He was cheerful; but his early extravagance had subsided. The Commandant's hands seemed to shake. There was a note of agitation in his voice.

'To the safe arrival of the vessel *Penalty*,' the Commandant said.

He had got through half the liquor at one gulp while the Admiral stood, gazing at him, barely conscious that he hadn't joined in the Commandant's toast. Then the Admiral brought the glass to his mouth and wet his lips; but he didn't drink.

'*Penalty*?' he said, showing his bewilderment. 'Why drink to the vessel *Penalty*?'

The Commandant was convivial again. His eyes shone, bright with some recognition of private reward.

'You didn't give me the news of *Penalty*,' the Commandant said. 'That was your offence.'

He had taken his seat. The Admiral took the first sip of drink and found himself stooping gently onto the chair.

'The vessel *Penalty* did stop here on its way to San Cristobal,' the Admiral said; 'largely a cargo of women. But nothing that would be cause for news.'

The Commandant was smiling as he raised his glass, urging the Admiral not to delay with his drink. The Admiral drank freely, letting his eyes wander across the deepening shadows that spread over the portraits of his kingdom's heroes. He needed their presence as a guide to the inscrutable wishes of the Commandant.

'Tell me,' he said, keeping his voice to a whisper, 'what is there special about the vessel *Penalty*?'

'A fortune,' the Commandant answered. 'I have my fortune there.'

The Admiral pondered the Commandant's secret, at once eager to learn and distrustful of any revelations that might come later.

'It would be an honour to eat with you on the *Reconnaissance*,' the Admiral said, and promptly finished the liquor that remained in his glass.

Sasha watched the small boat pushing through the early dark. He would have liked to go ashore, because he had never set foot on an island; and that's what he thought islands were really made for. They were made in this way, so that you could feel what it was like to have the sea under you and all around you while you went on living like people on real land. He couldn't believe that any small portion of earth which was encircled by water and named an island could be real land. What happened to people who had been lost on such a place? There was a limit to the distance they could walk. And what would they decide when they had reached the edge, which would never be very far away?

The boy couldn't imagine an edge to the continent of Lime Stone. The land came down to the sea there too, but this was different. The size of the Kingdom was like the ocean itself. You would never reach any point that could be called the edge. This was the reason why he wanted to go ashore: just to feel what it was like when you lived so near the edge. Sasha might have expressed his curiosity before; but his private game was over. After the episode with Ivan, he could never start on any pursuit of collecting views again. Now he saw the Commandant's boat draw near, and he was glad he hadn't left the ship. He had discovered something he didn't know, something he might never have got the chance to know. He discovered that he was lonely while the Commandant was away. He didn't know it would be possible for him to miss the presence of the Commandant; yet that is what had happened. He was anxious for the Commandant to come back.

And he had learnt something else during the Commandant's absence. He was thinking of Pierre, and the way the carpenter had moved about the ship after the Commandant had gone. In a way, everything had grown more nervous. The boy couldn't explain what he meant; but there was an edge in the air. And sometimes it felt dangerous. The men took no chances with Pierre, who had orders to supervise the scrubbing of the deck. It seemed the men had forgotten the other Pierre who played the flute and was a man for fun. Now they regarded Pierre with a distant and slightly frightened curiosity.

Sasha had never imagined the carpenter in this way; that he could bring about this quiet and nervous respect in other men. It was the first time he had ever heard Pierre threaten anyone. He had heard Pierre tell one of the men that he would break his neck if he let the bucket fall from his hands a second time. Sasha thought it might have been a joke, the kind Pierre was likely to make, but Pierre wasn't smiling on this occasion, and it didn't look as though he would smile for a very long time to come. Then the look on the man's face told Sasha he was right. The man behaved as though Pierre had already broken his neck.

Sasha was glad he didn't go ashore. He didn't believe that a visit to the island could have produced anything equal to the thrill of what he had witnessed on the ship: the strange, fearful power of something hidden in Pierre, like a calamity kept out of sight.

The boy heard a shout of voices announcing that the small boat had arrived. Surgeon and Steward were hurrying from the Commandant's cabin. They separated in different directions before coming down to the lower deck. Sasha watched the small boat sway and dip with each new charge of a wave tossing it up against the ship. The men were now loud in their welcome as they lowered the ropes. They looked so attentive and efficient. It might have been a special parade. Then Sasha saw Ivan's legs swing through the air and land him firmly on the deck. The men were very quiet now as they watched the Commandant hoist himself up the ladders, making a leap onto the deck. He had let Ivan go first. It seemed so strange, Sasha thought: that the Commandant should give pride of place to the painter.

Then there was an uproar of voices, and the Commandant was laughing as no one had ever seen him laugh before. The men continued to stamp and shout with joy; and Sasha found himself clapping and wondering whether he did so because the Commandant looked so happy or whether it was at the news that they would all feast on the deck, and the Admiral Badaloza of Dolores would be their guest.

The cooks were the heroes of the night. Everyone applauded their labours. Their cooking had no precedent in the experience of the men. The tables of kings on the most celebrated of festive gatherings had never been graced with such a delicacy and power of flavour. Every tongue had been captivated; but if the applause was a historic experience, it was nothing to compare with the studied modesty of the cooks.

'It is the occasion makes the man,' Duclos had said in his reply to the Commandant's toast.

Later his assistant was to judge the matter in a more sceptical tone.

'The stomach is the seat of favour,' the young cook said; and then added, as though it were a matter for the strictest confidence: 'Feed a monster well, and he may yet smile.'

'God provides, and the human hand decides,' Ivan said; 'what happens is a matter of character. The cooks are men of some character.'

'Let a man discover his opportunity,' Baptiste said, 'and the result will always be a matter for surprise.'

'Some praise must fall on Pierre,' said the young cook; 'his supervision was an example of command.'

'Thank you,' said Pierre.

Baptiste didn't acknowledge this tribute. He wouldn't let their attention be distracted from the achievement of the cooks.

'What is superlative must stay that way,' he said; 'the feast was superlative.'

'And not without due supervision,' Pierre said sharply. The tone was almost caustic.

'What is superlative is superlative,' said Baptiste.

'Superlative is a fitting title,' a voice said. 'I pay my dues to that. The cooks came superlative.'

'Those who can't eat must praise,' a man said. 'Some born to do, some born to witness. When I witness excellence, I praise. Tonight I am nothing but praise.'

Listening to this chorus of applause, the boy, Sasha, was thinking how different everything seemed when the men had joined to speak well of someone. It might have been the presence of the Commandant, who had eaten with them like any common hand on the deck. But the atmosphere was no less friendly now that the Commandant had left, taking the Admiral back to his quarters. The air of the feast remained hypnotic, almost sacred. Any voice that had dissented from this note of satisfaction would have been inviting a curse on itself. Sasha almost felt dizzy by the novelty of the occasion. He had never seen such a quantity of food, nor felt such excitement as when he tasted the bronzed neck of the guinea fowl. He had been served a whole one, small, yes, but the size was not noticed in the excitement of his discovery that it was whole. All his eating had been of the parts of some kind of meat: legs, wings, a head, the neck, or the fins of the black angel fish, which he adored; he had never had anything whole. It gave him an impression of completeness that was out of all proportion to the size of the bird. He felt lost away from the Commandant, but it was a delicious sensation—as if submerged by the jubilant promise of the men's voices.

Some huge reservoir of good feeling had sucked him in. This too was a kind of knowledge, a kind of learning that entered through the pores of the skin, never to be let out again, dispersing and going deep inside where words and argument could make no lasting contact. That's why it was so difficult sometimes to tell some truth about yourself, to dig up this kind of learning, which had let itself in through the pores of your skin, resisting every effort of memory to be brought out again. He heard someone say: 'When a thing like this happens, nothing can undo it. If I never eat again, tonight will still be tonight.'

The space above his head was thick with tobacco smoke. The wide rings bellied in and burst, making a new formation of cloud, great saucers that cracked and slithered down, until a breeze swallowed them out of sight.

Someone was going to make a speech, but it seemed he had forgotten what he wanted to say. He was looking at Pierre, who sat opposite him; and it seemed that Pierre was somehow the cause of this lapse of memory. Sasha recalled that it was the man whose neck Pierre had threatened to break if he let the bucket fall again. The man had given up his attempt to speak. It was as though the words had got blocked up somewhere in his throat. The meaning was clear to his mind; but a passage in his throat would not let any noise through.

Suddenly he smiled, waved his hand respectfully around the deck, and sat down. There was tremendous applause.

'A magnificent silence,' said Pierre. 'A magnificent silence.'

The man was laughing, as though he understood what Pierre meant. He laughed like a drunk when Pierre repeated this tribute to his silence. Now everyone was laughing, not in mockery, but rather from some vague awareness that the episode could only be appreciated in this way. And the boy puzzled over this laughter. It was not about rejoicing. And yet he could not deny that it was the same sort of laughter. It seemed they would never stop.

Night. It's night, yes, but it was happening again. Ivan could hear the crush of pebbles in his ears. He must have journeyed through this tunnel of earth before; touched these blades of corn, the blossoming seeds of pepper scattered over the ground. His vision was happening again. Not the stars, no. Not the stars. It was a spell of daylight that had suddenly opened his eyes onto the moon. Ivan could see a fleet of ships move grimly through the sudden fires of a morning. They grew tall and menacing with welcome as they came towards the shore. The native hands were busy collecting wood for fire, wood for war. Their hands were hot and sorrowful after a last embrace; then a wild surprise of good-byes consumed their sight. The natives of San Cristobal were dividing for the purpose of defence. Many would not meet again. But they had opened the earth with spades, leaving behind as many graves as there were hands among them. And they were numerous. Ivan marvelled at this lack of weariness in their hands. It was incredible how much digging they had done. Each grave was many times the ordinary height of a man; then they covered the hole with a deceptive turf of dirt and leaves. Ever so easy to enter, an enemy would have little chance of getting out from the ground that would follow after him. Such was their strategy of defence before making for the tunnel which took them underground and out of sight. Ivan must have been there before. He knew this wind that sang to him from the corners of the moon. The ships had sunk to the floor of the ocean. And the island was there. Dull and grave in the morning. But the moon had put a shadow over his eyes. He heard the voices calling to him; but he wasn't sure where they came from. His trance had obliterated all evidence of the men on deck.

'Ivan.'

'Ivan, Ivan.'

'Ivan.'

Then he recognized the music of Lime Stone. Someone was singing while the men collected around him, impatient for his powers to tell their future. The singing came abruptly to an end after Pierre had spoken.

PIERRE: What's the moon saying tonight, Ivan?
DUCLOS: Come on, come on! What is it you see up there?
PIERRE: Why do you go dumb, Ivan?
  'It isn't easy to read,' Ivan said after a long pause.
DUCLOS: It is never easy to read the moon.
PIERRE: Quiet, quiet. And let Ivan get it over.

Ivan seemed to have some misgivings; but such a watchful silence reigned over the men that he felt it might have been dangerous to delay them.

IVAN: I notice a change ever since we drop anchor here at Dolores. The moon was getting larger and larger with every mile we advance to San Cristobal.

DUCLOS: You think it's a different moon?

PIERRE: It's the same face that looks down on Lime Stone.

IVAN: It is the same face, to be sure. But I can't read it too smoothly these days.

PIERRE: Nights, nights, Ivan. What's wrong with you? It is only at night that you read the moon.

MARCEL: If you can't read it, you can't read it. But what do you see in it? Can't you see anything at all?

IVAN: It seems.

PIERRE: Quiet, quiet, and hear Ivan.

IVAN: I see the island. San Cristobal, it must be. I see the island exact in shape as I hear it described by the men of Lime Stone who have been here before. Exact ... in shape, size, and colours. Exact.

DUCLOS: Go on, Ivan. It seems the stars are letting you down these days.

PIERRE: Nights, Duclos, stars make night light. Make them say something, Ivan, something to please our waiting.

IVAN: You can't bribe the stars, Pierre. But I see there ...

PIERRE: Quiet, quiet, and hear Ivan. Let's hear Ivan.

BAPTISTE: Stars and moons! Say, Marcel, pass me some liquor and put a stop to my hearing. It makes a man furious to hear such talk on the eve of arrival. San Cristobal is but a day away from Dolores, a favourable wind allowing. The liquor, Marcel!

DUCLOS: What are you furious about? Tonight should make any man relax.

BAPTISTE: Relax? I have done nothing else all my life. And you, you.

MARCEL: Be careful, Baptiste. For a moment you sound moon crazy.

BAPTISTE: But I have my own moon. Right here inside my head, inside my skull.

DUCLOS: I think Marcel is right.

BAPTISTE: What do you say, Duclos?

DUCLOS: That Marcel may be right. The moon is on you.

PIERRE: Leave him alone. It is Ivan we must hear. Go on, Ivan, what was it you see?

DUCLOS: The island, Ivan. You say you see San Cristobal, exact as you hear it described.

IVAN: San Cristobal?

PIERRE: You say you see it, Ivan. Exact. Go on, go on. What else do you see?

IVAN: Exact, exact. It is like a turtle in shape, with a black shell flashing rainbows over the ocean. The sea makes horseshoes into the coast, round and round to the far end, where the earth is like an orchard of spices high up; and below, far, far down moving to the heart of the land, the cane is waving like spears ... there's a lake, sky blue on top, with a coral floor of stones. It sparkles like ice....

PIERRE: Go on, Ivan. We are hearing you.

BAPTISTE: I know the lake, Ivan.

IVAN: The trees hang like hair over tall springs of sulphur.

BAPTISTE: That's where the rheumatics go for cure. I know them.

PIERRE: Why do you stop, Ivan? What is it you see now? What is it, Ivan? Tell us.

IVAN: I see a footpath not wider than my hands spread out. It climbs around the trees up and up to a cliff that hangs white and sacred as a cross over the sea.

MARCEL: Do you see anyone?

PIERRE: What people?

IVAN: I see a woman.

DUCLOS: Now we are getting somewhere.

PIERRE: Be quiet, Duclos, or we'll throw you to the sharks. What people, Ivan?

MARCEL: How many would you say?

IVAN: One woman.

DUCLOS: She won't be enough for this crew.

PIERRE: Give us some facts. What is she doing?

IVAN: She is standing on the cliff with a jar of leaves in one hand. Now it looks like wine, but it could be blood that looks

like wine. The leaves are melting into wine. And the colour is
blood.

BAPTISTE: Blood, you say?

MARCEL: I don't like the colour of what you see, Ivan.

IVAN: I tell you what I see.

DUCLOS: The moon is going under cloud. Here, Ivan, have a
drink until she comes out.

BAPTISTE: Go on, Ivan, you may need it. Have a drink.

MARCEL: He is still gazing.

PIERRE: But he can't see the moon while it's under cloud.

MARCEL: Have a drink. We will wait.

IVAN: There was a cloud where the woman was standing.

DUCLOS: You mean a shadow.

IVAN: No.... There was a cloud where the woman was standing.

PIERRE: Whoever saw a cloud on the ground?

IVAN: I saw it then. Drifting up to hide the ship in her hand.
She was holding a ship in the other hand.

DUCLOS: A ship? Holding a ship?

BAPTISTE: Not a ship, Ivan.

IVAN: It is a ship, Baptiste. Exact in shape and build.

BAPTISTE: In shape and build?

IVAN: Exact like ours. Like *Reconnaissance*, Baptiste.

MARCEL: The stars are letting you down, Ivan. The native women
have no such knowledge of a ship like ours. You can ask
Baptiste. Or Boatswain, if you choose.

IVAN: The woman is not native, Marcel.

MARCEL: What do you say?

BAPTISTE: What is she, then?

IVAN: Of Lime Stone, to be sure.

DUCLOS: Of Lime Stone?

IVAN: The Lady ...

MARCEL: Go on, Ivan, Ivan.

BAPTISTE: Ivan, Ivan, go on. Ivan.

But Ivan didn't speak again; and the men were suddenly distracted by the sound of voices that came from the Commandant's cabin. The Admiral was in high spirits as he stumbled
through the dark towards the lower deck. He was full of admiration for the enterprise. His attendants were waiting in two boats

below; but the Admiral seemed reluctant to bring this celebration to an end. He was about to descend the ladders, then paused to embrace the Commandant in a final gesture of farewell. The officers stood close behind, their hands raised in salute. Pinteados alone had remained in his cabin; but his absence was hardly noticed by the men, who had been intoxicated by the splendour of the feast.

The Admiral was still elaborating on the virtues of the Commandant: the genius that could combine austerity of command with such a liberal feeling for his men. The Admiral was halfway down the ladders, but the men could still hear his voice in a rhapsody of praise. The moon rode over the cloud to show the small boats carving through the water towards the shore. The Commandant waved for the last time, then turned to applaud the men for their loyalty to the enterprise.

'Tomorrow, with the earliest wind,' the Commandant shouted, 'favourable or otherwise, we sail on San Cristobal.'

The men were loud with praise. And the boy, Sasha, thought how everything was different now. It was a rare thing for the Commandant to announce a plan in the presence of the general crew. Sasha's private game was over, but it seemed his secret learning of the men would never come to an end.

EIGHTEEN

Priest had assembled the crew at dawn. The sky was a battlefield of light, sun and moon fighting for supremacy over the hills. The clouds were a regiment of scarlet horses in the east. And back of the hills, over an orchard of coffee trees, the moon was falling. The air shivered where the light opened like fingers, pale and twisted, until the mountain arranged its peaks like a chain of hands held high, surrendering their final postures to a sudden burst of sunlight. It was the subtlest drama of sun and moon they had ever seen, two territories of light alive at once in the same dark tower of sky. This was how dawn happened over the gentle hills and valleys of the islands. The wind came fresh and amiable, like the touch of hands. There was an echo of birdsong in every breeze, a feel of leisure in the pace of the wind. Less than a day away, the island of San Cristobal would emerge from a long coast of sand and pebble where an ancient tide of seahorses had ridden and left a signature of hooves around the island. And everywhere the waves would show a breed of blue fish that had to fly for safety.

They had arrived; would soon finally arrive. And Priest, never forgetful of his office, had been schooling his flock in the discipline of prayer. But he had sensed a gradual decline in the men's enthusiasm for his calling. They had been listening out of habit. There was no evidence of terror in this gentle bay; and their lack of fear had reduced their need of Priest and the service he had rendered in more perilous zones. The men were eager to be on their way. They heard the clap of the wind where hands were beginning to slacken the sails.

The boy had arrived with an order from the Commandant. It was like the day of their departure from Lime Stone, when he had seen the men in a sudden fever of work as he went with the orders for the officers to meet in the Commandant's cabin. Priest, Boatswain, and Steward. In that order. Yet everything was different here. There was no hidden menace in the waters that lapped almost without sound up the ship's bow. Sasha had left the Commandant seated at the council table, a huge pile of charts and papers crowding his gaze. But his mood was gay. There was no atmosphere of emergency in the cabin. They had arrived, would finally arrive within a day or two.

Priest walked slowly behind the boy, who had come to a halt outside the Commandant's cabin. There he would wait until it was time to summon Boatswain.

The Commandant had got up to receive Priest into the cabin. There was a hint of mischief in his welcome.

'If we are cursed with a calamity, I shall know who put it there,' the Commandant said.

His bow was slow and deliberate. Priest smiled. Or rather, some instinct ordered a parting of his lips.

'It is a fair day,' he said, clasping·the Commandant's hand in his.

The Commandant used both hands to return his greeting. But his manner was soon grave again. It changed rapidly, like the rivalry of sunlight and the clouds racing outside.

'It will be a cheerful day,' said the Commandant, 'or else I know who has been at work.'

'Out of our hands, Commandant. The temper of the winds is quite out of our hands.'

'In a manner of speaking,' the Commandant said, 'but we have a duty. Nature will sometimes bend to your feeling.'

'In a manner of speaking, as you say,' Priest said. 'Sometimes the manner makes the event. I can agree there.'

'You do not go all the way?'

'I do not go beyond my station,' Priest said. 'There is a higher power than my willing.'

'And so there is,' the Commandant agreed.

He had gone back to his seat. Then Priest sat; a smile passed like shadow over his mouth, and his eyes closed briefly in prayer. The Commandant calmly observed his face, as though it were a map of remote and indefinable frontiers. He wanted to put Priest at ease, to make him feel a necessary part of every plan which now concerned their immediate future. The time had come to reveal his intentions; to clarify the principles that would govern their daily living on San Cristobal. He had selected a large sheet of paper from the pile of documents on the council table. He brought the page close to his eyes, blocking Priest from his view. He was reading slowly, gravely, hearing each syllable arouse some echo of danger from the past. He continued reading as though he had forgotten, for a moment, the importance of this meeting with Priest. He was reading his own writing like a child new to the alphabet, forever on the lookout for some error:

First and foremost in all our calculations was the safety of our sister ship, the vessel Penalty, *then lawfully moored in the capital harbour and waiting in disguise until all agents under the pilot's direction had discharged every item of provisioning.*

Avoiding all conflict with the Law ...

The Commandant paused and lowered the sheet of paper.

'I need you,' he said, relaxing his glance as he looked towards Priest. This admission was so abrupt and so unexpected that Priest leaned forward to confirm his alarm. He was about to ask the Commandant whether all was well, but the Commandant was quick to dispel any fears about their future. Priest's smile had surfaced.

'Your need is our service,' Priest said. 'That's why we are here.'

'It's about the men down below,' the Commandant said, moving with deliberate caution towards his meaning. 'I get reports about their impatience to arrive.'

'I know,' Priest said, and it seemed he was about to rise from his chair. 'This impatience, as you say. It has even cast a certain shadow on some of the officers. They suspect such exuberance in their subordinates.'

'It's about the men down below,' the Commandant said promptly. 'The officers are another matter.'

He seemed indifferent to any news about the officers.

'Of course,' Priest hurried, as though his memory had played him a trick for the Commandant's amusement. 'You have been liberal with them to a very great measure. There can be no complaint. Not that their impatience shows complaint. I would not say it goes that far.'

The Commandant had raised the sheet of paper like a screen between them. He had continued to read his own writing, timing the moment he would make his meaning clear. And Priest waited, eager and speechless, as he watched the gradual movement of the Commandant's head behind the screen of paper:

Avoiding all conflict with the Law, Penalty *had put out to sea, though some portion of her cargo was to enter without any truthful declaration of content or purpose. In all matters affecting my ultimate ambition, Pinteados had become the very shadow of my ears on land, as he was now to prove the eyes that would steer me from the thieves of the sea....*

In all matters affecting my ultimate ambition ...

The Commandant steered the paper down his face until it rested on the scar which showed the base of his chin.

'I have the ultimate proposition which I would like you to

247

sanction,' the Commandant said.

'My sanction, Commandant!' Priest struggled to conceal his astonishment.

'Yes, your sanction,' the Commandant assured him. 'It comes within your care, I would say.'

'A spiritual matter, I take it.'

'In a manner of speaking, it is,' the Commandant said.

Priest looked relieved. He felt the holy authority of his office come to his aid. But it was brief.

'A spiritual matter, to be sure,' the Commandant repeated. 'It concerns the sexual appetites of the men down below. These must be satisfied, you will agree.'

Priest felt his eyes burn wet. He could barely see where his glance was fixed on the Commandant's face.

'Do you speak of normal practice, sir?'

'I speak no other way but normal,' the Commandant said.

'This is most extreme,' Priest ventured.

'The result must be made normal,' the Commandant replied. 'The vessel *Penalty* will be waiting with a cargo of women when we arrive at the Isles of the Black Rock.'

Priest was embarrassed by his failure to understand. He considered the globe on the cabin table, entreating the future to school him in his duties.

'A cargo of women,' he mused. 'Forgive me if I think of the effect on the men.'

'That's why I need you,' the Commandant said. 'The matter must be done in a way that does not make for a general looseness of feeling.'

His tone was free of mischief. He had subdued Priest by exorcising all his previous fears.

'What do you propose, sir?' Priest asked.

But he couldn't be sure the Commandant had heard. The sheet of paper had come between them again. The Commandant was reading more quickly now, his eyes racing feverishly ahead of what he actually saw. It was his memory which served him as a guide:

I had determined to cause this crew of former strangers to break free and loose from the ancient restrictions of the King-

dom of Lime Stone, and I declare it was my pride and no less to build from this battalion of vandals and honest men alike such an order as might be the pride and example of excellence to Lime Stone herself; that I would plant some portion of the Kingdom in a soil that is new and freely chosen, namely the Isles of the Black Rock, more recently known as San Cristobal. For I have seen men of the basest natures erect themselves into gentlemen of honour the moment....

He had given his attention back to Priest.

'What do I propose, you ask?' the Commandant said, returning the sheet of paper to the pile of documents. 'What would you propose for these women who are waiting at San Cristobal?'

Priest was clawing his nails along the table. Suddenly he checked himself and made an effort to smile. Now his voice went hoarse, sore with apology for his failure to understand.

'You wouldn't be thinking of a forced union?' he asked.

'To be exact, yes,' the Commandant said sternly. 'A forced union made holy.'

'The situation sounds most abnormal, sir.' Priest was stammering. 'It never came my way before.'

'But you have known more abnormal situations,' the Commandant said. 'To be born again is not normal, or was it just an agent of malice who reported you eaten by cannibals on the coast of black cargoes? But here you are, Priest. Alive and ready to be my shepherd of the islands.'

Priest couldn't speak, shuddering in every muscle as he heard the Commandant reveal this intimate knowledge of his history. He had hoped no evidence of his history would threaten his future on this enterprise. But the Commandant knew and was using his knowledge to some deliberate purpose. In no circumstance could he now think of resisting any plan which the Commandant willed him to execute. The Commandant knew; and he had served warning that his knowledge could be made lethal as any weapon of war.

Priest was collecting his hands, rehearsing them slowly for an act of prayer. He felt the wooden crucifix hang more heavily from his neck.

'And the men, sir?' Priest said. 'How will they respond?'

There was a hint of impatience in the Commandant's reply.

'An early reluctance, yes,' the Commandant said, 'but they will bend.'

Priest nodded. An insect was ferreting through the hairs of his armpit. But he refused to recognize the appeal of his body. His composure had become absolute. He nodded again to the Commandant.

'Tell me my duties, and I am at your service.'

'You will prepare the ground,' the Commandant said, paying tribute with a smile. 'Remember, we have broken loose from the restrictions of Lime Stone, and therefore free from all previous philosophies of the Kingdom.'

His glance had found the wooden crucifix which rested on the slope of Priest's stomach. "Who else could make the matter appear in holy order?" he was thinking. But the crucifix had halted his speech for a while.

'To reverse all previous philosophies,' the Commandant now said. And his eyes darted from the pile of documents to the door. 'I do not accept the old order that such a plantation as ours must first be built by men; and seen to be safely established before women may honourably join them in daily living. You see the importance of the *Penalty*'s cargo, or do you not?'

His eyes had darted at the door, and Priest knew that this was a signal that it would soon be time to go.

'I understand,' he said, making to rise from the chair.

'Then who else could make such a matter appear in holy order?' the Commandant said.

And Priest acknowledged the privilege that was conferred upon him. He understood and gave the Commandant's boldness his silent blessing. The *Penalty*, with its cargo of women, would be their secret: the Commandant's and his.

He was bowing again as he reversed cautiously through the door. Outside he could hear the screaming voices of the men who were labouring joyfully down below.

NINETEEN

Now the sun was truly launched. It had burnt up the last precipice of cloud. There was no wind at all, and the heat had struck
without warning. The sea sparkled: the sky was a mountain of
blue rock. The morning poured like rain through the cabin port.
The Commandant felt the taste of salt on his lips; but he showed
no awareness of the heat. He had decided against any interview
with Steward. But he had sent the boy to summon Boatswain. At
the first promise of a wind he would give the order to sail; but
he had experienced some vague sense of guilt when he thought
of Boatswain, who had not quite recovered from the shock of the
Commandant's orders against receiving any cargoes of black flesh.
The familiar taste of the salt air now softened his feeling towards
Boatswain. The smell of the islands reminded him of some old,
forgotten debt of loyalty to him. He pondered the globe on the
council table. The charts dazzled his memory with names. He was
battling against the sentiment that was leading back to his earliest
encounter with the Isles of the Black Rock. There was a glint of
water in his eyes as his gaze rambled over the sheet of paper he
had taken from the council table:

*More than twenty summers ago, it was this same isle of gold
that gave me my first glimpse of the yellow metal. My very first
Voyage it was, when I was eager and knew what it was to be a
beast before the prey of great fortune; second to none in exercising the terrors that forced the Tribes to volunteer their services
to us and all men who had brought them no less a reward than
a knowledge of the true light. We had to drive them like cattle
from the fields and pastures, leaving ripe grain to rot, and a mighty
famine that would overtake even the unborn....*

The Commandant had halted with his reading. He thought

he heard a footstep outside the door, but no one was there. He shook the moisture from his eyes and quickly finished his reading:

Now my ambition is in reverse; and I reckon it is a more noble preference to plant some portion of Lime Stone in the virgin territories of San Cristobal. This purpose I declare to be absolute and true....

'Virgin territories.' He was talking to himself as though he had suddenly discovered some error in his meaning. But there was a sound of footsteps approaching; and he quickly put the paper out of sight.

When Boatswain entered the cabin, the Commandant was pouring himself a drink. The door was open, and they could hear the sound of voices contending on the lower deck. The Commandant didn't get up; and Boatswain, who was familiar with the charts that hung round the room, selected one for his special attention.

'Drink?'

'As you wish, sir,' said Boatswain.

The Commandant filled a small cup with wine while Boatswain continued to refresh his memory from familiar details on the chart. There was no sound to his movement as he turned away and followed the Commandant's invitation to sit at the opposite end of the table. The Isles of the Black Rock were near and vivid as human voices in their ears. San Cristobal curled like a pebble in the Commandant's hands.

'You remember San Souci?' the Commandant asked.

'Speak of memory, sir,' said Boatswain, raising his cup in a mutual toast.

'And Belle Vue?' the Commandant added.

'San Souci and Belle Vue,' Boatswain mused. 'And Morne, Chacachacare, and the Demon Coast.'

There was a look of melancholy and daring in Boatswain's eyes, a pride of nostalgia for shared secrets. He had made as many voyages as the Commandant himself.

'San Souci!' the Commandant said, filling Boatswain's cup with wine again. 'You came between me and my grave at San Souci.'

'It was in my own interest, sir,' said Boatswain, 'then as now.'

The Commandant understood his meaning and was cordial in rebuke.

NATIVES OF MY PERSON

'It was a bigger feeling,' he said.

'I was good as finished if the Commandant had expired,' Boatswain said. 'I felt strong interest there. With the Commandant gone, I had as much future as a corpse. That's the truth.'

'You had a bigger feeling,' the Commandant said. 'I know it as a certainty.'

But Boatswain refused this tribute to his virtue. He was appealing to the charts for evidence against himself.

'A whole life you put at my disposal, sir,' said Boatswain. 'Let the natives dig that dagger into your back at San Souci, and I would have been less than rotten cargo.'

'You had a bigger feeling,' the Commandant insisted. 'You have covered any debt to Lime Stone with your service.'

'A long time ago,' Boatswain said. 'That was a long time ago.'

A ragged sound of music drifted up from the deck. The voices had put an end to Boatswain's interest in the charts. He wanted to concentrate on matters that were near at hand. His attention was divided between the Commandant's exuberance and the dark omen of the painter's vision. Now he was like a man whose presence suggested that a whisper was the safest way of being heard. Some instinct of foreboding ruled his judgment. To be alive was to be warned.

'Commandant!'

'What is your trouble?'

Suddenly it seemed that Boatswain's memory had sprung a leak. His silence was like a temporary loss of face.

'Catch a breath and tell us,' the Commandant said. 'Tell it your way.'

'Thank you, sir.'

'No gratitude,' the Commandant advised; 'just tell it your way.'

'Down below,' Boatswain began, and he looked horrified at the prospect of visiting misfortune on the ship.

'Come straight to the business, Boatswain.'

'The matter is this, and no more,' said Boatswain; 'I carry no tales, sir, but I feel you may arouse rebellion by the favours you allow the men down below.'

'Speak for your own division,' the Commandant interrupted.

'So I speak,' Boatswain went on. His manner was solicitous and precise.

'They eat superior. The music never stops. They know of your instructions against punishment at the officers' hands. But their impatience to see San Cristobal. I do not like their eagerness to be on land.'

'What do you advise?' the Commandant said. The challenge was too abrupt. It made Boatswain feel like a rival if he dared to reply.

'I seek an opinion, sir,' said Boatswain. 'Suppose they turn such exuberance to their advantage. I mean, suppose they were to join in open insult to the officers when we are on land.'

The Commandant appeared a little distracted; and Boatswain got the feeling that he had betrayed his mission. He needed some assurance against a threat to his status.

'It is their taste for argument,' he said. 'Not that it could ever reach a point beyond the Commandant's orders, but I would say a harmony of feeling would be safer.'

The Commandant surveyed the cabin, his eyes making a slow, patient inventory of the furniture. Then he slapped his hands against the table as though some arbitrary power of instruction had got beyond control in its desire to be heard.

'You have a command, Boatswain, remember that.'

Lucid as daylight, the words had awakened Boatswain from any premonition of danger. The reproach conferred a surprising boldness on Boatswain's reply.

'I have a command, as you say. That I know.'

'Then use your head,' the Commandant retorted.

'Even to answer insult with a life?' Boatswain demanded.

'Whatever the circumstance,' the Commandant advised, 'use your head. And never treat the unexpected as emergency.'

Boatswain recognized that their interview was drawing to a close. By the authority of his glance towards the door, the Commandant had given him an obvious and familiar signal. This moment was the dead end of any future speculation. Boatswain rose from his seat and stood erect.

But there was a gradual change in the Commandant's mood. He had felt again this stubborn force of loyalty as he observed the dark, menacing scowl in Boatswain's face. Boatswain's eyes had grown sullen and heavy with brooding, docile and troubled by some secret fear. The Commandant couldn't resist the urge to come to his aid.

'Most of the crew are not like us,' the Commandant said, pawing gently at the chart. 'We have been out here before, you and me, on the same expedition. I am relying on your experience.'

'Yes, sir,' Boatswain said, responding quickly to the tone of comradeship in the Commandant's voice.

'I want you to keep a close watch on the younger men.'

'I know how they think, sir; I can manage them.'

Already the hint of equal participation had made Boatswain sound more cheerful.

'Whatever your rank and mine,' the Commandant continued, 'our business is the same. You must make that clear to every man.'

'I know when to speak to them, sir,' Boatswain assured him.

Boatswain was an officer again, a man on the inside, preparing himself to show disdain at any rumour of trouble. But the painter's visions were still getting in his way. He could feel the weight of some private terror threaten his composure.

'It's been a very long journey,' the Commandant comforted, 'but it will be the last.'

'I hope so, sir,' said Boatswain.

The Commandant glanced at the bowl of wine and thought of offering him another drink; but he had sensed Boatswain's eagerness to be relieved.

'Tomorrow we should see the coast of San Cristobal at dawn,' the Commandant promised.

'Yes, sir.'

'Any confessions of trouble can safely wait,' the Commandant said. 'Now I would advise an interval of peace. Take to your cabin if you wish, and rest until the men announce the coast of San Cristobal.'

The Commandant nodded towards the door.

'At your service,' said Boatswain, and briefly pondered the charts before going.

TWENTY

But the painter's vision had robbed Boatswain of any hope of peace. He thought he saw a ghost in every glance. It had driven him to seek refuge in Priest's cabin. He had come to make a final confession before their arrival at San Cristobal. Boatswain considered the large wooden crucifix sloping forward from the timber beam in Priest's cabin. The silver head, with its circle of thorns, gave an illusion of massiveness, as though it would fall at the slightest shudder of the room. He saw nothing but that head and the beam which supported it, climbing past the ceiling. He would have preferred to talk to the dumb statue alone, but he had already put his request to Priest. He wanted an assurance that required no promises on his part—that's what Priest was there for.

Now he became suspicious. Perhaps this was part of the Commandant's strategy; for a moment he saw Priest as a sort of channel through which every recorded privacy passed on its way to the Commandant's attention. Perhaps Priest served a purpose other than his calling. Instinctively, Boatswain thought of a bargain; could he buy Priest's silence against any knowledge the Commandant might order him to reveal? The thought of such a conspiracy made him tremble: to conspire against the Commandant and insult the crucifix by inviting its chosen messenger to be an accomplice.

'You suspect too much,' said Priest. 'Or if I may put it another way, you trust too little.'

He steadied Boatswain's hands and looked into his eyes as though he were appealing to a child. Boatswain felt the cold, gentle fingers caress his hands: the mysterious aura of the crucifix was wrapping its silver crown about his wrists. He might have been in chains: he could hear the scream of a voice hounding him to damnation, and the chase of feet pursuing him to the limits of the earth.

But Boatswain still believed the evidence of Ivan's eyes.

'The painter saw her ghost,' he said, imploring Priest to exorcise his fear.

'You are a man of the faith,' said Priest, 'but you trust too little. When did it happen?'

'When did what happen?' he asked.

The question had suddenly freed Boatswain from the power of the crucifix. He was brought back to the domain of mortal judgment.

'I mean your loss of faith,' said Priest. 'When did you feel it start to die?'

'To die,' Boatswain stammered. 'When? What started to die?'

'You burden yourself too much,' said Priest; 'whatever your fear may be, you cannot bear it alone.'

'I was alone,' Boatswain said sharply. He had startled Priest by the abruptness of his manner. An aggressive insistence on facts now influenced his judgment.

'We should pray together,' Priest said.

He shoved Priest's hands away and stood.

The cabin suddenly appeared more spacious. The light swam through the porthole and washed the room. The air felt clean and sharp everywhere.

'You know why I am on this ship?' Boatswain said, staring at Priest.

'Why are all of us on this ship?' Priest said. 'Each has his reason, but all are joined by the same need. You are here to serve the Commandant.'

The words had made no impression on Boatswain. He might have been waiting for Priest to finish some small private chore other than speech. He didn't hear anything but the sound 'Commandant', which brought his attention back to Priest.

'What about the Commandant?' he asked, and as quickly he had decided to ignore the question.

'I want you to listen to me,' he said. 'With your own ears, not the Commandant's. And carefully. Because I warn, Priest. There will be danger if I am betrayed.'

'Do I look a traitor?' Priest said, appearing to rebuke him.

'Did you ever serve at Little Aberlon?'

Priest was slow to answer. The name was like an adder in his ear. It was the office he had held before making his first Voyage to the coast of the black flesh.

'I knew Little Aberlon,' Priest admitted. His voice was cold; and his eyes drew narrow. The mouth puckered up, grim and defensive. 'I believe it is much in the news at this moment.'

'I made it,' said Boatswain.

'What do you mean, you made it?' Priest queried. 'Little Aberlon is a church and a town.'

'I mean the news,' Boatswain said. 'I don't know who made the church. But I made the news. That I did.'

Boatswain looked at his hands, splaying the fingers wide and crushing the joints until he heard them creak.

'It is there they must have found the Lady,' said Boatswain.

Priest felt a clot of air suddenly harden in his throat.

'You mean the Lady of the House?' he whispered.

Priest could not recognize his own feeling. His voice was an astonished mutter directed to no particular purpose.

'I did it,' Boatswain said, and looked at his hands as though he was depending on them to verify everything he was going to say.

He could feel the bewilderment of Priest, who had quietly walked past him and taken a seat on the bunk. The light crowded the porthole, sweeping the ceiling clean of shadow. Boatswain's face was grave; his eyes had the blunt, immobile look of stone.

'Did you say you killed her?' Priest said. This was simply his way of getting Boatswain to continue.

'With these,' Boatswain said, raising his hands, as though they were unknown tools he had hired for the occasion.

'But I don't understand,' Priest said. 'We have been at sea. Away from Lime Stone.'

'Compare the time it took for report to reach us,' Boatswain explained. 'We hadn't left when it happened.' He was defiant.

'And even if that be true,' Priest argued, 'Antarctica's vessels reported the death of those responsible.'

Boatswain raised his hands again and stared, as though he was imploring his flesh to speak.

'They took men,' Boatswain said, 'but they were not responsible. That I can assure you.'

'But what am I hearing?' Priest said. And his voice grew to a shout. 'Why do you want to take this burden on yourself? Are you out of your mind?'

'I may be mad to confess it now,' Boatswain answered, 'but I was not mad then. Will you listen?'

Priest conceded. He drew his body up and started to spread his hands out level over his knees, but he couldn't finish, as though clothes resisted his touch, were forcing his attention back to Boatswain.

'There was a saying in Little Aberlon,' Boatswain said, 'I don't know if you ever heard it. "Keep what you catch and catch what you can." '

'A code for cannibals,' Priest interjected.

'You know it?' Boatswain continued. 'Life was as the saying goes. That was the code among men who were blessed from birth with honour, men you had to hold in great praise for the reputation the nation gave them. "Keep what you catch, and catch what you can." Such men push me into my crime. I swear it to be so.'

Priest was silent. He had heard a note of personal doom in the name Little Aberlon. He was Lazarus come back to life, once shepherd of Little Aberlon, the small seaport that had grown fabulous with the rewards of adventure. Half the fortunes of the trading vessels were concentrated there: to the anguish and fury of the rest of Lime Stone. The taverns multiplied overnight. Men deserted their homes and congregated all day under the marquees. No one could tell who remained to supervise the offices which they had been chosen to occupy. They drank amidst a loud and repetitive licentiousness. Fortunes flooded their throats. Their houses, stately and overwhelmed with the spoils of privilege, served them as kennels, where they retired in the early morning to sleep. Affairs of state were conducted from the beds of concubines. Negotiations for the fitting of ships were sealed by the passing of a rumour. One slip of paper had the power of winds to sail men to the conquest of lands they had never seen. One signature could drive families to their doom. Men gambled irrationally. Debt was like a plague devouring the heart of any reasonable living; yet the miracle of spending reigned, like the hills that hovered above the sea, spreading a wild and dizzy magnificence over the town.

Priest was startled when Boatswain broke into his fearful recollection of Little Aberlon.

'A genuine poetry of corruption,' Boatswain said, 'that's what the Aberlon estate was when the Lady hired me, like you would choose a stud, to service her. Three times a week at night, and twice in the afternoon. I was grinding away, just for a chance to make contact with her husband. All I wanted was to get a word to the Lord Treasurer through her special privilege. I was a man who had to start from down below. There was no other way.'

'Heavens be merciful,' Priest exclaimed.

'Whatever you may judge,' Boatswain said, 'that's how it was. She put me to ignominious tasks, to pleasures that would condemn your hearing to hell. And all I wanted was to make contact. I was under sentence of death if I dare break it off. I don't have to tell you what power went with that family. Her husband didn't wear a crown, but hell would have been paradise if he had caught me. I was feeding her pleasures under sentence of death; and I daren't give it up. She wouldn't let me. She was plain and raw as any whore in speech: "You can choose between my cunt and your own grave," she would say. I decided there would be a grave, but not mine.'

Priest's lips trembled as he made the sign of the cross. He had difficulty focussing attention. More outrageous than Boatswain's confession of murder was the incredible account of his relation to the Lady of the House. Her husband had given distinguished service to the Kingdom, an heir to great office in affairs of state. Priest had never heard any scandal attached to the Lady's character. She was left much to herself, it was true; but that was the normal predicament of wives who had married into such status. There were many rumours of adulterous living in these circles; but this aberration had grown beyond the point of sinful error. It was the custom of the Kingdom among people of the same honourable rank.

'I think she just wanted to defile everything,' said Boatswain. 'I get the secret of the matter now. It reached me late, but it reached me all the same. She was hoping he would find us. That's what she wanted. Two pleasures at one go. The pleasure I give her and the pleasure of having her husband witness what she had come to. She chose me to defile him. There was that mentality in her. To defile! And it's how the church came to receive her corpse. She made me do it even there. With the altar for witness and all the holy saints in attendance, she would order me to bore into her. Under sentence of death she would order me to join in that defiling. And it was on such occasion that I felt these hands come closer and closer around her throat, till there was almost nothing between them but a kind of wet rag. I just left her there and made for safe shelter. I went into hiding. I was in hiding until it was time for this enterprise.'

Priest had grown very calm. This was perhaps the third change of emotion which he had experienced since Boatswain started on this confession. Boatswain's admission had alarmed him. He had a premonition that Boatswain was agitated by other matters. Perhaps the fateful prospect of the journey had put a strain on his reason. But the mention of Little Aberlon had given an air of reality to Boatswain's claim. Priest couldn't bring himself to believe what he was hearing, but he felt persuaded to listen. Then the matter changed again. Boatswain might have committed a murder, but his association with the Lady of the House was so improbable in the context of Little Aberlon and the Aberlon estate as he knew them. Yet Boatswain's harrowing detail had overwhelmed his doubt. In fact, it was no longer a question of doubt or certainty which exercised his mind. Priest could think only of the implications for the *Reconnaissance* and their enterprise.

'Boatswain.'

'Have you gone sick?' Boatswain asked. He thought he saw Priest's skin turned to green. An awful shadow of illness seemed to disfigure his complexion. His lips moved, but Boatswain could hear no sound.

'Shall I get the surgeon?' Boatswain asked.

Priest shook his head. He couldn't endure the presence of anyone else in the room.

'Where did you leave the body of the Lady?' Priest asked.

'In the church,' said Boatswain. 'Beneath the very altar she would desecrate.'

'May the Lord have mercy,' said Priest, making the sign of the cross once more.

If Boatswain's fate was to travel under sentence of death, Priest felt that his own lot was, perhaps, more anguished. He travelled under the sentence of being alive. He didn't know what he should advise. It seemed his training had deserted him. An excess of prayer may have rendered his powers of spirit feeble. The plague of living had got at him too. He glanced at Boatswain and thought, "Here is a dereliction, a total dereliction of person. But who am I to judge?" And he could find no answer that would appease his fear. One thing was sure, the Commandant would have to be warned before they caught the first wind for San Cristobal. *Reconnaissance* would have to be prepared for the vengeance of the House.

'Did she ever tell you any secrets of the House?' Priest asked.

Boatswain didn't appear to be listening.

'Did she ever tell you anything?' Priest asked again.

Boatswain shook his head. It had become other than part of his body. A weight that swung sideways when he heard Priest's voice.

'You don't remember anything at all?' Priest repeated.

'I never listened,' Boatswain said, as though he wanted to take leave of all speech. It was a task he couldn't cope with.

'Not a word you can remember?' Priest insisted.

'Yes,' Boatswain said. 'Sometimes she would say, "You are late." Another time she would say, "I am ready." I remember that. And her body lying naked for me to enter.'

Boatswain crushed his hands and stared up at the crucifix. He could feel his tongue move: slow, heavy, swimming in moisture. His lips were wet. An idiot's dribble leaked slowly down his chin.

'"I am ready,"' he repeated; 'that's what she would say. Then the animal I was would turn on. I was at my labours again.' He raised his hand to wipe his chin.

'Forgive us our sins,' said Priest, crossing himself.

'I deserve forgiveness,' Boatswain said. 'I had one reason. I wanted a chance to prove I could cope. I could make a future if I got that chance. What greater reason should make a man sin? I wanted to prove my honour, and there was no other way.'

Boatswain held his head with both hands, steering his glance around the limits of the room. He was soliciting pardon on behalf of the virtue which had trapped him into this fatal encounter. It was his supreme virtue to seek a chance. He would find again the skill and power he had once known. He had fought against his country's enemies. He had assisted in the plundering adventures that had brought glory to Lime Stone. He had a hand in the fortunes which had built its name: San Souci, Belle Vue. He was not without a record of service. The Commandant could be his witness.

'May her soul rest in peace,' said Priest, anticipating the vengeance of the House.

'She had no soul,' said Boatswain. 'A woman who would defile a man in that way. What soul is there to save?'

Boatswain's hands had come alive. They argued for him, emphasizing his right to redemption. He had been fortified by this secret knowledge of himself as a citizen who had served. If there were men who might commit themselves to some bestiality of need—a necessity of circumstance—it was also true that there were few so honoured by the virtue which had urged him to seek a chance.

'I had no other reason to kill her,' Boatswain said. 'It was the only way I could show myself as I was, show I was more than what I was doing. But she was nothing. Nothing but the pleasures she was feeling. What else could she be? Just defiling everything fortune gave her, defiling her husband, defiling his honour in the land. Just born to defile.'

'Forgive us, Lord,' said Priest.

'You waste your breath,' said Boatswain. 'I murdered her to save myself in my own eyes. But it was no punishment for what she was doing. To spare a holy wish for such a harlot!'

'Think of the men they have executed,' said Priest.

It was an astonishing reminder. It might have been the voice of the crucifix ordering Boatswain to consider the fatal punishment that had followed on his action; but he seemed unable to afford any thought at all. Priest's voice had wiped Boatswain's mind clean of everything except his knowledge of the man he was, the honour he had sought to prove.

'The men they hanged!' he said, turning his eyes away from Priest. 'You can't blame me for that. How was it my fault?

Answer that. Would you ask me to bear that, too? Now, would you?'

Priest heard the sombre pulse of the sea, and wished there was no territory but this sky, calm and without end.

'You must pray,' he said, walking towards Boatswain. 'It is not easy, but the answer is in the effort. Just try to say: "Forgive us." '

Boatswain heard the voices from the deck. The men were preparing the ship for early departure. He had to concentrate on what was immediate. A pace beyond the door a world would confront him with other tasks. He had to meet his division with the armour of dignity in which his office had trained him. He was in charge of men whose obedience was the test of his power to command. He knew this was what Priest might be thinking. You can't face men under your command in such a state of uncertainty. Fear made them more attentive. They noticed everything. The only way to gain the approbation of your superiors was to pay attention to their change of mood.

'You think I'm harsh?' Boatswain asked, in search of his confidence.

'Harsh it must be if that's your way,' Priest consoled. 'The result is what matters. It is the purpose behind your action. Be harsh if that's your way.'

Boatswain felt some consolation in this reflection. In a way Priest was expressing his own way of seeing things. There was nothing like the agreement of an equal in such a crisis of uncertainty. This assurance from Priest was enough to make him know his power again. Now he could appear on the deck, stride towards the forecastle, shout names, order his division to assemble, order them to disperse. He could be seen and heard for what he was: an officer, and therefore a man on the inside. Whatever fatality endangered his past, he had to anchor his future on this understanding.

'There is no wickedness a little time wouldn't put out of mind,' he said.

'Think only of your duty now,' Priest warned.

In a way, Boatswain resented this. He avoided any show of irritation, yet he felt he should let Priest know that he was at ease in his office.

'The first lesson is to threaten the lower orders against taking liberties,' he said. 'I have made every man master that.'

But the past was nudging discomfortingly at his memory again. Boatswain couldn't resist the parallel with the Lady of the House; she allowed no liberties, either. He performed according to her wish; like the men now under his command, his wish was their performance. They were there to execute his purpose. It grieved him to think that he couldn't avoid the example of the Lady of the House; that the memory of her was like the very principle which applied to his relations with the men.

'But you must never trespass on their rights,' he started to lecture Priest. 'It is the second lesson I apply. You train your subordinates to exercise their expected rights. Then they take no liberties. It works.'

'I've seen it work,' said Priest, smiling. He tried to look more cheerful as he listened to Boatswain, who was thinking: "Why is it always my turn to make things clear?" This impulse to reveal was a defect. It was not a trait he had noticed in Steward. And Priest, too, didn't let feeling give way too soon to speech. Even now it was there: that subtle wariness of manner that obscured his intention. Almost a lack of passion. Perhaps the habits of his holy calling had built these delicate shadows that obscured his eyes. "He has heard a lot," Boatswain thought. "He has heard more than I will ever know. It's the privilege of every priest. To enter the common burdens of his flock, whatever their station."

Boatswain checked himself. An air of defensiveness had grown over him. The old suspicion had invaded his sense of loyalty; but he couldn't resist it. He wondered about Priest. Did he keep everything he knew to himself? Was it placed wholly at the service of his calling?

'It is time I go,' said Boatswain. His voice was weary.

'I will think on all you have said,' Priest told him; and his tone was heavy, grave, and distant.

'I am ready,' said Boatswain; and suddenly he thought he had heard the Lady's voice. Her words had become a part of his own flesh, secreted in the hollow of his mouth, defiling his tongue.

Music came up from the deck. The men were singing. The ocean was an organ with the sound held low behind their voices.

They were exercising their rights as they got the ship ready for sailing.

As Boatswain was about to leave the cabin, Priest put a hand on his shoulder and asked: 'You are sure it was the Lady of the House?'

Boatswain's reaction was fearsome. He had thrust a hand up to the side of his head. His fingers twisted and probed up the side of his face, feeling for his ear. Priest hadn't anticipated such agitation. He watched Boatswain's agitation and regretted that he had spoken further. Priest said, by way of putting him at his ease, 'We'll speak about it another time.'

He was patting Boatswain's shoulder: the wise and casual reminder of an elder. The gesture displeased Boatswain. A moment ago Boatswain was ready, nerves adjusted to their customary steel. He had directed the stages of his approach to the men who were working outside. The past had given him time off; left him alone to sort out the austerities of command as they applied to each situation that might arise. Now he could feel Priest's hand like a crutch warning him of weakness. So gentle and solicitous in its encouragement, that hand was nevertheless a rebuke.

Boatswain had to take it away, but without any obvious display of resentment. The problem of timing was forever urgent in this kind of encirclement; behind him was the candour of his confession to Priest; around him, like the weight of the hand on his shoulder, was a power of knowledge that might be passed on to the Commandant.

Yet his most urgent thought was the safety of his command. His relation to the officers would determine how his own division of men chose to see him. There seemed less than an embrace of equality in Priest's gesture. But freeing himself of Priest's hand put Boatswain's habit of perfect timing to its severest test. He hadn't moved a step since Priest had touched him; the silence perplexed Priest, who was expecting another revelation. Boatswain suspected this too. Priest must have been preparing for another confession. Then Boatswain did what he had to do; and he did it without a word and without any trace of agitation. He simply took Priest's hand away from his shoulder. First he lifted it up. This might have been the first stage of an elaborate strategy. Then he steered the hand down to Priest's side and left it there.

Like an item of furniture that he had returned, not waiting for an answer.

Immediately thereafter, Boatswain departed. He went straight to his cabin. Priest looked at his hand as though it were a foreign limb. He was overwhelmed by the simple, deliberate phasing of Boatswain's departure.

Boatswain did not leave his cabin. His authority had wilted; the private rehearsal of orders for his men had been abandoned. He wouldn't face his division in this state of agitation. He decided to stay away from the deck.

The rain started lightly, like a noise of birds' feet above his head. Boatswain searched the cabinet for liquor. His hands knew every corner; yet the spaces deceived him, offering objects that he didn't want. When he found the bottle, he put it to his head and tried to drink. But he had forgotten to release the stopper. He returned the bottle and closed the door to the cabinet. The door banged and trembled where he had stayed it with one hand. Silence now started the strangest sensations in his head. Under his temples, soft and noiseless, the beat of air and blood made a cool, familiar drumming, a pricking of needles teased his ears. He watched his massive hands like poles growing up from the table to support his chin. They made a lock around his throat. This was the part of his body which made him watchful of danger. He let the sound of drizzle distract his attention, and the needles multiplied in his ears, and the drum expanded its noise under his temples.

That's how it was the night he took a final look at the Lady of the House. Forgetful of crime, he kept asking her body why she had done him such an indignity. He had probed the face, barely hopeful that it might come alive in order to answer his deepest need. Why had she done this to me?

Boatswain walked to the door of his cabin. For a moment he felt he ought to get out in the open air. There was a promise of courage in his legs. Then he hurried back and shut the light out from the room. Some new fear had come over him. He was terrified by the accumulated evidence of Ivan's visions. It was as though the Lady of the House had come alive to give evidence of his failure to be a man on the inside. Some dormant force of courage was ordering him to state his case, to reveal the larger history of his life.

"... tell them, you must tell them," he heard his history declare, "I was a man of parts, of many parts. Now all in pieces. But it is important that they know I was a man of parts. Of many parts.

"In the matter of repute. A man thinks he is flying high with a power of service behind him. Then a change of circumstance tells him otherwise. He was only floating. I was at the centre of many a victory. Issues that would decide the point of conquest once and for all time. You would think such service would be to your credit unto eternity.

"It is a hard lesson, that. To witness moments of glory made ordinary and of little account. I was at the centre of many a victory. But men recall the fact, then judge it to be of no importance beside events that come later. And you start from a position of one who is down below. I've known it in a painful way. People remember what happened only as a way of diminishing the man who made it happen. I say: listen to me; but all hearing is cut short by superior explanation. Someone answers: 'Yes, of course, the facts are as you say; but you couldn't see it wasn't so important.' Then a man has to make a boast to prove his point; but already he is diminished. It would take some drastic action to restore dignity. In his own eyes, that is. Argument exhausted me. In the end I would feel a weariness take me down. I had to settle in the position of men from down below. It would take some drastic action to call proper attention to my meaning.

"Now. I must tell them now. They have to know. Not later than this moment they must know. Tell them Boatswain was more than what is happening here. You must say it. I must tell them. A man of many parts. Now all in pieces. Tell them. Tell. You must. Them. I must. Tell them. A man of many parts. I must tell them."

The sea rolled in his ears. His cabin enclosed him. His eyes wandered everywhere, eager to learn the meaning of these objects that slipped into hiding at the slightest intrusion from his glance. The chair would not allow his gaze to trespass where it stood. A force of touch went out from his seeing and submerged these recent and familiar presences. The cabinet had departed when he turned to rescue his liquor from the shelf. He thought of an ancient friendship that had suddenly obeyed some impossible law of betrayal. But the cabin was there. Like a miraculous mouth that opened above the ocean, it took him in and covered him over; and a solitude, close as skin, squeezed his throat and tightened his fingers where they had rested idly over the scorching, wet column of his neck. "That I was a man. Of many parts. San Souci, Belle Vue, the Demon Coast."

This solitude was a cage. It allowed no recognition of the creature it contained. Words might burst it open, but now all forms of language had deserted Boatswain. There was the touch of fire and moisture over his hands; yet he could hardly feel where his fingers marched and ploughed through the slush of blood that covered his face. He was doing terrible damage to his skin. His hands grew hotter and more active: an ignorant, merciless surgery that butchered through his flesh, snapped cords of veins, and halted when it came to a surface of bone. His nails were sharp and sure as knives.

Climbing out from the mouth of his cabin, he had arrived at the door. He was alarmed by the power of the sun that held him there, gazing without sight into its eye. His eyes fixed on the bullets of sunlight. Boatswain couldn't recognize the slow, dazed gathering of men below. His hands were clasped in the sign of prayer, as though the sun had built an altar before his eyes. And the men looked up from below, pondering the disfigurement of Boatswain's face. His blood ran like a river into his mouth. His eyes shifted when Surgeon and Steward appeared. They pretended to be undisturbed as they walked towards him. The duties of command had trained them against panic. They paid no attention to the men below, although Steward was of the opinion they should be ordered away.

'Bloody nuisance,' said Surgeon, 'letting himself go in this way.'

'A lucky chance we are so near,' Steward said.

'Shall we order that lot out of the way?'

Steward glanced quickly below. 'I would agree.'

He was about to give the order when the voices gave out an alarm. The men had rushed forward to break the fall of Boatswain's body, somersaulting through the air.

'The Lady of the House was nothing but a whore,' his voice kept crying out. 'Was nothing but a whore.'

The men stretched him out over the hatch and waited for some instruction from Surgeon, who stood, stupefied, as he listened to the frantic raving that came from below.

'Was nothing but a whore,' Boatswain's voice continued to cry out. 'The Lady of the House was nothing but a whore.'

'To his cabin,' Surgeon shouted.

Steward remained still, reflecting on the silence and alarm of the faces that gazed towards the Commandant's cabin. They were waiting for an order from the Commandant, who had witnessed Boatswain's fall, and heard the oaths he swore against the Lady of the House. Priest stood beside him, fearful of what might happen next. But the Commandant said nothing at all. He returned to his cabin, and closed the door.

TWENTY-ONE

COMMANDANT: Fasten the door.
PINTEADOS: It's a furnace here.
COMMANDANT: The door, Pinteados; I say fasten the door.
PINTEADOS: You're all sweat, sir.
COMMANDANT: The door, I say.

The Commandant was ordering the night to take possession of his cabin. Pinteados could barely see his way back to the Commandant's desk.

COMMANDANT: How do the officers treat this scandalous news?
PINTEADOS: They whisper.
COMMANDANT: Is that all?
PINTEADOS: I believe they confer. But I am not included.
COMMANDANT: And the men down below?

PINTEADOS: Silence. They are waiting for the order to sail. But all is silence there.

It seemed a long time before the Commandant spoke again. Pinteados mopped the heat from his hands and tried to discern some shape of a face on the other side of the desk.

PINTEADOS: But nothing has changed with Boatswain's revelations.
COMMANDANT: Everything, Pinteados, everything has changed.
PINTEADOS: Everything?
COMMANDANT: I say everything.
COMMANDANT: I have a new order.
PINTEADOS: You have other plans?
PINTEADOS: An order?
COMMANDANT: Yes. We will proceed no further.
PINTEADOS: How do you mean?
COMMANDANT: I mean what I say. No further.
PINTEADOS: No further? We will not go on to San Cristobal?
COMMANDANT: That is the order.

Pinteados strained for some recognition of the face that spoke to him. He could make little sense of what he was hearing. He was used to the Commandant's extremities of mood displayed in moments of tension; but this instruction was beyond reason. It was too complete a waste of effort and daring to be final.

COMMANDANT: You knew?
PINTEADOS: Did you speak, sir?
COMMANDANT: You heard me speak.
PINTEADOS: Of Boatswain and the Lady?
COMMANDANT: Did you know?
PINTEADOS: Yes, sir.
COMMANDANT: And you never told me.
PINTEADOS: It was no part of my bargain.

Pinteados could hear a movement of hands over the desk. Nervous and irritable, the low pounding continued. He tried to imagine the reaction of the officers and men when they heard the Commandant's order. Boatswain had confused them; but this decision of the Commandant would confound all sense.

'You knew of Boatswain and the Lady?' the Commandant said again. 'Even before we put out to sea.'

PINTEADOS: Yes, sir, I knew. Even then.

COMMANDANT: And you kept me in the dark?

PINTEADOS: As I say. It was no part of my bargain.

COMMANDANT: Is that all you can say?

PINTEADOS: You know my way. I go no further than I agree.

COMMANDANT: But the gravity of such news, man. Her treacherous intercourse with Boatswain! How could you hold your tongue, Pinteados?

PINTEADOS: I thought it a matter the Lady could explain.

COMMANDANT: What explanation could excuse such treachery? Did you hear, Pinteados? Did you have a full knowledge of her depravities with Boatswain?

PINTEADOS: But this ship, Commandant. How do you explain this ship?

COMMANDANT: The ship, you say.

PINTEADOS: Yes, this ship. The Lady gave you the only chance fortune had left you. She gave you this ship, Commandant.

COMMANDANT: You see that as sufficient recompense for what I must feel?

PINTEADOS: She gave you back your life, Commandant. What meaning can Boatswain's story have beside the weight of such giving?

COMMANDANT: You would condone the Lady's treachery, Pinteados. Is that your meaning?

PINTEADOS: I see nothing to condone, sir. Except it be the treachery to her husband and the House. She gave you this ship. Forgive me to repeat such fact. But we made the enterprise because she gave this ship. Can you imagine a gift more perilous for the Lady?

COMMANDANT: You ask me to condone what I hear?

PINTEADOS: Think of the Lady, sir.

COMMANDANT: Pinteados!

PINTEADOS: I'm here, Commandant.

COMMANDANT: We shared a partnership.

PINTEADOS: That we did, sir. This expedition is not a fact I can forget.

COMMANDANT: I forget nothing. Do not rebuke me with forgetting.

PINTEADOS: How did we acquire this ship, sir?

COMMANDANT: I forget nothing, I say.

PINTEADOS: Forgive me if I go beyond my station, sir. Maybe you do not forget. Then there is something wrong with the way you remember.

COMMANDANT: I entered no bargain for this ship.

PINTEADOS: I agree, sir. It was an absolute and pure giving on the Lady's part.

COMMANDANT: You would pin me down to that.

PINTEADOS: And that alone, Commandant. It is the only fact. This ship. It was your life. And the Lady's gift.

COMMANDANT: And Boatswain's revelation! You do not recognize her treachery there?

PINTEADOS: I believe otherwise.

COMMANDANT: You knew?

PINTEADOS: I say I knew, sir, but I had no cause to interfere.

COMMANDANT: You would have seen me accept such a humiliation in the dark?

PINTEADOS: I think the Lady would be light enough. She is alive and waiting in San Cristobal. I saw her safely concealed on the vessel *Penalty*.

COMMANDANT: Alive and waiting, you say. After such criminal conduct with Boatswain? How can you reason on her behalf?

PINTEADOS: I reason from the fact, Commandant. She gave this ship.

COMMANDANT: That is your absolute answer? Her giving?

PINTEADOS: What other, Commandant? What other fact would there be? You have a long history with the Lady; long before she could ever conceive of marrying anyone else. A long history of feeling her legal marriage couldn't end. Why, sir, why should she give the ship?

COMMANDANT: You choose your answer. I have chosen mine.

PINTEADOS: I think you go against the truth, sir.

'I think you have said enough,' the Commandant concluded. Pinteados obeyed. He had never engaged in such a conflict of opinion with the Commandant. He hadn't lost his habit of neutrality; but he wasn't prepared for the effect of Boatswain's story on the Commandant. A day ago Pinteados had begun to enjoy a sense of elation. He felt his power as an agent in this stupendous drama of intrigue and secrecy; an accomplished success that was moving towards a climax he favoured. This history of feeling which had endured danger and long separations to unite finally the needs of the Commandant and the Lady of the House. He had borne unique witness to an event that was the fruit of love, astonishing and yet inevitable. He had come to think of it as the worthiest journey he had ever made. It gave style and a certain grace to all the coarser negotiations that made up his bargain. Now Pinteados felt as though his skill was about to desert him. He continued to strain for some sign of the face before him. The Commandant's voice emerged from the oppressive darkness of the cabin, tired and desperate, as though great age had come suddenly upon it.

'You may open the door.'

Pinteados felt a moment's relief. He wanted to relax his eyes.

'Thank you,' he said.

He had been deceived by the sound of the Commandant's voice; there was no noticeable change in his face. Stern and resolute as he had always known it; the chin pointing fiercely down, as though it was guiding the whole head to some fixed clearing of ground below. Pinteados waited at the door. He had known this moment before: when conversation with the Commandant was over. You were delayed by its incompleteness. Then you were allowed to judge the moment of your departure.

'I'll break the news myself,' the Commandant said.

PINTEADOS: The news?
COMMANDANT: Yes. My order stands.

'We'll change course?' Pinteados was pleading.

COMMANDANT: You will proceed no further.

The Commandant's chin tilted his head up to the ceiling, and the lids of his eyes came shut. It was an obvious cue for his return to solitude.

Pinteados said: 'At your service, sir.'

274

The pilot paused outside the cabin, reflecting on the secretive gathering of the men below. They were all naked to the waist. Pinteados could see the powder maker's hands charting maps on the air. 'What a waste of enthusiasm,' he thought. After so many months of hazardous labour, they would have to start again. Knowledge of their return to Lime Stone would be like a law of doom deciding all their future.

TWENTY-TWO

"... whatever you are, it is you ... whatever ... it is you I love ... whatever ... I love you...."

"What other fact could there be ... what other ... she gave this ship, Commandant, she gave you back your life ... what other fact ... what other ... you have a long history with the Lady ... a long history of feeling...."

"Whatever you are ... it is you ... I love you...."

The Commandant had not moved from the council table; but his body had grown light as air, feeble with memory. A symphony of birdsong had sailed him homeward across the dubious victories of his youth and over the empty moorland of his inheritance. Now he lay wounded and forgotten in the small cabin of space where she had once kept her jars of leaves that measured every voyage he had made. But the jars were no longer there. In the moment of his deepest crisis he had found her gone. Her little cabin of space, once sacred with the leaves that measured every mile of his return, was finally empty. She had refused to come back.

The orchestra of birds was outside his window again. Each note startled; a tune nested in his ear. Soft and nervous as cloud the echo would loiter; his hearing was a cage wide open to this variety of sound. He didn't know the names of these birds that assembled every morning outside his window, pecking at his sleep, alerting him to the swift arrival of the light that was shaping a reflection of leaves and branches, pressing through the shutters to build a fortress of shadows above his head. A perfume of wet grass, mown by the first winds, startled his smell. His head was a house of song. His eyes were still weary from the long inertia of sleep. He didn't want to look up where the window would open onto the fugitive masks of clouds and the same hard curve of sky. As though he was afraid to recognize what was familiar in this urgent and harmless gift of birdsong. He lay still, wounded and forgotten in this small room that was her cabin of space.

What were they saying? What crisis had recruited these birds, ordered their migration to pause and argue in such variety. He could hear them, ever so near, surpassing all other sound. He was unwilling to exercise his eyes. Was it the early effect of long sleep or a superstition that the birds were soothsayers of the air? He didn't care to look up, because he might recognize the feathers uniquely labelled with colours he couldn't name, yet vivid and deceptive as his dreams. Convalescence had discovered a new energy in him. Ever since his fifth Voyage, he had never slept without the solace of dreams.

'Are you awake?'

Was it reluctance or a failure to recognize? Perhaps his illness had left some permanent defect which made him hear some other sound than the birdsong which was receding from outside his window. He couldn't think of any urgency that would warrant interruption at this hour. Perhaps he might have said something by way of recognizing that he was awake. But his voice, like the birds, was absent. He decided to answer with his eyes. He was seeing her. He saw her. His eyes had come suddenly clean as the sky. He had seen her. She had come back.

'If I woke you...'

'How long,' he was asking.

'I'm sorry,' she went on. 'I didn't want to wake you.'

'But when,' he was asking again, as though he had to give his awareness some final recognition; 'when did you come in?'

She said: 'Were you asleep?'

'I didn't hear anyone,' he was saying; and then in soft yet decisive change of voice he said what he meant. 'I didn't hear you enter.'

She said: 'How are you?'

And he replied in the same tone of curiosity: 'How long were you here?'

Then she got up from the chair, as though she were surrendering it to a stranger, and walked towards the door. She returned slowly, and he experienced the first conflict of astonishment and relief. She had been sitting when he saw her. He looked at the chair half an arm from the bed, then decided that it would be natural and safe to look at her. He tried to raise himself into a sitting position; but the pain released a current down his back, and halted his movement. He was at ease again on his back. Leisurely, he pointed to the chair, hoping that she would see this invitation to sit as a gesture of appeal. Every nerve was cautious to preserve the calm he recognized in her manner. There was no evidence of an effort in anything she did. She had taken the seat again.

'It must be over a year,' he said.

'Two years and five months,' she said.

'So long?'

'To the day,' she added. She was smiling. She had given up trying to count the leaves that measured his absence.

He didn't know what freedom he should give his appeal; but it was the way she smiled, soft, reflective, yet warm with attention. He had seen her the way he wanted her to be. There was no warning of recrimination in these fleeting, yet homely signals of welcome which their eyes bestowed on each other.

He said, barely fearful of consequence, 'Kiss me.'

And she saw his arm curve for embrace; and again she smiled and took his hand, and gently leaned it for a moment against her mouth. As gently, she returned it to the bed.

The birds had deserted. A stale wind died in the trees; and a slow procession of dry leaves followed. He watched them flutter past the window; and wondered where the birds had gone.

'The Expedition was a failure,' he said.

'Why do you say that?'

'Didn't you hear?'

'Some portion of the news,' she said.

'Everything was lost,' he said.

'But you survived,' she said.

277

Her voice was crisp, dry: not a breath wasted. Her eyes were dazzled by lakes of sunlight which had started to bring the room to full attention. Her room once sacred with its heaviest burden of dead leaves.

'What was the company?' she asked.

'Three vessels,' he said. 'Three. And everyone gone under.'

She noticed the slow decline of enthusiasm in his voice. How familiar! It was his way of avoiding details. Sometimes it happened when he wanted to protect someone from his lack of knowledge: an enquiry that might have prompted him to say what he did not really know.

'People think there were only two,' she said.

'There was a third,' he said, 'a foreign bargain. But it suffered the same fate.'

Should he tell her what he could remember of the wreck? He was never sure whether it was an error of judgment or the price which was always paid for an act of heroism. It was the thought of heroism which suddenly diverted his attention from the past. He wanted to concentrate his mind on the miracle that had happened while he was asleep. She had come, after all. She had come back.

He said: 'I know I should have sent word to you.'

'I wasn't expecting it,' she said.

'Perhaps. But I wanted to.'

'What difference does it make?'

'There is a difference,' he said, trying to force a judgment against himself. The voice was barely audible when he repeated: 'I know I should have.'

She said: 'You will be all right.'

He raised his legs and felt a looseness of movement, like air or water hurrying under his skin. His toes moved freely in exercise. His ankles were about to dance. There was a feel of remedy probing his limbs. The pain had gone to sleep. He had cradled his hands under his back, coaxing the muscles to reply. Then he lay quietly and waited for her to lead him into talk. It was natural and safe to draw attention to his body. It lay there, lame and relaxed, an object of solace and promise.

'I'm lucky to be here,' he said.

Now he was surprised by the casual tone of reminiscence.

278

'You've been in greater danger before,' she said.

'That's true,' he said, and wondered whether it was his body which had spoken. He was recovering from this obscure circumstance of speech when she rose from the chair. Still calm, almost serene, she paced for a while about the room as though she were collecting intimacies from the items of furniture that she recognized. He was afraid to lead her into talk. Trusting to his feebleness of limb, he said: 'I thought it would be my last journey.'

'That's not the first time,' she said.

'If the Expedition was a success,' he said, 'it would have been the last voyage.'

'Then you will have to go again,' she said.

He was reluctant to follow her now. But he wanted to hear her through. He was testing his legs again, considering the liberties his body could take. There was warning of regret in every risk.

'Would you want me to go?' he asked.

And he saw her smile again. Vivid and dubious as the litanies of the birds.

'You will do what you decide,' she said.

Safe and natural, he thought. That's how he wanted her to be. Her visit deserved a meeting that was made of perfect moments, and he disciplined his reply to achieve that end. The atmosphere of word and gesture: every item of mood should build up to a revelation of his need for her. He wanted her to see that it was now impossible for her to break with him. All previous failures must be converted into the very substance of their love.

'You look very different,' he said.

And she answered after deliberate pause: 'You haven't changed.'

Should he argue some virtue to the contrary? He had hoped gradually to influence her towards some recognition of a change in himself. He had survived a period of extreme decisions that had modified his harshness and his ebullience with people. Now she hinted that she had detected nothing that would support this view. He decided to let it pass. Instead, he observed her closely, trying to name the points of difference he had drawn to her attention. He had never played the game of compliments with her. Now it was easy to avoid doing so.

'I think you're not so plump.'

'That is true,' she said.

'I hope you weren't ill,' he said.

He thought he saw her eyes change colour. They'd gone dark. Or was it the deception of shadows? But there was no shadow over her mouth: a nervous contraction of the lips. He knew her body like a map. From memory. In a moment of tension her brow would come smooth, immobile. The skin would look fragile as paper. He thought he saw this; but there was a difference. There was no fever in her eyes.

'I know I should have got word to you,' he said.

'Tell me about the Expedition.'

It seemed she was determined to ignore his apologies. This, too, was some proof of change. There was a time when she would seize on his work to demolish any argument in his favour. He didn't want to be distracted from his own impulse to analyze these changes; yet it seemed safer and more natural to follow her wish.

'They were a very brave crew,' he said, 'full of resource. Equal to any emergency in battle with nature or the enemy. But courage failed when they had to act against superior orders. We were to avoid the routes to the West because the House of Trade was negotiating a Treaty with Antarctica. I decided to ignore the directives of the House.'

'You were against the Treaty?' she asked.

'I was for peace, but the time was wrong,' he said. 'That my last journey should end in such a concession! I could not accept it.'

'And the men didn't understand?' she asked.

'They were for me in argument,' he said, 'but they feared the judgment of the House. The loyalties divided this way and that. When the enemy ships challenged us to divert, some were not sure whether they ought to resist. Some decided otherwise, but they fought with a certain restraint. The result was inevitable. You can't mix enthusiasm and restraint. The enemy would have made a bargain, although their numbers were superior. We were offered free escape, and without unfavourable report. But only on condition that we surrendered every item of cargo. I gave orders to set fire to the two ships most richly endowed. We reached our own waters in the third. Then the weather took over and forced those who remained to abandon.'

'They might have made you prisoners,' she said.

'Their Admiral was against it,' he said.

'How do you know?'

'Their pilot told me,' he said. 'He deserted and was with me until the night before our rescue.'

'There is rumour the House will not bring you to trial,' she said.

'The Kingdom is divided on the terms of the Treaty,' he said. 'That may be their reason. I am a card that can be played either way.'

'You will survive,' she said.

'Not to my liking,' he said.

There was a trace of harshness in his tone. The first signs of irritability appeared. His future was gravely in doubt, as it had never been before; illness and the enmity of the House had brought a certain end to his career; yet she continued to answer him with an assurance that made his worry seem trivial. She had made herself remote by this attitude of casual prophecy. He might have protested; but his instinct was on the side of reconciliation. It warned him to avoid any obstacles to this reunion.

To preserve these moments; to help the miracle of her visit towards its own final perfection. She had come back. He knew what he wanted to happen; but he didn't know the form of request his words should take. He was surprised by the total reversal of roles that now influenced their drama. She appeared to give her attention wholly to the details of the Expedition, and the consequences of his action. The future she offered was exclusively the province of his work. As though she had come to accept that all important and lasting priorities were concentrated in him.

And the thought grew, tempting him to make his need known: "She makes no mention of us." But it seemed premature to give himself to words, to test the miracle of her coming by asking whether she had come to stay. He chose silence, because it seemed more appropriate to his fear. It couldn't be long before her decision would be made known.

Remoteness was her way of keeping watch over the subtlest changes in his mood. She had followed his hands travel up his body and come to rest, aimless and resigned, over his brow. A spell of lethargy had closed his eyes. His body was imitating the fearful placidity of a corpse.

She said: 'I believe the third ship was not lost.'

He had heard her; but there was something novel and menacing in her insistence to call attention to the Expedition. He tried to make a secret of the curiosity she had aroused.

'Impossible,' he said.

'So it seemed, but it may be true.'

'You heard this?'

'Reliably,' she said.

He couldn't support his restraint any longer. "Reliably," he thought, and struggled with the conclusiveness of such an answer.

'What a strange knowledge for you to have,' he said, 'and reliably.' He heard himself laugh, as though his body was conspiring to bear false witness to his feeling.

'You sound like a voice from the House,' he said; and tried to support this conspiracy of laughter; but it failed. He recognized a fearful certainty of purpose when she spoke again.

'You're right,' she said. 'My information comes through the House.'

'What did you say?'

'You heard.'

'So I did.'

'And you've never known me to betray serious matters with a joke.'

The voice was familiar. His instinct was to protect himself from its meaning.

He said: 'That's true.'

'Then you must believe me,' she said. 'The third ship was not lost.' She paused and added, 'It will be yours again.'

It would have been natural to make further enquiries about this novel connection with the House; but his habit of defensiveness had been restored. He had always forbidden himself to trespass on a privacy. It was partly the confidence she had trained him to accept, partly a protection for his own tendency to obscure his motives. But there was a difference. There was no aggressiveness in her delivery, no breach in this formidable calm that selected her words, converting the most improbable news into a natural gift of fact. It was like an act of discovery when he realized that his body had overcome his fear of pain. It had raised him up into a sitting position.

He looked towards the window, as though he wanted to summon some neutral witness to what was happening here. He reflected on the recent departure of the birds, the calm that had come with the dumb shadows collecting in his room. Soothsayers of the air! He needed a superstition to partner this refusal to believe what he had heard. "The third ship. It will be yours again." Yet he couldn't decide what was the central fact of her revelations: was it news of the third ship, or this unlikely connection that she claimed to the House?

He could sense a gradual drift of judgment take him further and far away from the consequences of the Expedition. It might never have happened. He was preparing himself for some recovery of hope. To preserve these moments. It was necessary to deny the Expedition any claim on his attention. To help the miracle of her visit to its final perfection. It seemed that the Expedition had never taken place. There was no departure, no separation. She was here. In that chair. There had been no absence, no lapse of contact. For she had always been there. In that chair. Her little cabin of space forever sacred with the harvest of dead leaves.

'I can't imagine you anywhere else,' he said, and kept offering his gaze, like a bribe, to the chair. She heard him and collected his meaning without reply. 'If it's true,' he continued, looking to the window for witness again, 'that I was absent so long.'

'Two years and five months to the day,' she said.

'Then how did I survive without you?' he asked.

She said: 'You always survive.'

'What a waste,' he said, 'and worse than waste. Unnecessary. There was no necessity.'

'You will always do what you decide,' she said.

Everywhere his flesh seemed to warn of risk; a convulsion like the ocean ploughing for a bed it had never known. She could sense this tremor that seized him, a wave-like asphyxia binding him to silence. To preserve these moments! But his restraint snapped, broke into a freedom of speech he could barely recognize.

'And you?' he asked her, daring this miracle to bear fruit. 'What will you decide?'

'I have,' she said; 'I have decided.'

The answer was swift, resolute, too precise for reflection.

'You have?' But he was really talking to himself.

'Yes,' she said.

Now his career altered its former meaning; imposed different proportions on his sense of achievement. An eternity of mornings! The huge fruitless impermanence of nights! The false refuge of work!

'You will stay?' he asked.

'No.'

Discovering again the child's note of injury, he spoke.

'You're not leaving me?' he cried.

And she answered again: 'Yes, yes.'

She had been married without ceremony that very morning. He didn't yet know that he was speaking to the new Lady of the House.

TWENTY-THREE

'I'd give my share of fortune for a rumour.'

'I make it four days of waiting without any order to sail.'

'Today is nearer five.'

Many silent calculations followed, and the men waited for someone to break the pause. It made them more nervous.

'Four or five, it's more fearful than the month it took us to leave Lime Stone.'

'But he had good reason then,' a voice came to the Commandant's defence.

There was an air of diffidence as they looked to the man for some explanation.

'We were not idle,' it came. 'Provisioning the *Reconnaissance* was work enough to keep our attention off danger.'

There was agreement, at first fitful; then they gave themselves freely to a recollection of those slow mornings that woke them off the forbidden coasts of Lime Stone.

'And the pilot, Pinteados,' someone reminded them, 'we were waiting for Pinteados to arrive.'

A solitary glance was turned in the direction of the pilot's cabin; but it aroused no curiosity among the men. They were wholly obsessed by this failure to discover what might have gone wrong.

'This delay is not natural.'

A voice had started to ask about the Commandant's health; but the question seemed unreal, almost absurd. It lacked the necessary power of consistency, and failed to gain attention. It was almost natural the way the men ignored such a speculation.

'Is it some strategy, you think?' someone suggested. 'Would the delay be a kind of strategy?'

'The Commandant must break his silence,' a man replied, 'or we will never know.'

'It isn't what I'd call a just punishment,' his neighbour said. 'To keep us in the dark about such delay.'

But they didn't think they were quite alone in their fears for the future.

'What about the officers?'

'Boatswain is the only certainty,' someone said.

'The only certainty?'

'In his ignorance,' the voice went on, 'he is confined to cabin. And alone. Doesn't know if the ship is here or hereafter.'

There was a general reluctance to consider the plight of Boatswain, whose collapse was probably the cause of this delay.

'We ought to let the officers know our feeling,' a man repeated, and his voice was strangely militant. 'If the delay warns of disaster, let it be so. But they must not keep us in the dark.'

All eyes turned on him, afraid and hopeful that he might have known more than he had said. They waited for him to go on; but some vague anger had made it difficult for him to speak.

'You think it means disaster?' They were pressing him to come to their aid with news.

'Let it be so if it is so,' he said in a tone that was near prophecy, 'but we have a right to know.'

There was a look of disappointment in some faces. But the prophet had been spared further attention when another mariner arrived and took his place among them. Each new arrival offered a promise of some revelation. But the newcomer was average.

'How many days do you reckon?' he asked.

'Tonight makes five since the feast,' a tolerant voice informed him.

'And we were to sail with the first wind next day.'

'Favourable or unfavourable,' the newcomer said. 'Those were the Commandant's words.'

The sky was soft and clear. A remnant of cloud hung low, drifting seaward. The sunlight struck with power over the bodies of the men who had collected in small groups over the deck. Their eyes were bruised and weary from the heat. The air was still, empty of all sound except the hushed and fearful murmuring for news.

Sasha appeared on the deck, but he was careful to avoid any meeting with the men. He kept his eyes on a torn loaf of bread, squeezing the damp crusts between his fingers. He had picked his way between the groups. Now the boy stood with his shoulders crouched against the waist of the ship. A marvel had stolen his attention as he looked at the wide, bright arc of sky and had a vision of the ocean turned upside down, a frozen blue.

A bird plunged across his line of view, breasted the water, and swiftly journeyed forward in its ascent. Sasha followed the bird in flight, and went on rolling the pellets from the crust of bread. He didn't want to hear what the men were saying. He swung his head level, and gave all his attention to a trail of roots drifting towards the ship. He counted the pellets of bread crust and waited for the bird's return.

'Do you see that?' one of the men was asking. The gathering had got his meaning wrong.

'Would the boy have some knowledge of our delay?' a voice enquired.

'Not the boy,' said the other. 'Look there! To the right!'

The heads made a stolen movement towards Surgeon's cabin.

They saw Priest leave Surgeon's cabin. He must have been in consultation with Surgeon. Priest stood outside, uncertain where he should go. He showed no interest in the speculative glances of the men below. Suddenly Priest started walking in the direction of Steward's cabin. Now he looked more assured, as though the purpose of his mission had been restored.

'Only the officers can make our feeling known,' a man started. His voice was hoarse with protest; but it seemed that he had found some solace in the appearance of Priest on the upper deck.

'Which one of the officers should we speak to?'

'What would it matter who among them interceded? They are all equal in office.'

The wind blew a spray of spit into the man's eyes. He was about to swear at the offender; but the men had started a quiet dispute over his question. Then one voice made its sombre conclusion. 'But the officers have no special privilege when the Commandant is in this mood.' He had gained support from those who sat near.

'It's true. So I observe in the first days. And it's no less so now.'

'But this is different,' a voice argued. 'In the full heat of sailing, the Commandant could be left alone.'

He realized that this line of argument had some influence on their attention. 'This is different,' he went on. 'To be idle and without known cause! As though the reason for your labours had suddenly come to an end. But the enterprise is not over. Or is it?'

'What do you mean about the enterprise at an end?'

There was a look of exasperation on the face of the man who had spoken.

'Why this delay?' he continued. 'We are entitled through the officers to know the Commandant's reason.'

There was an appeal for challenge in his tone of voice; but the men had to retain some measure of confidence in the outcome of the enterprise.

'Perhaps the officers know,' someone said. 'Maybe they are in agreement with the Commandant's waiting.'

This view, acceptable as it might have been, produced an effect of disquiet on everyone. They had no experience of consultation between the Commandant and the officers. They knew he would never summon more than one officer at a time for any talk that pertained to the conduct of the ship. This was the Commandant's method; and the men had learned it by their close and habitual observation of the traffic that passed in and out of the Commandant's cabin. The order of arrivals might vary; but the officers had never been seen to enter or leave the Commandant's cabin together.

'You say the officers are in agreement,' a man had challenged. 'But I see no officer go near the Commandant's cabin since Boatswain's collapse.'

'Except Pinteados,' someone said.

'I didn't witness that,' the voice argued.

'To be sure, I saw.' The rejoinder allowed no chance of error. 'It was the very day Boatswain did such injury to himself.'

A few voices came to the man's support; and after an interval of reflection, the pilot's visit was confirmed.

'Maybe Boatswain is the cause. Perhaps the Commandant is grieving for the injury done to Boatswain by his own hands.'

'I think it otherwise. It is a deeper grief I suspect.'

'Would there be some plot afoot? Is that your meaning?'

'Could it be that the Admiral of this island is forcing the delay?'

'Speak plain!' someone ordered.

'As I say. Could it be the delay is outside the Commandant's decision?'

'And keep us in the dark? Why should the Commandant exclude us if the issue is about our own defence?'

'He might fear we lose our judgment, and retaliate out of turn.'

'Then it would be a judgment lost with honour. I fear the Commandant is too liberal in his affection for foreigners. The feast was a grave error. To feed that foreign dog whose appetite was to subvert our enterprise to San Cristobal. What better cause for an open fight? To be frank, I was never in favour of any Treaty. The Admiral, you say!'

The voice broke into a violent cough. The man's hands began to swell. Someone was trying to restrain his rage. Fear of the Admiral's intervention had influenced them to a sudden power of loyalty on behalf of Lime Stone. This fear was no more than a speculation, offered in their presence. It had no source outside this tight gathering; but it was enough to bring a smell of blood into the air.

'I can hear my sweat boil,' the man said, trying to subdue his coughing.

'A day or so from our destination,' another intoned. 'Just a day or less from our destination.'

'I swear there is some plot afoot,' the agreement followed.

'The Commandant must make his intentions known.'

'What's our numbers?'

'Enough. Few or plenty, I say we are enough.'

'To be sure, we are enough. But the Commandant must give an order.'

'Look,' a voice interrupted. 'To the left! See what I see.'

'Now, that is most unusual.'

The heads were stealing their movement again as Priest halted outside the pilot's cabin. The men thought he looked undecided about his visit; and his hesitation increased their belief that some emergency had been visited on them. Pinteados was never known to receive anyone in his cabin.

'I have never witnessed such an event.'

'Never in daylight, as I remember.'

'The officers must know the meaning of this delay.'

'I didn't see Pinteados at the feast. Do you remember?'

'Pinteados at the feast?'

'No, no. The pilot was never present at the feast.'

'What logic would you make of that? Foreigner refusing to welcome foreigner.'

They were waiting for someone to offer a reason for the pilot's absence. Their suspicions grew; but it seemed more difficult to detect the real target of their anger.

'Whatever the danger,' a voice advised, 'the Commandant's safety is our first duty.'

'I stand by that.'

'Until there is word from the officers,' a familiar voice started to warn. 'Our first loyalty is to the Commandant's defence.'

'His personal safety and defence.'

For a moment it seemed these warnings of a plot had given way to their unique devotion to the Commandant.

Pinteados watched the land from his cabin port, contrasting the frozen twilights of his northern shores with the crimson bars of sunset that stretched across the porthole. He saw the breakers chase up the shore, leaving blue fragments of a rainbow on the stones. He was trying to imagine the first footsteps that had trodden these sands, bargaining for welcome at the earliest signs of native habitation. The hills were windless. Soon the vivid folds of evening would abruptly disappear. The weather would go black. A silence of graves would settle over the island. He thought: "This might be the last supper of its kind." He heard Priest arrive.

'Should I close the door?' Priest asked.

Pinteados thought otherwise. He invited Priest to sit. Priest gave little indication of his mood. Like Pinteados, he seemed remote from events, impervious to surprise. Pinteados remained standing; but he had turned his back to the porthole.

'We've never met like this before,' said Priest.

The remark was too obviously true for comment. Pinteados showed no inclination to be drawn. His cabin was secluded territory: a cell which had reminded him every day of his long and friendless sojourn in Lime Stone. He inhabited his solitude like skin, incapable of any other possession but his own. His silence was a fortress that had grown with the daily exercise of avoiding intercourse with those to whom he could not risk a confidence. But his gift for listening had selected him for special privilege. A foreigner in a hostile land, he was to learn that native rivalry would find in him a proper instrument of mischief. Lime Stone had conferred assignments on him that no native would ever undertake. The pilot had become a vast agency of secrets, a central intelligence that could detect and chart the minutest traces of subversion in the kingdom. His power was wordless, invisible.

He regarded Priest with an air of harmless unconcern.

'You have seen Steward?' he asked.

'Yes. And Surgeon, too,' Priest added. 'I spoke with each about the vessel *Penalty*.'

'Separate or together?'

'Separate and alone,' said Priest. 'As you advised.'

Pinteados pondered the novelty of his decisions. Alone with Priest, in the familiar secrecy of this cabin, he was conscious of breaking the habits that had ensured his protection against men. He had solicited Priest's aid in making a disclosure that was to remain a secret between himself and the Commandant. No one else on board had known of the strategy that would reunite the officers and their wives. This was the pilot's bond of secrecy with the Commandant.

'Your information had perplexed me more than the cause of this delay,' said Priest. 'I didn't know their wives would be on the vessel *Penalty*.'

'You knew of *Penalty*?' Pinteados asked.

Priest was hesitant. He thought the question was a trap.

'Yes,' said Priest, and suddenly tried to reverse his answer. 'Very recent, I should add. There was no knowing beyond the propositions the Commandant put to me. That I would prepare the ground between our men and the strange cargo of women who would arrive at San Cristobal. It didn't sound a natural course of action. Until you told me about the wives of Steward and Surgeon.'

Pinteados gave no sign of further interest in the ship; it was clear to Priest that the pilot's knowledge of *Penalty* must have been complete.

'Surgeon wouldn't believe me until I gave him the substance of my interview with the Commandant,' said Priest. He paused. 'Would you have known Surgeon's wife?'

The pilot ignored what he had heard.

'And Steward? How did he take the news about his wife?' Pinteados asked, avoiding any answer to Priest's enquiry.

'With the same distress,' said Priest. 'I'd say there was more agitation in Steward's refusal to believe.'

He paused again. Priest tried to consider what passion had driven the two women to arrange for such a surprising reunion with their husbands. The hardships of such a voyage were not negligible for a man. There was something heroic about the loyalty that could make them risk such dangers in order to overcome a temporary divorce from the company of their husbands. Priest reflected on the pilot's motives in breaking the news at this time. But the Commandant's proposition had assumed an honourable aspect in his judgment. To assist the women in such an act of heroism! And in the cause of their proper marriage!

If the Commandant was often harsh and intransigent in his orders, he was not without a generous heart.

'It makes the delay more difficult to understand,' said Priest. 'To know that the wives will be waiting.'

Pinteados walked over towards the door. He looked up at the drooping sail and then towards the deck, where the boy Sasha was throwing the pellets of bread into the sea. The pilot waited to see the descent of birds. The boy was also waiting to see them dive for the pellets of bread. Then Sasha ran off towards the bow. Pinteados returned slowly to the table, drew up a chair, and leaned towards Priest. It was an atmosphere of whispers.

'Now you've seen Surgeon,' Pinteados ventured, 'Would he have shared any confidence with you about the delay?'

Priest had been preparing himself for some other kind of question. He offered Pinteados his smile, negative and friendly. You could never tell what surprise the pilot might spring.

'I have no such knowledge of the Commandant's thinking,' said Priest, without hiding his alarm. He looked like a man who was about to make a decision, grave, reliable, and at ease in his caution. But he was trying to make some sense of the pilot's question.

'How would you decide?' Priest asked, talking to himself.

'How would they decide?' Pinteados insisted. And everything was suddenly made easy.

'I put the same question to Surgeon and Steward,' said Priest. 'How would they decide if the Commandant had to change his plans.'

'You expect some conflict between yourselves and the Commandant?' Pinteados asked.

'To the contrary.' Priest hurried with his answer.

He couldn't afford such suspicion to rest with him. He showed his astonishment that Pinteados should have been thinking in this way. He had come too near to the completion of the enterprise to encourage such a charge against his loyalty. The same would be true of Surgeon. Priest couldn't imagine any circumstance that would make for an obstacle between Surgeon and the fortune that would reward their arrival at San Cristobal. Nor would Steward's ambition to surpass himself allow of a defeat at this late hour in the enterprise. But the pilot's question continued to stir some doubt in Priest. Did Pinteados foresee a conflict? And of what kind? He had the impression that Pinteados, too, had been puzzling over the Commandant's delay. Anxiety had made them equal. He wanted to probe the pilot's knowledge; but he had to guard against any suspicion that might attach to anything he said.

'Our mission is almost accomplished,' Priest began.

'Almost,' Pinteados said quickly.

The pilot's answer had increased his doubt. Priest was sure the Commandant would break his silence soon. But Pinteados had made him conscious of some conflict that might force the officers to make their allegiance known. Priest tried to imagine some circumstance that might divide their wishes.

How would he react in an open dispute between the Commandant and the officers? Was this the point of the question Pinteados had asked him earlier? He didn't want to appear to be in need of the pilot's advice; but doubt had restored him to his habit of compromise. It was urging him to ask Pinteados what he would do if such conflict should arise.

'How would you decide?' Priest asked; and he felt the pilot's glance alert him to the risk he might be taking.

'Decide?' Pinteados said, curious to hear what he meant.

'In a conflict between one officer and the next,' Priest said lamely. 'Between Steward and Surgeon, to be precise?'

Priest had the feeling that the pilot had seen through this subterfuge.

'I would do whatever is required,' Pinteados said.

'And who would determine that?' Priest went on, forcing a note of cheerfulness.

'The circumstance,' Pinteados said. 'It is always the circumstance.'

Priest was nodding. He wanted to acknowledge some wisdom in this answer; and to confirm it.

'I too follow my duty when it is made clear,' said Priest.

He felt a little ashamed at his failure to ask the question that had really started his doubt. He had switched the conflict to Surgeon and Steward, although he knew there was no opposition of interests between them. He thought the delay had already begun to ruin his judgment.

'It's time we move,' Pinteados said. 'I think I hear the bell.'

The pilot stood; then started walking wearily towards the door. The bell rang again. Pinteados looked up for the sail again; but the light had gone. It was habit that guided his eyes towards the masthead. The dark was burying every sign of movement on the deck. He could barely discern the island of Dolores, like an enormous tomb emerging from the ocean. What would Steward do? And Surgeon? For a moment Pinteados lingered on the different motives that had made him break the news that the officers' wives were on the vessel *Penalty*.

Priest was waiting; but the pilot appeared to be lost in reflections he was never likely to share. Pinteados had never really thought of himself as one of the officers. Now he was content to bear witness to their choice. What would they do? Caught between a promise of fortune and the erratic decision of the Commandant whom they had always obeyed! Priest stared in amazement at the pilot and wondered what sinister schemes were prolonging his delay.

'Time to eat,' said Priest as he might have done to a forgetful child.

Steward lingered in the bow, resenting the familiar summons of the bell to dinner. He wished for some reason that would excuse him from the company of Surgeon, who stood beside him. Yet he couldn't afford to be alone. He daren't act, unaided, in the decision which was slowly maturing. He had to solicit Surgeon's agreement without appearing to be in need of his support. Boatswain could no longer be regarded as an officer whose opinion might decide an issue. The past had taken over his judgment, forcing him into revelations which had brought about his downfall. There was no final decision about Boatswain's future; but he could no longer be seen as an officer, and a man on the inside. It was necessary to know what Boatswain had said; but it was impossible to forgive him after you had heard it. He judged Pinteados to be unreliable. No one could say what service Priest would offer. Priest had taken shelter in his vocation; and all his calculations had remained obscure. The thought of Priest made Steward burn with rage. Not Priest, but the content of his message. On the eve of their arrival, with fortune and the promise of glory almost within their grasp, Priest had revived the fears that the enterprise had helped him to overcome. He had set a plague on Steward's plans. His wife was there again, like a shadow that wouldn't let go. In attendance always. Before and after. Supervising every effort that might provide an escape to freedom. For a moment he was at a loss to decide which was the greater fear: retaliation from the House of Trade and Justice, or Priest's secret warning that he would have to meet his wife on the island of San Cristobal.

Surgeon was waiting for him to speak. He was sure that Pinteados and Priest had arrived in the dining cabin. They were waiting. Surgeon thought it was an error to be away while these two were together. But he wanted Steward to lead the way. Surgeon gave no hint of his intentions but his experience told him that he should make this close association with Steward appear to be of some consequence. And he thought how subtly the nature of compromise could change. There was a time for total concealment. Now the circumstance required that his secret should take the form of open acknowledgment. He suspected some allegiance between Pinteados and Priest; and his fears had found a strategy in his association with Steward. They must move together; and they must move to some purpose. He was impatient to hear Steward, who waited, still and obscure as the night.

Surgeon said: 'Any news?'

'What news?'

'Why this delay?'

Steward paused, selecting his answer.

'I have no news,' he said, refusing to make known Priest's recent information about his wife.

Surgeon hoped that talk might suggest to Steward that they should be going; but he made no move.

'Would you have news?' Steward asked.

'None,' said Surgeon.

Surgeon must have turned; for Steward heard the voice come from another direction.

'No news at all?' Steward asked.

'None.'

'No word from Pinteados?'

'None,' said Surgeon.

'And Priest? No word from Priest?'

'None,' said Surgeon. He felt the abruptness of his answer; then added as he turned, 'except a warning.'

'Warning?' Steward echoed him.

And Surgeon quickly found an answer that would conceal his ultimate fear.

'It's about the men down below,' said Surgeon. 'He thinks we ought to keep closer watch than ever.' Surgeon had found an answer that was plausible: a truth which would serve to conceal the truth.

Steward pondered the warning, and restrained himself from making a reply. Suspicion of the men had brought Priest's message of his wife to mind. He weighed the risk of silence against the risk of making enquiries that might reveal the source of his worry.

'You haven't seen Priest?' Surgeon asked.

'Yes,' said Steward, finding a refuge in Surgeon's own reply. 'He warned me also to watch the men.'

For the moment it seemed that neither would have any knowledge to share that went beyond this warning. They had found in the men a temporary rescue from the news of their wives. Steward, too, started to get the feeling that they shouldn't prolong this waiting. Seized by a suddenness of intention, he took a step forward; then paused as though his foot had come upon some obstacle in the dark. But he could feel some urgency of decision push him forward. He had to maintain the initiative; to confront Surgeon with a certain change of emphasis. If he was going to achieve Surgeon's support, he must appear to take the lead. Together they made their way to the dining cabin.

Surgeon looked at the shoulder of deer, a wrinkled surface, dark brown and stiff from too much cooking. A row of cloves traced a black border around the meat, like a procession of beads. Little cones of dripping collected on the plate. Surgeon observed the prunes, twisted and black with age. But his hands remained idle. His eyes could only notice things. He was waiting for someone to say something, to rescue him from the spell of his inertia.

Steward had changed his usual place. He had taken Boatswain's seat, with Pinteados at his left. Priest stayed where he belonged, at the head of the table, and ate quietly. Now and again he would glance at Pinteados; but there was no response. Pinteados, as always, concentrated on the dinner. This silence was to his liking. He was the foreigner: heedless of dangers, remote from any crisis that might be shared by those around him. The Commandant's plight weighed on him; but here among the officers, he had decided to pledge his skill to the principle that had always ensured his survival. He would do whatever the circumstances required. The thought kept recurring to him: this might be the last supper of its kind. But he couldn't tell who would confirm this feeling, what circumstance would prove that he was right.

Steward kept reminding himself of his duty. He had to make a break from his normal habits of caution. Not in private, as he had done with Surgeon. His decision must assume the boldness of initiative. He must set the mood, influence all doubt in the direction he had chosen; for he had made a choice. He had been liberated from his own caution. This was partly his reason for occupying Boatswain's seat. There was something daring and contradictory in this gesture. He was taking his place at the centre of dangers which would soon mature. It was Steward's duty to cultivate an atmosphere of crisis. Yet he seemed sceptical of his own judgment. He would have spoken earlier; but he distrusted his timing. Each word might be a reflection of the meaning he wanted to conceal. He worried over this conflict of needs: how to make his decision known while he guarded the reason for his choosing.

Then the officers heard him speak. Surgeon looked a little alarmed by the strength and certainty of Steward's voice. Pinteados showed no signs of hearing anything. But Priest couldn't disguise the look of enquiry that he abruptly turned on Steward.

'Glad, you say?'

'Yes,' said Steward, 'I'm glad of the delay.'

'Each man to his own way,' said Priest.

'I am saying,' said Steward, and the tone of authority was not lost on anyone, 'each of us should be glad.'

Priest wanted to make a retreat from further questions; but Steward had captured his attention. He was hoping that Surgeon would intervene.

'I would agree, if you mean that a rest is welcome,' said Priest.

He had scarcely finished when Steward took the initiative again. His manner was sharp, corrective.

'It's no time to rest,' he said. 'There is only time for a decision.'

'A decision?' said Priest.

'A decision,' Steward assured him. 'That's what I say.'

Steward's eyes were bright; his hands shook. A quiver of nerves made his mouth shudder. His lips were tight.

'You have some special knowledge?' Surgeon asked. His voice was docile.

'He must,' said Priest. 'He must have news we haven't heard.'

'None you don't know,' said Steward. 'Boatswain's warning is enough.'

Priest was about to speak; but Steward halted him. Surgeon was startled by the excited thrust of Steward's hands, demanding to be heard.

'Boatswain was not a man who would betray,' said Steward. 'But he had no instinct for being an officer and a man on the inside. That's why he broke. You witness how he broke.'

'So I did,' said Surgeon. He looked relieved.

'You say he warned us,' said Priest; 'what do you mean?'

'I pay attention,' said Steward. 'I always pay attention to the men. They will never be the same again. Never.'

'You suspect trouble among the men?' Priest asked.

Surgeon switched his glance to Steward.

'I do not suspect,' said Steward. 'I tell you what I see. They had no right to what they heard. Boatswain's collapse is the end of obedience. It was a warning. Better to have it now. Who knows what kind of rebels such weakness would make after our arrival?'

Steward paused, considering his effect on Surgeon. He wondered how long it would take for them to share this danger he was trying to cultivate. He wanted them to see the men down below as the only threat they could not overcome.

Surgeon was feeling a gradual release from his inertia. Some kind of appetite was emerging. He was making signals across the table. Priest passed the goblet. Steward watched where Surgeon's hands trembled above the glass. The wine ran a stain over his fingers. Then he felt a warmth spread slowly out from the back of his tongue. He was grateful Steward should have come to his rescue with such foreboding. Surgeon wanted to remind himself that he was still a man of cunning; resourceful in crisis. He was recovering from the shock of Priest's message: that arrival at San Cristobal would bring him to a meeting with his wife. Her presence was there. Ahead. She was what was awaiting him. He would be travelling towards a promise of inconvenience, a harvest of tortures more fearsome than any the disfigured wrecks of Severn had known. Now Surgeon tried to compose himself. Steward had given the danger of the men a meaning that would provide him with some escape to freedom.

Surgeon felt the glow of the wine die slowly in his mouth. Looking at Pinteados, he saw the intimate domesticities of his own past reflected in the foreigner's presence. The pilot knew too much about his failure. He had a dangerous vision of Pinteados on the deck, protected from death by the necessity of his skill. Surgeon felt a momentary elation as he realized that the foreigner's presence might not be necessary any more. He was gradually recovering his confidence; he could learn to ignore Pinteados.

'Priest must give us some guidance here,' said Surgeon.

'We must be guided in our own interests,' said Steward.

Steward was asserting his duty to retain the initiative.

'I see no argument there,' Surgeon assured him. 'Our interests must come first.'

Priest was gazing at his hands. He might have been expecting a sign, some hint of enlightenment that would protect him against their displeasure. He couldn't give any warning of his loyalties, because he wasn't sure what these ought to be. He wished Pinteados would come to his relief. A simple word of assurance might have been enough. But the pilot had buried his attention in silence. Grave, profound. Pinteados had excluded himself more thoroughly than any wish of Surgeon could have achieved.

'We are officers, and therefore men on the inside,' said Priest. 'That is what Boatswain did not remember. It is what we must never forget.'

He had looked up, but he wouldn't let his glance rest on anyone. He appeared to be at ease in this role of mediation: a man who knew how to provide a sense of companionship to those who had grown too solitary. He had a way of disturbing the habits of excessive brooding.

'This enterprise is about to bear fruit,' Priest went on. 'It could be the discovery of a future beyond anything you had imagined. I do not mean to go against your feeling. I do not argue against your interests. But you honour me with a plea for guidance. I advise you to remember who you are. As officers, and therefore men on the inside, you must consider what you do. Whatever the nature of your intentions. Consider what you do.'

He had felt his confidence return. Now he was looking at Steward; a subtle shift of the eyes included Surgeon. When Priest made a pause and lowered his head, it was as though he had transmitted a certainty to the pilot that he could never be forgotten.

Steward didn't know how he should reply; but he was influenced by his new sense of duty. He had to take the initiative. He must not be suspected of uncertainty, a loss of command over his own intentions. He, said: 'The men are no longer in the dark. They will never be the same.'

Surgeon hadn't anticipated these fears which Steward had insisted on bringing to their attention. But it was necessary for him to support them. He would have supported any means that provided him with a reason for escape from the future of the enterprise, from a reunion with his wife. Yet he felt it necessary to reduce the importance that Steward had given the men. He couldn't appear to be acting from a fear of the men. But his fear could be dignified beyond argument if he could give it a more impressive origin. He would offer the most absolute authority.

'I do not disrespect Steward's warning,' Surgeon said, 'but there is a greater threat. I am thinking of the House of Trade and Justice.'

'So what do you propose?' Priest asked.

'It is a matter for your guidance,' said Surgeon.

Priest despaired of any intervention from Pinteados. He was on his own; and instinct plunged him into the safest risk.

'We must bring this to the Commandant's attention,' Priest said. 'He has made no reference to events in Lime Stone.'

'I propose we ask to be relieved,' Steward insisted.

The effect surpassed all expectations. The atmosphere had changed. This was no longer a crisis Priest was hoping to mediate; it was like a call to mutiny. Priest couldn't restrain his glance. He looked at Pinteados, and made no secret of his need. There had to be an opinion from the pilot.

But Pinteados had returned to his original habit of self-exclusion. He had judged the emphasis of their argument; and he would take no further part in what they were about to pursue. He was the foreigner again: impervious, remote, and devoid of all interest in their personal destiny. He thought, for a moment, of the boy, and the men who were down below. The Commandant was too painful a memory for him to brood on in the presence of these officers.

Priest watched the pilot stir, and waited for him to say something that might reduce the dangers that Steward had threatened. But Pinteados was beyond entreaty. He wiped his hands across his mouth. He stood, and looked down at the empty plate for a moment. Then he walked out of the dining cabin. There was something ominous about the pilot's departure. Priest couldn't avoid recalling the night he had seen Pinteados walk away after his long and remorseless disclosure about the life of those who were confined to Severn asylum. There was nothing different about this atmosphere, except the absence of the Commandant. Their argument had a similar edge of temper. It had sprung from a similar need to test their courage against the pilot's illicit claims to power. Now it was the Commandant himself whom they had chosen as the pinnacle of their achievement in protest.

Priest felt momentarily abandoned. He was wringing his hands under the table, trying to distract his attention from the crisis that Steward was determined to release. Perhaps it might help to recall the promise of a future that the enterprise had inspired them to pursue. He knew where their ambitions were most delicate and sensitive to persuasion.

'It feels safer to be officers and men on the inside,' said Priest, appearing to speak for himself alone. 'And I think we have reached a point which says forward. There can be no other direction after you cross this point.'

Steward seemed to waver; but Surgeon wouldn't allow any bribery of privilege to detract from the urgency of Steward's challenge.

'We are officers and therefore men on the inside,' Steward said quickly, 'and it's only duty that prevented me from launching this challenge before. I would go further. It's duty that now makes any danger seem normal to me.'

'How well I know that feeling,' said Priest. 'On the inside you learn to treat danger as your natural calling.'

He noticed that his observation had found some favour with Steward, who now recognized in Priest his own style of neutrality. Priest wanted to make it clear, without too obvious commitment, that he was not opposed to their feeling; but he could not identify the prestige of an officer with their approach. They were all men who had been promoted from different levels of deprivation to the unexpected privilege of being officers and therefore men on the inside. Any recollection of the past would confirm the progress they had made. Their new status was more exacting than that known to men whom a natural inheritance of wealth and privilege had brought to power. Their origins always suggested that they would have to surpass themselves in action as well as in the manner of their acting. Boatswain had offered them an example that must be avoided.

'Crossing that point of promotion,' said Priest, 'you can't choose to go back. As officers and therefore men on the inside, you have to stay there; dig yourself in, even though some delay of circumstance does not let you move forward. But you can't go back. You have a status that forbids you to go back.'

Priest was superb in his new role as an advocate for adventure. He had dispelled any dangers about the Commandant's delay from his mind, letting his eloquence strike at the officers' wish to be relieved. He had freed his hands from under the table. They came to his support, lean and eloquent in appeal, as he spread them wide.

'Crossing that point,' Priest began again.

But Steward felt his initiative urge him on. He had to rebuke the silence Priest had trapped them into. A voice filled his skull with familiar predictions of ruin attending all his effort: "Where are your plans now? What have you ever done?" His wife had become a permanent noise in his ear.

'Crossing that point,' Steward argued, hoping to improve on what Priest had said, 'everything will depend on the force working against you. I see it clearly. The House of Trade and Justice will declare its vengeance. The Commandant knows it, and that's the cause of his delay.' Steward had excluded his wife from any list of dangers. The House of Trade had taken her place as the main source of danger. The politics of duplicity now ruled his private feeling.

Priest felt his authority slip. Premonitions of vengeance were never far from his mind after he had heard Boatswain's story. He looked towards the seat that Pinteados had vacated; a word from the pilot might have been enough to help him refute these fears, which Steward had now converted into certainty. Steward could still hear the absent and familiar voice of his wife prophesying doom for all his efforts. He kept a firm grip on his reactions. He had to resist those intrusions from the past. It was the nearness of the future that warned him against the blandishments of Priest. Priest was about to speak; but Steward raised an arm to signal that he was not finished.

'Whatever the Commandant's record,' Steward explained, 'he has never taken such liberties before. It is breaking loose without authority of the House that makes the difference. He will have to reckon with a force of vengeance he has never known before.'

Priest looked morose, and wished for Pinteados by his side. The pilot would have an answer for the despairing counsels of Steward. Then Priest decided he must offer some hope for the future of the enterprise. He spoke as he thought Pinteados might have done.

'The Commandant is not one to yield,' said Priest. But he wasn't sure what impression he wanted to convey.

'They won't let him go free and on his own,' said Surgeon, who had found a new advantage in the difficulties Steward had predicted. 'Either the House with all Lime Stone will bring the Commandant to his knees. Or ask Antarctica to do them that favour. If necessary, the two will join to crush him. What do you think the Treaty was made for?'

Priest showed signs of defeat. The vengeance of the House was enough to darken any further prospects for the enterprise.

But the combination of Lime Stone and Antarctica obliterated all trace of hope from his thinking. No courage would be mad enough to offer resistance to such a marriage of major powers. For the first time Priest really thought about the men who were down below. What judgment would the common mariners pass on these admissions of defeat? But it was useless to solicit a judgment from men who had no experience of the conflicts that raged among those who were officers and therefore men on the inside. Priest had no previous experience of such despair. Speech had deserted his earlier passion for arguing in the Commandant's defence. He had even come to think of the delay as a form of strategy. Until this moment!

'You mean our enterprise will result in waste?' he asked, almost indifferent to what anyone might reply.

'It will result as the major powers decide,' Surgeon said. 'They can crush him by sheer threat alone. Without firing a single shot. Just agree that he has no claim to further negotiation with either power.'

And Steward heard himself whispering under his breath: 'Like the Lord Treasurer and me refusing to negotiate with my wife. In the matter of the girl, Tate de Lysle and I have agreed.'

Steward saw Surgeon glance at him, and he quickly said: 'No claim to further negotiation with either power.'

He was expecting some private rejoinder from Surgeon; but Priest had spoken.

'And if the Commandant were to propose a favourable conclusion?' Priest suggested. 'Would they still want to crush him?'

Steward wouldn't allow any alternative to the gloom that had descended on their future.

'A favourable conclusion would never be to the Commandant's favour,' Steward said. 'That's what breaking free means. The odds change when you withdraw your protection from a major power. It is superior force that decides. The Commandant knows that. I repeat, it is the reason for his delay.'

'With a favourable conclusion,' Priest said wearily, 'some of us would still be on the inside. We might yet retain some measure of personal authority.'

Surgeon felt that he and Steward had now won their battle to bring Priest around. Surgeon was amazed, almost humbled by the fervour which Steward brought to the conflict that had arisen between themselves and Priest. It could only be a matter of time before they achieved a total harmony of feeling.

'I can't see the Commandant taking orders,' said Surgeon. 'Not after he had achieved the enterprise.' He decided to accord Priest some chance of satisfaction. 'It is not a small triumph by any scale. To settle San Cristobal, as was his plan.'

'He would never take orders,' said Steward.

Priest kept his eyes down, avoiding the look of triumph in Surgeon's eyes. He studied his hands, as though they were ships ploughing a passage forward, crawling feebly over the table. He had lapsed into a state of meditation. Slowly he raised his head, and his eyes showed some brief miracle of optimism.

'Forbidden to reach forward may be no worse than refusing to go back,' Priest said. 'I'd say stay put. If the enterprise has worked itself to this point, I suppose I would be happy to stay put.'

There was no conviction at all in his voice; and he spoke as though his interest had found an audience elsewhere. Steward thought he detected the echoes of a desperate man in these consolations. He refrained from making a reply.

'In the circumstances, it would be my right,' said Priest, indifferent to anyone's attention. 'After all that's happened from Lime Stone to this point, it is only natural I should want to remain an officer and a man on the inside. Whatever future this delay may mean, I am an officer and a man on the inside. That must not change.'

Abruptly he got up and made his way towards the door.

When Priest left the dining cabin, Steward felt some new fear of indecision come over him. His nerve had been strengthened by the opposition Priest had provided; in argument he had discovered fresh sources of conviction. But his failure to convert Priest had left him with a sense of foreboding. He started to question the wisdom of his initiative. To be relieved! He tried to anticipate his own conduct in a meeting with the Commandant.

Who would make the challenge to the Commandant? And what would be the stages of any conflict that would follow? He paid no attention to Surgeon as he brooded on the future of his initiative. It was too late to betray his call to action, too soon to prepare himself for a reunion with his wife. But he was seized by reflections on the waste of his days. He was about to rob his future of every ambition the enterprise had promised to fulfil.

'What a tragic timing it would be for us,' Steward said, 'if the Commandant achieved his purpose. Without interference from the House, and to the general applause of the Kingdom!'

But Surgeon had fortified himself against any doubt that might arise. His judgment was precise and cold as his voice.

'My admiration would be with him all the more,' he said.

'But we would provoke the opposite,' said Steward. 'Remembered as those who went soft.'

'It would be a heavy memory,' said Surgeon, abandoning his appetite for further adventure. 'But not worse than what lies ahead.'

And Steward heard his wife's voice again like a prophecy of doom on all his effort.

'It's an awful temptation,' he said; and thought: "To come so near in sharing the Commandant's glory if all went well." But he didn't trust himself to any further utterance of what he was feeling. Surgeon considered the silence that had grown between them, and thought he had found the safest way to fortify Steward in their resolution.

'Should we postpone our meeting with the Commandant?'

There was a sharp rivalry of glances. Then Steward decided it had to be his moment of triumph.

'The matter is decided,' Steward said. 'We must inform the Commandant that questions of the law weigh heavily on us. We do not accept responsibility in his name, and demand to be relieved.'

'When do we move?' Surgeon asked.

'Immediately,' said Steward, 'and with every precaution for success.'

He ignored Surgeon's nod of approval. He had taken the initiative again.

'The boats are ready?' Baptiste asked.

'They could lower at a moment's warning,' said Ivan. The painter was no longer fearful of consequences.

'Then find Duclos and make a final check on the men's feeling,' said Baptiste.

Ivan turned away and was soon swallowed up by the night. There was an edge of moon crumbling slowly and without light into the sunken ridge of sky. A nervous traffic of feet moved about the deck. Men whispered and dispersed, bearing fragments of news. No one could verify what he heard. Rumour was everywhere. There was a hunger for orders that might plunge them into some kind of action.

Baptiste sat alone, waiting for a decision from the men. He had already made his choice. It seemed his life had been one long and dangerous reflection that led him always forward to this moment. Ever so free! He felt his freedom near and beyond, like the night making its vast stride across the ocean. A day ago this waiting had made him weary. But his moment had come. It was here, a message that had always pursued him. The officers had ceased to exist. The Commandant was a fact outside memory. The powder maker was alone and free; generous in his attention to the private moon that blazed away in his skull, returning him to the springs of ancestry, the humble treasure that was his father.

'My first and only hero,' he mused.

He heard a voice alert him.

'I want to speak with you,' said Sasha. The boy had been waiting for some time, judging the moment he would speak.

Baptiste was slow to recover from the ecstasy that had brought his father back to life. He recognized a note of defiance in Sasha's voice.

'Something you have to know,' the boy insisted.

'About the Commandant, I suppose.'

'The officers,' said Sasha, who struggled to control his breathing. 'They've all gone into the Commandant's cabin.'

'Into the Commandant's cabin?' Baptiste repeated.

'And without warning,' said the boy.

'Without warning?'

'The Commandant gave no permission,' said the boy.

'Gave no permission,' Baptiste whispered.

Baptiste spoke like a man emerging slowly from a trance. The boy felt utterly defeated by this apparent lack of interest in his news. Baptiste remained silent. He had no advice to give Sasha. The powder maker looked up at the sky. There was no trace of light against the enormous black roof that swept everywhere over the ocean. Ever so free! He could hear his name in a race with the wind. The boy had gone. There was nothing he could do for Sasha. He had to prepare himself for other emergencies. He heard the footsteps approach. This delay was like a clock he had forgotten to consult. It was there, a souvenir of time. He heard Ivan's voice bending its whispers into his ears.

'Duclos will soon be here,' the painter said, and paused. Baptiste was calm beyond belief.

'Speak plain,' he said. 'How many have you spoken to?'

Ivan had lowered his body to a crouch. He feared the silence that had come between them.

'It may not be too late,' the painter said, 'but there is a bad division among the men.'

'You say the boats were ready?' Baptiste asked. His voice was quiet and sure.

'Yes. They could lower at a moment's warning,' Ivan said. 'It may not be too late. The officers are consulting with the Commandant. Or so it seems.'

Baptiste had purged his memory of any evidence that had to do with the officers or the Commandant.

'The men,' he said; 'how do the men feel about my plan?'

'I heard Duclos speak with them,' Ivan said, trying to postpone his answer.

'What's their feeling?' Baptiste asked again. There was no agitation in his voice.

'You know, it is never easy for the poor to act without proper orders,' Ivan said. 'Alone, a man will show he is willing. Together, they get frightened by your kind of decision.'

Ivan wished he could get a view of the face he was addressing. It was impossible to imagine Baptiste in such a state of calm, indifferent to the dangers he was proposing. It seemed his sense of power had made him patient. He was determined to put the painter at ease.

'How many do you suspect of weakness?' he asked, and Ivan felt a hand graze his shoulder. Baptiste had got up. Ivan climbed slowly up to face him.

'None are really weak,' the painter said. 'It is your plan which puts a double weakness in some faces.'

Ivan waited, trying to judge the effect of his report about the men. Baptiste didn't come to his aid, however, and the silence embarrassed the painter.

'They feel weak not to think like you,' Ivan said, 'and weak at the thought that they should betray the Commandant.'

'Cowards!' Baptiste hissed. 'Cowards!'

The word came in a mutter; and Ivan realized that the powder maker's mood had changed. He felt an urge to defend the men against this charge.

'Mutiny isn't so simple a command,' the painter said.

'I won't be gagged by words,' Baptiste replied.

Ivan was familiar with these bursts of temper. He had already decided what he was going to do. He would take orders from Baptiste in support of the plan to lower the boats and set out for San Cristobal on their own. His loyalty to Baptiste wouldn't allow of any alternative if the enterprise was endangered by some conspiracy between the Commandant and the officers. He thought only of the dangers for the common hands below.

'Whatever my feeling,' Ivan said, 'our strength is not the same.'

He hoped to tame the powder maker's mood by some expression of reverence for his courage. If some men were indecisive, it was simply because they weren't sure the plan would work. And what would be the consequences of such a failure? Ivan was trying to offer himself as a common example of a man who could be afraid. It was his strategy for making Baptiste see that there was nothing cowardly about the indecision he had observed when Duclos argued with the men.

'Any man wants to be sure what side he is on,' said Ivan. 'Let the plan work, and you are in command, then my gun and me will be alike before your orders. That's how common men always reason.'

'You too?' Baptiste said, as though he had heard some blasphemy. 'But you trust the Commandant without condition.'

Ivan understood what was intended by this charge. It expressed insult and a sense of betrayal. He felt some stir of dignity; a sudden impulse urged him to answer Baptiste in his own defence. But always it was the interest of the common men he wanted to preserve. The plan had become more important than any momentary triumph in argument with Baptiste. The painter realized that something had changed inside him. Baptiste had given him a taste for dangerous commitment. He was no longer the painter who had started out from Lime Stone: a man who stood for safety, the apostle of patience among the men who were down below. Baptiste had ignited some other instinct in him. But Ivan was not simply supporting the plan to lower the boats and desert the ship before the officers and the Commandant made their strategy known. It was no longer just a matter of giving his support to Baptiste. The plan had become an absolute necessity for the fulfilment of the painter's vision. Baptiste himself could not surpass this fervour for success that had converted Ivan, the visionary, into a man of fruitful action. The painter saw himself in a sacred partnership with Baptiste. Ivan had discovered in this delay the true meaning of that moment that Baptiste had always spoken of: a special opportunity had arrived, and he was ready to offer his life in the service of great events. He was a humble partner in the plan, the quiet and terrible conscience of each common mariner down below.

'We have no time to lose,' Ivan said, and there was still an infinite gentleness in his voice. He took a step ahead of Baptiste. 'Those who want to be captive here are free to stay. But we are for the ocean and San Cristobal.'

For a moment Baptiste seemed uncertain of his presence on the deck. The painter's voice might have been the sound of his own dreaming. Stretching his hand out, as though he had to make sure of his surroundings, he let it rest for a while on Ivan's shoulders. He wanted to applaud, as he had done when the Law failed to find his father. But he couldn't find words that would name his pride. He pressed Ivan's arm as they moved forward. They were going down below, where the men had gathered in a whispering controversy over their future. They would have to choose between the strategy of the Commandant's delay and the powder maker's plan to lower the boats and continue the enterprise to San Cristobal on their own.

Three lamps hung from hoops of iron around the belly of the ship. But the light was too feeble to reach the base of the timber beam where Baptiste and Ivan had arrived. They waited, unseen. A brief arc of light discovered the cook, Duclos, who was speaking amidst constant interruption.

'It would be a treachery to the Commandant,' a voice was

saying. 'What's more, I never did like the look of Baptiste.'

'That's not important,' someone answered. 'Let Baptiste look after his own face.'

'It's made for hanging, I'd say.'

'Then go hang Baptiste,' the voice came back. 'That is not my business.'

Duclos tried to intervene; but several voices were now raised in the dispute about Baptiste.

'Rumour says the Commandant may be in conspiracy with this foreign Admiral,' a man reminded them. 'That's my business.'

'And the officers, too,' someone added in support. 'What amity could there be in such private consultation with the Commandant? And all together.'

'I wage a bet the Admiral will arrive before daylight. They brought us on a dirty job.'

'Criminal dirty, if what you say is true.'

'Never,' a voice was protesting. 'The Commandant would never disgrace the name of Lime Stone to win a favour from a foreigner of Antarctica.'

'And the pilot?' the man protested. 'What's the pilot, if not a foreigner? And you forget the Treaty. What is the purpose of the Treaty if not to reach general favour?'

'Treaty or not,' the voice insisted, 'the Commandant would never join a foreigner to commit treachery against his own blood.'

'I stand by that,' someone conceded. 'Whatever makes the delay, the Commandant is no coward. Consult his record in open conflict with Antarctica and you will see.'

'That's true. And it is known he fought against the Treaty.'

Duclos couldn't be heard over the chorus of agreement which had brought the men to the Commandant's defence. He judged it was time he returned to the deck; but he was afraid to report his failure to Baptiste. He was about to make a final effort, but he had waited too long. Someone ruled that Duclos had spoken long enough.

'The Commandant will hear of this,' a voice was warning. 'That you tried to make rebellion against his command. That you ask us to pollute the name of Lime Stone and the reputation of the Commandant, which everyone in the Kingdom honours.'

Baptiste now felt a heat spread across his back. His sweat ran like a river over his eyes and into his mouth. Doubt had not got the better of him; but he had started to feel some threat to his purpose. He was trying to count the voices that might be on his side. He wanted to calculate his strength before he joined in open challenge with them. Suddenly he heard a sound like feet stampeding, and the crush of bodies pressing backward. The powder maker had swung his body around from behind the timber beam. The men were alarmed by the sudden apparition that had leapt so fiercely out of the night. Without warning and murderous in its aspect of command. Some thought it was a ghost. Those who were not near believed the Commandant had arrived. Baptiste now stood in a full arc of light shouting a gospel of abuse and hope at the men. They stood silent, overwhelmed by the tyrannical fury of the powder maker, contradicting all their loyalties as simple men of Lime Stone.

'The honour of the Kingdom, I hear you say!' Baptiste made a brief pause, as though he wanted each syllable to spell out his contempt of their illiterate understanding. 'The reputation of the Commandant, I hear you say!' And his voice waited again until he had completed the movement of scything the light with his hands. 'So what is your share in the wealth of Lime Stone? Go on, speak! What is your share in the continent where, even now, tonight, mothers and children are clawing like crabs for food. Go on, speak!'

The voice waited, and the hand was brandished like a sword.

'Go on, speak,' Baptiste continued, jeering at the men. 'Where do you stand in the conscience of the House of Trade and Justice? What is your place in the affections of the Commandant himself? Go on, speak! Name your region. North? Is it the East? South or West? Name it. Whatever name you honour it with, I tell you now the same fevers mutilate your villages. Hunger is no less savage. The same hands of authority organize your decay. They name you adventurers for the purpose of turning you into common animals of prey.'

The powder maker's voice was waiting. His hands were withdrawn slowly, like warriors come happily to rest.

'Name it, I say,' Baptiste was coaxing them. 'Different in age and ambition, you travel with the same experience. Your service

in the name of Lime Stone is a lifetime's robbery against yourselves. So I say it does not matter what is the cause of this delay.
I speak to a different purpose. The enterprise must be made ours.
We shall lower the boats against any orders from elsewhere. And
go forward to San Cristobal on our own.'

The powder maker's mouth had remained open. His lips were
still making an effort to speak; but his voice had died in the
solitary burst of gunshot that exploded from above. Striking like
a bolt of thunder breaking up the sky, it spread over the night
an echo that covered the sea. The sound had paralyzed all movement down below; louder and more decisive than any answer of
cannon fire the men had ever known, it had started a new terror
in every eye. The men continued to gaze, unseeing, at the startled
shadows that the lamps had swung on the timbers that climbed
above their heads.

Baptiste was the first who showed the distance between him
and the men. He had come into full view, a stride ahead of Ivan,
when they heard a fresh report of gunfire from above: two rapid
explosions tearing through the night. The sound died with little
trace of echo. A ripple of voices broke through the silence; and
the first signs of recognition showed on Ivan's face. He had seen
Baptiste; and beyond the heaving edge of light he could detect
the face of Marcel. The fisherman stood sombre and attentive to
the conference of whispering that had begun around him.

Baptiste realized there was no logic to their waiting, but he
couldn't decide what orders he should give. The whispering had
subsided. Now he saw the gradual movement of feet coming
towards him; but the men were concentrating their attention
elsewhere. The movement of feet continued, soft and nervous
as the march of shadows. Sasha came into view, and the men
waited for the boy to speak; he stepped forward into the light,
and the men came abruptly to a halt. They had seen the gun
that the boy was carrying. He gripped it firmly with both hands,
held high and away from his body. There was a look of power
and terror in Sasha's eyes, as though he had discovered in the
weapon some necessary and fearful truth that burnt his hands.
But his voice was calm, as though he had detached his feeling
utterly from the news he had brought.

'They have killed the Commandant,' he said. 'Surgeon and

313

Steward. They have murdered the Commandant.'

A babel of voices came tumbling around the boy. The men had entered into a state of frenzy with their questions. There was no pause in their appeal for enlightenment. But the boy didn't speak again. He turned away and walked through the opening of the timbers up the lower deck with the gun for company.

'To the boats!' Baptiste shouted; and then, more quietly, his voice was heard: 'Now is our moment to lower the boats.'

TWENTY-FOUR

EXTRACT FROM VOYAGES OF BAPTISTE,
NATIVE OF LIME STONE

If it may happen that I come to judgment before the majesty and opinion of the House of Trade and Justice, then I would have such authority as there be test my decision by these facts as I set them down. I was the agent and foremost advocate of what the common hands decide. That I do not deny; nor feel any shame nor degradation of conduct to declare it. After five days of waiting, and no just reason sent down for such delay, I in collaboration with such as were of the same mind deserted the Reconnaissance to continue the enterprise as we see fit and in accordance with the honour and prestige of our labour. The divisions could not get any officer to give a firm command; but rumour kept me fully aware of the reason. Some portion of the news might have been false. That I cannot argue. But there was a general opinion among us that the officers were against the completion of the enterprise. Some hands advised waiting until we had reliable word about their reason. But there was no consultation either by conversation or direct order. Therefore we started to suspect a betrayal of some kind was upon us.

The Commandant passed all his waking hours in the dark,

*allowing no opinion to reach him and denying all hands of en-
lightenment from the obscurity of his cabin. But rumour gave
me sufficient warning that certain officers were agreed on a course
of action which went wholly against my conscience and the judgment of the men on my side. These said officers would exploit
the Treaty by making a friendship with the Admiral Badaloza of
Dolores and for the purpose of abandoning the enterprise. I had
this fact from reliable source. Like others down below, I never
found favour with the Treaty, even before these events came to
threaten us. Some would have taken a position on the Commandant's side and against the officers. But as I say, there was no
word allowed from his obscurity. We decided therefore to act on
our own authority.*

*I know it is a fearful thing for common folk to act on their
own orders. Such independence has always put a terrible tremor
to the heart of all known authority. But it was an act of justice,
considering the labour we had supplied to the enterprise and the
expectations spread among us by the Commandant himself. We
were too near to the completion of such a labour to give ourselves
over wholly to such waste. And, as I repeat, without any instruction or word of reliable promise from the officers. I reason that
the officers were busy attending to their fears, whereas the common
hands were too far gone in the just expectations of the future to
be distracted by the officers' interests, which, considering the
nature of their intrigue, could not be to the ultimate honour of
the common hands.*

*In the evening of the fifth day of delay I had special report
of their appointed council with the Commandant. There was a
feeling the Commandant would open the conflict with the
officers. But I was no longer trustful of any favourable result, and
preparation had gone too far to halt the lowering of the boats.
Even before we touch water and start to row through that
fateful passage on to San Cristobal I had decided there could
be no returning. So when report reached us through the ship's
boy that the Commandant had been murdered, my duty became
abundant and clear. Yet even at that tragic moment there were
men of the opinion that if by some reversal of fate the news was
in error and the Commandant and officers had pursued us with
assurance that the enterprise was not over, that the promise which*

315

started this fateful journey would be restored, then they would very likely accept the old arrangement, conceding obedience to the officers as before. I cannot prove that such would be the real outcome; but I observe that in moments of extreme decision, some men will imagine an excess of hope against the evidence of all known fact.

...I would have it known for the benefit of record that there be one man among the officers who at this time venture to give us benefit of his knowledge. It was Pinteados, the pilot, a foreigner whose conduct in the entire business we cannot fathom. Believing him to be the least in importance in our business, it so happened he intervened in a way most suited to our interests. I cannot declare his reason, any more than I can put on record the just cause of the officers' decision to terminate the Voyage, and in such mortal dishonour. For if I may repeat, the Treaty with all its particulars on paper was never a matter of conviction and acceptance with me and those of my experience which would come to a just majority. If such be taken as disloyalty to the House, in defence I would argue on behalf of others and myself that the Kingdom was never without division over the fate of the Commandant. And there would be many voices of influence raised, for one reason or another, on behalf of my action.

'You may report what I say,' said Pinteados, 'but I sign nothing.'

'The authorities will want to hear some witness to these events,' the Admiral said.

'I repeat,' Pinteados replied, 'I put my name to nothing.'

They had found no one below the decks. The air was heavy with rotting odours lifting from the open casks. Rats had started to forage among the relics of food. The Admiral kept sniffing, slapping the back of his hand against his nose. Pinteados walked ahead, avoiding the timbers as he led the way back to the upper deck. He could hear the Admiral swear as he stumbled close behind. Then his head showed above the pump, and he felt the wind press him forward. The sky was coming forward to meet him: it seemed so near. The pinnacle of the mast was disappearing into a curve of hard blue rock. The wind clapped him again: a touch of hands, hot and strange. Some desert heat had spread out from the back of his neck, making a thirst in his eyes and

over the sudden grooves of salt forming under his chin. The
Admiral had come up beside him.

'They have all gone,' he said, and inspected the horizon. 'Every
man.'

'I saw no one below,' Pinteados said. His tone was mockery.

The Admiral seemed to puzzle over the pilot's remark. Of
course, they had seen no one below. He had borne the pilot's
discourtesy with unusual calm.

'Did you advise them to go?' the Admiral asked.

Pinteados gave the sky his attention again.

'I knew what they were going to do,' he said.

The Admiral worried whether he had got the pilot's meaning
right.

'You didn't advise them?' he asked again.

The tone had changed to interrogation: a warning of details;
but the voice suggested that there was room for compromise.
Pinteados had ignored the offer. He had robbed his interest of
everything except the skull of blue rock that burned above the
masthead. The Admiral was losing patience; but he thought it
would be useless to show his displeasure. Instead, he tried to
coax the pilot.

'The other matter is more important,' he said. 'A great tragedy.
No way to avoid a report of these events. The tragedy is too
great.'

'You will do your duty,' Pinteados said.

'And you will do yours,' the Admiral agreed.

They had returned to the Commandant's cabin, which was
now ablaze with sunlight. A brilliance of morning raged over
the charts and pierced the globe that rose like a human head
from the council table. Broken shadows of blood burnt black
along the edge of the table. The trail continued over the floor,
swerving past the small bed, until it reached the door. A blank
sheet of paper lay curled in the far corner. Dry stains covered its
surface like cakes of mud. It was less than an hour since they
had disposed of the bodies.

Pinteados looked a little dazed. He resented this fierce illumination that uncovered every object for his gaze. He didn't want
to repeat this visit to the cabin; but he had experienced a
momentary failure of will when the Admiral made his request

for a final inspection. The Admiral's attention was curious and vague. Now it would ramble; then focus with astonishing alertness on some detail that was minor, almost irrelevant beside the weight of what Pinteados would always remember: the swift and squalid end of a great career; the Commandant buried by foreign hands and without any trace of ceremony. It was as though some new need for participation had been born in Pinteados; so that the Admiral appeared to be the absolute real foreigner to the drama Pinteados was trying to re-create. The Admiral had started his enquiries again.

'And the boy's action?' the Admiral was asking. 'What was the boy doing in the Commandant's cabin?'

'He understands nothing,' Pinteados was saying to himself. The Admiral looked so eager and zealous in investigation, as though some manic hunger for evidence was the only appetite he had ever known. Pinteados watched him and felt an awful punishment of boredom descend on his silence. His interest was kept alive only by his awareness of the Admiral's lack of connection to this room.

'And why would the boy kill Steward and Surgeon?' the Admiral persisted. 'Would the officers have offended the boy at any time?'

Pinteados didn't answer. The Admiral thought the pilot was ignoring him; but Pinteados couldn't answer. Instead he was calculating how he might demonstrate what had happened. He began to walk in silence from the end of the council table over to the small bed, counting each step before he started on the next. Then he made three long, slow strides from the small bed, and finished on the far side of the table. He had taken up his position again. He didn't speak until he noticed the Admiral's failure to understand what he was witnessing.

'Admiral!' Pinteados said on a note of obvious disdain. 'If you or I had shot the boy, the Commandant would have killed us in that instant. Such an event is too large for what you call offence. Do you understand?'

The pilot paused; and the Admiral thought he should come to the rescue of his own dignity. He began to nod his head in a wise and casual acknowledgment of what the pilot had been saying. 'And if we must repeat for the last time,' Pinteados said irritably, 'there was a gun under that bed.' He was pointing towards the small bed; but the Admiral was no longer present to the pilot's mind. Pinteados might have been talking to himself, re-creating a memory that was strictly private.

'The boy arrived at the first sound of Steward's gunfire,' the pilot explained. 'He saw the Commandant sprawled out in his own blood. There!' The pilot pointed. 'He saw the Commandant sprawled out there.' Pinteados was withdrawing his hand as he continued. 'The boy walked to the bed, that small bed. There!' The pilot's hand struck out again. 'There,' he emphasized. 'And the boy sat down. Simple as waiting, he just sat down. No one paid him any attention, until seconds later Surgeon and Steward both collapsed. There!' The Pilot's arm circled the air, and suddenly his voice became low and grave. 'The gun was under that small bed. There! But no one knew. No one but the boy and the Commandant knew about the gun. Under that bed.'

Pinteados turned away and walked towards the door. He looked out over the deck, as though he was appealing to the sea to put its distance between him and the Admiral. He returned to the table, brooding on the shocking splendour of sunlight that enlivened the Admiral's eyes. Pinteados wanted some relief from the tragic intimacy of this room. He had begun to feel some novel sense of outrage at the events that had put an end to the enterprise in this room. Some weird and sinister absurdity had blossomed from the deaths that happened here. He might have recovered his need to talk if the Admiral could understand the affliction which had plagued the Commandant and the officers, and hurried the enterprise inevitably to its doom.

'It's time we went elsewhere,' Pinteados said walking towards the door. He wanted to put the cabin forever out of his mind as he made his way down to the lower deck. The Admiral was hurrying close behind. It seemed that his dignity always failed him when there were no words.

'There must be some report,' he said.

'Of course,' Pinteados replied. 'My witness you can have, but I sign nothing.'

The pilot came out to the deck and watched the sea heave and tumble where the Commandant's body had been buried. He thought he heard the dead voice of Steward scream its echoes across the ocean. The bleeding skull of Surgeon had surfaced, and its laughter alarmed the sea. Pinteados could see Surgeon's skull, scarlet with blood, and the sound of gunfire reverberated like insane laughter through the empty ship. And the Commandant's cabin had come alive, familiar and vivid with the memory of those tortured faces he had seen in the cells of Severn asylum. The pilot wanted to leave; but he couldn't move. He stood rigid and wordless, living again, stage by incredible stage, the final encounter of the Commandant and his officers.

The council of officers had been brief. Pinteados was alone with the Commandant when they arrived. Surgeon and Steward had come in together. But the dispute didn't begin until Priest took his seat. Priest must have foreseen what would happen, but he was powerless to influence the result. Like Pinteados, he kept himself aloof from the conflict that was threatening. He could never decide on a course of action until he was sure his duty would meet with general approval. But this was an impossible demand to make in an atmosphere where strength was on trial; and every argument had sprung from a hostile temper. Priest withdrew, hoping to bury himself in the habit of silence and prayer. But his hands had forgotten the shape of the cross. He could not pray, even with his hands.

Pinteados might have been able to rescue the Commandant and the officers from the fatality which was to follow. But he was stupefied by what he knew: the Commandant's instructions which he, alone, had received; they would proceed no further. He knew both the Commandant's instruction and the demands of the officers who had spoken in his presence the evening before. The Commandant and the officers were united by the same fear, motivated by the same wish to bring the enterprise to an end. And yet this common agreement of feeling had now become the soil for their antagonism. And Pinteados kept thinking—could only think—that he couldn't recall any history of enemies who had produced such a furious conflict as this rage of temper that proceeded from their agreement of feeling. And he alone knew what was obvious. They could not find the courage to accept a reunion with their women. Different in status and intention, the absolute deficiency they shared was a common failure to accept reunion with their women.

'It was a pure accident of timing,' Pinteados said in a sudden appeal for the Admiral's attention. 'There would have been no tragedy if the Commandant had spoken first.'

The Admiral welcomed his change of manner. The pilot's voice was less harsh, as though regret had made him amiable.

'When the act is mutiny,' the Admiral said, 'the lower orders always speak first.'

'But was it mutiny?' Pinteados asked. 'Their demand was to be relieved. The Commandant's decision was similar. He would proceed no further. But Steward made his challenge before the Commandant let his orders be known. A pure accident of timing.'

The Admiral reflected, prolonging his vague, almost habitual search of the horizon. The ocean was empty. The near swell receded from the ship and sank far away into a monotonous stretch of green sea.

'We couldn't suggest mutiny in the report,' the Admiral said.

Again there was a promise of future collaboration. But Pinteados showed no interest in the substance of any report which the Admiral might prepare. His memory of the Commandant was too recent; it stirred some loyalty in him, and a fresh grief for the intemperate mood that had brought about his death.

'The Commandant was not one to yield,' said the Admiral.

'It was their manner of speaking which provoked him,' said Pinteados. 'Fear made them bold, and fear was now so great, there was no limit to their boldness. Such fear is a fatal weapon of attack. The Commandant knew what was happening; yet he could not restrain himself.'

'He was a man of dangerous pride,' said the Admiral; 'I saw it at work in the last expedition before this enterprise.'

The Admiral now looked at Pinteados, renewing his hidden offers of comradeship. But the pilot was determined to exclude these reminiscences from his interest. Yet he responded to the Admiral's challenge.

'That's where it began for me,' Pinteados said. 'The Expedition.'

'I recollect,' the Admiral said.

'The price of desertion was my meeting the Commandant,' Pinteados said. Now he returned the Admiral's stare. 'I do not regret that time.'

They were caught in an exchange of scrutiny: the Admiral's

eyes exploring for some concession, some hint of compromise on the pilot's part. Pinteados wanted him to learn the daring and ruthlessness of the foreigner who had surrendered all claims to ancestral roots. He wanted to convey the meaning of absolute denial.

'This was the ship that went astray,' Pinteados said. 'The one you couldn't account for. Neither you nor the House of Lime Stone.'

The Admiral smiled and slapped his hands against the timbers. The moment for negotiation seemed very near.

'We remember,' he said.

'You can include that in the report,' said Pinteados, giving warning of his skill.

'You advise that?' the Admiral challenged.

'You will do your duty,' said Pinteados, 'but I sign nothing.'

Pinteados would remain firm and impersonal in his dealings with the Admiral. He knew the stages of calculation: the hints and suggestions which the Admiral would now employ to establish an atmosphere for bargaining. The value of the ship was at stake. The enterprise was still a matter of secrecy; no item of cargo was listed. There was no record that might verify the events of the last few months. The future of the ship—its value and any assignments that would follow—these intricacies of negotiation could be settled finally by himself and the Admiral. But Pinteados couldn't distinguish the motives that made him at first so resistant to the Admiral's hint of a bargain. He wanted to share a different experience with the Admiral, and the thought worried him how personal witness was the only reliable knowledge anyone could offer; and at the same time it was a kind of knowledge most difficult to communicate. He could devise no method that would help the Admiral share in the events he had witnessed. He was safe while the Admiral's offers of a bargain remained open. But he would have liked to share in a different kind of collaboration. Maybe he had wanted, at last, to be part of another's understanding. But the Admiral's company was useless for this purpose.

The Admiral's feeling for the tragedy was limited to a certain admiration for the Commandant, a recognition of a daring and authority he would never attempt. But the real tragedy of the Commandant would always escape his intelligence. Otherwise

322

Pinteados might have asked him to consider the extreme decisions the Commandant could make. He was thinking of the case of Boatswain. To the pilot's amazement, the Commandant had given an order for Boatswain to attend the council of the officers; it was the first time the latter had been released from confinement. It was as though the Commandant would discover in Boatswain's presence some source of his own strength; a fragment of certainty that what he did and felt derived from his interest in honourable conduct. Boatswain, whose story had precipitated a collapse and set the final signature of waste on the entire enterprise, had become the Commandant's example of support. During the council of officers, Boatswain was the only man to whom the Commandant would concede an opinion. He had invited Boatswain to say whether he wanted to be relieved. But Boatswain was too far gone to discover his own meaning. He was a man who had lost contact with what he did. He kept up an incoherent babbling about the Lady of the House. How he had killed her; and how the Kingdom had to be cleansed of all who would defile its honour. He had killed the Lady: that's all he could remember or value. He had dignified his error by according it a purity of purpose. For the rest, he sat in a stupor of silence: utterly disconnected from himself, from his meaning.

Now Pinteados was trying to shake himself free from the spell of this improbable union between Boatswain and the Commandant. It had revived the dereliction and torture of those faces he had met in Severn asylum. The pilot's memory suddenly grew fertile, irresistible; returning to the drama of men in acts of violent self-denial. This would be his last memory of the Commandant alive. The way he sought to justify himself through the futility and senseless ardour of Boatswain's support.

Pinteados turned to the Admiral and said: 'It makes me think of Surgeon. As never before.'

Again the pilot's impulse to bear witness made him forgetful of his audience. The Admiral had no idea what he was talking about. For a moment he judged that Pinteados might have been feeling the strain of what had happened.

'What should I report about Surgeon?' the Admiral asked.

But Pinteados didn't know how he should begin to explain

his meaning. Yet he went on, indifferent to the Admiral's lack of understanding.

'There was a kind of relief on the Commandant's face,' Pinteados said, 'whenever Boatswain spoke. That was enough. He found in Boatswain the same comfort I think Surgeon found in me.'

'You gave Surgeon comfort before he died?' the Admiral said, echoing by habit the words he had heard. He was offering new gifts of appreciation to the pilot.

And Pinteados replied, as though he had discovered in the Admiral the perfect conscience he had been seeking to receive his knowledge.

'That is true,' he said, 'I gave Surgeon the same comfort Boatswain gave the Commandant. I could feel Surgeon's relief that night I told him of my intercourse with his wife. He was enraged until he heard the worst. Then he was at ease. He could make peace with himself after he had heard the worst about his wife.'

The Admiral listened, ignorant and solicitous, calculating the chances of an allegiance with the pilot.

'I feel it was the same with the Commandant,' Pinteados said. 'Somehow Boatswain ruined his hope, and gave him comfort with his ruin.'

Pinteados felt the Admiral's hand embrace him. The mood had changed as they walked towards the ladders. The Admiral's boat waited below.

'What's to be done with Boatswain?' the Admiral asked. He had already decided to be rid of any obstacle that might interfere with his plans for the pilot.

'Let Priest decide,' Pinteados said.

The Admiral warned himself against any risk of argument. He had agreed that business might be more speedily conducted on their return to his quarters.

'To be sure,' he said, 'we'll let Priest decide.'

Pinteados made no reply; and the Admiral was quick to protect himself against any chance of error.

'It's the strain of a great tragedy,' he said, inviting Pinteados to lead the way.

Slowly, rocking to the swell that encircled the ship, they descended into the Admiral's boat.

The drama of the *Reconnaissance* had certainly enlivened the Admiral's duties. These mornings were so familiar: languid and slow. The heat had anaesthetized his senses. Daily he would stare through a dull haze, blinded by the flaming citrus that garrisoned the foot of the hills: a still, mute cluster of low-hanging fruit. Farther inland the vegetation would be busy with frightened deer and the slow vagrancy of cattle. The Admiral had been dying from a lack of duties until the *Reconnaissance* arrived. His brain had gradually come awake. Now the future of the ship excited his imagination. Could he make a deal with Pinteados for the ship? He could barely restrain his gratitude for the enterprise that had brought the pilot to his shores. He tried to give notice of his respect for the dead.

'Whatever their conduct,' he said, 'there was some bravery in them.'

'Under instructions,' Pinteados answered. 'They are the bravest under instructions.'

The pilot didn't appear to share his enthusiasm. The Admiral was curious, fearing any signs of disagreement.

'So near,' he said, 'to come so near and end in such tragedy.'

'It's a sickness of the spine,' Pinteados repeated. 'Their bravery will work only under instructions.'

'But they had some experience of command,' said the Admiral.

'They were only on the inside,' Pinteados said, 'no further. They were men who would settle for nothing else. To be on the inside was enough. To be within the orbit of power was their total ambition. But real power frightened them. To shine on the inside, within the orbit of power! There they were at home. But they had to avoid the touch of power itself. The women are absolute evidence of what I mean. To feel authority over the women! That was enough for them. But to commit themselves fully to what they felt authority over. That they could never master. Such power they were afraid of.'

'The Commandant had no fear of power,' the Admiral said, constant in his support of the dead.

'He was different,' said Pinteados. He paused, as though he had to guard his tongue from blasphemy when he spoke of the Commandant. Then he added: 'He too had a sickness of the spine. Different, but with the same sickness.'

'He was unusual,' the Admiral insisted. 'Most unusual, to be sure.'

And Pinteados agreed.

'Unusual he was,' said Pinteados, 'but of the same breed. A great pity he should be of their breed. Yet he was. No man ever rises far above the deficiencies of his type. Yes, he was great, I say. But of the same breed.'

It displeased Pinteados to offer the Commandant as typical of the officers; but it was his conviction. The Admiral noticed the pilot's change of temper. It seemed he wanted to rid himself of all interest in what was behind him. The enterprise was over. He would annihilate all memory of the Commandant by turning attention to his own survival. Experience had confirmed his judgment that he was safer without any claims to a national pride. He wouldn't hesitate to dispel any illusions of common birth and history, which the Admiral might have been nursing for their future. His native Antarctica was a name; its history was a label that was no longer relevant to this creation of himself as the absolute foreigner. The Admiral would have to learn the silence of this foreigner: a man who would make no claims beyond the practice of his skill, whose interests came to an end with the certainty of his survival.

They had leapt from the boat together, and started leisurely up the burning slope of pebbles towards the Admiral's quarters. Pinteados felt the earth resist his step. He kicked a patch of dirt over the threshold of the door; then paused, admiring the blue curve of the bay. The admiral had gone ahead. He was waiting, rehearsing the burden of courtesies he would have to endure in order to persuade the pilot. There was a vandal's pride in his embrace when Pinteados entered. But the pilot had become alien as the dead officers he had survived. His greeting was remote as the touch of stone.

Pinteados said, 'The vessel *Penalty*? How many days ago?'

'*Penalty*?' the Admiral was enquiring in reply. He was taken by surprise.

'She would have put down her anchors some days ago.'

The Admiral started to suspect some rivalry of interests was at work.

'That's where the men are heading for?' he asked.

'The women,' Pinteados said calmly; 'that's where the women will be waiting.'

The Admiral looked relieved. There was male mischief in his smile.

'Yes, I remember,' he said; '*Penalty* had a cargo of women.'

Pinteados was gradual in everything he did: he was looking around the Admiral's room with its treasure of heroic faces: men whose names Antarctica had made familiar as an alphabet. Pinteados did not want to sojourn here. Abruptly he turned his attention on the Admiral. His voice was sharp as the sound of brass.

'To business,' Pinteados said.

'Business?' The Admiral made some show of his alarm.

'Yes,' said Pinteados, impatient of delay. 'The future of the ship *Reconnaissance*. That's what is on your mind.'

'To be sure,' the Admiral conceded. 'We have some business to conclude.'

Some hidden fire had assailed the Admiral's eye. He saw his future at anchor not far away. He was sure he could arouse some fruitful bargain with the pilot. And Pinteados realized again that a wordless and invisible power had been conferred upon him. The ship was his secret; and his secret was the Admiral's last ambition.

The Admiral felt it would be wasteful to delay his meaning further.

'You feel there's no need for a report?' he asked.

'You will do your duty,' Pinteados said.

The Admiral struggled quietly to detect the substance of the pilot's warning.

'If *Reconnaissance* was the Commandant's personal property,' the Admiral began, appealing to the dead faces of Antarctica, 'and since we share in a common heritage of the same kingdom, I would propose—'

Pinteados had heard enough. He signalled the Admiral to join him in a brief interval of silence. The proposal might have been sound; but the future would have to follow the pilot's direction.

'If the truth must be known,' Pinteados said, '*Reconnaissance* belongs to the Lady of the House.'

The Admiral felt a burst of air explode inside him.

'You mean,' he stammered, 'we must report this matter to the House of Trade and Justice?'

'We must report to the Lady,' Pinteados said.

The Admiral thought there was some mischief in the pilot's answer. He had grown irritable and disconsolate.

'To the Lady of the House,' he shouted; 'what difference does it make if report must go to Lime Stone?'

Pinteados was removing his thumb from his ear. Gradually he was surveying the ancestral faces that hung a pride of Antarctica around the room. He was giving the Admiral a chance to compose himself.

'We report to San Cristobal,' Pinteados said.

'To San Cristobal!' The Admiral's stomach was relieving its bubbles of air again.

'We report to San Cristobal,' the pilot said. 'The Lady of the House is waiting there.'

The Admiral heard the air increase its bubbles in his stomach. Pinteados was beyond his comprehension.

'And you,' the Admiral asked; 'what about you?'

'I shall be around,' Pinteados said. 'While my skill lasts, I shall always be around.'

'In what zones?' The Admiral was begging.

'In any zone.' Pinteados smiled. 'Everywhere and in any zone.'

The pilot was resolute about his multiple choice of direction.

EXTRACT FROM FINAL VOYAGE OF PRIEST,
NATIVE OF LIME STONE

A whole world broke into fragments, and before my very eyes. I saw it and without the help of my Lord could never measure the true meaning of such ruin. To bear witness to the collapse of all order and to feel the foundations of every necessary belief crumble. Men imagine they can with patience or superior force recover from such a fall from grace; but it is wicked innocence that would encourage such optimism in their own powers. What sign was given by these deaths I can never without the help of my Lord signify. Why did my own strength fail when there was greatest need of my service?

And my punishment was more terrible than any the Comman-

dant could have known before that shot of gunfire blasted his breath away forever. I had lost all power to pray; to make a simple appeal for Your mercy; humbly to say, forgive, forgive him and us, my Lord. I could not name that word which might place such ruin within the orbit of Your mercy; had forgotten in that moment the entire history of my meaning as a shepherd entrusted with your flock.

And so he died (the greatest man of Lime Stone) without any effort on my part to intercede. I saw the two foreigners, Pinteados and the Admiral Badaloza, lower his body, still wet with the blood of his wound, into the sea, and the water was leaping like a white fire from hell, and I the last citizen of his Kingdom to bear witness to this unchristian burial could not name that word which would restore him and his assassins to the orbit of Your mercy. He died, the greatest man in the Kingdom, died alone and without aid, as the boy who was his favourite must now live. For the boy has discovered his safety in the barrel of a gun. My punishment is more terrible than any the officers could have known before they turned this boy's loyalty into act of murderous revenge. And I could not name that word which might bring the boy into the orbit of Your mercy; humbly to say, forgive, forgive him and us, my Lord. And even now, as I write these words on paper, and watch the alphabet perform its duty under the guidance of my hand, even now I can feel no spirit touch my tongue to name that word which might bring me within the orbit of Your mercy; to say, forgive, forgive me, my Lord. And all my past, the whole history of my service, has finally deprived me of all meaning. I watch the words I can no longer name, and realize I am simply exercising with the alphabet. My life has been nothing but a fruitless exercise with the alphabet.

To be born again! I want to pray for the boy and the future of the women who are waiting. But I have lost the power to name that word which would bring them within the orbit of Your mercy.

Why does my strength fail when there is greatest need of my service? Never can the shepherd of the coast of black cargoes be born again. My body is already like a corpse, nameless and without any memory of its former substance. I shall not survive this day. I am ready for unholy burial. And I know my end. Never can the shepherd of the coast of black cargoes be born again. Never.

3
The Women

TWENTY-FIVE

STEWARD'S WIFE: You say your hair changed colour?

LADY OF THE HOUSE: Many times. Almost like leaves, according to season.

STEWARD'S WIFE: My change would come too. But in the eyes. I couldn't predict what they would see. I couldn't tell where the seeing started, or how, or when it would stop.

SURGEON'S WIFE: Like my hearing. Always the distance was deceiving me. How near was the sound with an echo heard so far away. His voice was in my ear; but the syllables were coming from elsewhere.

STEWARD'S WIFE: It was my eyes. They put an end to my hearing. Bells and water. I would hear only with my eyes. I could only see. But I didn't know how he would appear. How my eyes would offer him.

SURGEON'S WIFE: It was the other way with me. I gave up seeing. Memory hoarded everything through my ears. I could never see again who was behind that laugh.

STEWARD'S WIFE: But you helped him. He couldn't have joined the enterprise otherwise.

SURGEON'S WIFE: Would you say you helped your husband?

STEWARD'S WIFE: I gave him back the ring as proof of my own security.

SURGEON'S WIFE: Was it a bargain?

STEWARD'S WIFE: Bargain? Was it a bargain?

SURGEON'S WIFE: My husband wanted me out of the way. That was different.

STEWARD'S WIFE: Maybe it is the same. I agreed a way must be found to help him go. You agreed too. We both came to their rescue.

SURGEON'S WIFE: It was what I had to do. He was a piece of my person.

333

STEWARD'S WIFE: It is the same. My husband had become that too: a native of my person. Whenever there is a crisis, we must choose against our interests.

SURGEON'S WIFE: That's how I chose. I didn't think of a bargain. There was no room for victory in our future. I simply chose on his behalf. I had to.

STEWARD'S WIFE: And if you had chosen in your interest?

SURGEON'S WIFE: I would have offered him false evidence of a false charge.

STEWARD'S WIFE: He had a charge against you?

SURGEON'S WIFE: Yes. I was frigid. That was my sickness.

STEWARD'S WIFE: Mine was envy and a greedy ambition.

A wave of hot air whistled through the mouth of the cave. Strange noises startled the fern and the fallen dry leaves. A shudder of hands, groping over the prickly fists of agave. Icicles of steam dripped from the ceiling of rock: wet eyes with the red veins of the soil, melting slowly where the wives sat: their voices rising from the wide-open skull of earth: fragile and melancholy presences, barely visible in the black embrace of the cave. They were serene as the night that travelled through this tunnel of earth.

SURGEON'S WIFE: We are waiting.

STEWARD'S WIFE: Yes. We are waiting.

SURGEON'S WIFE: Their arrival. They will arrive.

STEWARD'S WIFE: You mean their return.

LADY OF THE HOUSE: Arrival and return. It is the same.

STEWARD'S WIFE: How will you explain? About our departure? With the vessel *Penalty*.

LADY OF THE HOUSE: We may not have to explain.

STEWARD'S WIFE: Our presence will cause some alarm.

SURGEON'S WIFE: That's true. If the foreigner hasn't spoken.

LADY OF THE HOUSE: He won't speak. Unless they can pay his price.

SURGEON'S WIFE: What will his price be this time?

STEWARD'S WIFE: He may make it impossible. How? I don't know.

SURGEON'S WIFE: I have no way of judging him.

STEWARD'S WIFE: I don't wish to judge him.

LADY OF THE HOUSE: He observes. He calculates his service. He demands his price. There is nothing about it to allow a judgment.

SURGEON'S WIFE: In a way, he is like my husband. Except that he does not deal in people.

STEWARD'S WIFE: He refuses to make any personal claim.

SURGEON'S WIFE: Where is our sister?

STEWARD'S WIFE: Where are you?

LADY OF THE HOUSE: Here. I am always here.

The temperature changed. There was a smell of rain. A chill swept briefly over their hands. It grew cold where fingers paused to probe the emptiness of the air.

SURGEON'S WIFE: It is like home here. So familiar.

STEWARD'S WIFE: The waiting is familiar.

SURGEON'S WIFE: And the night. The same smell. The same sound of absence.

STEWARD'S WIFE: Yes. It is easier on my eyes.

SURGEON'S WIFE: And my hearing. My memory seems less fearsome.

STEWARD'S WIFE: What's home, after all?

SURGEON'S WIFE: Home is how you are. How you have always been.

STEWARD'S WIFE: Home: mine was so friendless. Like an empty hall waiting for an audience.

SURGEON'S WIFE: He made no entertainment for you?

STEWARD'S WIFE: My husband suspected any gathering of men who might claim his friendship.

SURGEON'S WIFE: Was he solitary by nature?

STEWARD'S WIFE: He wasn't without escapades in his youth. And some, rumour says, bore him grievous fruit. But he was afraid that any confidence might be used against him.

SURGEON'S WIFE: Suspicious?

STEWARD'S WIFE: In excess, I would say. He had trained himself to judge any gesture of collaboration as a pretext for some future theft. So he closed his doors against all offers of comradeship. It made me weep for him. To watch his eyes. They had lost all natural moisture. His face became a desert: harsh, sterile, unvisited. I would weep for him.

SURGEON'S WIFE: Did he know?

STEWARD'S WIFE: Did he know?

SURGEON'S WIFE: About your weeping?

STEWARD'S WIFE: Yes. He was familiar with my tears. But he

335

thought they had some other source of grievance.

SURGEON'S WIFE: My husband was the opposite. A gathering had the effect of expensive polish on the right kind of wood. Company made him shine. At home or in public.

STEWARD'S WIFE: Your house was never empty?

SURGEON'S WIFE: Often. But not if he chose it otherwise.

STEWARD'S WIFE: Where is our sister?

LADY OF THE HOUSE: Here. I am always here.

SURGEON'S WIFE: The heat makes you silent.

LADY OF THE HOUSE: It is familiar.

STEWARD'S WIFE: Like home.

SURGEON'S WIFE: They would come in the evening. His company. All of the same learning and skill. My husband's house was like a school. Sometimes I would forget the indignities done to me when I saw them in such close collaboration. Discussing prescriptions for every sickness the Kingdom might suffer. But I could not understand. Their talk was in words that always went beyond my learning. The medicines had foreign names. I could never understand. But it didn't matter. I felt they had a wholesome purpose. To heal whatever sickness the Kingdom was suffering. To build a group of New World men. It was such a noble sight. Men of learning collaborating on a plan. And my husband at the centre of their attention. He was always like that. It was his natural place. At the centre of their attention. I would serve them food and drink. But I could not partake of their analysis. Their talk was always above my understanding, although I was the substance of their concern. I and all who might be victims of any sickness in the Kingdom. To hear them predict the future that could come if circumstances allowed their plans to operate, it was like waiting for heaven. I was proud of my husband and his group of New World men. In spite of the indignities done to me, I couldn't help seeing them with some favour. Maybe it was their ambition for the health of the Kingdom which stirred my feeling. It made me forgive my husband's lack of attention. His interest had been given to a larger love. I did not think this was an error if his learning persuaded him that way. Until the night you know of. That laugh! That the indignities done to me by those who were his friends should provoke that laugh. I could not reconcile the horror of that laugh and the love which made him put his learning at the service of the Kingdom. I couldn't see him any more. My eyes went wrong. I couldn't see the man behind that laugh.

STEWARD'S WIFE: You say he got you out of the way.

SURGEON'S WIFE: Horror came natural. Ever since that laugh. When I woke up and realized my surroundings. That he had arranged my imprisonment among the tortured and lunatic of Severn asylum. For a moment I was amazed. Until I heard that laugh. And every terror in front of me turned normal.

LADY OF THE HOUSE: So it seemed to me when I heard of the divisions in the Kingdom. Every rumour of calamity lost its surprise. Disorder was normal. Everywhere. Not only in Severn. But outside. Everywhere.

SURGEON'S WIFE: I don't know which discovery was the more terrible. That night I heard him laugh. Or the morning he came to Severn asylum.

STEWARD'S WIFE: To Severn?

SURGEON'S WIFE: Yes. He came there.

STEWARD'S WIFE: Illness makes for reconciliation.

SURGEON'S WIFE: He came for other reasons. He came to explain about his plans. The first time in all our personal history that my opinion was to be of some account. There was a crisis.

STEWARD'S WIFE: But how could you help in matters of learning you didn't understand?

SURGEON'S WIFE: I could. I did.

STEWARD'S WIFE: How? You had no experience of their skill.

SURGEON'S WIFE: My surroundings made me acceptable as mad, and my madness would be put to some service. That was the favour he came to ask.

STEWARD'S WIFE: I don't follow such reasoning.

SURGEON'S WIFE: He was in crisis.

STEWARD'S WIFE: With the plans?

SURGEON'S WIFE: With the authorities of the House of Trade and Justice.

STEWARD'S WIFE: Was he in opposition to the House?

SURGEON'S WIFE: He and his friends, who came at night. They had taken great stores of medicines from the House. They had a plan to negotiate profits elsewhere.

STEWARD'S WIFE: They stole?

SURGEON'S WIFE: They didn't call it by that name. He said they were trying to transfer ownership.

STEWARD'S WIFE: He told you that?

SURGEON'S WIFE: The morning he came to Severn asylum. Five months to the night since he put me out of the way.

STEWARD'S WIFE: But what could you do?

SURGEON'S WIFE: Exactly what I did. I put my madness at his service.

STEWARD'S WIFE: You were not mad.

SURGEON'S WIFE: But I was qualified by my residence. To be in Severn was enough credential. As you would never question my husband's learning. So no authority would put a doubt on my madness. Severn had given my word total proof of anything I said. And my husband's crime was so large, only madness would explain the attempt.

STEWARD'S WIFE: What did you do?

SURGEON'S WIFE: I took responsibility. That was the first thing I did. Accepted the responsibility that was my husband's. I carried out his instructions.

STEWARD'S WIFE: What could he ask of you in such crisis?

SURGEON'S WIFE: To take his place. That's what I did. I confessed to the offence against the House of Trade and Justice.

STEWARD'S WIFE: But you knew nothing of those matters.

SURGEON'S WIFE: I learned everything I had to know. Where the property was kept. How it was taken. Where the agents of conspiracy had stored it. The plans for future distribution. The volume of profits that would follow. I learned everything I had to know.

STEWARD'S WIFE: You took his place?

SURGEON'S WIFE: Completely. And in everything I made his innocence absolute.

STEWARD'S WIFE: Did you tell the foreigner of this?

SURGEON'S WIFE: Everything. It was the price for my husband's escape. And my place in the *Penalty*. My hearing. As I say. Your voice is in my ear, but the words seem to come from elsewhere.

LADY OF THE HOUSE: It is the cave. The rock plays with echoes everywhere.

STEWARD'S WIFE: At least your husband knew why he ran away.

SURGEON'S WIFE: He knew that. Whatever interpretations he may offer later.

STEWARD'S WIFE: Mine was different. He too was a man with a plan. But he worked alone.

SURGEON'S WIFE: And he had committed no crime against the House of Trade and Justice.

STEWARD'S WIFE: No. It was the reverse. The House was about to commit a crime against him.

SURGEON'S WIFE: Did they accuse him without reason?

STEWARD'S WIFE: They had reason. When certain maps disappeared, their reason pointed to him.

SURGEON'S WIFE: But he was never known to steal.

STEWARD'S WIFE: That is true. But the maps that disappeared were maps which had been stolen from my husband. They were his in the first place. When they disappeared, the House decided that my husband had recovered them. You might say he had recovered them by theft.

SURGEON'S WIFE: Did they accuse him of stealing his own property?

STEWARD'S WIFE: If you put it that way, I agree. He knew nothing of the disappearance, but he refused to argue his innocence. He was going to hang himself, instead. His silence was as good as confession.

SURGEON'S WIFE: He wanted to die?

STEWARD'S WIFE: He wanted to preserve his pride. That's how he was. To deny the charges would mean that he had put himself on an equal footing with those who accused him. He simply refused to speak. To the end he would hold himself above argument. This was how he saw his virtue. Always to be above argument.

SURGEON'S WIFE: Yet he fled. Wasn't that an injury to his pride?

STEWARD'S WIFE: If the House had caused him to flee. But I decided otherwise. I offered to support the accusation of the House.

SURGEON'S WIFE: You accused him?

STEWARD'S WIFE: Yes.

SURGEON'S WIFE: You mean you lied against him?

STEWARD'S WIFE: I did what I had to do.

SURGEON'S WIFE: But you lied against him.

STEWARD'S WIFE: How did you come to your husband's rescue?

SURGEON'S WIFE: I had to lie, it is true. But that was to save him.

STEWARD'S WIFE: My case was the same. A different circumstance, but the same result.

SURGEON'S WIFE: I do not understand.

STEWARD'S WIFE: I knew him. I knew what I had to do.

SURGEON'S WIFE: What's that? To tell a lie against him.

STEWARD'S WIFE: I had to provide him with a cause for retaliation. That's what I had to do. And this is what I did. I offered to give evidence against him.

SURGEON'S WIFE: You did that?

STEWARD'S WIFE: Yes. That's what I did. And so I became a witness for the House. It was my judgment that challenged his pride. Not punishment of the House. He would accept the punishment of the House. But he could never allow my judgment the same privilege. His pride wouldn't allow it. And he fled.

SURGEON'S WIFE: Yet he was innocent.

STEWARD'S WIFE: Yes. And I was glad he was innocent. He was always proud of his innocence. Like he would be proud to know I had failed in my support of the House.

SURGEON'S WIFE: You saved him from the House?

STEWARD'S WIFE: It was my failure which saved him.

SURGEON'S WIFE: Did you tell the foreigner you had lied against your husband?

STEWARD'S WIFE: Yes. I did what you said you had to do. I told him everything. It was the price for my place on the *Penalty*.

LADY OF THE HOUSE: And the girl? What of your husband's passion for the girl? I have very particular reason to enquire. How did you accept his passion for the girl?

SURGEON'S WIFE: The girl. It was not in your nature to suspect the girl?

STEWARD'S WIFE: No.

SURGEON'S WIFE: His fondness for the girl! You said it didn't provoke you to suspect?

STEWARD'S WIFE: Did I say no?

SURGEON'S WIFE: You said no.

STEWARD'S WIFE: It was there. Yes, I should say yes.

SURGEON'S WIFE: You are not sure?

STEWARD'S WIFE: Yes. Now I would say yes. It made me suspect.

But I know now that you can suspect in two ways. You can suspect what is. Or what might be. You can suspect what might be. You can suspect that without any feeling that it is so. I don't think I felt it might be so. I didn't suspect what might be.

SURGEON'S WIFE: She didn't impress you to be such a person?

STEWARD'S WIFE: In the beginning?

SURGEON'S WIFE: In the very beginning.

STEWARD'S WIFE: In the beginning the girl was like a gift. There was no time to notice her as a person.

SURGEON'S WIFE: But his fondness. He could make her whatever she was not. With his fondness, I mean. You couldn't avoid notice of his fondness.

STEWARD'S WIFE: The girl was like a gift, I say. The circumstance of her coming, you see. I didn't know how to challenge him any more. He had shut me out from any influence on his life. He allowed me no opportunity to talk to him. Until the girl. The afternoon she came. And the circumstances of her coming. She was my only chance to talk with him. The girl was no more than a gift. In the beginning, that is.

SURGEON'S WIFE: It changed? After the beginning, I mean?

STEWARD'S WIFE: What changed?

SURGEON'S WIFE: I suppose I mean if your feeling changed?

STEWARD'S WIFE: You mean there was a change in my feeling for the girl?

SURGEON'S WIFE: Maybe. That's what I mean. There was a change in you?

STEWARD'S WIFE: You might say so. Perhaps. But I don't know. Maybe it was the circumstance. The girl made some change in the circumstance that came after. And with the change of circumstance, I changed too. I needed her to stay.

SURGEON'S WIFE: But his fondness!

STEWARD'S WIFE: No. His fondness was nothing. I mean, there was no challenge for me in his fondness. The girl was only armour. His fondness for the girl was only a way of shutting me out from all attention. That I was sure of.

SURGEON'S WIFE: But what did your eyes force you to see?

STEWARD'S WIFE: The girl. Yes, I saw them. But I had changed already. Before I saw them in that way.

SURGEON'S WIFE: It couldn't provoke you any more?

STEWARD'S WIFE: Provoke? Provoke, you say? I went out of my mind. Almost. Because I couldn't believe he could ever be so blind. Shameful blind. The girl was afraid. That is what my eyes forced me to see. How blind he was to this fearful feeling in the girl. Silence was the only service she could offer to save herself. He saw her silence as enjoyment and support. His blindness! Blind. Blind. His blindness saw the girl's fearful silence as support.

SURGEON'S WIFE: She couldn't complain?

STEWARD'S WIFE: Exact. She couldn't complain.

SURGEON'S WIFE: It is awful to be powerless to complain.

STEWARD'S WIFE: She was powerless, as you say. Powerless to complain.

SURGEON'S WIFE: She couldn't complain to anyone?

STEWARD'S WIFE: To whom?

SURGEON'S WIFE: Not you?

STEWARD'S WIFE: I needed her to stay. She knew that. How could she complain?

SURGEON'S WIFE: Not even to you?

STEWARD'S WIFE: Not to me, nor to my husband. We were the only authority her fear could call on. And each made her powerless to complain.

SURGEON'S WIFE: You say your husband didn't see she was afraid?

STEWARD'S WIFE: Didn't. Couldn't. Wouldn't. The difference can't matter. He was just a power of blindness.

SURGEON'S WIFE: Where is our sister?

STEWARD'S WIFE: Where are you?

LADY OF THE HOUSE: Here. I am here. The girl, you say. The girl came to your rescue. In your own house. The girl came to your rescue. And she died. When I came to the rescue of my servant, he tried to kill me.

SURGEON'S WIFE: You say you came to your servant's rescue?

STEWARD'S WIFE: How?

LADY OF THE HOUSE: I told him about the enterprise. His early ambition was to be Boatswain of some enterprise.

STEWARD'S WIFE: In spite of what he did?

LADY OF THE HOUSE: Yes. There was no case for revenge. None at all.

STEWARD'S WIFE: But he tried to kill you.

LADY OF THE HOUSE: To stop my breathing, that is all.

STEWARD'S WIFE: He left you in that church for dead.

LADY OF THE HOUSE: But I was never alive in his eyes. The very first intimacy we knew. It was with a corpse.

SURGEON'S WIFE: You had known him in that way before?

LADY OF THE HOUSE: Yes.

SURGEON'S WIFE: You mean there was infidelity with him?

LADY OF THE HOUSE: Infidelity! What crime does a gravedigger commit against a corpse? I say my first intimacy was as a corpse.

STEWARD'S WIFE: I would not have believed that from any tongue but yours.

SURGEON'S WIFE: How did you meet him?

LADY OF THE HOUSE: He was a man who had been ignored. Made voyages that brought him no rewards. A man whose service was remembered, but whose name was never known. He was a shadow in search of its original self. That's what I recognized the first afternoon he begged to speak with me. He wanted to pay his way back to recognition. He was a servant with no particular duties. He did whatever was left undone.

STEWARD'S WIFE: Who was going to recognize him in this role?

LADY OF THE HOUSE: He calculated according to the customs of the Kingdom. He knew who my husband was. Some contact with my husband might be the first stage of his journey back to life. So he came as a servant, but my husband has never recognized a servant. Not in my memory of him.

STEWARD'S WIFE: So he chose you.

LADY OF THE HOUSE: It was his only chance.

SURGEON'S WIFE: And you helped him?

LADY OF THE HOUSE: No. I made no contact for him with my husband.

SURGEON'S WIFE: You refused him?

LADY OF THE HOUSE: I refused his offer. You see, he wanted to pay his way.

STEWARD'S WIFE: But he had no resources.

LADY OF THE HOUSE: He thought he had. And the most important kind.

STEWARD'S WIFE: What could he offer you?

LADY OF THE HOUSE: Rumour.

SURGEON'S WIFE: Rumour?

LADY OF THE HOUSE: Yes. It was a price surpassing any fortune he had known. He had knowledge which he thought I needed: knowledge of my husband's personal affairs. That was the bargain. To inform me of my husband's infidelities. That was the sum of his resources. A knowledge which he thought I needed. When I refused, I had never seen such poverty in a human face: a poverty beyond any absence of money. If you can imagine the wealth of the trading ships, of the Kingdom itself, converted, at a moment's misunderstanding, into air. Abundant and of no use at all. That was the entire meaning of his eyes: his hands deprived of usefulness, his memory a total waste of effort. Some creature that saw its species come to an end. So I put my hand out as you would reach to touch a corpse. In sympathy.

STEWARD'S WIFE: Pause a moment.

LADY OF THE HOUSE: I tire you?

STEWARD'S WIFE: No. Just pause a moment.

SURGEON'S WIFE: It is the chill. The cave is sweating.

LADY OF THE HOUSE: I can feel it too.

STEWARD'S WIFE: What did he do?

LADY OF THE HOUSE: As I say. He was my first intimacy with a corpse.

SURGEON'S WIFE: How did he put that to you?

LADY OF THE HOUSE: He didn't speak.

STEWARD'S WIFE: No?

SURGEON'S WIFE: Said nothing at all?

LADY OF THE HOUSE: His poverty had no other language but to throw its massive weight upon me. I felt his flesh like dead earth some animal was shovelling. Trying to bury its future in a hole it could not enter. To know intercourse with a corpse!

SURGEON'S WIFE: You are so calm.

LADY OF THE HOUSE: Calm?

SURGEON'S WIFE: Your voice. It is so calm.

STEWARD'S WIFE: And your husband?

SURGEON'S WIFE: Did you keep this secret from your husband?

LADY OF THE HOUSE: I told my husband to transfer the servant from the stables to the house.

STEWARD'S WIFE: You kept the servant?

LADY OF THE HOUSE: Kept? I elevated him.

STEWARD'S WIFE: Why did you have him promoted from the stables to the house?

LADY OF THE HOUSE: He was my game with death. It is the only logic I can give those afternoons. I was rehearsing how to die.

SURGEON'S WIFE: What a despair.

LADY OF THE HOUSE: Despair?

SURGEON'S WIFE: To accommodate your pleasure to a corpse. Turn your body into a grave.

LADY OF THE HOUSE: It was discovery. A terrible discovery. The truth is no occasion for despair.

SURGEON'S WIFE: Then he tried to kill you.

LADY OF THE HOUSE: To stop my breathing.

STEWARD'S WIFE: But why?

LADY OF THE HOUSE: His poverty had no other language.

SURGEON'S WIFE: He must have been without all religion.

LADY OF THE HOUSE: It was the other way. He was overcome by religion. He was going to kill in the name of his religion. The arrangement in the church at Little Aberlon was not an accident. It is famous for its treasure: a house of heroes. All the names that he idolized are buried there. Gold and honour are made immortal in that little church. I wanted to break the news of his release in the company of the dead: the names that had taught the Kingdom how and why they prayed. I had arranged for him to set to sea again. But he didn't want to go.

STEWARD'S WIFE: He refused.

LADY OF THE HOUSE: He rebelled against the circumstances. His loyalty to the House. The voyage was a robbery against the House. To join a ship that left the land without authority of the House. He found language now, and it was really bold. My whore's bed, to use his words, was innocence, holy innocence, compared to this treachery. To persuade him to such treachery. It was my ultimatum which brought that poverty into his eyes again. I told him he would have to choose. Either he set to sea again, resume his original wish to find his way to some life again, or be ready to follow the multitude of vagrants who infested the land. I was bringing his service as my corpse to an end. I had deprived him of his dignity, he said. That was his reply. And there was such an animal fury in his hands.

345

SURGEON'S WIFE: I think she is not well.

STEWARD'S WIFE: Are you in pain?

SURGEON'S WIFE: She is not well.

LADY OF THE HOUSE: It will pass.

STEWARD'S WIFE: I can scarcely breathe.

SURGEON'S WIFE: It changes so sharply. This weather!

STEWARD'S WIFE: Very sharp.

SURGEON'S WIFE: Are you still there?

LADY OF THE HOUSE: Yes. Where else?

SURGEON'S WIFE: I am here.

STEWARD'S WIFE: It will pass.

SURGEON'S WIFE: It always does.

STEWARD'S WIFE: Only to come back.

SURGEON'S WIFE: It is almost over.

LADY OF THE HOUSE: Almost. I feel a little light in my throat.

SURGEON'S WIFE: A light? In your throat?

LADY OF THE HOUSE: Yes. My tongue is loose again.

SURGEON'S WIFE: It's gone.

LADY OF THE HOUSE: Yes, I think it's going.

STEWARD'S WIFE: He fled.

LADY OF THE HOUSE: Fled?

STEWARD'S WIFE: The servant! When he thought you were dead.

SURGEON'S WIFE: You were as good as dead.

STEWARD'S WIFE: And all alone.

LADY OF THE HOUSE: He thought we were alone.

STEWARD'S WIFE: Thought?

SURGEON'S WIFE: Who else was there?

LADY OF THE HOUSE. Not present then. But somewhere. The foreigner!

SURGEON'S WIFE: The foreigner?

STEWARD'S WIFE: The foreigner! You say the foreigner was around?

LADY OF THE HOUSE: The foreigner was there.

SURGEON'S WIFE: And your husband? Where was your husband?

LADY OF THE HOUSE: Where was my husband?

STEWARD'S WIFE: You think your husband knew? About the servant?

LADY OF THE HOUSE: No more than he would choose to know.

He knew my need was elsewhere. That was enough to make him lose all interest in anything I did.

STEWARD'S WIFE: Even to share his privilege with a stranger, and a man from down below?

LADY OF THE HOUSE: Better a man from down below than one who was his equal. He knew my need was already matched with someone he could never surpass. Therefore he allowed the degradation of my intercourse with a man who had no rank at all. It was the remedy for my husband's lack of quality. My disgrace was the safest way he could promote his pride.

STEWARD'S WIFE: I do not understand your choice of Tate de Lysle. There was a husband who had no likeness to anything I would want to call a man.

LADY OF THE HOUSE: Choose? How do women of Lime Stone choose? I knew a man who was my fortune. At daybreak, in deepest night, you name the hour or season made for love and loving, and we knew it, richer than any heaven could afford. Under the most humble abode, in the commonest bed, with the plainest fodder humankind could endure: name any example of inconvenience, any obstacle of deprivation you can remember of your own or another, and we could transform it into a richness which all the wealth of Lime Stone could never equal. He was my kingdom, my grace and altar. I could rejoice with weeping, laugh in anguish, accommodate the sorest disappointment as though it were a sudden gift of luck. Simply to know that he was there. This was reward enough. He was the only road I really chose to travel. We could inhabit any crisis without question. We were partners in eternity.

STEWARD'S WIFE: It is the Commandant you speak of.

LADY OF THE HOUSE: Yes.

SURGEON'S WIFE: But he didn't die.

LADY OF THE HOUSE: No. But he had to bury whatever was alive. He buried himself alive.

SURGEON'S WIFE: He deserted you?

LADY OF THE HOUSE: No. That might have been less painful. Desertion would have been easier to bear. He simply took himself away. Not a literal separation, as you say. For a long time he remained. We stayed together; fed our appetites as before. But his presence had become a separation in itself.

347

I saw him; held him; nursed and embraced him as before; laughed at him; fought and quarrelled for him. But he—my only kingdom—was no longer there. He had given way to a ghost; some shadow that was familiar, and I could not touch. "Don't you love me any more?" I would ask; and his silence would last and last, deep, and so final, like the triumph of a grave.

STEWARD'S WIFE: When would he speak?

SURGEON'S WIFE: On what occasion?

LADY OF THE HOUSE: Only to say that he was going away. Whenever he had orders from the House to sail from Lime Stone. Briefly, he would say that he was going away. Very briefly.

SURGEON'S WIFE: And on his return?

LADY OF THE HOUSE: On his return?

STEWARD'S WIFE: Long absence sometimes makes an arrival easier.

LADY OF THE HOUSE: He didn't distinguish between arrival and return. Didn't or couldn't or wouldn't, I do not know. He had lost all sense of difference between the coming and the going. To come and to go: these were only names for the same activity. On each arrival, or return as you call it, I would see him; and couldn't imagine that he had ever broken that silence while he was away. I would hold him; embrace him; humour him; curse him; harass him; or even try, in moments of bitterness, to ignore him. My choice of conduct made no difference.

STEWARD'S WIFE: Didn't he miss you?

SURGEON'S WIFE: During a long absence, would he miss you?

LADY OF THE HOUSE: His absence was no longer a matter of time. A year; months less than a year. Two years. He had no sense of such measure. He was there, or he was not there. And when he was there, it was his silence which I recognized to be unchanged, changeless.

STEWARD'S WIFE: You think he loved you always?

SURGEON'S WIFE: Do you still love him? Like you describe?

LADY OF THE HOUSE: His power of ownership over me has never changed. That's the limit of my certainty. That's why I am here.

SURGEON'S WIFE: You love him.

STEWARD'S WIFE: She loves him.

SURGEON'S WIFE: How could you choose Tate de Lysle after what you knew?

LADY OF THE HOUSE: I made no choice. When I decided to leave the Commandant, I had surrendered whatever power I had to choose. I could only offer myself for a rescue. How do women of Lime Stone choose after what I knew? It is our need for rescue which some men cannot afford, and only husbands are able to provide. Tate de Lysle was a born husband: rich in possessions and impotent at heart. My perfect rescue. Suffering had given me a novel taste for atmospheres of comfort; and any heart but the Commandant's was useless to what was left to me. Gabriel Tate de Lysle came to my rescue, and for a minimum of service in return. He could rummage like a common dog for his sex outside. But his status required a Lady for his parlour. Do you find this strange for a woman of quality from Lime Stone?

STEWARD'S WIFE: It sounds familiar.

LADY OF THE HOUSE: Familiar, you say? It was natural law among those I knew.

SURGEON'S WIFE: There are exceptions.

LADY OF THE HOUSE: To be sure, there are exceptions. But it is difficult to know how many, since their names can never make news.

SURGEON'S WIFE: It is a dreadful thought.

STEWARD'S WIFE: To remain unknown?

SURGEON'S WIFE: No. To be a wife whose union with her husband is that of common whore.

LADY OF THE HOUSE: It would be more dreadful if the reverse was not also true. To be a husband whose generosity to his wife is no different from a whore's.

SURGEON'S WIFE: Hardly a point of difference, as you say.

STEWARD'S WIFE: None, I would agree.

SURGEON'S WIFE: How do they survive it without going mad? Husband and wife in the role of whores? And the keepers of whores? How? How?

LADY OF THE HOUSE: Because their whoredom is also the whoredom of the House of Trade and Justice. It is the national principle of the continent of Lime Stone. What safer consolation or protection can a citizen have than to know that his private vice is the nation's religion?

STEWARD'S WIFE: You speak with some authority, I know.

LADY OF THE HOUSE: Absolute, I assure you. I was not a Lady of
the House by name alone. There's not a Gentleman of high
rank in the trade and politics of the Kingdom with whom I
have not shared a criminal confidence. I lived among them;
fed them; and wined them; witnessed their robberies in public
and personal affairs alike. And that's why I was able to arrange
for *Reconnaissance* to sail without any record of its departure
in the House. I could arrange it because I knew those rivals
of my husband who dared not refuse my wish. Now they believe
my disappearance may be an act of murder, and some even
wish it so; but they cannot make this public; or a fresh war of
accusations will be waged. In the name of the Kingdom. The
first voice to be raised will be the first to be accused. Who
killed the Lady of the House? And the answer will be given
as thunder follows lightning. The questioner is up for question-
ing. In the issue of *Reconnaissance* and the Lady of the House,
no questioner is safe who puts his question.

STEWARD'S WIFE: And you risked all this for love?

LADY OF THE HOUSE: For one man.

STEWARD'S WIFE: For his arrival or return?

LADY OF THE HOUSE: Simply to have him here. I would ask no
more than to have him here.

STEWARD'S WIFE: This weather!

The heat had grown suddenly fierce. The cave seemed to shrink
and close like a skull, bracing the air with currents of steel. They
gazed towards the mouth of the cave, which was briefly whistling
a noise, in and out, like wind caught under a door. A splinter of
light showed the distance between them, now paved with a hot,
white slab of haze. The heat had started to drip: soft points of
water slipping tediously down to the floor of the cave.

SURGEON'S WIFE: The weather, you say.

STEWARD'S WIFE: This weather. The moment it goes, I recognize
something.

SURGEON'S WIFE: It's like home.

STEWARD'S WIFE: Something familiar. The moment it goes, I feel I
have known it before.

SURGEON'S WIFE: It's so fierce. I feel I am crushed forever.

STEWARD'S WIFE: But it doesn't last.

SURGEON'S WIFE: It never lasts.

LADY OF THE HOUSE: Its power is in the contact only. Then everything evaporates.

SURGEON'S WIFE: It is familiar. The same absence which shock leaves behind.

STEWARD'S WIFE: Absence?

SURGEON'S WIFE: Yes. It has the same smell.

STEWARD'S WIFE: It is like home here. As you say.

SURGEON'S WIFE: The waiting is familiar. Like home.

STEWARD'S WIFE: The absence.

SURGEON'S WIFE: Like home. The same sound of absence.

LADY OF THE HOUSE: Yes. And the same smell of absence.

SURGEON'S WIFE: Then why? Why?

STEWARD'S WIFE: You ask why?

SURGEON'S WIFE: Yes, why? Why did we follow them here?

STEWARD'S WIFE: Yes, why follow them here?

LADY OF THE HOUSE: Because we are a future.

STEWARD'S WIFE: A future, you say?

LADY OF THE HOUSE: A future, I repeat. We are a future they must learn.